LOVE IN THE LOW COUNTRY

Debby Mayne

Forget Me Not Romances, an imprint of Winged Publications

ISBN-13: 9781718046566

CONTENTS

Love in the News

A Fall'N For You novella

Debby Mayne

Forget Me Not Romances, a division of Winged Publications

Chapter 1

"Hey, Evan, can you hand me the remote?"

Without saying a word or looking up, Evan picked up the TV remote and gave it to his dad. Jonathan narrowed his eyes as he studied his son whose gaze remained transfixed to the gaming device he hadn't put down since he finished his homework.

School had just begun a month ago, and Evan was already slammed with more homework than Jonathan ever remembered getting at that age. But he almost always got it done before dinner. He'd hesitated to let Evan go into the advanced program for gifted kids, but the guidance counselor seemed to think he needed the challenge.

Jonathan watched his son for a minute before speaking up. "Don't you think you've been playing with that thing long enough?"

Evan held up a finger. "Hold on just a second, Dad. I have one more level to get through before I can talk to you."

Jonathan reached out and snatched the device from Evan's hands. "That comment just earned you a break from this thing."

"But Dad—" Evan's forehead crinkled as he finally nodded. "Okay, I get it."

"Good. Why don't you help me with the salad?"

"Salad? Why do you keep making me eat salad?"

Jonathan thought for a moment about how Evan's mom Samantha used to fix a salad before dinner every night. At first, he wasn't crazy about it, but once he realized she was doing it to make sure he ate properly, he loved her even more.

"It's good for you. It has vegetables."

"That's lame, Dad. I had vegetables on my sandwich …" Evan pointed to the broccoli in the colander. "And we're having them with dinner."

"Lame or not, we're having salad."

Evan shrugged and started placing everything in the salad bowls that Jonathan had set aside. "Bleu cheese or ranch?"

Jonathan grinned. "Whatever you have."

The sound of the music on TV, announcing that the five-minute brief was about to start caught both of their attention. Jonathan liked catching the most important events of the day, while he suspected the anchor was the reason his son looked up.

Carrie Marshall was absolutely gorgeous with her shoulder-length brown hair that glistened under the studio lights and twinkling eyes that one of the other newscasters mentioned changed from green to brown, depending on what she was wearing. He focused on what color they were tonight. Brown. Nice. Just like his.

"Dad, have you ever thought about dating?"

That simple comment startled Jonathan. "I've already done that. Your mother and I dated before we got married."

"I know, but I'm talking about now. You're not exactly getting any younger."

Jonathan chuckled as he shook his head at his son whose wisdom seemed much older than his age. "Where did that come from?"

"Noah told me his parents are afraid of not having someone to get old with after they got divorced, so they date a lot."

"I think it's different for us."

"What do you mean?" Evan paused. "Just because Mom died?"

"Yeah, something like that." Jonathan had married the love of his life, and he couldn't imagine finding anyone to take her place.

He just wished Evan could remember her, but she'd been in a fatal car crash when their son was still a baby. Jonathan squeezed his eyes shut at the painful memory of that night when she'd run to the store to pick up a few things from the grocery store. Evan was taking a nap, while Jonathan sat on the sofa watching a football game.

When the call came to let him know there had been an accident, and Samantha was in the hospital, he had no idea she'd never return home again. By the time he and Evan got to the hospital, she'd gone into a coma. The medical team did everything they could to save her, but the injuries were too severe. At that moment, he became a single parent—something he was not prepared for.

As soon as Evan poured the dressing on the salads, they sat down at the kitchen table. Evan fidgeted with his fork for a few seconds before looking at his dad. "Oh, there's something I forgot to tell you."

Jonathan lifted an eyebrow. "And what's that?"

"You have to be at the school the day after tomorrow."

"Are you in trouble, son?"

Evan shook his head and dropped his gaze. "No, nothing like that. It's just that … we have a special guest, and the teacher said she needs help, so I told her—"

"You told her I'd be there?"

"Yeah, and it's really important. You *have* to be there."

Jonathan leaned back and laughed. "Okay, I get the picture. I've scheduled a couple of people to work mornings all week, so I should be able to get away. What time do I need to be there?"

"By 9:00."

*

Tom's shadow over Carrie's the next day caught her attention. "We got a call from Baker Creek Elementary School, asking for someone to talk to some fourth grade classes."

Carrie smiled at Tom, her production manager. "So are you going?"

A mischievous grin flickered on his lips as he slowly shook his head. "No. You are."

"Me? I don't know how to talk to fourth graders. You've always done that."

"I know, but it's your turn." He set his coffee mug down on the desk and folded his arms. "They asked specifically for you."

She let out a nervous laugh. "They clearly made a mistake. I haven't been doing my job long enough to know what I'm doing, let alone tell a bunch of kids—"

"You don't have to say much. I'll get a bunch of station goodies together and help you make some notes."

Carrie opened her mouth, but she knew that arguing with Tom was futile. When he got something in his head, there was no changing his mind.

"When do they want me?"

"Tomorrow morning at 9:00."

She pulled her lips between her teeth and stared down at the floor. She'd planned to meet someone for coffee before work, and now she'd have to cancel. It wouldn't have been so bad if this hadn't been the third time she'd done that to this guy. They'd been chatting online after seeing each other's profile through the dating service. The first two times they were supposed to meet, she'd chickened out. This time, she decided that a coffee meeting before work would be safe and convenient because she had to be at the station by 10:00.

"You'll do fine, Carrie." She glanced up and saw his concerned fatherly expression. "You're good at every single thing you attempt, and I have no reason to think this would be any different."

He clearly didn't know she was planning to meet a guy from the dating site, and she certainly wasn't about to tell him. Quite a few of her friends had met their spouses that way, but Tom came from a different generation. She doubted that he'd understand.

Tom gestured for her to follow him. "Let's go round up some swag. Kids love free stuff."

An hour later, Carrie had two boxes filled with all kinds of things from the station—from pens and notepads to Frisbees and bouncy balls. As they pulled things from the storage room, she started to relax about her change of plans. Chances are, things wouldn't have worked out with the guy from the dating site anyway. She had reservations about him before, which was why they hadn't met yet. Maybe this was saving her from an embarrassing situation that would have been difficult to get out of.

"Why don't you go on home right after your segment?" Tom asked. "You've been jittery ever since I told you about tomorrow morning." He paused and grinned. "Go home, take a bubble bath or whatever you do to relax, and get some sleep. You'll do just fine."

"I'll be okay."

"Oh, I know you will. I've always had confidence in you."

The five-minute news brief went by quickly. She barely had time to cover everything that had happened that day, which was a good thing. It was always much more difficult to deal with slow news days because she had to fill the time with adlibbed content.

Tom was right there by her side as soon as she took off her mic. "Great job as always. Now get outta here and don't come back until after you talk to the kids at the school."

All the way home, she thought about what to say to the guy she was supposed to meet and finally decided to be direct. "I'm sorry, but something has come up at work and I can't make it for coffee."

As she expected, he didn't take it well. "Sounds like you're not ready to do this dating thing yet, and I can't wait around forever," he said. "It's time for me to move on and meet someone else. Have a nice life."

She pressed the OFF button on her phone and dropped it onto the table. Well, that sounded final. Oh well. It wasn't like she would miss the guy since all she knew about him was what he'd put in his profile and the few things he'd told her via email and a couple of brief phone conversations.

*

The next morning, she put on some slacks and a comfortable top and applied bare minimum makeup since she'd need to freshen it anyway before her segment aired later. All the goodies were still in boxes in her car, so all she needed to bring was a lightweight jacket for the slightly cooler temperature and her briefcase.

The lady at the school reception desk smiled and asked her to wait for someone to come for her. As she waited, she looked out the window and thought about what she was missing. Her loneliness had intensified over the past several months, and she wasn't sure what to do about the feeling.

As soon as that thought struck her, she let out a low chuckle. That was a new one for her. The very idea of her becoming a mother seemed as strange as flying to the moon.

"Must be thinking some good thoughts to be laughing this early in the morning."

The sound of a strange man's voice behind her made her turn around. She smiled at him but didn't say anything.

"I'm here to escort someone to my son's class. You wouldn't happen to be …" He paused and made a face as though he couldn't remember something important.

She swallowed hard as she forced a smile and extended her hand. "Hi, I'm Carrie Marshall, and I believe I must be the person you came for."

"Yes, Carrie, you most certainly are. I'm Jonathan Hanks, and my son is in the first class you're speaking to." The way he looked at her as he spoke gave her an odd sensation in her belly. "You're the news lady, aren't you?"

She nodded. "I do the news brief every evening."

"And you do a mighty fine job of it. In fact, even my son likes to watch you, and until you started, he had no interest whatsoever in the news."

Her cheeks flamed, so she tilted her head forward so her hair could cover the redness. She wished she'd put on more foundation. "I'm glad he enjoys it."

"I have to admit, I like it too. There's something about the way you deliver the news …" He glanced down at the boxes she'd placed on the cart. "Are those yours?"

She nodded. "Yes, I brought some things to hand out to the kids."

"You clearly know this crowd. They love people who bring them surprises."

A nervous giggle escaped her throat. She needed to watch herself around this guy—especially since he clearly had a family. The last thing she needed was to let her instant attraction to him show.

*

The sound of her laughter sent a sensation shooting through him that he hadn't experienced since Samantha died. And he didn't mind the feeling at all.

He stopped and gestured toward a classroom door. "Here we are, Miss Bell's second grade class." He leaned over and whispered, "Don't be afraid. I'll protect you."

As she tossed her hair back, he caught a scent that reminded him of strawberries and cream. She smiled. "Thanks."

She looked him directly in the eyes, and within seconds, he felt as though someone had slammed him in the gut. Those eyes of hers seemed to see inside him, and he knew that it wouldn't take much to completely lose himself in her gaze.

Chapter 2

Jonathan noticed how she looked around the room before going up to the front and speaking. He suspected that had something to do with her journalistic training—sizing up a crowd before making a move.

"I'm so happy to be here," she began. "Some of you may have seen me on TV when I deliver the news headlines in a feature segment called 'News Briefs.'" She smiled. "And if you haven't seen me, please encourage your parents to tune in to channel 2 tonight at 5:30 PM."

As she spoke, every single child in the class seemed mesmerized. He had to admit, she sounded like an angel as she explained the processes in the newsroom.

She finished by asking for questions. Nearly all the boys and a few girls raised their hands. He couldn't help but chuckle to himself.

One of the boys had a mischievous look on his face when she called on him. Jonathan remembered that Ethan said this boy was a troublemaker, so he braced himself for stepping in to help Carrie.

"Have you ever seen a dead body … like after someone has been murdered?" the boy asked.

Carrie didn't seem the least bit flustered as she slowly nodded. "Unfortunately, yes, but that's not very common. Most of the time, the police have taken care of that before I arrive."

Jonathan let out a sigh of relief—partly because the question could have been worse but mostly because she handled it so well. He leaned against the edge of the teacher's desk as she looked around the room again. Then her gaze met his, and he felt as though he'd been turned inside out.

*

Carrie wanted to kick herself for looking directly at Jonathan. The warmth of his dark brown eyes sent her senses into overdrive, and she found it almost impossible to look away. She was thankful when he broke the gaze.

"What happens if the bad guys come after you?" one of the boys asked. "Do you get to shoot them?"

"No, I don't shoot anyone. It's my job to report the news, not make it happen."

She alternated between calling on the boys and girls, and she was amazed by the differences. Tom had warned her, so she was prepared for whatever came at her.

"I want to be on TV when I grow up," one of the little girls in the front row asked.

"Then start thinking about how you can do that. Do you want to be an actor, singer, show host, or TV reporter?"

"I don't care. I just want to be on TV. How do I do that?"

Carrie nodded. She never thought about being on TV when she was a little girl. All she wanted to do was be a reporter, and the TV thing happened after she got her first job. She explained how she'd gotten a job as a news copywriter. One day the anchor was sick, so she was asked to fill in.

"Were you scared?" another little girl asked.

"A little. But I knew that the public needed to know what was happening, so I took a deep breath, sat down at the anchor desk, and did what I had to do."

That started a whole new set of questions that she was able to answer without too much thought. It was about her journey, and she never minded sharing her experience with anyone who wanted to know.

The teacher finally gave a sign that it was time to move on to the next class. She stopped talking, pulled the first bag out of the boxes she'd brought, and handed out some of the goodies.

Once she was finished, Jonathan gestured toward the classroom door. "I'll walk you to the next class."

She picked up her briefcase and followed him to the door. As soon as they got to the hallway, she let out a deep breath. "Those kids are amazing. Which one was yours?"

He lifted an eyebrow. "You couldn't tell?"

"Well …" She smiled as she thought about the boy who looked like a mini-Jonathan. "If I go by looks, I'd say the little boy in the second row, right behind the large globe. He has a lot of your features."

"Bingo. That's my son Ethan."

"He didn't ask any questions."

Jonathan's grin widened. "That's because he's smitten."

"Smitten?"

"Yeah, with the pretty lady talking to his class."

"Oh." Now she wasn't sure what to say.

"I hope I didn't embarrass you." He took a few more steps and then stopped at a door at the end of the hall. "When was the last time someone walked you to class?"

"It's been a few years." She tilted her head back and laughed.

*

After Jonathan introduced her to the next teacher, he headed back to Ethan's class to say goodbye. He leaned over his son's desk and whispered, "You set this up, didn't you?"

Ethan wouldn't look him in the eyes. "Let's talk about it later, Dad. We're getting ready to have a math test."

"We'll discuss this when you get home."

Ethan still didn't look at him, so he straightened up, said goodbye to the teacher, and headed toward the school office to check out. The receptionist asked if he was coming back to help with the Fall Festival.

"I'm not sure. I'll talk to Ethan and see if he even wants me here."

The receptionist laughed. "I'm sure he will. It's not until sometime during middle school that most of the kids don't want anyone to know they have parents."

Jonathan thought about her comment as he went out to his truck. He remembered being embarrassed by his mom and dad when he was in seventh or eighth grade. When one of them brought him to school, he always had them drop him off on the corner a block away. Now that he was a father, it made him cringe to even think about acting that way. A sudden urge to call his dad came over him.

"How's the hardware business, son?"

"It's practically running itself. I just left Ethan's school. The teacher wanted me to come in and help out with someone who came in to speak to the kids."

"I remember those days. You had me come speak to your class about my job as a firefighter."

"Yeah." Jonathan remembered too. "I thought you had the coolest job in the world."

"You might have thought it was cool …" Jonathan braced himself for what his dad always said. "But in reality, it was the hottest job in town."

Jonathan let out a chuckle. "I knew I could count on you."

"Yep. That old joke will never change." His dad paused. "Why do I get the feeling there's something else you called about?"

Jonathan let out a nervous chuckle. "Um … I think Ethan is trying to play matchmaker."

His dad belted out a laugh. "Why would he go and do something like that?" He paused. "Are you being overbearing? Because if you are, he might think you need something … or someone to take the pressure off him."

"I don't think so." Jonathan pondered the possibility. "Well, maybe."

"Then stop it."

"It's not that simple. He's the only other person in the house, so when I have something to say, he's it."

"Maybe that's why he's trying to play matchmaker. Has he fixed you up with anyone?"

"I'm not positive, but I think he's working on it."

"So tell me about it. I'm all ears."

Jonathan told his dad about watching the news with Ethan and then next thing he knew, the woman from TV was in the classroom. It wouldn't have been so suspicious if Ethan hadn't made such a big deal of making sure he was there.

"He sure is a fast worker, if he saw her one night and got her to the classroom the next morning."

"It didn't happen that fast. He's been watching ever since she started doing the news brief on Channel 2."

"Oh, wow. No wonder Ethan's smitten. I've seen that girl … What's her name? Carrie something-or-other?"

"Carrie Marshall."

"She's a real looker." His dad cleared his throat. "And smart as a whip from what I can tell. I told your mother I thought she was a great addition to the news."

"That's all beside the point. I'm not sure what to do next."

"That's easy, son. Ask her out on a date. You sure have gotten rusty, haven't you?"

"What if I don't want to ask her out?"

"Are you kidding? You don't want to ask her out?"

Jonathan shuffled his feet as he thought about it. "I didn't say that. I just don't want Ethan to think he can manipulate me."

"Listen to me, son. Ethan isn't trying to manipulate you. He cares about you, and he doesn't want you to be lonely."

"But his mother—"

"Ethan doesn't remember his mother. Everything he knows about her is what we've told him."

"But his other grandparents—"

"They don't want you to be miserable either. In fact, I saw Donald last week, and he asked about you. He says Ethan is worried about you, but we didn't have much time to discuss it. Now it all makes sense. Ethan must have talked to them about your loneliness."

"I never told him I was lonely."

Again, his dad laughed. "You don't have to tell anyone. It's obvious to the people who love you."

"Okay, well, I've got to run now."

"Think about what I said. Your son loves you, and he'll do anything to make you happy."

"Yeah, well …"

"Call me in a few days and let me know how things are going with you and that news lady. Goodbye, Jonathan."

After he got off the phone, Jonathan rocked back on his heels and pondered the conversation. His dad was right. He was lonely. But he never realized Ethan was aware of it. He needed to do a better job of disguising his feelings.

He went to the hardware store and saw that everything was running smoothly, so he took the deposit from the safe and headed for the bank. It was a bright, sunshiny day, and there was a crispness in the air that reminded him of college … when he'd met Samantha.

The first time he saw her, she was walking across the expansive lawn of the Student Union building. She was dressed much nicer than the other female students. While most of them wore jeans or some sort of stretchy pants, she had on a cute little skirt that showed off her stunning legs. He found himself breathless as a gentle breeze lifted her long dark hair off her shoulders. Right then, he knew he needed to meet her.

He wasn't able to make it across the lawn before another guy approached her. She smiled up at him in a way that let Jonathan know they were already friends. He hoped that was all, but he suspected there was more to the relationship than that based on the admiring gazes from the guy.

It took him a week to work up the nerve to approach her. When he got within a few feet of her, she glanced up at him and grinned, showing off her heart-shaped lips and sparkling white teeth that were slightly crooked—just enough to add character to her face.

"Hi there. I'm Jonathan." As soon as he said that, he groaned at his lack of creativity.

She continued smiling. "Hey, I'm Samantha."

Her hint of a southern accent took him by surprise. "Nice to meet you, Samantha. I've seen you around."

Her smile widened even more. "I know. I've seen you watching me."

He slapped his forehead. "Sorry. I'm not normally a stalker, but I couldn't help …" His voice trailed off as he realized he was heading into territory he couldn't get out of.

"Don't worry about it. I've been watching you too."

"You have?" Now his voice squeaked, so he cleared his throat. "I hope in a good way."

Samantha slowly nodded, and at that very moment, he knew she was the girl for him. Now all he had to do was convince her he was the guy for her.

It didn't take long before she admitted she was in love with him, and she actually said it before he told her how he felt. By the end of the next semester, right before he graduated, they were engaged, even though she was still a junior. They'd planned to wait to get married, but Samantha's grandmother found out she had terminal cancer, so they moved up the date. And not one single time did they have any regrets.

Their marriage was wonderful … not always perfect but overall as good as Jonathan could hope for. When they found out they were having Ethan, both of them were over the moon. Jonathan had never seen a more gorgeous pregnant woman. His wife positively glowed.

Chapter 3

Carrie narrowed her eyes as she looked at Tom. "They want me to do an appearance at their Fall Festival?"

"Yup."

"Why did they ask me?"

He shrugged. "Apparently, you made quite an impression on the kids. The principal said a group of them came into the office and requested you, just like they did before." A twinkle formed in his eyes as he smiled, folded his arms, and leaned back. "I told you that you'd slay it."

"Whoa, wait a minute. What do you mean by the comment *just like they did before*?"

Tom avoided her gaze for a few seconds before looking her in the eyes. "Exactly that. They got together and decided they wanted you to come talk to their class."

"That's odd." Carrie sighed. "Think about it, Tom. These are kids. How many fourth graders do you know who would want a news person to come and talk to them?"

"How should I know? Kids are getting smarter all the time." Before she had a chance to continue questioning him, he gestured toward the door. "Now get back to work. We have more news rolling in by the minute."

Carrie held his gaze momentarily before nodding and leaving his office. As she strode past the pool of copywriters, she sensed their amusement. Everyone else clearly knew something she didn't … or at least it felt that way.

Throughout the remainder of the day, her mind flitted back to her presentation at the elementary school. Images of the children actually listening to her, the man who came and got her from the reception area, and his son who was quiet but extremely attentive … so much so that she couldn't get his expression out of her mind.

He acted as though he thought he knew her. When she said something related to her newscast the night before, he nodded. And when she told an amusing story about something that had happened to her on the job, he was the first to crack a smile … a warm and friendly smile.

The presentation went well in the other two classes after that, but the first one continued to stand out in Carrie's mind. And it didn't hurt that the seriously good-looking man with the easy manner and purposeful stride had walked her to and from that classroom.

She worked with the copywriters to prepare for her news brief. It took longer to synopsize the news than it did to write the original copy. Some things were difficult to put into 20- or 30-second sound bites, but she managed to do it day after day.

Her mind took her back to when she told the children how difficult it was to write short. Jonathan's son had nodded while the rest of the kids made comments that they'd much rather write short than long. She explained how she still had to get the message of what had happened that day without losing its meaning, and she gave an example so they'd understand. The teacher interjected with her own experience during college exams.

Snapping fingers behind Carrie yanked her from her thoughts. "Must be a doozy of a daydream to have you so spaced out."

She smiled up at Tom. "This is a crazy day."

"Does it have anything to do with your school visit?"

She didn't want to lie, but she also didn't want to let him know that her thoughts lingered on one specific little boy and his dad. "I'm sure it does. Things always seem different when I change my routine."

*

After dinner last night, Jonathan had noticed strange behavior from Ethan. It was normal for Ethan to pick at his food, so he was instantly suspicious when he dug in and didn't say a word until he finished every last bite on his plate.

"What's going on, sport?"

Ethan shrugged. "Nothing."

"You must've been hungry."

"Yeah."

Okay, so Ethan didn't feel like having a conversation, which would have been fine if he hadn't been acting so strange otherwise. Not only did he eat more than usual, he wouldn't look Jonathan in the eyes.

"What's going on, son?"

Ethan shrugged again. "I have a bunch of homework."

"It didn't look like as much as usual to me." Jonathan leaned toward his son to get his attention. "I saw it on the board this morning. It shouldn't take you more than ten or fifteen minutes to do."

Ethan opened his mouth but quickly shut it. "I think I want to read tonight."

That wouldn't have been alarming if it hadn't been for how Ethan acted during Carrie's news brief. "So what did you think of seeing Ms. Marshall on TV after having her talk to your class today?"

Bingo. Ethan's face turned bright red. He'd finally found the path to discovering what was going on with his son.

"Well?"

"I guess that's kind of cool."

"Yeah, I agree. What did you think about the way she looked in person versus on TV?"

"She looks the same." Ethan pursed his lips and frowned. "May I be excused?"

Jonathan leaned back in his chair as he slowly nodded. "Sure. Let me know when you're ready to go to bed, and I'll come up and listen to your prayers."

Ethan got up from the table, carried his dishes to the sink, and left the kitchen. Jonathan remained sitting there, trying to figure out what had happened to have his son acting so weird. He wasn't a teenager—or even what he'd call a preteen yet—so he couldn't blame it on hormones.

After more than an hour without hearing from Ethan, Jonathan couldn't take it any longer. He had to talk to his son. So he went upstairs, walked down the hall to Ethan's room, and knocked.

"What do you want?"

"Ethan, you know better than to talk to me like that."

Within seconds, the door opened, and Ethan looked up at him with a contrite expression. "Sorry, Dad. Did you need something?"

"Yes, I do." Jonathan nodded toward the room. "Mind if I come in?"

Ethan glanced over his shoulder and then backed away. "Sure, come on in."

"What's going on?"

Ethan sat down at his desk, picked up some papers, and shoved them into the top drawer. "Nothing."

One thing Jonathan knew was that his son wasn't typically a secretive person, so when he had something he didn't want anyone to see, he wasn't good at covering it up. "What did you just put in there?"

Ethan's face turned an even brighter shade of red, and he quickly glanced down. "Um …" A pained expression covered his face when he looked back up.

Jonathan took a deep breath as he pondered what to do next. He didn't want to be an overbearing father, but he didn't want his son to keep things from him. "You know you can talk to me, right?" He paused and held his son's gaze. "I won't judge."

"But—" He cut himself off as he clearly had some mental processing to do.

"I love you unconditionally, and there's nothing that will make that go away."

Ethan slowly nodded. "I know."

"So if something is bugging you, I want you to come to me with it. I might not have all the answers, but maybe the two of us can come up with some solution."

Ethan's lips twitched into a half smile. "Thanks, Dad."

"So, is there anything you want to discuss with me now?"

"No."

The abruptness of Ethan's reply shouldn't have surprised Jonathan, but it did. It was clear he wasn't ready to open up about whatever was bothering him.

Jonathan took another glance around the room before backing toward the door. "I guess that's all I have to say for now. Finish up whatever you're doing. It's almost bedtime."

"Okay."

Jonathan closed the door behind him and took a few steps toward his room, when he heard the drawer open and then slam shut. It sounded like Ethan had gone back to his secretive mission, whatever that was.

*

The next morning, Jonathan drove Ethan to school and then headed for the hardware store. It had taken every ounce of self-restraint to not go back home and look for clues about Ethan's behavior. He'd worked hard to establish trust with his son, and he didn't want to break it. The only thing that would make him look was if Ethan started acting out or causing trouble.

He'd run a sales ad for a toolbox filled with the basics for anyone who was starting out. He had a variety of colors, including pink for the girlie types, navy for the more masculine guys, and red-white-and-blue for those who were more patriotic. With the holidays coming over the next several months, they were slammed with customers—mostly parents buying for their adult children—asking for these toolboxes. It was good to stay busy.

Instead of leaving for lunch, Jonathan ordered a few pizzas to be delivered for him and his employees. He'd hired a great group of people who were steadfastly loyal, and he rewarded them in as many ways as he could. They'd been there for him when his wife died, and they didn't mind helping out when he wasn't sure what to do as a parent. As tempted as he was to ask what to do in his current situation with Ethan, he decided to wait.

But Maryann, one of his full-timers, let him know she was aware of something going on. "What's bugging you, Jonathan?"

He chuckled as he met her gaze, amazed by the fact that she was only about ten years older than him, yet she had more wisdom in her little finger than he figured he'd ever have. "Just normal stuff."

"Like what?" She put her slice of pizza down on the paper plate and leaned back in her chair. "You know I'll do what I can to help."

"Well …" He pursed his lips. "It's Ethan. The problem is that I don't know what the problem is."

She smiled. "Ethan's a little bit younger than my kids were when they affected me this way, but he's also a precocious kid."

"Yeah, that he is."

"What's he doing that has you so baffled?"

Since Jonathan didn't have any secrets, he figured there was no harm in telling Maryann what was going on. "He's not doing anything wrong, but …"

"That's the problem. He's being too good, right?"

"I don't even know if that's the problem. He's just not being himself."

She gave him a look of concern. "When did this start?"

Jonathan thought back and tried to pinpoint a time, but he couldn't. All he could think of was that night when Ethan couldn't take his eyes off the TV, and then he acted strange when Jonathan went to the school to help out with the speaker.

"Do you think it has anything to do with that?"

Jonathan shook his head. "I can't imagine how that could be the case."

"You never know with kids. A lot of them are smarter than us, and they keep us on our toes."

"I know, right?" Jonathan stood and carried his paper plate over to the trashcan. "I'd better get back out there and see how we're doing on the toolkits."

The instant Jonathan hit the sales floor, he was busy assisting customers with the sale items, leading them to other items to supplement the kits, and answering questions. That was one of the things he particularly enjoyed about his business. There was always something to do.

Maryann offered to continue working after her shift ended. "I don't want you to be late picking Ethan up from school."

Jonathan often brought his son to the store and set him up on the Internet in the office so he could do his homework. "Thanks."

She grinned. "It's good for me too. Wesley and I are still working on the master bathroom, and the extra money helps."

As Jonathan drove to the school, he thought about Maryann and her husband. They were always working on some sort of project around the house … often more than one at a time. The last one was a complete kitchen remodel. Wesley was handy, but he was also heavy-handed, so Maryann did most of the finishing work. The two of them could have gone into the remodeling business, but she said she didn't like the uncertainty of it.

When he reached the school, his heart sank. There stood Ethan, right beside the principal, and neither of them looked happy.

Jonathan took a deep breath and lowered the window on the passenger side. He leaned over and smiled at the principal. "Good afternoon, Ms. Bateman."

She nodded before glancing down at Ethan who blurted, "I'm sorry, Dad."

"Sorry for what?" Jonathan narrowed his eyes as he held his son's gaze, and then he looked at the principal who opened the car door for Ethan.

"Tell your dad what you did."

The pained expression on Ethan's face made Jonathan's heart hurt. He looked just like Samantha when she was upset.

"C'mon, Ethan. I don't want to have to pull it out of you. What did you do?"

"I sent the letter to Channel 2 without permission."

"What letter?" Jonathan again switched his gaze to the principal.

"The one asking for Ms. Marshall to come."

Jonathan shook his head. "I'm sure this makes sense on some level, but I'm missing something."

A hint of a smile crossed Ms. Bateman's lips as she closed the car door and leaned over. "Apparently, he and some of his friends thought it would be a good idea to bring Carrie Marshall here …" She gave Ethan a motherly look. "Apparently, he wanted you to meet her."

"Oh." That sort of explained Ethan's strange behavior, but there were still some holes that needed to be filled in. He looked directly at his son. "Why?"

Ethan shrugged. "I don't know. I guess I just thought she was pretty and smart and nice … just like you said Mom was, and you're lonely."

"What makes you think I'm lonely?"

Ethan rolled his eyes. "It's obvious."

Ms. Bateman's lips twitched, but before she went into a full-blown smile, she pulled her lips between her teeth. Jonathan supposed it would be amusing to someone else, but his son calling him out on being lonely embarrassed him.

In spite of the fact that his face flamed with the humiliation, he looked at Ms. Bateman. "I'm terribly sorry about this. I'll talk to him and make sure this never happens again."

"You really don't have to apologize," she said. "I thought you should know about it, and he shouldn't be doing this without asking permission or at least letting someone know …" She cleared her throat. "But we're actually happy to have someone from the TV station get involved with the school. In fact, they've sent us some paperwork to fill out so they can adopt us."

"Adopt you?"

She nodded. "Businesses adopt schools all the time. They participate in events and do other things to help the school."

At least something good might come of this. But still, he didn't want Ethan to overstep, and he needed to learn that this could have backfired. In fact, on a personal level, it did because he'd lost some of the trust they once had.

Jonathan assured Ms. Bateman that he'd deal with the issue, and she smiled. "I'm sure you will. By the way, are you available to help out with the Fall Festival?"

"Sure. What do you want me to do?"

"We have several things for you to pick from. First, we need some able-bodied people to help build the booths, and then we need people to work at the concessions. After it's over, everything has to be taken down."

"Yes, I'll be happy to help."

"I'll put your name down. What do you want to do?"

"All of it. Whatever you need." After all, it was the least he could do after Ethan's shenanigan.

Her smile widened. "Wonderful." She turned to Ethan. "You're a fortunate young man, Ethan."

Jonathan watched Ethan's face turn red as he made a quick nod. He clearly didn't know what to say.

As soon as Ms. Bateman straightened up, Jonathan pulled away from the curb. They rode in silence all the way to the store. "We would go home and talk about what happened, but the ad brought in a lot of people."

Ethan blinked and swallowed hard, indicating he was still nervous and unsure of what to expect. Good. That was how it should be after what he did.

He set Ethan up in the office and pointed to the computer. "If you have to get on the Internet, fine, but no messages to the TV station."

"I just have some spelling words to study, a chapter to read for history, and a page of math."

Out of the corner of his eye, he spotted someone standing in the doorway, so he straightened up. "Hey Maryann. Need something?"

"There's a call for you on line one."

"Can you take a message?"

"You might want to take this one. It's Carrie Marshall from Channel 2."

Chapter 4

Carrie had been torn about calling Mr. Hanks after she learned what his son had done. It was actually sort of sweet, and she was flattered that his son thought so highly of her. But she mentally put herself in Ethan's dad's position and decided it was best to deal with this directly.

She'd managed to squelch her feelings, until she heard all the details of his wife's death. Apparently, Tom had gotten to know some of the school administrators over the past couple of days, and they'd shared this information with him. There was no doubt in her mind that Tom saw this as a matchmaking opportunity, and the funny thing was that it didn't bother her in the least.

As she waited for him to pick up the phone, her heart hammered. Mr. Hanks was an extremely good-looking man, and he appeared to be kind if his gentleness with the children was any indication. She'd learned from the principal of the school that he owned the hardware store, so she assumed he was handy too. The combination of all of that made him seem almost perfect.

When he finally came on the line, she opened her mouth to talk, but all that came out was a squeak. She cleared her throat.

"I'm so sorry about my son," Mr. Hanks said. "I can assure you it won't happen again."

"That's quite all right." She wanted to tell him that not only was it okay, she wouldn't mind getting to know him better. But she couldn't. "I just wanted to let you know that we'll be working at the ticket booth together."

"Did Ethan—?"

"No, I don't think so. Apparently, the station manager and the principal set it up." She didn't want his son to get in more trouble than he was already in, so she felt like she needed to eliminate any thoughts that he'd done something bad.

"Do you want me to see if they'll change my duties or put me on a different shift or something?"

"No." The instant that word left her mouth, she realized it came out way too fast. But in reality, knowing he'd be there made the project seem rather enjoyable. If it had been any other situation, she would have dreaded it, but knowing she'd be working alongside Jonathan Hanks gave her something to look forward to.

He let out what sounded like a nervous chuckle. "If you're sure …" His voice trailed off, and she could hear someone talking in the background on his end. "I need to go now, but I'd like to call you later if you don't mind."

"Sure, that would be fine."

"Should I call you at the station?"

She thought for a second and decided to just go for it. "No, call me on my private cell phone."

After she gave him her number, she leaned back and closed her eyes. It had been a very long time since a man had gotten her flustered like she was now. And never had any man with children been the least bit interesting to her.

*

After Jonathan got off the phone, he got up and went back out to the sales area, where customers clustered around the stack of toolkits that had shrunk significantly. He noticed that most of the pink ones were gone, and they had an abundance of navy.

Maryann leaned toward him. "Looks like girls are holding their own these days." She laughed. "And they're not forgetting to keep it girlish." She lifted one of the boxes and pulled out a pink-handled hammer. "I would have loved one of these when I was younger."

Jonathan made a face. "Why not now? You're still a girl."

"Oh, I know, but I've got the perfect hammer in red. No one, not even Wesley, is allowed to use it."

"I see." Jonathan gestured toward the stack still sitting on the sales floor. "So now we have to figure out how to get these navy ones sold."

"I'm sure they'll sell as soon as we're out of the pink ones. Most girls are okay with navy, even if it isn't their first choice."

"Dad?"

The sound of Ethan's voice caught Jonathan's attention. He turned around. "Finished with your homework?"

Ethan nodded and walked toward the toolkits. "Those are really cool. Can you get me one?"

"Seriously?" Jonathan glanced at Maryann before returning his gaze to his son. "What would you do with it?"

Ethan shrugged. "Maybe you can teach me how to do a few things around the house."

Maryann grinned and gave a thumbs-up. "I think we just figured out what to do with these navy toolkits. Start 'em early."

Jonathan rubbed his chin as he studied his son. "Ya know, that's probably a good idea. You've always been such a good student, it didn't even dawn on me to get you into this kind of thing."

Ethan sighed. "Being smart doesn't mean I can't be handy too." A goofy look crossed his face as he added, "And I want to be a jock."

"A jock?" Jonathan laughed. "What brought that on?"

"Some of my buddies at school said jocks get all the pretty girls."

Maryann burst into laughter, in spite of Jonathan scowling at her. She tousled Ethan's hair. "Trust me, Ethan. I don't think you'll have any trouble in the romance department."

"Ew." Ethan's face puckered up. "Who said anything about romance?"

Jonathan grimaced. "Looks like it's almost time for the talk, son."

"No, I don't want that talk."

Maryann's eyes widened as she backed away. "You boys need some privacy. I'm outta here."

"You do realize there's more to pretty girls than just getting them to like you, right?"

Ethan gave his dad a yeah-right look. "I was just kidding. You know I wouldn't know what to do with a pretty girl if I caught one."

Jonathan couldn't help but laugh. "That's why we need to have a talk."

Ethan folded his arms and tilted his head as he gave his dad a long look. "So you think you know what to do with one?"

Jonathan bobbed his head in a nod. "Yeah, I like to think so."

"Then why are you so confused about Ms. Marshall? She's a pretty girl, and she likes you." Ethan paused and gave a closed-mouth grin. "A lot."

"How would you know?"

"Oh, I can tell. She looks at you real funny."

"I don't even know her very well, so don't go getting any ideas, kiddo. Why don't you pick out a toolkit, and I'll buy it for you."

"You don't have to buy it. You own the place."

Jonathan shook his head. "I might own the place, but it's not free. Which one do you want?"

All the toolkits were identical, but Jonathan knew Ethan liked having some say in his life. He walked around, opened a couple, and then lifted one from the stack. “This one looks good.”

“Okay, take that up to the counter and let Maryann know that’s the one I’m buying for you.”

As Ethan walked up to the counter carrying the toolbox, Jonathan could imagine his son following him around the house, learning how to fix what was broken. And that made him as proud as he was of Ethan’s stellar test scores at school.

Maryann approached him and whispered, “Why don’t you and Ethan go on home? I’ll close up.”

“I don’t want to—”

She held up her hand to shush him. “Trust me, it’s not an inconvenience. Wesley is cooking tonight, so all I have to do is show up.”

“Okay, if you’re sure you don’t mind.” He waited for her to nod before motioning for Ethan to get his backpack.

Once they got in the house, Ethan turned on the TV and put it on Channel 2. Jonathan grinned as he pulled the chicken out of the refrigerator to start supper. He actually wasn’t mad about his son trying to set him up with Carrie.

He’d barely gotten dinner in the oven when Ethan called out. “Dad, she’s gonna be on TV in a minute. C’mon, or you’ll miss her.”

*

“This has got to be the busiest news day ever.” Carrie looked over the information she needed to condense for the daily news brief, wondering how she’d get it all down to five minutes. “It’ll definitely be a challenge.”

“Good that it’s you and not me,” Tom said. “I couldn’t possibly talk that fast.”

She laughed. “No one can talk fast enough to say all of this. I’ll just have to give some teasers to get people to watch the longer broadcast.”

“Remember the last time you tried to do that?”

She nodded. “Do I ever. I can’t remember a time when so many people called in, complaining.” She glanced down at her notes. “But I don’t see that I have much of a choice. I’ll just warn them that it’s been a very newsy day.”

Tom gestured toward the small set. “Better get on over there, or you’ll surely have folks calling in.”

Carrie sat down behind the desk, took a deep breath, and glanced at her notes one more time. The teleprompter was set and ready to deliver, so the second the cameras came on, she began.

It took her every single second of her five minutes, but she managed to deliver all the news. Once she was off the air, she let out a deep sigh.

"Wow." Tom's eyes widened as he shook his head in amazement. "I'm blown away by how well you did that."

She let out another breath from puffed cheeks. "I can't believe I managed to say so much in such a short amount of time. I just hope we don't get a bunch of angry people calling in."

As if on cue, the studio phone lit up. Tom took the first call, and the assistants started picking up. This went on for about fifteen minutes, and then they tapered off.

Tom cleared his throat after he got off the call. "You spoke too fast. The caller said she'll forgive you this one time, but don't ever do that again, or she'll have to start watching Channel 5." He chuckled. "After I told her why you did that, she said you could have slowed down and taken ten minutes. She clearly doesn't understand scheduling."

"Can't get away with anything around here," Carrie mumbled. "But I did what I thought I had to do."

"And you did the right thing." Tom folded his arms and smiled. "Some people are never happy, so don't worry about it."

She nodded. One of the things she knew she needed to overcome was her desire to please everyone. She knew it wasn't possible, yet she continued to try.

"So are you prepared to face hundreds of elementary aged children at their Fall Festival?"

"As ready as I can be. I don't think there's any way to prepare since they can be so unpredictable." She didn't say the rest of what she was thinking—that she didn't know how to prepare for a little boy's attempts to fix her up with his dad. She couldn't help but smile as Mr. Hanks's image popped into her mind.

"At least you seem happy about it."

She shrugged. "I don't mind. It's all part of the job."

He chuckled softly as he narrowed his eyes. "Somehow this seems like more than that this time."

Carrie wished she was better at hiding her feelings, but she'd always been easy to read. "I really don't know."

"You'll do fine. You always do." Tom gave her one last fatherly smile before turning and heading back to his office.

She finished her work before going home to her apartment. Ever since college, she'd lived alone, but lately, loneliness had started creeping its way into her life. Part of the reason was probably the fact that most of her friends had gotten married over the past few years … and now she had to admit she wanted some of that for herself.

Never one to miss dinner, she prepared a meal of baked fish and steamed asparagus. People who weren't used to being alone always seemed surprised when she told them she cooked meals for herself most nights. Her childhood best friend said she never wanted to go to that much trouble since she was the only one there before she married her husband. Carrie wasn't sure she'd ever find a man to spend her life with, so she needed to take care of herself.

After dinner, Carrie turned on the TV and watched some cable news to catch some snippets of what she might have missed. Her dad used to tease her about being a news junkie. She denied it when she was younger, but now that she was in the business, it was okay to admit it. And she couldn't stand to miss anything.

Her phone rang, making her jump. She rarely got phone calls at this time, so she was tempted not to answer it since she didn't recognize the number. But her curiosity got the best of her, so she picked it up and clicked the TALK button.

"This is Jonathan Hanks. I hope I'm not bothering you."

"Hi Mr. Hanks. No, you're not bothering me. How are you?"

"Couldn't be better. I wanted to let you know how impressed my son and I are by your news brief earlier."

She belted out a laugh. "So you and your son like fast talkers?"

"You clearly had a lot to say."

"I did." She sure hoped he didn't hear her hammering heart. "How's your son?"

"Ethan's great. In fact, he's the one who turned on the TV … and he asked me to call you."

"He did?"

"Yes." Jonathan cleared his throat. She sensed that he had more to say, so she remained quiet. "Ethan would like to know … well, we'd both like to know if you'd be interested in a picnic at the park on Saturday … that is, if you're not busy."

"Picnic? In the park?" Carrie had never been an outdoorsy type, and he'd caught her off guard. She let out a nervous laugh. "Um …"

"Don't feel obligated. If you don't want—"

"Oh, but I do. I'd be delighted to join you and Ethan."

"Is it okay if I pick you up, or would you rather meet us there?"

"Sure, I'd love for you to pick me up." She'd held her breath so long she needed to inhale before giving her address.

After she told him where she lived, he said they'd pick her up around 10:30 on Saturday morning. "We'll bring all the food. Just make sure you're wearing comfortable clothes. It's supposed to be unseasonably warm, but since you probably have an in with the weather person, you're probably already aware of that."

She laughed. "You're right."

"Ethan and I can't wait to see you. Enjoy the rest of the week."

"I look forward to seeing you and Ethan."

After she hung up, she thought for a moment and decided to call her mom to let her know she wasn't coming over on Saturday. Normally, she had nothing to do on the weekend, besides go to church, so she'd established a habit of stopping by her parents' house.

"But we were counting on you," her mother said. "In fact, Matthew's mother called and said he'll be home for a few days. I thought—" She cut herself off. "Never mind."

Chapter 5

"Looks like you're getting what you want, son." Jonathan widened his stance, folded his arms, and looked down at Ethan. "Now I'm curious what you're gonna do."

Ethan tilted his head as he met his dad's gaze. "What do you mean, what I'm gonna do?"

"It's sort of like a dog chasing a car. What'll he do if he ever catches it?"

"That's a weird thing to say, Dad. What are you talking about?"

Jonathan sat down on the sofa beside Ethan and leaned forward, propping his forearms on his knees. "It's like this. You've been watching Ms. Marshall for a while now, and you got both of us to go to the school. It's obvious what's going on, but I'm not sure what you think will come of it."

Ethan gave him a shy look. "She's pretty, Dad."

"I know she is, but there are a lot of pretty women in this world."

"But she's smart too. You always said Mom was smart, so I know you like smart girls."

"You're right, I do." While Jonathan appreciated Ethan's logic and concern for his love life, he couldn't let his son feel responsible for making him happy. "Just remember that if I'm supposed to meet someone, it'll happen. You need to concentrate on school and sports … and other stuff boys your age do."

"Like being a good son?"

"Yes, but you can do that without finding me a woman."

"Maybe I won't have to." Ethan gave him a goofy grin.

"Why do you say that?"

"Ms. Marshall's going to the park with us on Saturday, and maybe you'll decide to marry her."

"Whoa, there, Ethan. Slow down." Jonathan stood and took a couple of steps toward the kitchen. "We're all going on a picnic together. That's all."

"But what if she has a good time and wants to do something else with us?"

Jonathan flashed a smile at his son. "Let's take this down a notch. As it is now, Ms. Marshall is a friend. Maybe after we go to the park, she'll become a very good friend."

"And—?"

"And nothing. Don't try to force anything, Ethan. I've done that, and it never works."

*

The rest of the week got even more hectic at the TV station. Between some of the city council business and the national news, Carrie had more than one day of talking fast.

"I'm thinking about entering you in the fast talk competition," Tom said. "I think after this week you can give that British guy … the fastest talker in the world … what's his name?" Before she could answer, he continued. "Steve Woodmore? You can give him a run for his money."

Carrie widened her eyes and slowly shook her head. "I have no desire to keep this up. If the news continues at this pace, I'm afraid we'll either have to hire Mr. Woodmore to deliver it or make the news brief ten minutes."

One of the production grips passed, held up a finger, gave Carrie a teasing glance, and turned to Tom. "Woodmore isn't the fastest talker anymore. A couple people have beaten his world record, so maybe he's in the market for a job."

Tom chuckled. "I just might give him a call. So what do you have for today's brief?"

They had one of their impromptu meetings before she sat down and wrote the news for the teleprompter. By the time she got home that night, all she wanted to do was flop down on her bed and sleep. But she'd barely gotten in her house when her phone rang. It was her mother.

"Are you still going out with that guy?"

"Still going out?" Carrie paused as she formulated something to say that wouldn't make her mother think it was more than just a friendship. "I wouldn't say we're going out, but we do have plans. Why?"

"You have plans, huh?" Her mother snickered. "In my book, that's going out. So what are your plans?"

"I'm going to the park with him and his son."

"His son?"

"Yes. He's widowed. I suspect this is more about his son wanting to hang out with a news personality than his wanting to go out with me."

"Oh, I don't believe that for one minute. If this man has half a brain, he'll know you're a good catch."

Carrie laughed. "Mom, you're incorrigible."

"No, I'm not. I just know you're an amazing woman who can get any man you want if you'll just look away from your career long enough to let it happen."

Carrie's jaw tightened. She was tired of her mother coming back to her with the same argument over and over.

"Let me know how the date goes."

"I already told you it's not a date."

"Okay, whatever you want to call it, let me know what happens. I'm not so sure you're ready to get involved with a ready-made family."

Carrie resisted the urge to let out what her mother always called a growl. Instead, she told her she needed to go.

After Carrie got off the phone, she sank back in her chair and thought about what her mother had said about not being ready to get involved with a ready-made family. Ten years ago, when she was twenty-five, that would have been the case. But now that she was in her mid thirties, she thought it actually sounded pretty good—especially if the child was as amazing as Ethan appeared to be.

The teacher had told her he was advanced for his grade level, and she'd wanted to have him tested to possibly promote him to fifth grade. But his dad had said no, he wanted him to be with other kids his age. So they'd come up with some extra lessons to challenge him. That said a lot about both Ethan and Jonathan, and she liked what she saw.

The rest of the week passed in a blur, with Carrie's only in-focus thoughts being about spending Saturday with Jonathan and his son. She pondered bringing something, even though he told her he'd bring the food.

After fretting about it enough to cause a sleepless night, she decided to just do it. Now all she had to figure out was what to bring. She was a decent cook, but she didn't want to mess up anything Jonathan had planned. So she decided to make a dessert. Even if he brought something sweet, she could send hers home with them later.

She thumbed through her cookbooks and checked out some recipes online to see what would do well at a picnic. Most of what she saw would make it look like she'd tried to hard, so she kept looking until she clicked onto a site with chocolate-dipped strawberries. That would be easy, and they'd be perfect for a picnic.

Strawberries weren't in season locally, but the produce manager said he had some really good ones that were imported. She purchased those and went to the baking aisle where she found all forms of candy coating—white, dark, and milk chocolate. Perfect.

On Friday night, she dipped strawberries, and once the coating was hard, she packed them in some plastic containers. After she was done, she picked up her e-reader and sat down to catch up on some of the magazines she'd downloaded. But it was impossible to focus on the words when her mind kept projecting her to tomorrow. Finally, she gave up and went to bed.

*

"Can we go pick her up now?"

Jonathan glanced down at his son who'd been jumping around the kitchen all morning. "It's still early, son. Why don't you go watch some cartoons?"

"Cartoons are lame."

"Then go play a video game." Jonathan couldn't believe he'd just said that since he'd been trying to get Ethan away from video games lately.

"You're kidding, right?" Ethan frowned. "You're just trying to get rid of me."

Jonathan put down the spoon he'd been using to stir the potato salad and turned to face Ethan. "Sorry, Ethan. I hate to admit this, but I'm nervous."

Ethan's face lit up. "You are? That's a good thing, right?"

"I'm not so sure it's a good thing."

"It is because it means you really like Ms. Marshall. I like her too."

Jonathan nodded. He'd learned a long time ago that his son could see right through him when he tried to hide his feelings. "I do like her, but I don't want to scare her away by showing up early or appearing too anxious."

Ethan's expression turned contemplative. "I don't get it. Don't you want her to know you like her?"

"Yes, of course, but I don't want to rush her. That might scare her away."

After a momentary pause, Ethan shook his head. "That wouldn't be good."

"So do you understand now?"

Ethan shrugged. "I don't know if I'll ever totally understand when it comes to girls."

Jonathan belted out a laugh. "You're not alone, son. Most of us have a hard time understanding girls, but that's part of the allure."

"And that's one of the things I don't get."

"But you really like her, don't you?" Jonathan persisted.

Ethan nodded. "Yes, but not because she's hard to understand. I like her because she's smart and pretty and nice and …" He shrugged again. "I think she's really cool."

"You and me and a lot of other people, I imagine. We just have to give her a reason to like us back."

"Is that why you're cooking so much?"

Jonathan lifted an eyebrow and gave Ethan a questioning look. "Is that a complaint?"

Ethan held up both hands and adamantly shook his head. "No, I'm not complaining at all. I love your fried chicken and potato salad and coleslaw and all that other stuff."

A half hour later, Jonathan was finished putting the final touches on the food and had everything loaded into the truck. "Ready to go, son?"

Ethan flashed a humongous grin. "I've been ready forever."

Jonathan smiled back and thought, *me too*.

Chapter 6

Carrie continued to pace back and forth, glancing out the front window each time she passed it. She'd been ready for almost an hour, and now her nerves were starting to get the best of her.

When she finally saw the white truck pull into her driveway, she had to resist the urge to run to the door and fling it open. Instead, she stood still and did one of the breathing exercises she'd learned before going on air for the first time.

Then she waited for the knock at the door before opening it. She expected Jonathan to be standing there, but instead, Ethan was on her porch, and Jonathan stood at the foot of the porch steps.

"Hi there, Ethan."

"Are you ready to go on a picnic?" Ethan's flushed red cheeks made him look like someone out of a Norman Rockwell painting. He glanced over his shoulder at his dad who gave him a clipped nod. He turned back to her. "Dad has made a ton of food, so I hope you're hungry."

"I am hungry." She took a step back and gestured for him to come inside. "Why don't you and your dad come on in while I get something I made out of the refrigerator?"

Jonathan cleared his throat. "You didn't have to make anything. I didn't want you to go to any trouble."

"I know, but I wanted to." She smiled back at him. "Besides, it wasn't any trouble at all. It's just chocolate dipped strawberries."

She saw Jonathan and Ethan exchange a glance before they both looked back at her and smiled. "In that case, we'll wait right here while you go get them."

As Carrie went into the kitchen, she pondered their reaction when she told them what she was bringing. Something strange had just happened. Then it dawned on her. Maybe they didn't like strawberries … or worse, one of them was allergic to them, but they didn't want to hurt her feelings. She let out a soft chuckle at that thought. After being in the newsroom for so long, it took quite a bit to hurt her feelings.

She came out with the container of strawberries and stopped in the doorway. "Do you guys not like strawberries?"

Ethan looked surprised, but Jonathan shook his head. "We both love strawberries."

"Oh, okay, that's good."

"Why do you ask?" Jonathan took the container from her and gently placed his other hand in the middle of her back to guide her toward the door.

She shrugged. "The way you two looked at each other made me think you might not care for them."

Jonathan's momentary silence concerned her, but Ethan spoke up. "Mom used to make chocolate-covered strawberries for Dad, and that's why we never have them anymore."

"Oh." Now it made sense. She'd brought back a memory that caused their reaction. "I'm so sorry. I had no idea."

"Of course you didn't know." Jonathan managed a smile. "I think it's time to try one of my favorite treats again. It's been a while."

"I don't want—"

"Don't worry about it. I think it's very sweet that you did this for us."

He helped her into the truck and then got Ethan settled in the backseat. The mood had changed, and they drove to the park mostly in silence until they arrived.

Jonathan glanced over his shoulder at Ethan. "Why don't you carry the strawberries? Ms. Marshall and I can get the rest of it."

They found a picnic table near the playground and start of the hiking trail and started spreading everything out. Jonathan and Ethan seemed to have a system, letting her know they'd done this before. So she tried to follow what they did so she wouldn't mess anything up.

"Are you always this adaptable?" Jonathan asked.

She grinned. "Not always. I just happen to know that it's important to turn to those with experience when I have no idea what to do next."

He contorted his mouth in a humorous way. "Yeah, it's important to get the picnic thing right, or the earth might tip off its axis."

"We wouldn't want that to happen."

Ethan looked back and forth between them before interjecting. "If that happened, we might roll off into the universe. That would be so weird."

"It would be more than weird."

"Yeah, we'd either burn up or freeze to death, depending on which direction we rolled."

Jonathan tousled Ethan's hair. "Why don't we try being a bit less morose? I suspect Ms. Marshall isn't used to that kind of talk."

"Oh, trust me, I'm used to all kinds of morose. Don't forget what business I'm in."

"So true."

Ethan tilted his head and studied Carrie. "Is all that stuff true?"

"What stuff?"

"All that stuff you talk about on the news."

She nodded. "Unfortunately, yes. We only tell what really happens."

Jonathan held up his hands. "We're supposed to be having a good time today. I'm sure Ms. Marshall doesn't want to talk about work."

"No, that's okay," she argued. "I think it's natural for children to have questions about the news … but if you don't want him exposed to so much tragedy …"

"If I could keep him from tragedy, I would, but it's everywhere." Jonathan hopped to his feet as he gave her a warm smile. "Why don't we hit the hiking trail?"

"Sure." She stood and dusted off her backside, while Ethan bounded toward the trail like a streak of lightning.

If they'd been anywhere besides Baker Creek, South Carolina, Carrie would have offered to stay with their picnic loot. But very seldom did people mess with things that didn't belong to them around here. In fact, very little of the bad news she reported came from this town. Most of her local information was positive and uplifting—like the *School of the Month* or the *Hero of the Year* awards. And the few times when she didn't have enough news to fill her slot, she'd been known to call the fire department to find out if they'd rescued any kittens from trees.

"You're a fast walker," Jonathan blurted. "Not many people can keep up with Ethan."

"I've had to walk fast to catch up with some of the people I interview." She made a wry smile. "They don't always want to talk to reporters."

"I can imagine."

"So what do you and Ethan normally do on Saturdays?"

He gestured around. "This or hang out at the hardware store."

"Sounds fun."

"It really is if you like that sort of thing." He moved a limb to keep it from hitting Carrie's face. "My dad was a builder, and he took me on jobs when I didn't have school, so I was around construction people most of my life."

"Is that something Ethan's interested in?"

Jonathan nodded. "Yes, but in a different way. He seems to like the engineering aspect, and he's incredible with numbers."

"He seems incredible in a lot of ways," Carrie said.

"I think so, but of course I would." Jonathan looked around. "And speaking of Ethan, he knows better than to get too far ahead." He called out for Ethan.

"I'm right here, Dad." Ethan's voice came from just around the corner where a patch of shrubbery blocked the view. "You'd think I was a baby the way you worry about me."

Carrie couldn't help but laugh. She'd been around enough parents to understand how difficult it was to let go. In fact, she wondered if she'd be much worse than Jonathan.

*

The sound of Carrie's laughter brought a smile to Jonathan's face. It felt right to be with her, chatting with each other while keeping an eye out for Ethan. It felt like he was part of a team again.

When she turned toward him, his breath caught in his throat. She was beautiful, but more than that, the way she made him feel when their gazes met nearly caused his knees to buckle.

She took another step and stumbled, but he reached for her and caught her before she fell. The instant they touched, he knew he had to kiss her.

He leaned toward her, and when she didn't resist, he continued until his lips touched hers. The pounding of his heart was powerful, and he didn't care if she felt it. This woman was special, and now that he'd had a taste of her, there was no turning back.

"Dad!"

Jonathan jumped back and ran his fingers through his hair as he turned toward the sound of his son's voice. "What do you need, son?"

Ethan pulled his lips between his teeth as his eyebrows went up. Carrie appeared flustered, and he could tell she had no idea what to do or if she'd been involved in something bad. He had to say something to diffuse her worry.

"Can't you tell I'm trying to kiss the girl?"

"Sorry, Dad, but I …" Ethan's voice trailed off as he offered a shy smile and turned away. "I'll leave y'all alone but when you're done, I want to show you something."

"Now where were we?" Jonathan took her hand in his and kissed the back of it.

"Doesn't that worry you?"

"Doesn't what worry me?" he asked.

"Your son. He saw us …" She pursed her lips. "He saw us kissing."

"Yeah, and do you have a problem with that?"

She crinkled her face and narrowed her eyes. "Should I?"

"No, not at all. In fact, I suspect he's feeling pretty good about things now. You do realize he orchestrated this whole thing, right?"

"I wondered if that might be the case."

"Do you want to know the details?" he asked. "My son is quite the matchmaker, and he didn't leave many stones unturned."

Carrie smiled but didn't say anything. He wasn't sure how she felt, but she didn't seem to mind the kiss.

"Dad! You gotta see this!"

Jonathan gave her an apologetic look and shrug. "Coming, son."

*

Carrie sighed as Jonathan ran ahead to see what Ethan wanted. His kiss had caught her off guard, and she enjoyed it.

When Jonathan and Ethan came back around the corner, she couldn't help but notice a snake dangling from a stick Ethan was holding. "Look what I found."

The sight of Ethan with the snake surprised her, but she wasn't the least bit rattled. Growing up, she had brothers who thought it was hilarious to put a black racer under her sheets. The first time she screamed, and after that she always found a way to get even with them.

Ethan held the snake out toward her, but Jonathan stopped him. "Don't shake it at her."

Carrie laughed, took another step toward Ethan, and held out her hands. "I haven't seen a black racer in a long time."

Jonathan's eyebrows shot up. "Aren't you scared?"

"Nope. I have brothers."

Ethan handed her the snake that gave a little wriggle but stopped. "I don't think he's feeling too good."

"I bet he's afraid." Carrie held it up to look at it a little more closely. "We should probably let him go. Did you know that they help keep rodents under control?"

Jonathan looked at Ethan who nodded. "I did a report on the benefits of snakes during my enrichment class."

"Enrichment class?" She tilted her head.

Ethan turned to his dad who spoke up. "That's what the school put him in when I said he couldn't go to fifth grade yet."

"Oh, I see. So why don't we let your little friend go, so he can get to work hunting rodents?"

Ethan looked at his dad, who nodded. "Good idea. We don't want the rats to take over, do we, son?"

"No." Ethan paused, glanced back and forth between Carrie and Jonathan, and walked over to the bushes a few feet away.

After Ethan let the snake go, Jonathan leaned over and whispered, "Good job. I can't believe you didn't scream."

"You're not likely to ever hear me scream." Carrie bobbed her head and smiled. "If you do, you'd better run."

"Which direction?" Jonathan asked. "Toward you or away from you?"

"All depends on why I'm screaming."

"Dad, I'm getting hungry. Can we eat now?"

"Sure thing." Jonathan gestured toward the trail going back to the site where they'd left the food. "After you."

All the way back, Carrie was fully aware of the man and boy behind her as their footsteps crunched the freshly fallen leaves. This was a day she knew she'd never forget.

*

Jonathan didn't waste a single minute before pulling the food out of the basket and opening the containers. Ethan got each of them drinks from the cooler.

"I can't wait to finish lunch so I can have one of the strawberries," Ethan said. "I've always wanted to try them."

"Sorry I deprived you all these years," Jonathan said. He glanced over at Carrie who appeared unsure of what to say or do. "I'm really glad you made them. The one time I tried to do it myself, the chocolate seized up and got all gloppy. I made a huge mess."

"Is that why you haven't had them in a while?" Carrie asked.

He hesitated for a few seconds before nodding. "Yeah, I waited a year, but when the nostalgia came over me, I had to try my hand at making them. Somehow I mastered the art of mixing potato salad and frying chicken, but the fine art of getting the chocolate on fresh strawberries somehow eluded me."

"Did you use a double boiler to melt the chocolate?" Carrie asked.

He shook his head. "No, I don't even know what a double boiler is. Maybe you can show me sometime."

Her lips twitched into a soft smile. "I'll be happy to."

"Maybe you can teach me some other things as well." As soon as those words escaped his lips, he realized how they might sound to Carrie. But she didn't flinch.

"I'm a pretty decent cook, but based on the way this food tastes, so are you. Maybe we can have a cook-off."

"Sounds like fun. Ethan can be the judge."

Ethan was so busy chomping down on his food he didn't say a word, until he finished the last bite of his sandwich. "Can I have a strawberry now?"

Jonathan glanced at Carrie, who nodded, before he turned back to his son. "Sure, but just one for now."

Carrie lifted the lid and extended the container to Ethan. He looked them over and pulled out the biggest one in the bunch. Both Jonathan and Carrie laughed.

Ethan nibbled some chocolate off the edge of the strawberry before opening his mouth wide and shoving half of the fruit into it. His eyes widened, and he managed to smile as he chewed.

"Like it?" Jonathan asked.

Ethan nodded and then swallowed. "Can I have another one?"

"Let's wait a little while." Jonathan turned to Carrie. "When he likes something, he can make it disappear faster than you can say 'stop.'"

Without wasting another minute, Ethan jumped to his feet. "Dad, can I go play on the swings?"

All it took was a nod from Jonathan, and Ethan was running off toward the playground. Jonathan chuckled. "So what do you think of hanging out with a man and his boy?"

"I like it." Carrie glanced off in Ethan's direction.

When she turned back to face Jonathan, he wanted more than anything to kiss her. And that was exactly what he did.

Chapter 7

Carrie woke up early Sunday morning and stretched but stayed in bed as she thought about yesterday's picnic. She couldn't have planned a more perfect day than the one she had with Jonathan and Ethan. Everything about it was a surprise—from the snake encounter to eating the food—and every single thing was delicious.

Ethan seemed to have an innate ability to know when to hang out with them and when to go play. Jonathan clearly loved his son, and it was obvious he spent quite a bit of time with him, based on how well behaved Ethan was.

Then there were the kisses. The first one surprised her, but once she realized what was happening, she allowed herself to go with the moment. But the second one … that was a real humdinger, as her mother used to say. It made her toes curl.

He'd asked her if she wanted to do something today. She told him she couldn't because of church. What she didn't say was that her mother had plans for her to get together with Matthew, but he really didn't need to know that.

"Maybe some other time." The disappointment in his voice was evident.

"Absolutely. In fact, why don't you and Ethan come over one night this week, and I can show both of you how to dip strawberries?"

"Perfect."

"I can cook dinner too."

"Even more perfect. By the way, what church do you go to?"

"Baker Creek Community Church."

He narrowed his eyes. "Isn't that the big one a block east of Main Street?"

"That's the one."

"Beautiful, smart, a good cook, and a church girl. Can't get any better than that." He took her hands in his and kissed her again.

Just as she closed her eyes and tried to remember the feeling, her phone rang. It was good while it lasted. She opened an eye, lifted her phone from the nightstand, and groaned. It was her mother.

"I just wanted to let you know Matthew was here yesterday afternoon. He asked about you."

Carrie repositioned herself up on her elbows. "How's Matt doing?"

"He's doing extremely well. In fact, he's moving back to Baker Creek."

"That's nice. Is he moving in with his parents?"

"No, of course not. He just bought a house close to downtown. I'm sure he'll tell you all about it after church."

"After church?"

"Yes, sweetie. I apologized for you having other plans, and I told him you'd love to go to lunch with him today."

"You didn't." Carrie didn't have anything to do after church, but she certainly didn't like her mother's interference.

"Look, Carrie. You and Matthew used to be so good together, and he's excited about seeing you again."

"But he's the one who broke up with me."

"That's only because both of you had to figure out life before you settled down and—" Her mom stopped, but Carrie knew what she was thinking. "At any rate, you need to see him. He looks even better than he did before he left for Atlanta."

"I'm sure he does."

"Well, I'd better run. Make sure you look nice for Matthew. He hasn't seen you in a while, so you need to make sure he likes what he sees."

After Carrie got off the phone, she went to the kitchen and fixed herself some coffee and toast. As she sat down at her kitchen table, she thought about Matthew and how she once imagined herself married to him. In her mind, they both had careers and a couple of kids who, like Ethan, were precocious and well behaved. Now that she thought about it, she realized how mismatched she and Matthew would have been.

He never liked her goals in life, and the fact that she had no intention of backing down caused some arguments with both of them saying things they couldn't retract. He finally said he had different ideas for his future, and then he left town to pursue his own dreams.

Although she had to admit she wondered what he was doing back in town, she had no desire to reestablish their former relationship, regardless of what their moms expected. Her mother would probably never understand, though, so she might as well face the fact that she needed to confront her.

She finally got up, put her dishes in the sink, and got ready for church. This was one of those times she wished she'd followed some of her old friends and joined one of the smaller, more contemporary churches so she wouldn't have to deal with what everyone else expected of her.

All the way to church, she imagined how it would be to see Matthew after all these years. What was it? Three years? She did some mental calculations and realized it had been at least four years.

She'd barely pulled into the parking lot when she spotted Matthew. He was hard to miss at six-foot-four, broad-shouldered, black-haired, and looking like he'd just stepped out of a men's fashion catalog. And right beside him were their mothers. She groaned.

Carrie was tempted to keep going, but they'd seen her, so there was no escape. She pulled into a spot on the edge of the lot, sat for a moment and stared at the patch of trees in front of her, and said a brief prayer for knowing how to deal with whatever she faced. Finally, she got out of her car and without looking in Matthew's direction, she walked toward the church, where dozens of people stood on the steps. But her mother was nowhere in sight.

"Carrie!"

She turned around at the sound of Matthew's voice. He came toward her with his arms open wide. "Hey, Matthew. It's good to see you."

He chuckled as he pulled her in for a hug and then let go. "Your actions don't match your words." He looked her up and down. "You look amazing. Being a celebrity agrees with you. I always knew you'd do something special."

She bristled at his words. "Matthew, you know I don't see myself as a celebrity. I just love being a reporter and telling people what's going on in the world."

"And you're on TV every night." He placed his hands on his hips and shook his head. "You are amazing, Carrie. You've always been gorgeous, but you're prettier now than ever."

His attention to superficial detail was exactly what bugged her the whole time they hung out. Their mothers had been good friends for years, and they'd hoped for Carrie and Matthew to bring the families together.

"So where do you want to go for lunch after church?" he asked. "Your mom recommended the Plucked Pig. She said they still have the best barbecue in town."

"I don't know." Why had her mother done this to her? She knew how Carrie felt.

"It sounds good to me, but if you have someplace else in mind, let me know. I don't really care as long as I'm with you. We sure do have a lot to catch up on."

The sound of the organ music sent everyone inside, including Carrie and Matthew. There really was no way of getting round the fact that he planned to sit with her.

*

"Hey, Dad, there's Ms. Marshall."

Jonathan had to force his breath to come out evenly. "Yes, I know. I saw her outside talking to some people when we came in."

Ethan leaned back and gave his dad a curious look. "You did? Why didn't we go say hi to her?"

Jonathan did a one-shoulder shrug. "I figured we could talk to her after church." He didn't want to bring up the fact that the man she was with had clearly laid claim to her, based on his body language and how they looked at each other. Even when Carrie gave him a look of annoyance, it was also one of familiarity.

"Who's that guy sitting with her?"

"I have no idea, but he's clearly a good friend of hers." It was hard enough not to look at Carrie, but his son was making it even more difficult.

"He must be a really good friend," Ethan said.

"Why do you say that?"

"'Cause he just put his arm around her, and only good friends do that."

Now he had to look, and sure enough, the man had his arm possessively around Carrie's shoulders. Jonathan felt as though someone had punched him in the gut.

He managed to sit through church without losing his mind, but he couldn't remember a single thing about the sermon once it was over. Even though Ethan wanted to go talk to Carrie, he thought of an excuse to get home.

"I'm not sure I turned off the coffee pot. Maybe we can call her later."

"But Dad—" Ethan frowned and stopped when he made eye contact with Jonathan. "Okay."

When Carrie told him where she went to church, he thought he and Ethan would just show up and surprise her. Now he realized that was the stupidest thing he could have done. He should have taken Ethan to the same church they'd been going to since Samantha died.

On the way home, Ethan brought up some points from the sermon. He was amazed by how much his nine-year-old son had grasped. "Do you think God really sees every single thing?"

Jonathan nodded. "There is no doubt in my mind that He does."

"How does he do that?"

"I have no idea."

Ethan pondered that for a moment before he nodded. "I reckon that's what makes Him God."

"Yep." Jonathan forced a smile and tousled Ethan's hair. "I reckon you're right."

"So what are we gonna do now?"

Jonathan had just turned the burner on the pot of soup he was heating up for lunch. He leaned against the counter beside the range. "I guess I'll call Ms. Marshall tomorrow and find out when she wants to see me again."

"That's not what I'm talking about, Dad. I just want to know what we're gonna do this afternoon."

"Oh." Jonathan turned his back to Ethan so his son wouldn't see his expression. "I guess we can either go back to the park."

"Or maybe we can go see Nana and Papa."

Jonathan nodded. "We can do that."

"If you give me your cell phone, I'll call and tell them we're coming."

"Hold your horses, Ethan. Let's have some lunch first, and then you can call them."

Jonathan looked at his son, whose expression gave away his disappointment. Before church, they'd discussed different ideas of what to do after the services, and Jonathan had told Ethan that if she didn't have plans, maybe they could hang out all afternoon.

Ethan was clearly smitten, but Jonathan had to admit to himself, not as much as he was. Carrie had stolen both of their hearts, but he should have figured there would be someone else. She was smart, pretty, interesting, and fun to be around.

As they ate their soup and sandwiches, Jonathan tried to steer their conversation away from anything that might bring it back to Carrie. He thought he was doing great, until Ethan put down his spoon and gave him an intense look.

Jonathan leaned back and met his son's gaze. "What's on your mind?"

"Why are you avoiding Ms. Marshall? I thought you liked her."

"I do. It's just that …" How do you explain something like this to a child?

"Are you jealous that she was with some other guy?"

Jonathan's eyebrows shot up. "Jealous?" He pondered that thought. "I don't think I can call it jealousy, but I might as well admit that I was disappointed. I was hoping she wasn't in another relationship."

"You mean you don't want her to have another boyfriend?"

Jonathan couldn't help but smile. "Yeah, that's what I'm talking about."

"Well, dad ..." Ethan gave him a big grin. "You just might have to fight for this girl."

*

Carrie decided there wasn't any harm in meeting Matthew at the Plucked Pig, but she couldn't continue letting him think there would be anything besides friendship between the two of them. As they sat across from each other in the booth, he reached across the table for her hand. She put both of her hands in her lap.

"What is going on, Carrie? I always thought there was something special between us."

"Matt ..." She wanted to be extra careful with her words because not only did she want to spare his feelings she didn't want to create an issue between their mothers who'd obviously had a hand in this. "There is, but it's a special friendship ..." She glanced down and then back up at him. "Nothing more."

"But I thought—" He pulled his hand back and pursed his lips. "There's someone else, isn't there?"

"No ..." She thought about Jonathan. "Well, maybe ..." She gave him an apologetic look. "Sort of, but nothing serious."

"You're confused about your feelings for this guy?"

She shrugged. "Not really. It's just too soon to know."

He folded his hands on the table and slowly nodded. "So I'm losing out to someone you just met, and you're not even sure about him."

Carrie hated being put on the defensive, but she still understood. "Look, Matthew, you can't really say anything since you're the one who didn't stick around."

He closed his eyes and slowly reopened them as he nodded. "Good point. Is there anything I can do to make up for what I did wrong?"

"That's just it. You didn't do anything wrong. You wanted to leave town, so you did."

"I'm sorry."

She smiled at him. "There's nothing to be sorry about. We're still friends, right?"

"Yes, of course. I still feel bad that I might have messed up an opportunity to see what might have happened between us."

"I'm fine."

"Yeah, I can see that. You got the job you've always dreamed of, you look amazing, and you seem to be moving into the romance department. It's exactly like you planned it."

It wasn't like she'd planned it, but she wasn't going to correct him and open herself up for an argument. If she'd had what she wanted years ago, she would have been in a much bigger city and anchoring one of the prime news segments. Now she was happy right where she was.

Matthew took a deep breath and slowly blew it out as he smiled back at her. "So tell me about this guy."

She shrugged. "There's not a lot to tell right now."

"Is he handsome?"

He was, but if she went solely on looks, Matthew would have won out. "He's very nice looking."

"Is he rich?"

She thought for a moment and then shook her head. "I can't be totally sure, but I don't think so. He owns a hardware store."

"Here in town?"

"Yes."

"He must be a handy type." He rubbed the back of his neck. "I get a pain just thinking about it."

She laughed. "He said he loves projects and fixing things."

"If that's the kind of guy you're looking for, then I hope you're happy with him."

That's just it. She wasn't looking for any type of guy. As for being happy with him, she couldn't even say that since she'd just been out with him once.

This conversation wasn't going anywhere, so she decided it was time to change the subject. "Tell me all about what you've been up to. How did you like Atlanta?"

His eyes lit up at the opportunity to talk about himself. She listened as he went on and on about how he'd worked hard and climbed the corporate ladder before he realized that wasn't what he wanted.

"So do you know what you want now?"

He nodded as he locked gazes with her. "Yeah, I was hoping what I wanted would want me back, but it's obvious that's not the case."

The server brought their food, so they turned their attention to eating. Carrie managed to lighten up the conversation a bit, and when they finished, she said she wanted to leave.

After he paid, they walked out to the parking lot and stood next to her car. "See you in church next week."

"It was nice getting to talk to you again, Matt."

He nodded but didn't say another word as she opened her car door and got in.

All the way home, she thought about their conversation, and then her mind drifted to thoughts of Jonathan and Ethan. That put a smile on her face. Now she wanted to see them.

Years ago, she would have waited for Jonathan to call, but now she figured she had nothing to lose by taking the initiative to make the next move. So as soon as she got home, she pulled up his number on her phone, and pressed CALL.

Chapter 8

Jonathan glanced down at his phone at the first sound of the call coming in. When he saw that it was Carrie, his heart did a little flutter.

"Dad, your phone's ringing."

"I know."

"Aren't you gonna answer it?" Ethan looked at the phone, and his eyebrows shot up. "It's Ms. Marshall. If you don't answer it, I will."

"No, I'll call her back in a few minutes."

The phone stopped ringing. He cleared his throat and picked up the now silent phone.

"Why didn't you answer her call?" Ethan frowned. "I don't get it."

Jonathan started to come up with an excuse, but Ethan was smart. He'd see right through anything Jonathan might concoct. "I'm not sure what to say when I talk to her."

"It's because of that guy she was with, isn't it?" Ethan tilted his head and gave him the same inquisitive expression Jonathan had perfected as a parent.

"Yeah, pretty much."

"Maybe she called to tell you about him."

"I doubt it." Jonathan chuckled. "She's probably calling about something related to the school's fall festival."

Ethan pointed to the phone. "You won't know until you call her back to see what she wants." He paused and gave his dad a sly grin. "Or maybe she doesn't want anything. She might just feel like talking to you."

Jonathan could only wish. "Maybe you're right." Or not.

"Call her back." Ethan picked up his dad's phone and handed it to him. "There's no point in waiting." He folded his arms. "You're not getting any younger."

"Well, then, I'd better call her back before I'm ready for the nursing home." Jonathan took the phone and laughed. "You sure don't let me get away with much."

"What is it you used to say when I did bad stuff?" Ethan tapped his finger on his chin. "What goes around comes around?"

There were times when Ethan's precociousness was almost more than Jonathan could handle, but it still made him smile. "Okay, I'll call her now."

"I'll go to my room to give you some privacy."

Before Jonathan had a chance to say another word, Ethan was gone. Jonathan pulled up Carrie's number and stared at it before he pressed the CALL button. She answered before the first ring ended.

"Um …" He wasn't prepared for her to answer so quickly. "Did you call me a few minutes ago?"

"Yes, I wondered what you and Ethan were doing this afternoon."

"We, uh …" What was she doing calling him after being with that guy in church this morning? "We thought we'd hang around the house and relax."

"Would y'all like to come over a little later? I'm making a big pot of chili, and it would be so much more fun to have someone to share it with." Her voice wasn't quite as steady as it was when he first called her back. "Unless you'd rather not."

Ethan would never forgive him if he turned down an opportunity to see her. "That would be fine … yes, we'd like to come over. What can I bring?"

"Just yourselves."

"Why don't I bring dessert?"

"Okay. Why don't y'all come on over around 5:00? I'll have some snacks out, and I can show Ethan some cool stuff in my backyard."

"Cool stuff?"

"Yes." She paused. "I have what's left of a butterfly garden, there's a squirrel run along the very back, and I'm getting several bird feeders ready for the winter."

"I'm sure Ethan will love that."

After he hung up, he stood still for a moment and rubbed the back of his neck. This whole situation confused him. He wasn't sure why she'd gone to church with that guy and then called him to come over.

"Dad?"

He spun around to face his son. "Hey, Ethan. Guess where we're going for supper."

"Out with Ms. Marshall?"

"Even better. She's cooking chili for us."

"But Dad, you cook the best chili. Did you tell her you won the Baker Creek Chili Cook-off three years in a row?"

"No, of course not." Jonathan issued a stern look at his son. "And I don't want you to say a word about it either."

"Why?"

This was one of those times Ethan acted his age. He was great when it came to understanding complex math concepts and grasping what his teachers taught from textbooks. But when it came to matters of the heart … well, that was different.

"It'll make her uncomfortable."

"But why?"

"She might think I'm judging her chili or comparing it to mine."

"What if I don't like it?" Ethan contorted his mouth and made a funny face. "I mean, it'll be hard for her to come close to yours."

"I'm sure you'll like it." Jonathan squatted a little to make better eye contact with his son. "Just remember who made it, and I'm sure it'll be the best chili you ever had—even better than mine."

"It can't be better than yours, but I won't say anything if you think it'll make her feel bad."

Jonathan smiled at his son who had taken on the role of being his best friend. Sometimes it worried him that Ethan was more mature than many adults he knew, yet he wasn't sure whether that was a good thing or a bad one. He liked the fact that Ethan did so well in school, and his vocabulary would rival almost anyone he knew. However, some of the parents he'd spoken to had said Ethan intimidated their kids. Jonathan would never want that.

"So what do we do now?" Ethan asked.

"We come up with a great dessert that will knock her socks off."

Ethan scrunched his face as he tapped his finger on his chin. "Bakery or homemade?"

"What do you think?"

"I'm sort of in the mood for pumpkin pie."

Jonathan nodded. "Yeah, me too … with a huge pile of whipped cream."

"Then c'mon, Dad. We need to go to the store and get started on it. We don't have all day."

Jonathan laughed as he picked up his keys and followed Ethan out the door. They had to work fast to get the pie made in time to be at Carrie's house by 5:00.

*

Carrie hadn't wasted any time getting the chili in the pot and simmering. She went through the house and straightened up.

Her phone rang a couple of times—once when Andrew at the station called to ask about a story she'd been working on and once when her mother wanted to know what happened with Matthew. She knew she'd have to answer sooner or later, so she figured she might as well get it over with.

"I told him we could be friends, and that's all."

"That's ridiculous, Carrie. I remember how you used to get all dreamy-eyed when he was around."

"Mom, I was a teenager then. I got dreamy-eyed about a lot of people."

"But Matthew was different. You've known him most of your life, and …" Her voice trailed off, so Carrie took over.

"And you and his mother are close friends. I'm glad y'all get along so well, but I wish you'd find something else to talk about besides Matthew and me. He and I aren't meant to be anything but friends."

"How can you be sure? You haven't given him much of a chance."

Carrie sighed. She wasn't in the mood for this conversation. She'd much rather be thinking about seeing Jonathan and Ethan.

"Will you at least see him again? Maybe do something casual with him? That way you can let things happen as they—"

"I see him at church."

"You know what I'm talking about, Carrie. You need to go out with him." Her mother paused. "You need to at least be open minded." Her mother paused. "Okay?"

"Sure."

"Why do I get the feeling you're trying to brush me off? Were you busy when I called?"

"Sort of."

"Doing what?"

"Cooking a pot of chili and straightening the house."

"Why? Is someone coming over?"

"Do I have to have a reason to cook dinner and get my house in order?"

"C'mon, Carrie. Just tell me."

"Okay, Jonathan and Ethan are coming over for dinner."

"You need to be careful about letting a strange man in your house, sweetie. How well do you know this guy?"

"Well enough to know that he loves his son, and he's been nothing but a gentleman since the day we met."

"I don't know about—"

"Mom, I promise I'll be careful."

"What if he—?"

"Please don't. I've been on my own for a long time, and I'm pretty sure I can tell a person's character after seeing him a couple of times."

"Call me after he leaves so I can sleep."

Carrie let out a deep sigh. "Okay, I'll call you."

After Carrie hung up, she leaned against the wall. Her mother's desperation for her to get back into a relationship with Matthew made her crazy. It all started back when Carrie and Matthew dated, and their mothers got the idea that they might wind up being mothers-in-law. They had family parties together, put together joint scrapbooks, and even talked about future grandchildren.

When Matthew moved away to Atlanta, both mothers went into mourning that lasted more than a year. They eventually seemed to come to terms with the fact that they'd have to settle for the friendship they always had.

In the back of Carrie's mind, she sort of wished Matthew had stayed in Atlanta a tad longer, although she knew his mother missed him something awful. Now that he was back, it would be much more difficult for Carrie to avoid their mothers' plotting and planning.

But no one had asked her what she wanted, so she knew she had to deal with what was there. It might get sketchy for a while because she couldn't be sure about what came from Matthew's intentions and what their mothers had concocted.

After pondering this for much longer than she wanted, she finished getting her house ready. Then she went out to the backyard and made sure there was plenty of birdseed and squirrel food to attract the animals so Ethan could see them. Maybe one of the salamanders would show up. They freaked her out the first time she saw them, but now she enjoyed them and hoped Ethan would too. Just the thought of that little boy brought a smile to her face.

She'd always been good with children, but there was something extra special about Ethan. He had a knowing look in his eyes that made him seem much older than he was. If she'd met him outside the classroom, she never would have imagined he was a fourth-grader because he acted more like a sixth or seventh-grader.

Carrie respected Jonathan's decision to keep him in fourth grade, but she wondered if Ethan would be challenged enough. However, she could tell the other children liked him, so maybe he was where he should be.

Then she laughed at herself. Who was she to be concerned about where Ethan should be? Not only was he not hers to worry about, she'd just met him.

One thing she knew, though, was that she did care what he thought.

She liked both him and his dad, and there was certain that Jonathan wouldn't do anything or be involved with anyone without considering his son first. And that made him even more attractive to her.

She'd dated single parents in the past, and she was always turned off when they didn't put their children first because that showed that their priorities were in the wrong place. It let her know that if she were to get involved with them, they'd think of themselves first—something that could easily destroy a relationship.

Being single wasn't something she wanted for the rest of her life, but she wasn't willing to settle for a man who had selfish tendencies. The more she thought about it the more she realized she wanted the love her parents had.

They got along pretty well most of the time. Even when they disagreed, they found ways to come to terms and move on without getting bogged down in petty arguments. Their marriage was very old school, with her dad working at a nine-to-five job and her mother staying home with the children. She did volunteer work until the perfect part-time job came along.

What Carrie didn't understand was why her mother wouldn't let go of the notion that she and Matthew would ever be a couple. She thought she'd made it clear that she simply stopped feeling it not long after he left.

Chapter 9

"What if she doesn't like pumpkin pie?" Ethan looked up at Jonathan with concern etched on his little face.

Jonathan gave his son what he hoped was a comforting look. "Who doesn't like pumpkin pie?" He paused and took a longer look at Ethan. "What are you so worried about, son?"

"I don't want to mess anything up."

"Ethan, you couldn't mess anything up if you tried."

"But I like Ms. Marshall, and I want—" He stopped talking and quickly tightened his lips.

"I like her too, and I think she likes us. But everything has to be natural, or it won't work."

"Won't work?" Ethan gave him a curious look. "What do you mean?"

"I'm assuming you want Ms. Marshall to be … a special friend. I think she will be, but we have to let it happen without forcing it, or it'll be uncomfortable for all of us."

Ethan chewed on his bottom lip for a couple of seconds before nodding. "I think I understand."

"Are you ready to go?" Jonathan lifted the pie from the cooling rack and gently covered it and placed it in a box.

Ethan nodded. "I don't want to keep her waiting."

Jonathan welcomed the silence that fell between them as they drove to Carrie's house. He had a feeling his son was as nervous as he was.

When they pulled up in front of her house, Ethan gave him a curious look as he pointed. "That car in the front is Ms. Marshall's, but who does the one behind it belong to?"

"We're about to find out."

Jonathan helped Ethan out of the truck and then got the pie out of the box. Then they headed up the sidewalk toward the front porch of the Craftsman style home that appeared to have been recently renovated. He knew a bit about this neighborhood—the fact that most of the houses had gone into a state of disrepair many years ago and that people had slowly purchased them and done major overhauls. He wondered if Carrie had bought the house before or after the improvements.

As soon as they got to the door, Ethan looked up at Jonathan. "Dad, I'm nervous."

Jonathan chuckled. "Want to know a secret?"

Ethan nodded. "Yeah."

"Me too."

*

Carrie had hoped to send Matthew home before Jonathan and Ethan arrived, so when the knock came at the door, she let out a slight groan. Matthew seemed as embarrassed as she was.

"I'm so sorry," he said. "Would you like for me to explain everything?"

"No, I can handle it."

"Do you want me to leave right away?" Matthew gave her a warm, apologetic smile. "Or I can stick around and get to know this guy."

She shrugged. "I don't know what you should do."

"Then we'll play it by ear." He gestured toward the door. "You'd better answer it, or they'll think you're not home."

She lifted her head, took a deep breath, slowly exhaled, and forced a smile. Then she opened the door. "Come on in." She met Ethan's wide-eyed gaze. "Hey, Ethan. It's so good to see you."

Jonathan looked around the room before his gaze settled on something behind her. The sound of Matthew clearing his throat added to her frayed nerves.

"Hi, I'm Matthew, a very old friend of Carrie's."

"I'm Jonathan, and this is my son Ethan."

Tension sizzled in the room as the men shook hands. Matthew gestured toward the kitchen. "Carrie has cooked some of her famous chili for you guys. You're gonna love it."

Carrie shot him a look, hoping he'd take that as a cue to leave. But he didn't. Instead, he continued talking about how great her cooking was.

The more he talked, the cloudier Jonathan's look became. She sensed him pulling back—something she couldn't control as long as Matthew was here. It was time to let him know she didn't need him here.

"Matthew, I think we'll be fine. Thanks for bringing that platter from Mom."

"More than happy to do it. She thought you might need it tonight." He remained standing in the same position.

Carrie gestured toward the front of the house. "I'll walk you to the door."

Matthew glanced over at Jonathan, smiled, and finally moved. "No, that's okay. You have company. Talk to you later, okay?"

"Sure." She would have said more if Jonathan and Ethan hadn't been standing behind her. Matthew could have left as soon as she told him she was having company. Instead, he asked if it was the guy she'd mentioned, and when she said yes, he said he wanted to meet him. Now she'd have to explain everything to Jonathan—something she shouldn't have to do this early in the relationship.

After she closed the door behind Matthew, she turned around and saw Jonathan standing there, still holding the pie he'd brought. She felt terrible.

"I am so sorry." She reached for the pie. "Let's take that to the kitchen."

"Did we …" Jonathan paused as he appeared to swallow hard. "Were you in the middle of something important when we got here?"

"No, Matthew just returned something I left at my mother's house. His parents live next door to mine. He's been gone for a few years, and he just returned to Baker Creek."

"Are you … is he …" He raked his fingers through his hair in what appeared to be frustration. "Do the two of you have something—"

"The only *something* we have is friendship." She smiled. "If we'd wanted anything more, we would have started years ago. Like I said, he was just helping my mother out by delivering the platter I left last time I brought food to her house."

She watched as he processed the information. As he finally nodded, she wasn't convinced he understood, but hopefully she'd be able to change all that.

"Smells good in here." Jonathan looked down at his son who clung to him, letting her know the little boy was as uncomfortable as his dad. "Doesn't it, Ethan?"

Ethan nodded. He looked up at his dad and then at Carrie.

She smiled back at him. "Hey, I have an idea. Let's go out to the backyard and see if one of my special critters will show his face."

Ethan tilted his head. "Special critters?"

She nodded. "Yeah, I have a couple of spotted salamanders that visit me from time to time. Maybe we'll see one of them this afternoon."

"Cool. I've never seen one in real life." Ethan had apparently forgotten his discomfort as she led the way to the backyard with Jonathan right behind them.

"See that tree over there?" She pointed to a tree in the corner of her yard. "During the summer, I have hundreds of tree frogs hanging around it."

"There must be water around here somewhere," Jonathan said.

"Yeah," Ethan agreed. "Frogs start out as tadpoles, and they need water."

Carrie nodded. "There's a creak that runs throughout the neighborhood."

As they chatted about tadpoles, frogs, and other creatures that visited Carrie's backyard, she found herself imagining what life would be like with a family. She didn't know Jonathan well enough to include him in the mental image, but he was right there … and so was Ethan.

"Ms. Marshall, I have to go to the bathroom."

She smiled down at him. "Just go in through the backdoor, past the kitchen, and down the hall on the left. It's the second door on the right."

"Thanks!" He took off running toward the house.

Jonathan shoved his hands into his pockets, glanced down at the ground, and then up at her. "You're really good with kids."

"Ethan is easy to be around. You've done a wonderful job with him."

"Thanks. He's been a real blessing." He paused. "Do you think you might ever want children of your own?"

"If they're as wonderful as Ethan, I'd like a houseful of them." The instant those words came out of her mouth, Carrie wanted to kick herself in the backside. She needed to be subtler.

He laughed. "You've only seen his good side."

"I can't imagine there being a bad side to Ethan." She stopped herself before she added that the same went for him.

"No one's perfect." He gave her a look that made her melt.

She cleared her throat. "Do you think Ethan's hungry enough to eat dinner now?"

"Probably. That boy gets up from the table hungry."

"Why don't we go back inside?"

As if it were the most natural thing in the world, he took her hand as they walked back toward the house. When they reached the steps, he pulled her closer. There was no doubt in her mind that she was about to be kissed.

*

Jonathan hadn't planned on kissing Carrie today. In fact, he'd decided to keep his emotional distance to protect himself and his son. But she was right there, being kind and loving, looking soft and pretty, and overall just looking downright kissable. He couldn't resist the urge.

Seeing that guy at her house when he arrived had shaken him up, but Carrie had explained well enough. She might not have had a spark for Matthew, but he was pretty sure Matthew carried some deeper feelings for her. And the fact that her mother had sent him over created even more questions in his mind.

When they walked into the house, Jonathan saw Ethan standing in the kitchen, waiting and watching, making Jonathan wonder if he'd witness the kissed. It really didn't matter, but it still made Jonathan uncomfortable thinking that he might have.

"Do you like celery with ranch dip?" Carrie asked Ethan. "I've found that it helps cut some of the spiciness and acidity of the chili."

Ethan gave an enthusiastic nod. "I love celery."

Jonathan chuckled. "Ethan likes anything with ranch dressing. That was always how I got him to eat his veggies when he was little."

Ethan propped his elbows on the counter. "You don't have to do that now because I understand how important it is to eat stuff that's good for me. My teacher says good food is the first building block of a healthy body."

Carrie lifted her eyebrows. She was impressed. "Wow. I don't think I knew that when I was your age."

Jonathan made a face at Ethan. "I didn't know either, but if I did, it wouldn't have mattered."

Ethan turned to Carrie with a serious face. "Dad always says that, but I can promise you he'll eat the celery … even without any dip."

Jonathan glanced over at Carrie who was clearly having trouble keeping a straight face. As advanced as Ethan was for his age, he still didn't have the maturity to know when to stop trying to sell Carrie on the attributes of his dad.

She glanced at Jonathan and then smiled at Ethan. "That's good. We want your dad to stay healthy, don't we?"

"Yeah, he's a bear when he gets sick."

This time, Carrie didn't hold back. She belted out a laugh that surprised both him and Ethan.

"I didn't mean that to be funny, so why are you laughing at me?" Ethan frowned.

"I know, sweetie, but I wasn't laughing at you. I was laughing because I think it's sweet for you to be so concerned about your dad."

Ethan lifted his shoulders and held out his hands, palms up. "Someone has to be."

This time, when Carrie laughed, Ethan chimed in, followed by Jonathan. As he stepped closer to his son, he thought about how much he enjoyed the three of them being together.

"Do y'all want to eat in the dining room or sit down at the kitchen table?" Carrie looked at Jonathan.

"Why don't we stay in the kitchen? It's cozy in here and—"

Ethan interrupted. "And it's closer to the chili." He paused as a look of concern crossed his face. "That is, if we're allowed to have seconds."

"You can have as much as you want," Carrie said. "That is, if it's okay with your dad."

Jonathan appreciated her deference to him. "It's perfectly fine with me. I have a feeling we'll both eat until we pop."

Carrie pulled her head back and made a goofy face. "Now that's a visual I can do without."

As they ate, they chatted about the upcoming Fall Festival at Ethan's school. Jonathan told her he'd be helping set it up and working one of the concessions.

Carrie listened and then put down her spoon. "I'm not sure what they want me to do. My boss just told me they want me to make an appearance."

"Maybe you'll be the Fall Festival reporter," Ethan said. "You can interview people, like my dad." He turned to Jonathan. "Wouldn't it be cool if you were on TV?"

Chapter 10

After Jonathan and Ethan left, she didn't have much to do since they'd helped her clean up. She reflected on their conversation about the Fall Festival. The memory of Jonathan's expression when Ethan mentioned her interviewing him for TV made her laugh.

She plopped down on the sofa and started thumbing through some magazines she hadn't had a chance to look at when the phone rang. It was her mother.

"Are they still there?" her mom asked.

"If you're talking about Jonathan and Ethan, no, they left about half an hour ago. Ethan has school tomorrow. Why?"

"Just curious. Matthew said the man is a nice guy, and his son seems well behaved."

It annoyed Carrie that Matthew felt he needed to report back to her mother, but she tried to hide her feelings. As her mother continued talking about how difficult life could be with a ready-made family, she found herself countering all the points in her own mind with thoughts about how much she enjoyed being with the man and his son.

She listened for a few minutes before changing the subject to food. Fortunately, her mother took the hint and let the conversation turn to her biggest passion.

After they got off the phone, Carrie flopped back on the sofa and let her mind wander to the time she'd spent with Jonathan and Ethan. It was relaxing yet fun—a combination that made her smile.

*

The next morning, Jonathan awoke with Ethan staring down at him, over the bed. "Need something, son?"

"Ms. Marshall is really cool."

Jonathan propped himself up on his elbows and smiled about the fact that his son was still thinking about Carrie. "Why do you say that?"

"She likes frogs and salamanders, and she feeds all the animals in her backyard. Most of the girls I know scream when they see wild animals."

"She's obviously not like most girls." As Jonathan uttered those words, he realized he'd been thinking that exact thought.

"When can we see her again?"

"She's going to be at the Fall Festival."

Ethan scowled. "That's a whole week away. I want to see her before that."

Jonathan sighed as he sat all the way up and put his feet on the floor. "I'll see what I can do, but we're both very busy."

"Doing what?" Ethan folded his arms and stared at his dad.

"Work. She mentioned that she has some big projects that she's working on, and you know we have a big sale at the store."

"Why don't we invite her over for dinner?" Ethan tilted his head and held out his hands. "We have to eat, right?"

Jonathan tried to think of a reason to say no, but he couldn't think of one. "Tell you what. We can invite her to come for dinner on Wednesday, but don't get upset if she can't."

"Why do you think she might can't?"

Jonathan couldn't help but smile at his son's choice of words. "I don't know. Maybe she's slammed at work."

"Well … it'll have to be late because she has her news brief when we normally eat. I can have a snack so I won't starve to death, and then we can have something yummy." Ethan paused and then looked up at his dad. "Can you make your famous chicken spaghetti?"

"Famous?" Jonathan laughed. "I don't know about famous, but yes, I can make that."

Ethan held up a hand and started pointing to his fingers. "We can have a salad with spinach and carrots and tomatoes because she likes that kind of stuff."

Jonathan couldn't believe how much his son wanted to impress Carrie. Ethan clearly had a little boy crush on the woman. If she hadn't been so sweet in person, he would have thought it was more of a fan crush than a real one.

"So when are you gonna call her?"

Jonathan glanced at the clock. "Let's give her a chance to wake up."

"I'm pretty sure she's awake by now. It's almost 8:00."

"Why don't I take you to school, and I'll call her at her office." That way, the conversation would be brief.

Ethan groaned. “But I wanted to hear you talk to her.”

Jonathan tilted his head and gave his son a closed-mouth smile. “Don’t you trust me?”

“I just want to make sure you don’t mess up.”

“Why don’t you just tell me what to say, and I’ll write it down?” Jonathan picked up a notepad from his nightstand. “That way I won’t mess up.”

“Okay.” Ethan tapped his chin with his index finger before telling his dad exactly what to say.

“Perfect.” Jonathan held up the paper and waved it in the air. “This is exactly what I’ll say.”

“Good. Now let’s go get breakfast.” Ethan tugged on Jonathan’s arm and pulled him toward the kitchen.

After a breakfast of eggs and toast, they got ready for the day and headed for the school. On the way, Ethan talked about all the things he’d show Ms. Marshall when she came over. Jonathan sure hoped he wouldn’t be disappointed.

*

Carrie had just sat down after the morning meeting when her cell phone vibrated. She didn’t always answer personal calls at work, but when she saw that it was Jonathan, she didn’t waste a second.

Her breath caught in her throat as he read the message from Ethan inviting her for dinner on Wednesday. After Jonathan finished reading it, he paused and then asked, “Well? Will you make my son the happiest little boy in Baker Creek and join us?”

Her mother had talked about having her over for dinner one night this week, and more than likely it would be Wednesday. And just as likely, she’d have Matthew there too. Carrie would much rather spend a few hours with Jonathan and Ethan than sit there awkwardly trying to deflect her mother’s attempts at matchmaking.

“I’d love to.” It was time to stop worrying about making her mother happy when it came to her love life.

“You would?” Jonathan’s voice cracked. “I mean, you don’t already have plans?”

“I do now. Tell Ethan I’m excited about seeing him again, and I can’t wait to see his rock collection.”

“You have just made my son one happy boy … or at least he will be when he finds out you’re coming.”

After they hung up, she finished putting together one of the stories she needed to cover later, and then she went to the break room for lunch. Tom glanced up from something he was reading and gave her a perfunctory wave before turning his attention back to the paper.

"Must be riveting." Carrie pulled her lunch out of the fridge and gestured toward the chair across from him. "Mind if I join you?"

He removed his glasses and smiled. "I'd be offended if you didn't. So how's the story going?"

"It's pretty much wrapped up. All I have to do is find some B-roll for one segment, and then we're all set."

"I'm sure glad I don't have to worry about your work. I hate having to nudge people who procrastinate." Before she had a chance to say another word, he continued. "By the way, I heard from the elementary school. They asked if we could send some more people to help out at the Fall Festival. I know you'll be speaking, but they want folks to help out with some of the booths to help generate more income. They seem to think that our reporters are celebrities who might draw bigger crowds."

"They're probably right." She took a bite of her sandwich.

"How about you? Are you up to spending a little time at one of the booths?"

She lifted a shoulder and gave a head bob. "Sure, as long as it's not a kissing booth."

He snapped his fingers. "You just ruined all the fun." He chuckled. "But seriously, if you can spend an hour or two at one of the booths, I think that would be a huge help to the school. I thought I'd have Dave from weather and one of the sports guys go as well."

Carrie nodded. "Dave's great with kids."

"He should be." Tom rolled his eyes. "Between their biological kids and the ones he and his wife foster, they have a houseful of them."

Back when she first met Dave, she admired him and thought he reminded her of Mr. Rogers. It wasn't long before she learned about his big heart and open door for anyone who needed love and support.

"The folks at that school sure do like you, Carrie. What did you do to get them asking for you all the time?"

She laughed. "Must be that special powder I sprinkle on myself every morning."

"Kind of like fairy dust?"

"Oh yeah." She pointed to the papers in front of him. "Breaking news?"

"No, it's just part of the 'Fall in South Carolina' special we're running. As soon as we put the word out, we got slammed with requests for a mention on air."

"They do what they have to do to get people coming."

"Including special requests." The smirk on his face sure was suspicious.

"Why are you looking at me like that?"

"You've been requested to attend and speak at several of the venues."

She smiled back. "Okay, that's fine. I enjoy getting out and about in the community."

"Good because I accepted for you, so you'll be out and about quite a bit over the next month or so."

"Um …" She narrowed her eyes. "I'm still doing the evening news brief, right?"

"Yes, of course. Ever since you've started, our ratings have skyrocketed for that time slot."

They chatted about some of the upcoming events she'd be attending and then went back to their desks. As Carrie finished wrapping up her report, she thought about how things had changed over the past six months. She'd finally realized her dream, but now that didn't seem quite good enough. Being with Jonathan and Ethan had planted a desire for something more basic in her heart. She wanted a family.

*

"Dad, please don't mess up tonight."

Jonathan glanced down at Ethan who hadn't stopped hovering since they'd been home. "Son, I've been making chicken spaghetti for as long as I can remember, and I don't think I've messed it up yet."

"I know, but this is a big deal."

"Even after getting to know Ms. Marshall, you still like her a lot, don't you?"

Ethan shrugged. "Sort of, but not as much as you do."

"What are you saying?" Jonathan straightened up and held his son's gaze.

"I don't know. You just look at her funny, and you smile a lot when she's around."

"So do you."

Ethan's eyebrows went up. "That's because you're smiling so big, I can't help it." Ethan paused. "And ya wanna know something else?"

"What's that?"

"She smiles a lot too."

"I'm sure she has lots of practice since she's on TV every night." Jonathan gestured toward the table that was perfectly set for three. "How'd I do?"

Ethan walked around the table, looking at everything very carefully. "It looks okay, but it needs something."

"Like what?"

"She had some flowers in the middle of the table when we went to her house."

Jonathan glanced at the table and realized his son was right. "Good catch. So let's go make a centerpiece."

"But we don't have any flowers."

Jonathan shrugged. "Then we'll have to work with what we've got."

They wound up with a structure made from some interlocking blocks and action figures they found in Ethan's toy collection. While making it, Ethan lit up with enthusiasm, but after they placed it on the table, he stood back and frowned.

"What's wrong, son?"

"It's not as pretty as the flowers she had on her table."

"Maybe not as pretty, but it's at least as cool."

Ethan bobbed his head. "Yeah, it is pretty cool, isn't it? Do you think she'll like it?"

Jonathan lifted an eyebrow. "She likes frogs, doesn't she?" After Ethan nodded, he added, "Then I'm sure she'll like the forces protecting the table."

They took some time out to watch Carrie's segment on the news. She closed with, "I hope y'all enjoy your evening. I have very special plans tonight, so I'm sure I will. Good night."

Ethan shot up out of his chair and pointed to the TV. "Did you hear that, Dad? She told everyone in the world that she has special plans."

Jonathan let out a soft chuckle. "She sure did."

Every now and then, between stirring the spaghetti sauce and making the table as attractive as possible, Jonathan glanced at the clock. Tension mounted until the knock came at the door.

Ethan didn't give Jonathan a chance to make a move before running to the door. "I'll get it."

*

Carrie couldn't have been happier to see anyone than Ethan when he eagerly flung the door open. Her mother had called her immediately after work, and the only way Carrie could get off the phone was to agree to come over tomorrow night. Her mom had already let it slip that Matthew would be there helping her dad fix a few things around the house.

"Hi, Ethan." She stepped inside the house. "Sure does smell good in here."

"That's Dad's spaghetti."

"Well, if it tastes half as good as it smells, I hope you have enough for seconds."

Jonathan appeared from around the corner, wiping his hands on a dishtowel, grinning. "Good to see you, Carrie. Dinner's almost ready."

Ethan looked like he'd eaten a pack of jumping beans as he bounced around her. "Wanna see the centerpiece we made? It's not as pretty as your flowers, but Dad says you won't mind because you like frogs … but it doesn't have any frogs because we don't want them jumping all over the table."

She tried to stifle a laugh, but it came out anyway. "I can't wait to see it."

"Then c'mon, it's over here in the dining room."

The second she saw the intricately designed warrior scene in the middle of the table, she let out a gasp. "Ethan! Did you put this together?"

His face turned bright red as he obviously tried hard not to smile. "I made most of it, but Dad helped a little."

"That is way cool!" She walked around to see all angles. "I used to enjoy putting those blocks together when I was a little girl …" She leaned over. "Don't tell anyone this, but I played with them after I was a teenager when no one was looking."

"You did?"

She nodded. "Do you have more that we can play with after we eat?"

He jumped up and down a couple of times as he nodded. "We have boxes and boxes of them."

She wasn't surprised. Ethan's precociousness had clearly been encouraged and fed by his dad. As she did more segments on schools and early childhood centers, she'd learned that building blocks of all types helped children develop spatial skills and enhanced other areas of learning.

"I hate to break this up, but dinner's almost ready. Go ahead and have a seat. I'll bring it out."

Carrie glanced down at Ethan and winked before looking at Jonathan. "We can help."

Without waiting for an answer, she walked straight into the kitchen with Ethan following right behind her. She didn't want to give Jonathan a chance to argue. It always made her feel better to participate because getting waited on seemed so awkward.

A couple of minutes later, they were seated at the table with serving platters and bowls clustered around the centerpiece. The whole setting felt so cozy she just wanted scream out how good it felt. Instead, she cleared her throat and looked at Ethan, who'd already bowed his head and folded his hands. So she followed.

Ethan said the blessing that was sweet, heartfelt, and on-point. After she opened her eyes, she noticed both of the guys watching her.

They passed around the dishes and filled their plates with spaghetti noodles, sauce, and salad. "This all looks so delicious, I'm not sure where to start."

Ethan pointed to the bowl of salad dressing. "Try the salad first. Dad makes the best dressing in the whole entire world."

Jonathan shrugged. "It's honey mustard."

She took a bite and was impressed. "I'll have to get your recipe for this. It's delicious."

"Easy recipe. Just honey, mustard, a few drops of olive oil, and a tiny bit of cayenne."

As she ate, she let Jonathan know how good everything was. "I've never thought about using chicken in spaghetti sauce."

"I substituted it one night when I'd promised Ethan we'd have spaghetti before I realized we were out of ground beef. I didn't feel like going to the store, and we had chicken …" He held out his hands. "And now it's our favorite."

After dinner, Ethan squirmed around in his chair before turning to his dad. "Can we have dessert now?" He looked at Carrie. "I made dessert … well, most of it anyway. Dad had to help me flip it."

"You flipped dessert?" She scrunched her nose and gave him a curious look. "What is it?"

Ethan glanced back at Jonathan, who nodded. "Pineapple upside-down cake. You put the pineapples on the bottom of the pan, so you have to flip it so they'll be on top."

"Oh, yes, of course. I'm glad you said something about that before I got more spaghetti, or I wouldn't have had room for dessert."

When Jonathan stood and picked up his plate, she started helping clear the table. He opened his mouth, but he quickly shut it when she started for the kitchen. Once they had all the main part of the meal put away, Jonathan told Ethan to go to his room to get boxes of blocks for later.

The second Ethan left Jonathan closed the distance between them, placed his hands on her shoulders, and looked her in the eyes. "Thank you so much for everything, Carrie."

The butterflies in her stomach fluttered like crazy as she allowed herself to get lost in his gaze. "I'm the one who should be thanking you. Dinner was delicious."

"I appreciate that, but not as much as I appreciate the way you are with Ethan … with us. You're one of a kind."

Silence fell between them momentarily, and then she knew he was about to kiss her. As his face drew closer to hers, she realized she could easily fall in love with this man. And she didn't have the will to fight it.

Chapter 11

Jonathan had only experienced love once before, and he didn't think he'd ever find that feeling again. But he was wrong.

From the first time he saw Carrie in person, there were sparks, and not just a small fireworks display. It was more like bombs and grenades going off. What amazed him was the fact that every single time they were together, his feelings grew more intense.

Ethan felt it too. After Carrie left their house, he told Jonathan that Ms. Marshall made him feel all squishy inside. He even asked if it would be okay to hug her next time he saw her.

Most of the time, Jonathan felt that he was doing a good job of playing both roles—of dad and mom—to his son. But when Carrie was around, he saw a different side of Ethan, letting him know that he was missing something very important in his life. That wouldn't have been enough to get him thinking about a long-term relationship with Carrie, but combining the way both of them felt around her actually sent his mind and heart to a place he'd long since buried.

Based on the way she kissed him back, she felt the same way about him. And she seemed to enjoy getting down on the floor and playing with Ethan. In fact, he was surprised by how much she seemed to enjoy the interlocking blocks and how intricately designed her structure was. Only someone who had experience could make something with so many parts.

One possible glitch in their relationship might be her secrecy. He'd asked if she wanted to do something with him and Ethan after she got off work tomorrow night, and her smile quickly faded. She told him that she had other plans and she probably wouldn't see him again until the Fall Festival. The fact that she didn't tell him what the plans were got his imagination running wild.

He woke up the next morning with Ethan standing over him again. “Good morning, champ. Hungry?”

Ethan nodded. “Starving.”

“Are we talking cereal starving or more like bacon-and-eggs starving?”

“Pancakes.”

Jonathan got up and put his hand on Ethan’s shoulder. “So you’re going for the big guns. Okay, I’ll rustle up some pancakes. Do you want bacon or sausage to go with them?”

“Bacon.”

As Jonathan prepared breakfast, Ethan sat at the kitchen table and talked about how much fun last night was. He started with the conversation during dinner and moved on to their playtime with the interlocking blocks. “I didn’t know girls liked that kind of thing.”

“Some obviously do.” Jonathan downed the orange juice he’d just poured. “Why don’t you get the syrup for the pancakes while I plate them up?”

Yes, both he and Ethan were smitten. Now all he had to do was figure out what else was going on in her life.

*

Carrie was eager to finish her segment and go to her parents’ house to get this thing over with. Tom had noticed that something was wrong, and he’d asked about it during lunch. At first, she hesitated, but she trusted him enough to give him a brief outline of her dilemma.

“Since you’ve talked to your mom about it, and you don’t seem to be making any headway, why don’t you have a conversation with Matthew?”

“I tried.”

He tilted his head, raised an eyebrow, and gave her a questioning look. “And?”

She shrugged. “It just seems awkward, ya know?”

“Can it be any more awkward than it is now?”

As soon as she got off the air, she went to her desk, wrapped up a couple of things, and headed for the door. Tom intercepted her in the parking lot. “Don’t forget what I said. If you have any hope of moving on, this thing needs to be dealt with. Besides, as a guy, I would respect a woman much more if she’d be direct about something like this.”

He had a point. Maybe she would talk to him tonight if the opportunity presented itself.

It happened more quickly than she expected. As soon as she pulled into her parents’ driveway, Matthew came from around the house carrying a ladder. He dropped the ladder, waved, and walked toward her.

She took a deep breath and smiled at him. "Hey Matthew. Can we talk?"

"Now?"

"Yes, if you don't mind. There's something we need to discuss as soon as possible."

"Okay." He glanced over his shoulder. "Should we go inside, or does this need to be a private chat?"

"Private."

He gestured toward his parents' house. "Let's go sit on my mom and dad's porch. Everyone is at your house."

Once they were seated, she took a deep breath. "I like you, Matthew. I think you know that."

He gave her a crooked smile. "But?"

"But that's all. We've been good friends for many years, and I'd like to keep it that way."

"I know you said that the other night before that guy came over." He glanced down at his feet and then lifted his gaze to hers. "If it weren't for him, would things be different between you and me?"

"I don't think so." She paused to think of a nice way to state her feelings. "Even if Jonathan and his son weren't in the picture, I'd still want to remain good friends with you, and that's pretty much all."

He nodded. "At least you're being honest with me." He took her hand and squeezed it before letting go. "And I'm fine with that. The problem is …" He grimaced. "Our mothers."

"I know. They're quite a team, aren't they?"

"They most definitely are." He stood and gestured back toward her parents' house. "We might as well go face them. Should I tell them that we'll always be good friends, but that's all, or do you want to?"

"Do we have to tell them anything?"

He chuckled. "I wish we didn't have to, but they need to save their energy for something they can actually accomplish."

"Why don't we just play it by ear? Either of us can tell them."

"Sounds good to me," he said. "Let's go."

They'd no sooner walked inside the house than both moms approached with humongous grins on their faces. "We saw you pull up, Carrie." His mother glanced over her shoulder at her mom. "It's so nice that you wanted some time alone with each other."

"Mom." Matthew placed his hand on his mother's shoulder. "There's something we need to discuss with you."

Both mothers' eyebrows shot up as their grins got even wider. "Sounds exciting."

"Maybe … or maybe not." Matthew pointed to the sofa. "Why don't y'all have a seat?"

As soon as the mothers were seated, Carrie and Matthew explained what they'd discussed. Their moms' smiles faded as they took it all in. Finally, Carrie's mother spoke up. "So there's no chance of—"

"No, it's not going to happen, so we'd appreciate your support in our …" Matthew glanced at Carrie who nodded. "In our friendship."

"If you're sure that's what both of you want," his mom said.

Carrie and Matthew spoke up at the same time. "We are."

Carrie's mother lifted her index finger to get their attention. "But if you ever change your minds, I want you to know that's okay too."

Dinner was awkward, with both of the mothers having to stop themselves in the middle of sentences. Carrie wished she could have recorded their conversation because one of these days she might look back on this time and think it was funny. But now, not so much.

After they finished eating, Matthew went outside and helped clean up from the projects he and his dad had helped her dad with. Carrie was stuck inside with their moms who continued acting strange. She was relieved when everything was put away.

Matthew came to the kitchen door and motioned for her to join him. "I just wanted to let you know that at your mother's urging, I volunteered to help with the Baker Creek Elementary Fall Festival."

Carrie laughed. "Why am I not surprised?"

"I just wanted to warn you so you won't think I'm not honoring my word."

She touched his arm and smiled. "Thank you for being so understanding."

"After meeting Jonathan, I was prepared for something like this. He seems like a nice guy."

"He is."

"How about his little boy?"

"I adore him too."

*

Jonathan had spent some time learning how to run the ticket booth as well as the game sponsored by his hardware store. He was still on edge as he wasn't sure what to expect when he saw Carrie. The last time they were together had been almost magical, but the more he thought about her secrecy the more concerned he became.

He'd barely arrived at the ticket booth when he spotted Carrie about a hundred feet away. He narrowed his eyes to see who she was talking to, and then his heart felt as though someone had ripped it from his chest. There was that guy, Matthew, smiling down at her.

He took a couple of deep breaths as he tried to clear his mind. Carrie was a sweet woman, and he didn't think she was the type of woman to play games. But he still needed to back off and give her some space since Matthew clearly had a place in her heart.

Since he was busy with the booths, the dad of one of Ethan's friends had agreed to take him to the festival and then bring him home to spend the night. That freed Jonathan up to do whatever was needed at the event.

Fortunately, he was able to compartmentalize the task in his mind, so he didn't think he showed his frustration and confusion. Then Matthew approached with a big 'ol honkin' grin.

"Hey, can we talk?"

Jonathan didn't want to talk to Matthew. "Sorry, pal, but I'm stuck here for a while."

Matthew nodded his understand. "I'll check back later. What time does your relief arrive?"

"In about an hour, but after I leave here, I'm working a booth."

"Your company's booth?"

Jonathan nodded. "I'll be there until closing."

"I'll see you there." Matthew left before Jonathan had a chance to say another word.

For the next hour and a half, Jonathan vacillated between confusion and a resolve to forget about Carrie. But based on how deeply he already felt for Carrie he knew the second option would be impossible.

When his relief arrived at the ticket booth, he made sure she had everything she needed before walking over to the game booth, where Maryann's husband Wesley gave him the rundown. "Maryann just left when things slowed down a bit. We've been busy off and on since we opened."

"Thanks. I appreciate all you've done."

Wesley held up his hands. "It's the least I can do to help the kids who'll be running this town when I'm old."

After Wesley left, Jonathan bent over to make sure there were enough prizes to replenish the ones hanging on the wall behind him. Then he stood up and found himself face to face with Carrie.

"Hey." He raked his fingers through his hair. "Enjoying the festival?"

She nodded. "I just finished speaking to that group under the tent. It's quite a bit different from being on air in a controlled environment with a bunch of cameras pointed at me."

"I can imagine."

She gestured toward the booth. "So I'm here to help out."

"Here? As in this booth?"

"Yep. As in this booth. Didn't Matthew tell you?"

"No, can't say he did." He should have known Matthew knew more about Carrie than he ever would.

She crinkled her face and gave him a hurt look. He had to turn around to keep from letting her expression stab him in the heart.

*

Matthew had told her that Jonathan was acting strange, but he didn't say anything about the anger that was clearly beneath the surface. If she hadn't committed to working his company's booth for the remainder of the evening, she would have said goodbye and gone home.

Jonathan continued acting as though he didn't even know her as people came up to play the game. She stood back and only interjected when he wasn't available.

She'd been there for about an hour when Matthew approached. "Hey, Carrie. Can you handle this place for a few minutes? I'd like to talk to Jonathan."

Jonathan shook his head. "But I don't—"

"Seriously, dude. We need to talk."

Carrie nodded. "Sure. I'll be fine."

Jonathan reluctantly left with Matthew, while she continued to stand there, speculating what Matthew might be saying to Jonathan. She didn't have to wait too long before the moms arrived—hers and Matthew's.

"Have they had that talk yet?" her mom asked.

"If you're talking about Jonathan and Matthew, that's what they're doing now. Do y'all know what this is all about?"

The moms exchanged a glance and then turned to her, nodding. "Apparently, Matthew thinks Jonathan is upset with him, so he's telling him that he's out of the picture."

Intense panic gripped Carrie's throat. "No. He can't do that."

Her mother planted her fists on her hips. "And why not?"

She lowered her gaze. "It might scare Jonathan away."

"Oh, I seriously doubt that." Matthew's mom laughed. "I've been watching him, and I don't think anything will scare him away."

"If you've been watching him since I've been here, you've probably seen how he's ignoring me."

The moms both burst into laughter. "You sure do have a lot to learn about men," Matthew's mom said. "That guy is so crazy about you he doesn't know what to do with himself."

Her mother glanced up and pointed. "Look who's walking this way. C'mon, let's leave the kids to work this out."

As the moms skittered off, Jonathan shook Matthew's hand and then turned to face her, a look of determination on his face. Whatever they'd discussed sure had changed his demeanor, and she didn't know what to do. So she just stood there with her arms dangling by her sides as Jonathan came around behind the booth and stood there looking down at her.

"Why didn't you say something?" he asked.

"About what?"

"I had the wrong idea about Matthew all along." He cleared his throat. "Well, I had the wrong idea about your feelings for him."

"What did he say?"

"That I should do this." He wrapped his arms around her, pulled her close, and kissed her forehead. "Carrie, there's something special between us. I've felt it since we first met, and Matthew told me you feel the same way."

"Oh, so that's what he wanted to discuss." Now she was more awkward then ever.

"I can't predict the future, but I think we have something special. How do you feel about hanging out with me and seeing where our relationship goes?"

Carrie blinked up at him and nodded. And then he kissed her—this time with more determination and feeling than the last time. They stayed locked in their embrace, until the sound of applause from outside the booth grabbed their attention.

The crowd split as Matthew approached carrying two caramel apples. "I knew this was a romance made in heaven when Jonathan mentioned that this was his favorite festival food." He laughed as he handed them the apples. "I remember it being yours too. I hope this is the first of many fall festivals for you two as a couple."

Carrie gave him a curious look, and when he smiled back, she knew he meant it. She turned to Jonathan who held out his apple to interlock arms. And then they took a bite.

"I guess this is our way of toasting our relationship," he whispered. "I have something important to ask you soon, but I want to wait for Ethan since it affects him too."

Epilogue

Carrie had never experienced such an odd combination of feelings in her life as she did now, waiting in the bridal room at the back of the church. Her mother had already gone to the altar and lit the unity candle with Jonathan's mother. Matthew had stopped by to tell her how happy he was that she'd finally found love, before helping to seat the guests.

A knock came at the door. She opened it to see her dad's proud face beaming back at her.

"Are you ready, sweetie?"

She swallowed the lump in her throat and nodded. "Ready as I'll ever be."

As she walked toward Jonathan who stood at the front with open admiration on his face, she knew her life would be changed forever. And nothing could have made her happier.

Ethan took his job as the ring bearer very seriously. He made sure his dad had the ring firmly in his hand before moving back to the position of being best man.

Tears formed in her eyes throughout the vows. Here she was, her life fuller than she'd ever imagined with the career of her dreams, but more importantly having a family. A year ago, she wasn't sure she'd ever find love, and now she had it in abundance.

As the words, "I do," came from Jonathan's lips, she let the tears fall. And when he kissed her, she allowed herself to melt in his arms.

Dear Reader,

I hope you enjoyed *Love in the News* as much as I loved writing it. Please take a couple of minutes to leave an honest review on Amazon or Goodreads.

Thanks!
Debby Mayne

Love at the Hug-a-Mug

A novella from the Mocha Marriages collection

By Debby Mayne

Forget Me Not Romances, a division of Winged Publications

This book is a work of fiction. The characters in this story are the product of the author's imagination and are completely fictitious.

Chapter 1

Bailey shifted from one foot to the other as she waited in the long line at the Hug-a-Mug coffee shop. She should have gone to Mr. Coffee Bean. The baristas weren't as customer friendly at the Bean, but there was never a long line.

Her best friend Martina nudged her in the side. "Don't look now, but that lady over in the corner is staring at us."

Bailey glanced around to see what Martina was talking about. "Are you talking about that sweet little old lady with the flowered dress?"

"I told you not to look."

"I don't care if she stares at me. I just want my coffee."

Martina rolled her eyes. "I can't believe how cranky you are first thing in the morning. You used to be so pleasant."

Bailey made eye contact with the woman in the corner who smiled. "Maybe you're right. I shouldn't have looked at her."

The line moved, and the woman with the long red braids and even longer order finally left the counter with a tall cold coffee drink topped with whipped cream and some chocolate shavings. "No wonder it took forever," Martina whispered.

"It actually looks pretty good."

Martina made a face and bobbed her head. "Maybe, but who can take anyone who drinks something like that seriously?"

"You know I like frothy drinks."

"Just proves my point." Martina laughed.

"Uh oh." Bailey tipped her head in the older woman's direction. "She's coming toward us."

"Maybe she's not—" Martina stopped midsentence and smiled down at the sweet face framed by loose tendrils that had fallen from the lady's bun. "Hi."

Bailey glanced down at the short woman with the big presence. "Did you want to talk to us?"

"Just you."

Bailey narrowed her eyes and pointed her thumb to her chest. "Me?"

"Yes, you."

Martina took a step back. "Do you need privacy?"

The woman chuckled. "Are you kidding? If I wanted privacy, do you think I'd be here?"

Martina's shoulders slumped as she cast a quick glimpse at Bailey before looking back at the woman. "Um, no, I don't suppose you would."

Without missing a beat, the woman stepped in front of Martina, turning her back to her, and looked up at Bailey. "I've been watching you for a while, and I think you would be perfect."

"Perfect?" Bailey didn't remember ever seeing this woman before, but she wasn't about to argue. "For what?"

"Before I continue, I need to know your name and your marital status." She glanced at Bailey's left hand. "I don't see a ring, so I assume you're single."

Bailey was about to give a vague answer when Martina spoke up. "Yes, she's single. Why? Do you know someone?"

A beatific look came over the woman's face. "I might."

"In that case, I'm single too." Martina tossed her chemically straightened, dyed red hair over her shoulder. "Whatever you have in mind for my friend Bailey … well, I'd like some of that."

The woman started to giggle, but suddenly she glanced up and a look of pure horror crossed over her face. Bailey turned around to see what had frightened the poor woman.

All she saw was a six-foot-something man with sandy brown hair, a determined look on his face, and a stride that had more swagger than all of the other guys in the Hug-a-Mug combined. Her knees grew weak.

"There you are, Aunt Mabel." He walked up to the woman, took her by the arm, and cast an apologetic look at Bailey and Martina. "Sorry if she was bothering you."

Martina didn't miss the opportunity as she shook her head. "Oh, she's not bothering us at all. In fact, we've been enjoying our nice little chat with your aunt."

His eyes twinkled with amusement. "I'm sure you have. She is very sweet …" He glanced down at his aunt. "But she's also constantly getting into situations that she can't find her way out of."

Mabel yanked away from his grasp, planted her hand on her hip, and scowled at him. "I'm just getting to know my new friends, Scotty. Why did you have to come in here and mess things up for me?"

"Mess things up?" He looked back and forth between Bailey and Martina. "Did I mess anything up?"

Bailey gave a half nod, while Martina vehemently shook her head no. He laughed.

Mabel took advantage of the lull in conversation and stepped closer to him as she shook her finger in his face. "I'll have you know, young man, that I am an adult, and I have the right to be wherever I want to be, when I want to be there."

"I know, Aunt Mabel ..." His face reddened as he cleared his throat. "It's just that Mom was worried when you didn't meet her on the corner when you said you'd be there."

The older woman glanced up at the clock on the wall. "Oops. Sorry about that."

Martina sighed. "I think it's sweet that your nephew cares so much about you."

Bailey couldn't help but miss the flirty tone in her friend's voice. She stepped back to get out of the way.

Mabel grabbed her by the arm and pushed her toward the man. "Scotty, I think you and this one—Bailey, is it?" Before Bailey had a chance to respond, Mabel continued. "The two of you would make a very cute couple. Isn't she pretty?"

Martina's eyebrows shot up as she gave Bailey a challenging glare. Bailey had no idea how to respond, so she just shrugged.

He grinned. "Yes, she is very pretty, but I'm sure she doesn't appreciate being put on the spot like this." He directed his attention to Bailey. "My aunt means well."

"I understand." Bailey glanced down at the floor.

The man extended his hand, and Bailey took it. "By the name, my name is Scott Nixon."

"Nice to meet you." Bailey gestured toward Martina. "And this is my friend Martina."

After Scott shook Martina's hand, he turned back to his aunt. "Mom is really worried about you. We need to let her know you're okay."

"I can imagine what my sister's thinking," Mabel said as she slowly stood, using the edge of the table to pull herself up. "I've seen her when she's got a bee in her bonnet, and it's not a pretty sight."

Scott grinned. "Then we'd better get going, or you'll have to deal with that not-so-pretty sight."

"Would you mind bringing me home to the retirement center? If your mother drives me there, she'll fuss at me the whole way, and I'm not in the mood for her fussin'."

"Of course I don't mind." Scott lifted his hand. "It was nice to meet you ladies." He started to lead Mabel to the door, but she stopped and turned around. "What are you doing, Aunt Mabel?"

"Hold your horses, there, Scotty. I don't want to be rude to my new friends." She smiled over at them. "It was nice to see you girls. You're both very sweet. Will you be here tomorrow?"

"I … uh …" Bailey wasn't sure what to say.

Martina nodded. "I will."

"What time?"

"Same time?"

"Good," Mabel said. "I'll see you then."

Scott waved and guided his aunt out the door. As soon as they were gone, Martina let out a soft chuckle.

"What?" Bailey asked.

"That has got to be the strangest thing that's happened to me today."

Bailey rolled her eyes. "It's only 8:30 in the morning."

"I know, right?" Martina glanced at her watch. "Sorry I can't stick around. I have an appointment with a new client this morning, and I have to pull up all the information before he gets there. See you here tomorrow?"

"I guess." Bailey knew that if she didn't agree to come, Martina would hound her and make her regret it. "Just don't expect to see Scott."

"Of course not." Martina faked a look of surprise. "I'm just excited that we'll get to see our new friend Mabel again. She's such a sweet lady, isn't she?"

"That she is."

After Martina left, Bailey turned her attention back to the line that had shrunk by only a couple of people. The guy in front of her turned around to face her. He appeared to be in his late forties or early fifties, and he had a kind look on his face. "Interesting."

"What's that?"

"Those people … your friend. That kind of thing never happens to me."

Bailey laughed. "It doesn't normally happen to me either."

*

As soon as Scott dropped his aunt off at her retirement center, he drove straight to the job site where he was in charge of the first of three new shopping centers in Summerville, South Carolina. In all the confusion back at Hug-a-Mug, he'd forgotten to get his much needed morning cup of coffee.

Oh well. He'd make sure everything was going as planned and stop off at a convenience store on the way to the real estate office where he'd meet his new realtor to discuss future sites for his company.

The foreman he'd hired had everything under control. "The only thing we need is the rest of the drywall. A pallet of it is supposed to be delivered later this afternoon. We have plenty to do until then."

Scott went back out to his truck and took off for the real estate office. He'd been away from Summerville for several years, and things had really changed. It used to be a sleepy little town not far from Charleston, but now it had grown so much he didn't recognize anyone.

He pulled into the parking lot of the real estate company that had relocated from the tiny office on Main Street to a large, standalone building on Old Trolley Road. He walked inside and took a long look around.

No one looked even vaguely familiar, until he glanced over toward the person walking toward him. No, it couldn't be.

She smiled and extended her hand. "Hi, Scott. When I got to the office and saw your name, I couldn't believe it."

"Martina, right?" He couldn't believe it either.

She nodded. "Did you get your aunt home okay?"

He laughed. "Yes, and she chatted all about you and your friend the whole way there."

"She's a sweet woman," Martina said. "Why don't we go back to my office, and I'll show you what I've pulled up. There are actually quite a few possibilities for your next site."

"Any of them look good?" he asked.

She glanced at him over her shoulder. "They all look good. Remember, this is Summerville, and this town is growing like crazy."

"True."

Martina maintained a professional demeanor throughout the meeting. He was relieved, but he couldn't resist asking about Bailey.

"Is your friend dating anyone?"

Her expression went from cool to amused. "Not at the moment. Why? Interested?"

He shrugged. "Maybe."

"Bailey is single, she's a merchandising manager of a large retail chain, and she loves animals, although she doesn't have any pets right now. Anything else you want to know about her to help you decide whether or not you're interested?"

He laughed. "That's pretty much all I need to know right now."

She leaned back in her chair. "So tell me about yourself, Scott."

"Well ..." He wasn't quite sure what to tell her, so he decided to give her a few facts. "I was born and raised here in Summerville. I went away to college, attended a private high school in Charleston, went to work for a real estate development firm in Atlanta, and then decided to branch out on my own."

She steepled her fingers and smiled. "Which is what brought you back to Summerville?"

"That's right." He stood. "I really need to get back to the site. If anything else comes available, let me know."

"I will." She followed him to the door of her office.

He could feel her gaze on his back as he left the building and got into his truck. It was obvious that she was interested in him, but he agreed with his aunt about Bailey being a better match.

Chapter 2

"You are not going to believe this."

Bailey chuckled. "Take a breath, Martina, and slow down." Bailey leaned back in her office chair and switched her phone to the other ear as she gave her friend a moment to relax.

"Remember Scott from this morning?"

"How could I forget?"

"He was here … at my office …"

"What was he doing there?"

"Looking at commercial property. He was my appointment this morning."

Bailey gripped the phone tighter. "Why didn't you tell me?"

"I didn't know. All I knew was that someone from Nixon Property Development would be here."

"Okay, so that was Scott Nixon."

Martina groaned. "I didn't even put it together."

"Did he remember you?"

"Of course he did … and not only did he remember you, he really likes you."

"How do you know that?" Bailey asked.

"I just do. Look, Bailey, you and I both know he's the best looking guy we've seen in a very long time. I would go out with him in a heartbeat, but I'm pretty sure you're the one he's interested in."

"No, I think it's his aunt who's interested in me."

"Why do you have to be so dense, Bailey? When he was here, his eyes lit up at the mere mention of your name." She laughed. "Oh, and he asked if you were seeing anyone."

"He did? Or did you volunteer the information?"

"I can tell this conversation is going nowhere." Martina paused.

"Where do you want to go for your birthday on Friday?"

"I haven't thought about it."

"You need to start thinking. This is your thirtieth. It's special, so I want to take you someplace nice."

"What if I have a date?"

Martina gasped. "Do you?"

"No, I was just kidding. I guess we can go to that new place on North Cedar Street."

"Okay, but I was thinking someplace more … expensive."

"It doesn't have to be expensive to be nice, you know," Bailey reminded her. "Besides, I like their salmon."

They finalized their plans for Friday night and then got off the phone. Bailey leaned back in her office chair. She'd managed to get most of her orders placed since she was the first to arrive in her office. Most of the other managers were out in the field this morning. She planned to go out later.

*

By the time Friday arrived, Bailey was ready for the weekend. She went straight to her apartment after work and got ready for her dinner with Martina.

On the way to the restaurant, Bailey's phone rang. She pulled into a parking lot and answered. It was Martina.

"Hey, I might be a few minutes late. Go ahead and get a table."

"Okay." Bailey pressed the OFF button and drove the rest of the way to the restaurant.

She'd been seated about a minute when she glanced up and saw Scott Nixon walking toward her. He stopped, nodded toward one of the empty chairs, and grinned. "Mind if I join you?"

"Um …" She leaned around and looked toward the door. "Martina is supposed to be here in a few minutes, but if you'd like to join us, I guess that's fine."

He grimaced. "Sounds like Martina didn't tell you I'd be here."

"She knew?" *Of course she did.* "Please, sit down."

"If you don't want—"

"No, I insist." Bailey thought about all the things she'd say to Martina later, but this wasn't the time to be rude.

She studied his smooth but masculine motions as he sank into the chair. When he looked at her, she felt her face flush with embarrassment that he'd caught her staring at him.

"I hear it's your birthday."

Bailey blinked and nodded. "Tomorrow is. I'll be thirty."

"I hit that one a little more than a year ago." He leaned back, held her gaze for a few seconds, causing another flutter in her chest, and grinned.

She licked her lips and smiled back. "You don't look half bad for an old man."

His eyes crinkled as his grin widened. "Thanks … I guess." He picked up one of the menus the hostess had left. "What do you recommend?"

"I've only had the salmon, and it's really good. Martina isn't much of a fish eater, so she prefers the steak or pork chops."

He put the menu back on the table. "Then salmon it is."

As attracted to Scott as she was, she didn't want to show it—at least not yet. Besides, this whole scenario could get quite awkward after Martina arrived. She leaned over and glanced toward the front of the restaurant.

"Looking for Martina?" Scott asked.

"I don't know what's taking her so long."

"Why don't you call her and ask?"

Bailey nodded as she pulled her cell phone from her bag. "It'll just take me a minute."

Martina answered on the first ring. "I'm doing my best to get out of here, but my client keeps having to call his wife before he signs the papers. In fact, he's out in the hallway doing that right now."

"Okay."

"Did … um …" Martina cleared her throat. "Have you seen anyone we know?"

"If you're talking about Scott, yes, he's sitting right here."

"Good," Martina said. "At least you're not having to wait alone." She paused. "Tell you what. Why don't you go ahead and have dinner with Scott? I'll come for dessert and to pick up the check."

"I—"

Before Bailey had a chance to argue, Martina said, "My client is coming back in now. Gotta go." *Click.*

Bailey held the phone out and stared at it before meeting Scott's sympathetic gaze. "Business."

"I hate when that happens." He continued looking at her as he folded his hands in front of him on the table. "But I can't say I'm disappointed. I'd like to get to know you better."

She blinked. Scott was probably the best looking guy she'd ever seen in her entire life, and he seemed very nice.

Over the next hour and a half, they chatted about everything that came to mind. Bailey was amazed by how easily the conversation came. The more they talked the more she liked him.

The server had just taken away their plates when Martina arrived, frazzled and clearly frustrated. "He never did sign the papers. I suppose I should have known that would happen based on the way he kept hedging." She plopped down and looked directly at Scott. "Sorry about that. So, how was your meal?"

"Delicious. Bailey recommended the salmon, and she was right. It was cooked to perfection."

Martina crinkled her nose. "I'm glad you liked it. I hope you left some room for dessert."

*

The next morning, Scott awoke with a smile on his face. Last night had been the most fun he'd had in a while. Bailey's beauty was matched by her sweet disposition, but there was something else he felt … a connection … a feeling that he needed to know more about her.

When his phone rang, he slid out of bed and picked it up off the chest of drawers. "Hi, Aunt Mabel. Everything okay?"

"Yes, but I was wondering if you'd mind stopping by and picking me up for church tomorrow morning. The bus is in the shop, so all of us are having to find rides."

"Of course, I'll be happy to take you. Do any of your friends need rides?"

"I'll ask. See you in the morning at 10:30."

"You don't want to go to the early service?" he asked.

"Not tomorrow."

After he hung up, he thought about Bailey and wondered if she went to church. Normally, that was one of the first things he discussed with women because he didn't want to get involved with anyone who wasn't a believer. But he'd let it slip his mind last night.

He squeezed his eyes shut. *Forgive me, Lord. I'll make it a point to ask her next time we talk.*

After he opened his eyes, he jotted a note to himself so he wouldn't forget that he was going to the 11:00 service. He and his family had always gone to the early service and then had brunch at the country club.

The day went by in a blur as he worked alongside the construction crew. During the week, his work schedule was filled with administrative duties, but on Saturdays, he enjoyed actually doing some of the manual labor. It brought him back to a simpler time when he could leave the site and relax at the end of the day, physically exhausted but knowing he'd been productive. Now it always seemed as though he juggled balls all week, and one of them could drop at any minute.

*

"Why are you acting so nervous?" Bailey asked. "You keep looking around like you're expecting someone."

Martina shrugged. "I just want to see who all is here."

"Looks to me like the same people we see every Sunday." When she noticed Martina trying to stifle a grin, she narrowed her eyes. "Wait a minute. What's going on?" When she glanced over her shoulder to see what had caught her friend's attention, she spotted Scott standing with his aunt and a couple of older women. "Did you invite him?"

"No. I didn't have to."

"What are you talking about?"

"I just happened to run into his aunt on Friday. She told me that he was such a sweet Christian boy, so I asked her what church he attended." Martina's smile widened. "When she told me that he came here, I told her that we do too."

"Why have I never seen him here before?"

Martina shrugged as she turned and gestured for Scott to join them. "You'll have to ask him."

Scott's aunt and the other women walked up to the front of the church, while he stopped beside Martina. "Mind if I join you?"

"Of course not." Martina jumped up and let him slide in beside Bailey before sitting back down. "Isn't it amazing that we go to the same church?"

He chuckled. "Yeah, but this is the first time I've been to the late service in a very long time. I wondered why Aunt Mabel insisted on changing." He winked at Bailey before turning to Martina. "Would you happen to know?"

Martina shrugged. "Maybe." She gestured toward the front of the church where the worship team had started to assemble.

Throughout the worship service, Bailey had to force herself not to pay attention to Scott and to listen to the message. After the final song, Martina leaned over. "I really have to run. Mama wants me to come help her pick out some new curtains for the dining room."

Scott's aunt and her friends approached as soon as Martina left. "Hey, Scotty, Edna's son is taking us back to the retirement center, so we don't need a ride."

As soon as she left, he turned to Bailey. "Looks like we just got set up."

Chapter 3

Bailey should have seen this coming—first, when Martina kept acting so nervous when they first arrived, and second, when Scott came walking in with his aunt. "Looks like it."

"I hope you don't mind." He gave her a hopeful look. "I'm fine with it."

She nodded. "Me too."

"How about some lunch?"

"You don't have to—"

Scott reached for her hand and covered it with his own. "I know I don't have to, but do you want to know a secret?"

She tilted her head to one side. "What's that?"

"I'm glad my aunt found you. If it weren't for her, we might not have ever met."

Bailey could have melted right there in the church pews, but she forced herself to remain upright. "What did you want for lunch?"

As he recited a list of places from memory, she watched how his expression changed with each one. He finally stopped and gave her a questioning look. "What?"

"You want a burger, don't you?" she said.

An odd expression crossed his face. "How do you know?"

"I can just tell by the way you lingered over that option. You raced past everything else."

He shot her a half pathetic smile laced with a humorous sound. "I can't believe this."

"Can't believe what?"

"A woman who can read my mind."

"Well," she said slowly as she gained control of her wobbly knees. "You did make it rather obvious."

He glanced around the church. "Something else is pretty obvious to me. We're the last ones standing in the sanctuary."

"Then we'd better get out of here. Let's go get some burgers."

When they got to the parking lot, she started toward her car. "Do you want me to ride with you?" he asked.

"Um … sure." She'd thought they would meet at the restaurant.

"Or you can ride with me." He rubbed his chin and looked around. "Even better, why don't I follow you to your place and pick you up from there. That way, we don't have to come back to the church later."

"Okay, that's fine too."

"Are you always this agreeable?" he asked.

"No, why?"

"Just asking. You go on ahead, and I'll be right behind you."

*

Scott had no idea where she lived, so when she pulled down a tree-lined street with small, single-family, cottage-style houses, he was surprised. Most of the women he'd known had lived in apartments or condos.

"Nice neighborhood," he said as she got into his truck. "How long have you lived here?"

"A couple of years. I got tired of throwing my money away on rent, so I finally broke down and bought a place."

"Smart move."

"How about you?" She had turned and positioned herself to face him as much as her seatbelt allowed. "Do you live in a house or apartment?"

He grimaced. "I'm still throwing my money away on rent."

"Oh. Well, that's not a bad thing to do if you're not sure you'll be staying in town."

"But I plan to stay."

She glanced out the side window before looking at him. "Which burger place are we going to?"

"I thought about several places, but there's one in Downtown Charleston …" He paused. "Are you up for a bit of a drive?"

"Absolutely. I love Charleston. Maybe we can walk around after we eat … unless you have to be back for some reason."

"Sounds like a good plan."

He could see her watching him out of the corner of his eye, but she didn't say anything else. Then his phone rang. He glanced at it before pulling over.

"My aunt," he whispered before pressing the TALK button.

"Just calling to check on you and Bailey," she said.

"We're on our way to lunch."

"Good. I knew the two of you would hit it off." He could practically hear her smiling.

"So you're admitting this was part of your plan—to get me to the late service so I would see Bailey?" He glanced over at the subject of the conversation, and she grinned.

"You got that right, Scotty. I didn't want to leave anything to chance … or you for that matter. That girl's cute and sweet. Someone's going to snap her up, and that might as well be you."

Now he couldn't help but laugh. "We'll see how it goes. Do you need anything?"

"Nope. At least not now. But I will expect a report at the end of the day."

"Okay," he said. "I'll take notes."

"Don't be ridiculous, Scotty. Just pay attention and make sure you don't miss an opportunity to kiss the girl."

After he pressed the OFF button, he looked over at Bailey who remained still but somewhat amused. He took a deep breath, leaned over, and pulled her a little closer. And then he planted a quick kiss on her lips.

When he pulled away, her eyes were open wide, and her mouth was slightly open. He chuckled.

"I needed to do that for Aunt Mabel."

"You what?" She licked her lips, making him want to kiss her again.

"She told me not to miss an opportunity to kiss you, so I thought I'd make sure I had something to report later."

"Oh." She turned to face the front for a couple of seconds before looking back at him. "Is that why you did that?"

"It's one of the reasons." He took her hand in his and gently stroked the back of it. "The other reason is that I wanted to do it. You look so sweet and pretty and … well, kissable."

"Okay." She smoothed the front of her skirt with her free hand. "At least you won't disappoint your aunt."

"Be on alert." He turned his attention back to his driving and pulled away from the curb. "I just might decide to do it again."

"I'm sure your aunt will be very happy about that."

"I know, and she's not the only one." He cast a quick glance in her direction. "It makes me pretty happy too."

*

The remainder of the afternoon was like a fairy tale. Bailey stood in front of her sink and reflected on sitting across from Scott in the restaurant, talking about anything that came to mind, and walking hand-in-hand with him through Downtown Charleston.

After lunch, they walked through the City Market, past the Pineapple Fountain overlooking the water, and stopped to look at the old church architecture. Overall, it seemed like a relaxing afternoon, but her insides were anything but relaxed.

Her phone rang, snapping her out of her reverie. Before she had a chance to say *Hello*, Martina started jabbering.

"I want to know every last detail … I mean everything … don't leave anything out. Where did you and Scott go this afternoon? Did you have fun? Was he dreamy?"

Bailey laughed. "We went to Charleston, had lunch, and walked around. Yes, we had fun … and what was your other question?"

"Did he kiss you?"

"I don't remember that being one of your questions. What did you say before?"

"Never mind what I said before." Martina's voice came out in a rush. "Just tell me, did he kiss you? Did it make you kick your foot up, like Doris Day in her old movies?"

Bailey sighed. She figured she might as well tell Martina, or she might never have any peace. "Yes, he did kiss me. Twice."

"Ooh, I want to hear all about it."

"Well, the first time was a surprise. We were sitting in his truck, and he kissed me to get it out of the way so he could tell his aunt he did it."

"Oh, come on," Martina said in a low growl. "He wouldn't have kissed you if he didn't want to. How about the second one?"

"We had just stopped to read a placard at one of the old churches. When I turned around, he leaned over and kissed me."

"Was it a long one?"

Bailey giggled. "Not terribly long, but it was nice."

"Nice, huh? I guess that's about as much as I'll get from you now, but don't think this is a closed subject. When are you going to see him again?"

"I'm not sure. He asked if I could go out on Tuesday, but I'm working late with one of the new store managers."

"Don't keep turning him down," Martina warned. "A guy who looks like that won't stay single long."

After Bailey got off the phone, she poured herself a glass of sweet tea and carried it over to her laptop on the table where she signed on to her email. She needed to stop thinking so much about her afternoon with Scott, or she might start worrying about the things that could go wrong.

But it was impossible not to think about him. Images of their afternoon together kept popping into her head. She finally closed her laptop and went to start some laundry.

The next couple of days seemed to drag. Every time Bailey's phone rang, her heart lurched. But when she saw that it wasn't Scott, a wave of disappointment washed over her.

Since she'd had to work late on Tuesday night, she didn't have to be at work until early afternoon on Wednesday. She slept an hour later than usual, so when she got up, she decided to have a big breakfast and skip lunch. She'd just finished eating waffles, eggs, bacon, and apples when her phone rang. This time it was Scott.

"Hey, I wondered if you'd be able to meet me for lunch."

Figures, she thought. She glanced at the plate she'd just cleaned and sighed. She remembered what Martina had said about someone like Scott not staying single long. "Sounds good."

He named a couple of places, and she chose one not far from her office. Then she quickly got ready and left. She still wasn't hungry, but she didn't want to miss out on seeing Scott again.

As soon as she parked her car and got out, he was by her side. It seemed that he appeared from out of nowhere. "Wow! How'd you do that?"

He pointed to his truck that was just a few spaces over. "I've been watching for you." He grinned as he placed his hand in the small of her back. "Hungry?"

Now that he'd come out and asked her point blank, she couldn't lie. "Not really," she said softly. "I had a big breakfast right before you called."

An odd expression came over his face and then he smiled. "Why didn't you say something?"

"I—" She glanced down and then looked back up at him. "I wanted to see you." She knew it was a risk letting him know how she felt, but anything else would be a lie.

"That's what I was hoping you'd say. I really missed you over the past couple of days." They walked into the restaurant. "Will you at least have a salad or some dessert?"

"I'll have coffee," she said. "After those two huge waffles with maple syrup, I'm afraid dessert would send me into sugar shock, and I wouldn't get much done this afternoon."

"I know what you mean."

They chatted about Summerville, Charleston, and other places he'd lived. Since she'd never lived anywhere else, she did most of the listening while he talked.

She glanced up at the clock. "I really need to get into the office soon."

"Do you have to work late again today?" he asked.

"Only about an hour later than usual. I've already put in quite a few hours this week."

"Do you feel like doing something later?" He looked directly into her eyes, melting her insides. If he kept looking at her like that, she'd never get anything done, so she glanced away.

"Sounds good, but it can't be a late night. I still have to be available to the new manager while she gets comfortable with our system."

"There's a potluck and concert at the church tonight. I'll pick something up at the deli so you won't have to worry about bringing anything. How does that sound?"

"Perfect."

Shortly after she got to her office, her desk phone rang. It was her mother, and she sounded frantic.

"Your father just heard a rumor about you. Please tell me it isn't true."

"A rumor? About me?"

"Yes. One of the guys he plays golf with said he saw you with Scott Nixon in town today."

"Well, yes that is true."

"How could you do this to your father?"

Chapter 4

After hanging up with her mother, Bailey was confused. Apparently, her father and Scott's dad had been best friends growing up. They'd even started a company together before her dad went into the Army. Apparently, they'd had a major falling out over how the company had changed in her dad's absence. There was something else about a shady deal—something she didn't understand.

Her mother seemed to think Scott was seeing her to get information. No matter what Bailey said to explain that it was his aunt who brought them together, she couldn't convince her mother that it wasn't some nefarious scheme that Mr. Nixon had concocted.

The last thing her mother had said hit her hard. As Bailey sank back into her office chair and closed her eyes, the words all came tumbling back into her head. "If you continue seeing the Nixon boy, you're showing your lack of support for your father. I think he would be terribly hurt if he ever found out."

For the first time in Bailey's adult life, she'd finally found someone who had the whole package of what she would want in a man. He was kind, gentle, intelligent, interesting, and fun. To top all of that off was the most essential thing—he was a Christian. And it didn't hurt that he was so great to look at.

"Bailey?"

She quickly opened her eyes and saw the office administrative assistant standing at the door looking sheepish. "Yes, Tracy?"

"I'm sorry if this is a bad time, but I wanted to remind you that we're having a conference call with one of the distributors in a few minutes."

"Oh, yes, of course." Bailey straightened in her chair as she glanced at the wall clock. "I'll be there a few minutes before it starts."

Tracy smiled and disappeared. Bailey sighed and said a quick prayer that she'd be able to focus on work until she left for the day. One thing she needed to remember was that she still didn't know Scott very well. Her parents had always been there for her, and they always had her best interests at heart. If she needed to end things with Scott, it was better sooner than later.

*

Scott couldn't believe the brushoff he'd just gotten from Bailey. Earlier, during lunch, she seemed to be as into him as he was her. But just now, she told him she wouldn't be able to go with him tonight. And when he asked if they could do something later in the week, she said no and asked him not to call her again. Ever.

Something had clearly happened to upset her, and he planned to get to the heart of it. Based on the sound of her shaky voice, he thought it must be pretty bad. In the meantime, he had to make sure his team was taken care of.

He headed out to check on the guys at the site. Just a few years ago, the sound of country music blared from boom boxes, but now, everyone was plugged into the music on their phones.

His foreman stopped when he saw him and yanked out his ear buds. "What's up, boss?" Todd frowned. "Looks like you have some bad news."

"No, everything's fine." At least it appeared to be on the job. "In fact, it all looks good."

Todd grinned and nodded. "We're on track to finish early. It helped that the inspectors came early."

Since there wasn't anything urgent that needed Scott's attention, he picked up a hammer and went to work alongside the carpenters. He'd long ago discovered that nothing helped with frustration more than physical labor.

At the end of the day, Scott was the last person to leave. He finally went home, took a shower, and changed into some clean jeans and a button-front shirt. Afterward, he took a long look at himself in the mirror before closing his eyes and saying a prayer for the right words. Then he went to visit Bailey in person.

All the way to her house, he tried to think of what could be going on with her to make her shut him out so quickly. But nothing came to him. It was so frustrating.

Within seconds of when he rang her doorbell, the front porch light came on, and she opened the door. Her red-rimmed eyes let him know she was upset about something. She just stood there staring at him.

He nodded toward the entryway. "May I come in?"

Her eyebrows came together in a quick frown, but then she nodded and backed away from the door. As he walked inside, he glanced around at the clean lines and noticed the lack of tchotchkes. This was exactly how he would have pictured her personal space.

She closed the door behind him, widened her stance, folded her arms, and locked gazes with him. "What do you want, Scott?"

"I'd like to know what happened. Everything seemed just fine … and then boom! It all went south."

A myriad of expressions crossed her face before she eventually took a deep breath, slowly let it out, and blurted, "Apparently, there's a family feud going on between the Nixons and the Hatchers."

"Really?" He tried to remember if anything was ever said about her family, but nothing came to mind.

She nodded. "Did you know that our dads used to be in business together?"

He shook his head. "When?"

*

As Bailey told Scott what her mother had said, she noticed his jaw tightening. But he didn't speak. He just remained very still and listened until she finished.

"I hope you believe me when I tell you that I had no idea about most of this."

"Most?" She narrowed her gaze, tilted her head, and continued staring at him. "So you knew some of it?"

He closed his eyes and opened them, shaking his head in what appeared to be frustration. "I'd heard bits and pieces of someone my dad used to work with. The details were rather sketchy, but they don't completely match up to what you just said."

"Well, apparently, the details are still vivid in my parents' minds, and they think you're trying to do something—"

Before she could finish, he closed the distance between them, took her hands in his, and looked down into her eyes. "Please trust me, Bailey. I would never do anything to hurt you. In fact, I would go out of my way to protect you. I just didn't know what to do until now."

"What do you mean, *until now*?"

"I have to talk to my dad. If something happened between them, I need to know. He's always been a shrewd businessman, but I never saw him do anything underhanded."

She shrugged. "I don't know what good that would do now—to talk to him, I mean. That happened a very long time ago."

"What I don't understand is why you would turn me away so quickly without at least talking to me about it."

She saw the pained look on his face. "I was going to talk to you …

eventually. But right after my mother told me what happened I had no idea what to say. It hit me hard."

"It's hitting me hard too," he admitted. "Would you like for me to go with you to speak to your parents?"

"No." The word came out quickly. "I mean, I think we're probably better off letting a little time pass before I say anything."

"But in the meantime …?"

She gave him a look of contrition. "We're probably better off not seeing each other until I figure out what to do."

He pulled his hands away from hers and shoved them into his pockets. "I don't think that's such a good idea."

"But—"

He gave her a soft smile. "What if some nice looking guy comes along and sweeps you off your feet?"

She grinned back. "He already has." She dropped her gaze after revealing something she'd been thinking but had no intention of saying—at least not now.

"Look, Bailey, you and I are obviously attracted to each other, and the only thing stopping us from having a … relationship is something that happened a long time ago … something totally out of our control. We shouldn't be punished for whatever either of our fathers did before we were ever born."

"I know." She'd thought about that. But her mother was adamant that Scott was probably doing the bidding of his father for some reason she couldn't figure out. "But my mother was extremely upset." She shook her head and grimaced. "I don't think I've ever seen her so distraught."

A thoughtful look came over Scott as he rubbed the back of his neck. "I wonder if Aunt Mabel knows about any of this."

"That's right. She was the one who initially brought us together. You don't think …?" Her voice trailed off. She didn't want to accuse his aunt of something she might not have done.

He chuckled. "No. Aunt Mabel is a romantic, not someone who would do something underhanded." He paused. "At least not in a mean way."

"I'm sure." Bailey couldn't imagine his sweet aunt being involved in anything rotten, but she didn't know her very well either.

"In fact, I think she'd be shocked if she knew any of this."

They stood in her foyer, gazing into each other's eyes for more than a minute before she finally glanced away. "I think you need to leave now, Scott."

He nodded and started to leave but stopped and turned to face her. "Mind if I call you?"

"Can you wait a while?"

"Of course. But I don't want to wait too long. I'd like to get back … get us back to where we were before all of this came to light."

This time she kept her mouth closed as she smiled and nodded. She followed him to the door.

"Good night, sweet Bailey. I'll force myself to wait before I call."

As she closed the door behind him, her heart felt as though it left with him. She'd never fallen so quickly for any guy before … or so hard. She knew that she could easily fall in love with him if she allowed it to happen.

*

Friday after work, Bailey went straight to her parents' house for dinner. She noticed her mom and dad exchanging glances as they ate, and as soon as they finished, her dad got up and went to the living room.

Bailey helped her mother clear the table. "Can we talk?"

"About what?" Her mother lifted her chin and pursed her lips.

"I think you know."

"If you're talking about that Nixon boy, there is nothing left to talk about. His family is no good, and I don't want my daughter getting involved with something she can't handle."

"Come on, Mom, you know good and well that Scott had nothing to do with whatever went on between my dad and his."

"He's still a Nixon, and I'm sure very loyal to his family."

"I'm sure he is loyal," Bailey agreed. "But that doesn't mean he would participate in anything underhanded, even if his parents wanted him to."

Her mother put the dishes into the sink and spun around to face Bailey. "What makes you think that? How well do you know this boy?"

Chapter 5

"I admit I've only known him a week, but so far I've seen nothing but good."

"A week, huh?" Her mother folded her arms and shook her head. "It takes a lot longer than a week to really know someone. You've always been way too trusting."

"So what are you saying? That I should stop trusting people?"

"No, of course not." Her mother let out an exasperated sigh. "Just be more careful and wait to form an opinion."

Bailey could tell that there was no point in arguing with her mother, but she had to try one more angle. "Why don't I bring him here so you and Dad can meet him?"

"No."

"So what you used to tell me about giving people a chance to explain doesn't count this time?"

"This is different." The lines on her mother's face deepened. "If you get involved with that Nixon boy, there is no telling how it would affect your father. His father did something so dirty and underhanded, we weren't sure if we would make it."

"That sounds pretty bad," Bailey admitted. "What happened?"

Her mother shuddered. "It was awful … I don't think I can go into the details. Just trust me when I tell you that your father might completely fall apart if you keep seeing that boy."

"So you really do think Scott might be doing something underhanded?" Bailey asked.

Her mother shrugged. "I don't know what that Nixon boy is doing. All I know is that his dirty rotten father said he would personally see to it that we would never win in business. Your father has finally reached success, and I'm concerned that they might want to take it away from us

... just like they did before."

"What could they possibly want that you and dad have now?"

Her mother took her hands in hers and squeezed them. "You."

"What on earth is going on in here?"

Bailey turned around and saw her father standing in the doorway. Before she had a chance to say a word, her mother spoke up.

"I was just telling Bailey how important family loyalty is."

"It is, but remember what you and I discussed before she got here?" He tilted his head forward and gave her mother one of those looks that Bailey knew held a private message.

Rather than stick around and risk being the cause of an argument between them, Bailey backed toward the door and grabbed her purse. "I think it's time for me to leave." And then before anyone could stop her, she took off.

Bailey was too antsy to go home, so she called Martina. "I need to talk. Can you meet me somewhere?"

"How do you know I don't have a date?" Martina asked.

"Do you?"

"No." Martina let out a chuckle. "But that's beside the point. How about meeting me at the Hug-a-Mug?"

"Sounds good. I could use a creamy caramel mocha—decaf, of course—with lots of whipped cream and chocolate shavings."

"Girl, there's so much sugar in one of those things it won't matter if you have full caffeine. You'll be up all night anyway."

"You're right. And the drink isn't the only reason."

"Ooh," Martina cooed. "Sounds like some good stuff. I can't wait to find out what it is."

After Bailey pressed the OFF button, she headed straight to the Hug-a-Mug where she was surprised to find a parking spot near the front. The owner once tried closing early, but customers talked her into staying open late. People needed their coffee and a place to unwind with their laptops.

Bailey had barely placed her order when Martina came walking in. She ordered plain decaf coffee and motioned toward one of the tables in the far corner.

As soon as they were seated, she leaned forward on her elbows, looked directly at Bailey, and widened her eyes. "What gives?"

"It's complicated. Wait until my coffee comes up, and then I'll tell you all about it."

The coffee shop wasn't crowded, so the barista was able to bring the order to the table. "Enjoy." She grinned before going back behind the counter.

Martina's eyes lit up as she focused all of her attention on Bailey. "So spill it. I want details."

As Bailey unfolded the details, Martina made little comments. After she finished, Martina leaned back and frowned.

"This is a very awkward situation. I agree with you—that Scott doesn't seem like the type to cause the kind of trouble your mother is worried about." She tapped her finger on her chin. "But you do have to be careful, and there is that family loyalty thing."

"Careful of what? I'm not going into business with him, and I don't have anything he would want."

Martina grinned. "Except you."

"Huh?"

"He wants you, remember?" Martina leaned back in her chair and took another sip of her coffee. "We have to figure out some way to get him to meet your parents."

"We?"

"Of course, we. You don't think I'm going to leave you alone during your time of need, do you?"

Bailey smiled. "You wouldn't be able to leave me alone, even if you wanted to. It's in your DNA to get involved."

"I know, right? Let's brainstorm what to do next."

Bailey sat there and listened as Martina talked about all the different things they could do to make her parents come around. Then she frowned. "But what if they're right."

"My parents?"

Martina nodded. "Yeah, what if Scott really is up to no good."

Bailey glared at her friend. "Why did you just say that?"

"I don't want to be all Pollyanna about this. Some people are good at covering up bad intentions."

"Yeah, you're right. I need to chill a bit and let things happen like they're supposed to."

Martina laughed. "Bailey, sweetie, you couldn't chill if you were stuck at the North Pole."

By the time they finished their conversation, Bailey felt more relaxed, knowing that Martina had her back. "I have a short training session in the morning for one of the new managers, so I guess I'd better get on home."

"Me too, only I have nothing to do in the morning but search for some houses for one of my new clients who's coming in next week."

"We're just a couple of business tycoons," Bailey teased.

Martina rolled her eyes. "With no personal life." She grinned. "At least that's my story. Yours may be different once we get this whole family feud thing figured out and solved."

*

Scott woke up on Saturday morning with Bailey on his mind. The fact that their relationship was moving along at such a fast pace and then came to such an abrupt stop left him feeling out of sorts.

He called his parents' house to see how they were doing and at least try to get some idea of his dad's relationship with Bailey's father. His mother answered the phone.

"How's everything?" he asked.

"Pretty much how it always is. Why?"

"May I talk to Dad?"

She let out a sarcastic laugh. "Are you kidding? What on earth would make you think he'd be home on a Saturday morning?"

"Mom, what's wrong?"

"Nothing."

He wasn't one to let things slide, so he decided to stop off at his parents' house and see if he could see what was going on with Mom and get some information about his dad. His dad had always been very closed about business related things, but maybe he could get his mother to talk.

When he pulled up in front of their sprawling suburban house, he thought about the success his father had attained and how it had enabled them to live in such a nice house. And he wondered if any of what Bailey's mother had said was true. None of the success was worth it if it involved anything underhanded.

His mother was having coffee in the kitchen … alone as expected. "Hey, Mom."

She smiled up at him and gestured toward the coffee pot. "Pour yourself a cup and have a seat."

Once he sat down, he looked directly at her and noticed a sadness he'd never seen before. "Okay, I'm here now, and I can see that something is going on. What's wrong?"

She sniffled as she gripped her mug with both hands. "What makes you think something is wrong?"

"Well, for starters, you look miserable."

His mother let go of her mug and covered her face with her hands. Seeing her like this ripped at Scott's heart.

"Mom, I'm here to listen if you want to talk about whatever it is that's bothering you. I know you don't want to put me in the middle, but I'm an adult now. I want to help."

After what seemed like forever, she finally dropped her hands and looked directly at him. "I don't know what is happening with your father. It's almost like we're strangers lately."

Alarm bells rang in his head. "Did something happen? Did he do something?"

"No, that's the problem. Nothing happened, and he didn't do anything … at least not with me. All he ever does is work. When he comes home, he never wants to talk. I asked him to attend one of the charity events that we go to every year, but he said he was too busy."

"Would you like for me to talk to him?" Scott asked.

"I don't think it would do any good." She cleared her throat. "Besides, he might get mad at me if he finds out I said something to you."

"I won't tell him that you said anything."

"Then he'll get mad at you for prying."

Anger welled in Scott. "So what if he gets mad. He has no reason to treat you like this."

She forced a half smile. "Thank you, Scott. You're a good son. So tell me what's going on with you lately?"

The timing didn't seem right to discuss what he'd come for. "Not much. Just working and trying to figure out what to get into next."

"Don't let your work take over your life, Scott. This is how it started with your father. He said he needed to work nonstop so we could have a good life and live in a nice house. I thought things would slow down, and we'd get to enjoy some of the good life, but that hasn't been the case."

Even though Scott didn't want to go into detail about what Bailey had told him, he wanted to take advantage of the opportunity his mother just presented. "Y'all have mentioned that he had a partner in the beginning. Who was it?"

"A man who was way too trusting. Your father said he didn't have the business savvy he needed to be successful."

"Can you remember his name?"

"Hatcher," his mother said. "Dan Hatcher. Maybe one of these days you can ask your father about what happened with Dan—if you can ever get him to sit still long enough."

"I intend to." The words came out much sharper than Scott wanted, so he gave her an apologetic look. He stood up and carried his mug to the sink. "Now how about I take my favorite girl out to brunch?"

"Who might that be?"

He walked back to the table, lifted his mother's hand, and kissed the back of it. "Who else but you?"

"Well, since you put it that way, how can I resist?" Her expression looked much less sad as she stood. "Just give me a little time to get ready."

"Sounds good. I have a few errands to run, but I'll be back in an hour, okay?"

"I'll be ready and waiting."

As soon as Scott got in his truck, he pulled out his phone and called his dad. "Hey, son, what do you need?"

"About fifteen minutes of your time."

"I don't—"

"Dad, I really need to talk to you. It's important."

"You're not in any trouble, are you?"

Scott sighed. "Not in the classic sense of the word, but it is important."

"Fine. I'm at the office, but I can't talk long. I have an appointment in an hour."

"Perfect," Scott said. "So do I."

When Scott walked in, he saw his dad at the desk, studying some papers in front of him. He glanced up and motioned toward the metal chair on the other side.

"So what are you so worked up over that you must talk to me right this minute?"

Scott took a deep breath, folded his hands, and met his dad's gaze with a steely one of his own. "I want to know about Dan Hatcher."

Chapter 6

His dad's face went pale, but he quickly recovered with a tilted grin. "Dan Hatcher, huh? What do you want to know?"

"What happened between the two of you when you first started this company?"

"We weren't a good business match, so we went our separate ways."

Scott felt his own jaw tighten. "Was it a mutual split?"

"Mutual split?" his dad repeated.

"Yes. Did he agree that you weren't a good business match?"

The older man blew out a breath, puffing his cheeks in the process. This was what he always did when he didn't have a ready answer.

"I want to know, Dad."

"Why?"

Since Scott expected total honesty from his dad, he decided to be honest with his reason for wanting to know. "Because I think I might be falling in love with his daughter."

His father pulled back and gave him an incredulous look. "You're kidding, right?"

Scott shook his head. "No, I'm one hundred percent serious."

"There are lots of single girls out there, son. Couldn't you have picked one with less—" He stopped and rubbed his temples. "What does she know about your past?"

"That's just it," Scott said. "It's not my past … or hers. It's between you and her father—something we shouldn't have to pay for."

"There is something called family loyalty, you know."

Scott narrowed his eyes and stared at his dad. "Yes, that's true, but I would like to know what I'm being loyal to."

"Okay, here's the short version. Dan Hatcher and I started this business. He wanted to move slowly, but I didn't see the need to move at a snail's pace. I mean, you don't hit success in business by holding back. You know that, right?"

"Not exactly. Don't forget that I took some time to learn my business by some of the best developers in the Southeast before I went out on my own."

His dad made a low grunting sound. "I didn't have that luxury. I had a family to support. I got an opportunity that he said he wasn't comfortable with because he didn't have enough information, and he thought something seemed fishy about it. We had a disagreement, and then he left."

"Why wasn't he comfortable with it?"

His dad shrugged, trying hard to appear nonchalant, but Scott saw through that. "Something about the owner of the other company not having a decent reputation and Hatcher had a bad feeling in his gut."

"Did he flat-out refuse to work with the guy?"

"Not exactly." His dad glanced down at the desk and then looked back up at him. "He just wanted to investigate some more."

"Investigate?"

"Yeah, like find out why the guy had a bad reputation and what we could do to protect our company. Those are things that can kill a deal before it ever gets off the ground."

"Did you check things out before you made the deal?"

His dad cleared his throat and glanced away. "The deal didn't go through."

"Then why did Mr. Hatcher leave? Sounds to me like if the deal didn't go through, he would have stuck around, since that was what the disagreement was about."

"You sure do ask some tough questions, son."

"I want to know the truth. Maybe you should give me the long version."

"I don't have time now." His dad looked at his watch. "I already told you that I only had a few minutes."

"Does Mom know the details?" Scott asked.

"Some, but you know how she is." His dad gave him a half smile, but when Scott didn't smile back, he grew more serious. "There was no need to discuss everything with her. I just told her that Dan and I were no longer in business together. She was fine with that, until Dan's wife quit calling or answering her calls."

"Wow. You let business get in the way of friendship." Scott stood up and backed toward the door. "I want the whole story when you have time to tell it. And I want it soon. This is one girl I don't want to lose, and if you wait too long, I'm afraid it'll be too late."

"Don't put all your eggs in this one basket, Scott. Date around. You're still young."

It took every ounce of self-restraint not to slam the door as he left his dad's office. When he finally got to his truck, he rested his arm on the steering wheel, lowered his head, and said a prayer that this would all get sorted out without a family rift. He had his doubts.

*

Bailey woke up early on Sunday morning. Between training a new manager and what happened with Scott, it had been a rough week. She felt like crawling deeper beneath the covers, but she knew that she needed to worship … especially when she felt this way.

Martina spotted her as soon as she walked into the church. Bailey smiled, and Martina waved her over.

Bailey gestured toward the pews. "Want me to find us a seat?"

"That's fine, but before you do, you might want to talk to Scott."

"Nah, that's okay."

Martina tilted her head toward Bailey and gave her a stern look. "He's looking for you, and besides, you can't keep running away from love."

"Who says—"

"There you are." The sound of Scott's voice behind her made her insides all quivery.

She slowly turned around, mentally lecturing herself to maintain her cool. She managed a slight smile. "Hi, Scott."

She couldn't miss the look of intensity in his eyes. "We need to talk."

"Okay." She glanced over toward Martina who was still talking to the people she was with when Bailey first got there. "When?"

"After church. It's important."

"I told my mom I would join them for lunch." Bailey knew that any conversation with Scott could cause her to lose track of time, and she wasn't about to upset her parents. "Maybe sometime during the week?"

"Any way I can meet your folks? I would like a chance to talk to them."

"I don't think this is a good time."

He opened his mouth to speak, but then he saw someone behind her and waved. Next thing she knew, his aunt stood beside them.

"I'm so happy to see you young people getting along so well," Mabel said.

Bailey couldn't think of a word to say, so she looked at Scott who appeared uncomfortable for a second before turning to his aunt. "I know church is about to start, but I have to ask you something, Aunt Mabel."

"Then you better hurry up and ask. You know I like to get seated as soon as the organist starts playing."

"Did you know anything about Bailey before you …" He looked at Bailey with a half-apologetic, half self-conscious expression. "Were you aware of who her father was before you introduced us?"

The look on Mabel's face quickly changed, making Bailey suspicious. Mabel quickly recovered. "Is her father someone I should know?" Her eyebrows shot up. "Is your daddy famous?"

Bailey shook her head before turning to Scott. "I don't think this is the time or place—"

"I know. I just had to ask."

"But I do know that Bailey is a sweet girl, so even if he is famous, it certainly hasn't gone to her head." Mabel gave her another beatific smile. "In fact, I think it's sweet the way she's so humble."

"Aunt Mabel, her father isn't famous. I just wanted to know if you knew who he was."

"If he's not famous, how would I know?"

"It's complicated." Scott looked back at Bailey. "May I at least sit with you during church?"

Bailey couldn't turn him down now … at least not in front of his sweet aunt. "Yes, of course."

Mabel giggled as she hobbled toward her group of friends. Scott leaned down and whispered, "If my aunt hadn't been standing there, would you have said yes?"

She shrugged. "That's a rather moot point, don't you think? C'mon, let's go sit down before Martina gives my spot to someone else."

Martina gave her an inquiring look but didn't say anything. Bailey didn't want to have to explain, but she knew she'd have to later.

Throughout the service, Bailey had to force herself to focus on the sermon. With Scott sitting right there next to her, it was difficult. His very presence reminded her of why he'd been on her mind, morning, noon, and night since they'd met. The chemistry between them had completely knocked her off her axis, and there was absolutely nothing she could do about it.

After the last worship song was sung, Scott placed his hand on hers. "I spoke to my dad about … you know, what happened between him and your dad."

She looked into his eyes. "And?"

"I have a feeling your dad has a good reason to be upset."

This surprised her. "Why? What happened?"

"I wasn't able to get the details." He squeezed her hand and shoved his hand into his pocket. "I'm not going to leave this one alone."

"It's probably better if you do. My mother was adamant, and I don't want you to do anything that will anger your parents."

"My mom isn't involved. It's just my dad."

"Then I don't want you to upset your father either."

"Maybe he needs a jolt," Scott said. "Something seems wrong in how their old business deal was handled, and I want to find out what it was."

"But why? It happened a long time ago—before either of us was born."

"That's just it. I refuse to be punished for something I had nothing to do with." His chest rose and fell as he took a deep breath and slowly let it out. "I want the opportunity to get to know you better … to see if there's something—"

"Scotty, I hate to bother you, but I need a ride home. Edna's car won't start, so her grandson is taking her. He doesn't have room in his truck."

"Of course, Aunt Mabel. I'll be happy to."

Mabel blinked as she looked at Bailey. "There's plenty of room for all three of us in your truck, isn't there?"

Bailey smiled at Scott's aunt. "I drove to church, and now I'm going to visit my parents."

"Oh, well then, I'm sorry I interrupted you."

"No, that's okay. I have to go now." Bailey looked at Scott. "Why don't you call me later tonight?"

He nodded. "You can count on it."

*

On the way to the retirement center, his aunt jabbered for a few minutes and then stopped mid-sentence. He could feel her powerful gaze as she directed it to him.

"What is going on between you and Bailey? I would have thought the two of you would be going strong by now. In fact, I thought you were, and then …" She scrunched her face. "Something has changed."

"It's a long story, Aunt Mabel, and I'm not sure I understand it."

"Just tell me what you know, and maybe I can help you sort it out."

Scott knew that Aunt Mabel had never been a big fan of his dad, but he didn't want to brush her off. So he decided to give her the basics and promise to tell her more, later.

"Apparently, my dad and Bailey's dad were former business partners, and they had a falling out many years ago."

He pulled up to a traffic light and looked at her. Her face turned pasty white, and her eyes widened. "You do know what happened, don't you?"

He shrugged and let up off the brake when the light turned green. "Just that they had a disagreement on some business deal that eventually fell through."

"Trust me, Scotty, it was a bad deal that your dad had no business getting involved with."

"What do you know, Aunt Mabel?"

She shook her head. "I probably should keep my big mouth shut, but you know how I am. It's just too good to keep to myself."

"What is it?"

"That guy your father wanted to go into business with was a crook, and your dad knew it. His business partner, Dan Hatcher, found out about some shady deals, so he refused to sign the contract."

"That's pretty much what I already knew … with the exception of the guy being a crook. It's probably not a good idea to talk about it anymore until I have more information."

"Well, Scotty, I just happen to have more information." She paused. "Maybe I should keep my big mouth shut, but considering your love life is at stake, I can't very well do that."

"What are you talking about, Aunt Mabel?"

"You know that guy your daddy wanted to do business with?"

He nodded. "What about him?"

"The deal didn't go through because the guy—the crook—wound up in jail over the last deal he got involved with." She gave him a moment to recover before adding, "Dan Hatcher was right, but your daddy was too stubborn and proud to admit it."

Chapter 7

"He what?" Scott pulled into a parking lot, stopped the truck, and turned around to face his aunt.

"I think you heard me just fine. Your daddy's partner knew about the guy's shady past, but would your daddy listen? Nope. And he just about got pulled into the mess. If it weren't for having to wait for his partner, he might have been in just as much trouble."

"What did he do?"

"It had something to do with transporting illegal substances." Aunt Mabel lifted her chin and folded her hands in her lap. "Terrible, terrible stuff."

"Illegal substances … you mean, like drugs or something?"

She nodded. "Something like that. Of course your daddy didn't know until it was almost too late. Your mama was fit to be tied, but your daddy told her the good Lord was looking out for him."

"I had no idea." He slammed his hand on the steering wheel. "No wonder Bailey's parents are so upset about her getting to know me."

"Now don't go throwing a temper tantrum over this, Scotty. You're too old for that."

"Sorry." He put his truck back in gear and pulled out onto the road. "After I take you home, I plan to pay my parents a visit. All this time I've wondered why my dad never went to church with the rest of us. Mom used to say it was because he was so tired. I suspect it had more to do with his business dealings." He paused. "And guilt."

"You're right, Scotty. Your daddy used to attend church religiously." She giggled. "That was a good one, wasn't it?"

He cast a curious glance at her. "What was a good one?"

"Church … religiously …" She made a face and swatted at the air with her hand. "Oh, never mind. You come across pretty clueless when your mind is elsewhere."

He cast an apologetic grin in her direction. "Sorry about that."

"No biggie."

He laughed. "Aunt Mabel, you are a piece of work."

"I know. But you have to admit I'm a classic."

"You got that right."

They rode along in silence for a few minutes, until he pulled into the driveway of her retirement center. He stopped under the awning over the circular drive so she could get out by the door. But she didn't. She just sat there.

"Aunt Mabel, what's wrong?"

She looked down and then raised her hands to cover her face. "I can't keep up this charade."

"What charade?" He took hold of her wrist and gently pried it away from her face. "What are you talking about?"

She looked him in the eyes. "I knew what I was doing."

"When?"

"When I got you and Bailey together."

"What do you mean, you knew what you were doing?"

"It might take me a while to explain, and I don't want to block the entrance." She pointed to a parking spot in the next aisle over. "You can park your truck, and we can either go to my apartment, or we can sit in your truck and talk about it."

"Talk about what?"

"My confession."

He did as he was told and parked the truck. "Why don't we go inside?"

She nodded. "Yes, I think that's best."

Once they got to her apartment, she fixed him a glass of sweet tea and a platter of store-bought cookies. "Maybe you'll cut me some slack if you're not hungry."

"Cookies before lunch?" He snorted. "This must be a big confession for you to forget what you used to tell me."

"You've always been nicer when you've had sweets."

"Okay, so what's your confession?"

His aunt sat down and shifted in her seat for a little while before picking up a pillow off the sofa and holding it in her lap. She gave him a shaky smile. "About two months ago, I had this sudden urge for coffee."

"Which is strange," he said. "You've always been more of a tea drinker."

"I know. Anyway, I was having coffee at the Hug-a-Mug when in walks this really cute girl chatting with her friend. I thought she looked familiar—"

He held up his hand. "Are you talking about Bailey?"

She nodded. "Yes. As I was saying, I thought she looked familiar, so I asked the lady who owns the place if she knew who that girl was. When she told me, I knew that the Lord had brought me there at that specific time."

"Let me get this straight." He narrowed his eyes and looked at his aunt. "The Lord gave you the urge for coffee at precisely that time?"

"Yes, but that's beside the point. Let me finish."

He leaned back and rested his folded hands on his abdomen. "Okay, please continue."

She scowled back at him. "Don't keep interrupting me."

"All right."

She took a sip of her own tea before continuing. "Years ago, when your daddy and Dan Hatcher had their falling out, your mama was distraught. She was very close to Darlene."

"Darlene?" he asked.

"Yes, that's Dan's wife ... Bailey's mother. As I was saying, when I found out who the girl was, I figured that was the Lord's way of helping me bring your mama and her friend back together."

In some strange, convoluted way, that made sense to Scott. He nodded.

"And the bonus was the fact that Bailey is such a pretty girl, and I thought you might like her."

Again, he nodded. "Yes, she is very pretty, but she's much more than that."

"I know. I found out that she goes to the Hug-a-Mug almost every morning before work, so I made it a point to be there as much as I could to observe. That girl is so sweet. One day I watched her pay for someone else's coffee when she discovered the young mother didn't have enough money."

"That's very kind."

"She always holds the door for people coming and going." Aunt Mabel grinned. "And she even gives her table to older people. I walked in one day, ordered my coffee, and turned around to look for a place to sit. When she saw me looking around, she got up, pointed to her table, and said she was just leaving. I knew she'd only been there for a little while because I was standing halfway down the block when she went inside."

"That was very nice of her."

"So that's how I brought the two of you together."

He shook his head. "Maybe so, but I'm missing a few pieces of this puzzle. You said you wanted to reconcile my mother and Mrs. Hatcher. And then Mom called me because she lost you."

She closed her eyes, and moved her lips in what appeared to be a silent prayer, and opened them. "That was all carefully orchestrated. In fact, I held my breath until you came walking in. I wasn't sure it would work." She rubbed her hands together. "But it worked beautifully, don't you think?"

"Maybe so, but how did that help bring my mother and her friend together?"

"Oh, that hasn't happened yet." She gave him a sly grin. "I got sidetracked when I realized you and Bailey would make the perfect couple."

"How did you know I'd come looking for you?"

"About a week ago, I just happened to mention to your mama that you and I had some sort of radar and magnetic pull ... you know that silly nonsense those New Age folks keep talking about?"

He laughed. "Like I said, Aunt Mabel, you are a piece of work."

"And now I have to help you solve this dilemma. I know what's going on, so it's time to finish my mission."

"Refresh my memory."

She rolled her eyes. "You sure do have a short memory. I need to bring these two friends back together."

"Based on what I've seen, that's not likely to happen."

"It will if we can get your daddy to apologize."

"We?"

Aunt Mabel nodded. "As much as I hate to admit it, I need your help with this, Scotty."

"I don't want to get involved with any schemes."

"Oh, it's not a scheme. We'll just have to do a little bit of planning to make sure they're in the same place at the same time."

"Like you did with Bailey and me?"

She nodded. "That's right, but it's not that simple since your mama and Bailey's mama are both loyal to their husbands." She tapped her index finger on her chin. "Somehow we need to show your daddy that apologizing is a manly thing to do."

"I still can't see him ever apologizing."

Aunt Mabel lifted a finger and gave him a stern look. "Don't forget the power of prayer and how the Lord knows exactly what needs to happen."

Scott stood up, grabbed a single cookie off the plate, and strode toward the door. "I'm glad you filled me in on all of this. Like you said, Mom is very loyal to Dad, and I doubt she would have told me any of this … and I don't think Dad would have admitted it based on the way he brushed me off yesterday."

"I never want you to lie, but you don't have to tell them where you heard all of this."

He smiled. "Gotta run. Give me a call if you need me for something."

"Oh, trust me, I will." She got up and followed him to the door. "See you soon, Scotty."

As soon as he left the retirement center, he drove straight to his parents' house. Sunday afternoons were the only time he could count on both his mom and dad to be home. He wasn't going to come out and tell his parents about his conversation with Aunt Mabel, but he planned to find a way to confirm some of the information with them.

One thing he didn't want to do right away was let Bailey know that Aunt Mabel had chosen her to help bring his mom and her mother back together as friends. He worried that might make her feel that he was using her and that he was somehow knowingly involved. How did everything get so complicated?

*

Bailey wanted to kick herself in the backside for telling Scott to call her later. That would only make things more difficult for both of them.

After church, she'd headed to her parents' house. They went to a different church that ended earlier, so she knew there would be a nice Sunday dinner waiting for her. Mom typically alternated fried chicken, ham, and pot roast—and all of those sounded good.

As soon as her mother saw her, she motioned for her to follow her into the kitchen. "I heard you sat with Scott at church this morning."

"Who told you?"

"Never mind who told me. I just don't understand why you would do this to your father."

"I'm not doing anything to Dad. Why don't you just tell me what this is all about?"

"I thought I did."

"What you said isn't a good enough reason for me to turn my back on the only man I'm even remotely interested in."

Instead of telling the details, her mother kept talking about family loyalty and how important it was for her to have it. She just wished she knew why seeing Scott wasn't loyal.

"Are you staying for dinner? I thought I'd change things up and have soup and sandwiches today."

Bailey had lost her appetite. "No thanks. I just wanted to stop by for a minute. I think I'll go on home now and get some laundry done."

"You could have brought it here."

"But I didn't. I'll call you later in the week."

Her mother tried to smile, but Bailey could see the sadness behind it. After she left, she stopped off at the grocery store and picked up a few things.

She normally didn't like to work on Sundays, but she needed something to fill her mind until Scott called. Her phone rang a few hours earlier than she expected, and she was happy to see his number on caller ID.

"Bailey, you and I need to talk." His voice was strained and clipped. "Soon. And in person."

"Okay," she said slowly. "When?"

"Now?"

"Do you want to meet somewhere?"

He let out a deep sigh. "I'd rather talk in private … unless you're uncomfortable with that."

"No, that's fine. Why don't you come over here?"

Chapter 8

By the time Scott arrived a half hour later, all sorts of things had flitted through Bailey's mind. She kept thinking about her mother's comments about loyalty.

As soon as she heard his truck in her driveway, she went to the door and flung it open. He got out, headed up the sidewalk, and stopped a couple of feet in front of her. She stood there and stared at his handsome but solemn face for a few seconds.

He nodded toward the door behind her. "Mind if I come in?"

"Sorry. Come on inside. Would you like something to drink?"

"Water would be good."

She motioned for him to follow her. "Let's sit in the kitchen and talk."

Once they had their water in front of them, Scott looked around. "It was smart to buy this place … good investment."

"It was a fixer upper when I first bought it, but it's coming along pretty well."

"If you need any help with anything, let me know."

She saw that he was having a difficult time getting started on the topic he came to discuss, so she prompted him. "What did you need to talk about?"

After a brief pause, he told her what he'd learned about their fathers. "I confirmed it with my parents this afternoon. Unfortunately, it turned out to be a big mess. Mom started crying, and Dad got angry about the fact that I brought up something that happened so long ago." He shrugged. "I wasn't surprised, though. I sort of expected some fallout."

"If you expected it, why did you do it?"

He leveled her with a gaze. "Because the air needs to be cleared for all of us to move on. It's the right thing to do."

She nodded. "I agree, but sometimes it hurts to dredge up buried pain, even when you're trying to fix it. Some things are better left alone."

"Some things, but not this." He traced his finger along the rim of his glass before continuing. "Like I said, it's the right thing to do, but that's not the only reason I'm doing this."

"What's your other reason?"

"I like you." He cleared his throat. "A lot."

"You know there are no guarantees that things will work out between us, right?" It hurt her to say that, but it was true. "I'd hate for you to upset your family for nothing."

"It's not for nothing," he said. "It needs to come out so it can be dealt with."

"What, exactly, do you expect your dad to do?"

"The right thing." He glanced down at the table and then up at her. "Whatever that is."

"As long as you know it won't be easy …"

"Seems like nothing is easy anymore."

She smiled and nodded. "You got that right."

They chatted for a few more minutes before he finally got up. She followed him to the door before he turned around to face her. "I have an early morning appointment with someone from the codes department. Mind if I call you sometime this week?"

"Of course I don't mind." She smiled as she held the door. "I'll be praying."

"Thanks."

After Bailey closed the door behind him, she leaned against the wall. As flattered as she was by the trouble Scott was going through, she couldn't ignore their parents' feelings. And she had no doubt that it would take quite a bit of work on Scott's part to get his dad to initiate anything that would change her parents' minds.

She lowered her head and prayed for the Lord's will to be done. And then she prayed again before she fell asleep.

The next morning, she got up early enough to spend a little time at the Hug-a-Mug with Martina who almost always started her day there. As soon as she walked into the coffee shop, she looked around and spotted her friend sitting at a table in the corner with Scott's aunt.

It was tempting to turn and leave, but Mabel saw her before she could get to the door. "We're over here, Bailey," the older woman called out. "Come join us."

Bailey met Martina's amused gaze. She hesitated for only a moment before she decided to join them because if she didn't, she'd seem rude.

"Your timing was perfect," Martina said. "We were just talking about you."

"I hope you were saying nice things."

Mabel chuckled. "What's the point of talking about someone if you're only saying nice things?" The twinkle in her eye made Bailey smile. "Just kidding. Of course we were saying nice things. I was just telling your friend here that I had you picked out a very long time ago."

Martina cleared her throat and turned to Bailey. "Why don't you go get your coffee? We'll be here for a while."

As Bailey walked toward the counter to place her order, she heard Martina whispering, but she couldn't make out what she was saying. She'd ask later. Bailey had always been able to pry secrets out of Martina.

When she sat back down with her coffee, the conversation became stilted. Mabel didn't say much. She just kept looking around and acting nervous. Then suddenly, her gaze settled on the door. Bailey glanced over her shoulder and spotted a well-dressed woman who appeared to be looking for someone.

Mabel lifted her hand. "Over here, Ingrid."

The woman smiled at Mabel as she walked toward them. "I don't know what's gotten into you, Mabel. You never used to like coffee."

Mabel waved her hand from the wrist. "Never mind what I used to like. I want you to meet my coffee drinking buddies Martina and Bailey."

The woman extended her hand to Martina first. "So nice to meet you."

When Bailey took the woman's hand, she added, "I'm Bailey—"

Mabel interrupted Bailey before she gave her last name. "Girls, this is my sister Ingrid."

Ingrid laughed. "Her much younger sister."

"I think it's pretty obvious." Mabel rolled her eyes. "When our parents brought her home from the hospital, I thought she was a gift for me. A live baby doll." She motioned toward the chair. "Have a seat, Ingrid. I'm sure Bailey wouldn't mind getting you some coffee."

Bailey nodded. "Of course. What would you like?"

"Decaf would be good."

"Come on, Ingrid. Decaf is for wimps. Go for something good. They have all kinds of yummy coffees with whipped cream and chocolate and even caramel."

Ingrid shrugged. "Okay, then whatever you think I'll like."

"Atta girl." Mabel looked at Bailey. "Get her one of those frothy drinks with the works. And don't forget the toppings." She tapped her chin. "I think sprinkles would be good … or maybe chocolate shavings." She nodded. "Yeah, make that dark chocolate while you're at it. I've heard that's good for the heart."

Bailey nodded. "I'll get her what I always get." The woman pulled out a credit card and extended it toward Bailey.

Bailey stood and smiled. "It's my treat."

"But—"

"Aw, Ingrid, let her take care of this. Some people just like to do nice things, and you should let them."

Ingrid shook her head and continued holding out her card. "I don't—"

"Did you not hear what I said?" Mabel shook her head as she turned to Bailey. "Can you afford this?"

"Yes, of course."

"Then it's settled. This is Bailey's treat." Mabel made a shooing gesture for Bailey to go on up to the counter. "Why don't you go with her, Martina? I have a few things I want to say to my sister, and I don't think you want to be here when I do."

Martina nudged her as they stood at the counter. "This is getting stranger by the minute."

"I know. They were whispering when we first left, but listen to them now." Bailey pointed her thumb toward the women they'd left at the table.

They could hear Mabel fussing at her sister, even though they were more than ten feet away. "Now don't go gettin' all testy on me, Ingrid. You know it's not a good idea to argue with me. I think it's time to step away from your pride and do what you should have done years ago."

Even after Bailey brought the coffee back to the table, the sisters continued arguing. Martina nudged Bailey under the table with her foot. When Bailey met Martina's glance, she saw the same look of what-do-we-do-now expression that she felt.

Mabel gestured toward both girls. "Can't you see how uncomfortable you're making my friends?"

Bailey expected Ingrid to keep arguing, but she didn't. Instead, she closed her eyes and lowered her head, only to be interrupted by the sound of footsteps coming toward them and a voice saying, "Mom, Aunt Mabel, I've been trying to call both of you. What are you—?"

*

Scott stopped in his tracks when Bailey turned around to face him. His heart sank as he thought about the possibilities of what might have been said.

"Hey, Scotty," Aunt Mabel said. "Grab a drink and join us."

"I don't think so ..." He cautiously turned to see his mother's reaction. To his surprise, she didn't appear upset. "Mom?"

She smiled. "Scott, I think you and I need to have a chat." She stood up, but before she left, she turned to Bailey. "It was very nice meeting you, Bailey." Then she smiled at Martina. "And you, Martina. I'm sure

I'll see you both again … soon."

Scott mouthed an apology to Bailey before following his mother out of the coffee shop. As soon as they reached the sidewalk, she spun around. "We're not going to talk here. Come to the house."

"Now?"

She gave him a clipped nod. "Yes, now."

Chapter 9

He drove straight to his parents' house, where his dad was waiting in the study. His mother walked inside, waited for Scott to follow, and then sat on the loveseat adjacent to his dad's chair. Scott wasn't sure what was about to go down, but he could feel the tension in the air.

"Okay, Ingrid, why did you tell me there was an emergency at home, when there clearly isn't—?"

"Oh, but there is." Scott's mother cast a brief glance at him before turning to his dad. "My sister set a trap—one that I couldn't get out of."

"If you can't deal with that senile sister of yours, I will." Scott's dad's words alarmed him.

"Aaron! That is totally uncalled for. My sister loves me, and she has my best interest at heart, even if she does have a rather … unconventional way of showing it."

Scott extended his legs, folded his arms, and studied the facial expressions on both of his parents. His dad looked angry, but his mother appeared different. She had a look of determination and hope on her face.

"One of the things my sister said was that the way we're acting is affecting our son."

His dad glared at her. "I see it differently. What our son is doing is affecting us. His disloyalty—"

"No, he hasn't been disloyal. He fell for a girl before he realized she was the daughter of your adversary."

"But still …" His dad's eyebrows had come together in one long line, something that always happened when he was at his angriest. "Scott, have you continued seeing that Hatcher girl, even after our talk?"

Scott swallowed hard. "Yes."

"Why would you do that to me?"

Scott's mother spoke up. "Stop it, Aaron. Quit acting like this is all about you. Your son deserves a life, and if you keep acting this way, one of two things will happen." She held up two fingers and touched each one as she spoke. "He'll either do what you tell him and be miserable, or you'll alienate him." She leaned forward to meet his gaze. "Tell me, Aaron. Do you want either one of those things?"

His dad looked down at the floor and shook his head. "No."

"Then what are you going to do about it?"

"I don't know."

"You have to do something, Aaron. You've ignored this problem, and look where it's gotten you."

Scott had heard enough. He stood up, brushed his hands, and walked toward the door. "This is going nowhere fast. I'm leaving."

"Scott!"

As the sound of his dad's voice echoed through the hallway, Scott hesitated only for a second before leaving. He couldn't sit there and listen to his dad's stubborn lack of defense.

Scott's thoughts swirled in his head as he drove around. He had to stop off at the job site to make sure everything was under control. Fortunately, it was, so he went home to gather his thoughts. He hadn't been prepared for what had happened that morning, and he had a lot to ponder.

Later that evening, he went back to his parents' house. His dad had calmed down quite a bit at first, but the more they spoke the more agitated he became. Finally, Scott pushed a little too far, and things got ugly.

*

"Earth to Bailey."

Bailey glanced up at the sound of her name by her office door. "Oh, hi Jenn. What's up?"

"Nothing much." Bailey's coworker Jenn tentatively stepped into her office. "Just taking a break and thought I'd stop by and see how you're doing. Anything you want to talk about?"

Bailey leaned back in her office chair. "Not really. So how's that new client of yours doing?"

Jenn grinned. "That bad, huh? Okay, I get it." She pointed to the chair on the other side of Bailey's desk. "Mind if I sit? Maybe we can brainstorm some new marketing strategies."

"Sure, that's fine. Have a seat."

For the next hour and a half, Bailey and Jenn talked about what they'd been doing and discussed ways to enhance their existing marketing plan. Bailey was happy to have something to take her mind off Scott.

After they finished their impromptu meeting, Jenn got up, turned to face Bailey, and smiled. "I sure hope whatever is bugging you gets worked out soon. I miss your sunshiny disposition."

Bailey grinned back at her. "I'll be fine."

After Jenn left, Bailey started thinking about lunch. At least she still had her appetite. She'd forgotten to bring something from home, so she pulled some of the takeout menus she'd collected from her bottom desk drawer.

She'd decided on a deli salad when her phone rang. It was Martina.

"Hey girl, what are you doing for lunch?"

Bailey glanced at the menus. "I thought I'd get something and bring it back to the office."

"Are you swamped?"

"Not really," Bailey said. "Why?"

"I thought maybe you and I could meet somewhere. How's the Eclectic Chef sound?"

It actually sounded good. Bailey loved their soups. "Okay, what time?"

"Can you be there in half an hour?"

"Absolutely."

As soon as Bailey got off the phone, she cleared her desk and put an out-to-lunch message on her email and office voicemail. Then she scooted out the side door of the office so no one would grab her for a chat.

Martina was waiting for her when she arrived. "Go ahead and place your order. You and I need to talk."

It took Bailey less than two minutes to place her order, get her drink, and sit down at the table. Martina didn't waste a second.

"Mabel feels terrible about what happened."

Bailey cleared her throat. "I don't know why. She didn't do anything wrong."

"Oh, come on, Bailey. You and I both know that she had more than one motive for bringing you and Scott together. The matchmaking was kind of sweet, but the deal between y'all's parents … well, she knows she should have kept out of that."

"Does she really?" Bailey tilted her head forward and gave her friend one of those looks that always managed to get the truth out of her. "Did she actually say that?"

"Well, not exactly." Martina fidgeted with her flatware.

"What did she say?"

"Okay, so she didn't say she regretted anything, but I'm sure she does, considering how things have turned out."

Bailey forced a smile. "Why are you so adamantly defending Mabel? Has she replaced me as your best friend?"

"No, of course not." Martina managed a sheepish grin. "But we both care about you and Scott."

"Don't worry so much about my relationship with anyone. I'm a big girl, and I can certainly take care of myself."

"I don't know about that, Bailey." Martina stopped talking when the lady at the counter called her name.

Bailey was thankful for the interruption. She got up from the table, accepted her order, and sat back down. "Can we talk about something else?"

"No, this is too important to ignore."

"Come on, Martina. There are millions of other, much more important, things we can discuss."

Martina contorted her mouth and glanced away for a couple of seconds before looking Bailey in the eyes. "Actually, this is important because Mabel isn't going to leave this one alone."

Bailey groaned. "What's she up to now?"

"I'm not sure, but I do know it involves you, Scott, and both sets of parents."

"Thanks for the heads up. What do you think I should watch for?"

Martina shrugged. "Mabel can be pretty crafty when she's motivated … and I think she's pretty motivated right now. Her sister, her brother-in-law, and her nephew are all angry with her right now. She feels terrible—"

"I don't want to hear about how bad she feels, especially since she's jumping right back into the same behavior that got her into trouble."

"I know, right?" Martina took a bite of her sandwich, chewed, and swallowed before looking back up at Bailey. "There is one tiny hint that might help us figure out her next move."

"What's that?"

"She mentioned something about taking advantage of being Scott's family's common enemy."

Bailey pondered that for a moment. "That's really not much of a hint."

Martina held out her hands and shrugged. "That's all we have to go on at the moment."

"Since we don't know much about that right now, let's talk about something else." Bailey paused to make sure Martina understood. As soon as her friend nodded, Bailey continued. "What are you bringing to the church potluck on Sunday?"

"I hadn't thought much about it yet. How about you?"

"A couple of things," Bailey replied. "Since I usually bring something healthy, I thought I'd shake things up and bring dessert too."

Martina chuckled. "Let's not get too crazy. People will think you've lost your mind."

"I know."

"What is this world coming to?" Martina blinked, and then her eyes widened. "Don't look now, but look who just walked in."

Bailey groaned when she saw Scott. It only took him three strides to reach their table, and when he got there, he looked directly at Martina. "After you called this morning and mentioned that the plot next to the other site was available, I decided to check it out. You said to let you know, and you mentioned that you were coming here for lunch, so I thought—"

Martina cleared her throat loud enough to interrupt him. "I didn't mean …" Her voice trailed off as her face turned crimson.

"Oh." Scott chuckled. "I think I know what's going on."

Bailey was tired of this, but she didn't want to take it out on Scott, who was clearly as caught off guard as she was. "Would you like to join us?" she asked.

He hesitated before shaking his head. "I appreciate the offer, but I'm supposed to meet one of my foremen at the site."

"Is it the location I told you about?" Martina asked.

"Yes. I didn't think it would work at first, but I decided to check it out again." He backed toward the door. "See you ladies later. Enjoy your lunch."

As soon as he left, Bailey turned to face Martina, who suddenly seemed enthralled by the small amount of her sandwich she hadn't finished. "Look at me, Martina."

Bailey wouldn't stop glaring until her friend finally met her gaze. "So you called Scott this morning?"

"I did." Martina hung her head with a sheepish look on her face.

"And you told him where you would be."

Martina nodded. "But I didn't tell him to come."

"You knew he would want to see that site, though, right?"

"Of course, but I still didn't—"

Bailey held up a hand. "I have another question. Did you tell him I'd be with you?"

A look of anguish washed over Martina's face. "No, I absolutely did not tell him I was meeting you here."

"Okay, you finally said something I believe."

"What?" Martina's voice came out in a shriek. She took a deep breath and started over. "Are you saying I lied to you … because I've never—?"

"No, I'm not saying you're lying, but I do think you're more involved with Mabel's plan than you're letting on."

Martina sat there and fidgeted with her napkin. The door of the café opened, and she glanced around in a nervous, jerky motion.

Chapter 10

A group of young, professionally dressed women came walking in and headed toward the order counter. When Martina turned back around, she appeared relieved.

"Well?" Bailey asked. "Are you?"

Martina finally looked directly at her. "Am I what?"

"In cahoots with Mabel?"

"Not exactly in cahoots."

"Then tell me exactly what's going on?"

Martina let out a long sigh and shook her head. "Okay, you win. I spoke with Mabel this morning right before I called Scott. Since I don't want to betray you in any way, I told her I couldn't get involved in a scheme ..." Martina smiled and paused. "But I told her I wouldn't interfere in hers." She continued explaining her conversation with Scott's aunt. "I told her it would be best if I didn't know all the details of anything she had planned."

Bailey didn't know whether to laugh or get mad at her friend. On the one hand, her friend was making all the right noise about not getting involved. But on the other hand, she knew that Mabel was still plotting, and since Martina said she didn't want to be a part of it, Bailey had the element of surprise working against her.

"I have to get back to the office in a few minutes," Martina said. "But there is one thing I want you to think about."

"What's that?"

"Are you going to let your parents keep you from being with the man who could possibly be the love of your life, or are you going to stand up for yourself and fight for him?"

Bailey felt an odd sensation in her chest. "There's really nothing to fight for since I've only been around him a few times. I figured it would be best to end something before it began."

Martina stood up and tossed her trash in the wastebasket. "I'm afraid it's too late for that. You're already smitten."

"Smitten?" Bailey grinned. "I haven't heard that word in a while."

"It fits, though, don't you think?"

"I'm not going to answer that."

"You don't have to." Martina leaned over and gave Bailey a hug. "Thanks for agreeing to meet me. I hope you're not too mad."

"I'll get over it."

All the way back to her office, Bailey thought about what was happening. As much as she liked Scott, she still wasn't willing to hurt her parents just to get to know him better. Why couldn't Martina get that through her head?

Fortunately, everything went well for the remainder of the day. She only had to deal with one issue, and it was something she had done many times.

The rest of the week was pretty routine, and she managed to stay away from the Hug-a-Mug until Friday morning. But she woke up craving a frothy mocha drink.

She decided to get there early, order her drink, and leave before Martina typically arrived. A different crowd was in the coffee shop—people she didn't recognize.

Good. She went straight up to the counter, ordered her drink to go, paid, walked over to the area to wait for the barista to make it, and lifted it off the counter before turning toward the door.

That was when she spotted Scott standing there watching her. Her heart thudded, and her mouth went dry. She forced a smile as she tried to walk toward the door without stumbling.

"I'm glad I got here early," Scott said. "We need to talk."

"Um …" She didn't have to be at work for another hour, so she didn't have an excuse, and she wasn't about to lie. "Okay."

"Maybe we should go someplace else so we don't get interrupted."

"No," she said. "We can stay here. Martina won't be here for a while, and I doubt your aunt will come this early."

"You have a good point." He allowed her to lead the way to a table and then followed her. "Is that why you're here at this hour?"

She smiled and gave a clipped nod. "I'm getting tired of the drama."

"Yeah, me too." He plopped down in the chair.

"Don't you want something to drink?"

"I got here when the place opened, so I've had more than enough coffee."

She stirred the froth into her drink and took a sip. "So why have you been here so long?"

He placed his forearms on the table and leaned toward her. "I stopped off at my parents' house again last night and had a long talk with them."

She didn't look directly at him. "I hope you had a nice time."

"Well, actually, it was quite miserable. They didn't like what I had to say. In fact, my dad ordered me to leave."

She shot her gaze directly at his. "That sounds serious."

"It is." He pursed his lips and cleared his throat before he started speaking again. "Bailey, I'm crazy about you. In fact, you're all I've been able to think about ever since I met you."

Her hands started shaking, so she put her drink on the table before she dropped it. He'd just admitted that he felt the same way she did.

"So last night I went to my folks' house and told them that if they didn't do something to make their relationship right with your parents, I would go have a talk with your dad on my own."

"You said that?"

He nodded and gave a half grin. "I did."

"What did they say?"

"My dad was furious. Mom told me that I needed to get over whatever it is that's going on. I told her that was impossible because I'm—well, I'm emotionally involved with you, and I want to see where this thing goes with us." He swallowed hard, but his gaze never left hers. "I took a big chance, hoping you felt the same way." He quickly grew silent.

Now she knew she had to say something—either to admit her feelings or tell him it wouldn't work and hope that her feelings would fade. She blinked a couple of times before nodding. "I do."

His cheeks puffed as he blew out a breath. "That's a relief." And then he smiled as he reached for her free hand. "I've never felt this way about a girl this quickly … or *ever*, for that matter."

"Do you have any idea what your parents will do?"

"I left when my dad told me to, but Mom called me later and said they'd been talking."

"I hope that's a good sign."

Scott looked up and did a double take toward the door. "Don't look now, but I think we're about to have company."

"Who?"

He waved and whispered, "My aunt."

Mabel didn't waste a second getting to the table. She pulled out a chair, pointed to it, and said, "Hey, Bailey. Mind if I sit here?"

"No, of course not," Bailey said. "I have to leave in a minute, but I'm sure Scott would enjoy your company."

Mabel turned to Scott. "I see the two of you have finally gotten together *on your own*. It's about time."

Bailey opened her mouth, but she was so stunned nothing came out. She gave Scott an apologetic look.

He took over. "Hi, Aunt Mabel. Want me to get you some coffee?"

"Nah, I had some tea before I left the house. I'm really not much of a coffee drinker, ya know."

"But I thought—"

Mabel rolled her eyes, stopping him mid-sentence, and then she grinned at Bailey who had stood. "It sure was good seeing you."

"It was nice seeing you too."

Scott nodded. "I'll call you later."

As Bailey walked to her office, she couldn't help but smile. Scott's admission got the last day of the week off to the best start ever.

*

After work that day, Scott drove straight to his parents' house. His mother had called and said they wanted to talk to him. After he pulled into their driveway, he put his truck in PARK, closed his eyes, and prayed for the issue between his and Bailey's parents to be resolved.

His mother stood at the door waiting for him as he got out and walked up the sidewalk. "Your father is in the study."

As soon as he walked into the semi-dark study, his dad got up, came around from behind his desk, and embraced him in a bear hug. "Son, I've been doing a lot of thinking … and praying."

Chapter 11

Bailey expected Scott to call sometime Saturday, but when he didn't by mid-afternoon, she came to the realization that she might not hear from him that day. She decided to ask Martina if she wanted to do something. She pulled out her phone, punched in her friend's number, and hoped that she hadn't made any plans yet.

"One of my clients is having a housewarming party, and I told her I'd stop by for a little while. I'd love for you to be my guest."

"Are you sure it's okay?" Bailey asked. Normally she wouldn't have wanted to go to a stranger's party, but she didn't want to be home by herself either.

"Absolutely. It's a come-as-you-are open house. We'll just go for a little while so I can drop off this plant I bought. Then maybe we can go hang out at the Hug-a-Mug."

"Let's go somewhere else, okay?" Bailey asked.

Martina laughed. "That's fine. I understand."

A couple of hours later, Martina arrived to pick her up for their girls' night out. They stopped off at one of the older restaurants in downtown Summerville for an early dinner before driving out to Martina's client's house.

"Wow! This is nice." Bailey looked around at the newer houses in a subdivision she knew about but had never been to. "They all look like mansions."

"They are. In fact, the commission from this sale is enough for me to put a down payment on that townhouse I've been looking at." Martina pulled up in front of one of the humongous brick houses. "And here we are." She got out of the car, opened the back door, and got the plant off the floorboard. "Esther told me she liked evergreens, so I decided this was as good as any housewarming gift."

Bailey followed her friend up the sidewalk and to the front door. "I hope I'm not underdressed," she whispered.

"You're fine. Black on black will go anywhere."

A woman who appeared to be in her mid-fifties answered the door. "Martina!" She pulled Martina in for an embrace before grinning at Bailey. "And who is this sweet looking young woman?"

"This is my best pal Bailey."

"Come on in. Martina, why don't you show Bailey around the house and then go on back to the kitchen for some refreshments? I'd like for you to meet some of my good friends."

As they walked around the house, Bailey oohed and ahhed over the size and details of the rooms. "They didn't miss a thing when they built this house, did they?"

"No, and Esther and her husband paid dearly for it too."

"I can only imagine."

Martina gestured toward the stairs. "Ready to go down and meet some of Esther's friends?"

"Sure, let's go." Bailey took a couple of steps before adding, "Let's not stay too long, okay?"

"Yeah, that's what I was thinking."

A few minutes later, they walked into the dining area where a buffet had been set up on the large, twelve-foot table. Esther spotted them immediately. She walked over, took both of them by the hand, and led them to a couple standing by the coffee urns.

"Aaron and Ingrid, I want you to meet these two darling girls."

As soon as Bailey made eye contact with the woman, she knew exactly who it was. She forced a smile and extended a hand. "It's nice to see you again, Mrs. Nixon."

The woman smiled back and nodded. "Bailey, you look lovely." She turned to Martina. "And so do you."

The man standing beside Mrs. Nixon gave her a curious look. "You know these girls?"

Mrs. Nixon lifted her chin. "Why yes, Aaron. This is Bailey *Hatcher* and her friend—" She scrunched her face. "I'm sorry, but I don't remember your name."

Martina looked at Bailey with wide eyes before turning back to the woman. "Martina."

"Oh yes, that's right."

"Bailey Hatcher?" The man narrowed his eyes. "Do you know—?"

"Yes, dear, this is Dan Hatcher's daughter." Mrs. Nixon placed her hand on his shoulder as if to hold him back.

He pulled away, scowled at his wife, and then turned to Bailey with a smile. "It's so nice to meet you. Our son has said some very nice things about you."

"He has?" Bailey's voice caught in her throat, so she gave her friend a panicked look for help.

Martina made a production of glancing at her watch. "We really need to leave now."

"It was nice meeting you, Mr. Nixon," Bailey said as she backed toward the door. "And it was good to see you again, Mrs. Nixon."

They said goodbye to the hostess and quickly left. As soon as they were outside, Martina started laughing. "I can't believe they were there."

"I can. The upper crust of Summerville has always been a tight bunch."

Martina nodded. "True. Esther and her husband are definitely what I would consider *upper crust*. They just sold one of the historical mansions to buy this place."

"I wonder why."

Again, Martina laughed. "They downsized."

"Oh."

"Where to?" Martina asked as she started the engine. "Can I talk you into the Hug-a-Mug?"

"In spite of the fact that I said no earlier, I need a decadent, gooey coffee drink after what just happened."

"Then Hug-a-Mug it is." Martina cast a brief glance in Bailey's direction. "But we'd better stick to decaf since it's so late."

"Yes, of course. I just hope we don't run into anyone … if you know what I mean."

Martina shook her head. "I don't think we will, but if we do, I'll figure out a nice way to leave."

Fortunately, the only people they saw at the Hug-a-Mug besides the owner and one of the familiar employees were people they didn't know. They chatted until Bailey finally said she needed to get home so she could get up for church the next morning.

*

Scott stopped off at his favorite bakery on the way to church. He picked up a couple dozen cupcakes and some dinner rolls for the potluck.

As he pulled into the church parking lot, his stomach roiled. Mom and Dad had said they might come to church today—something they hadn't done in a very long time. His dad had softened during their chat yesterday, and after they prayed together, he said he would figure out a way to make things right with Dan Hatcher. Scott knew that his dad was doing that for him.

He walked down to the fellowship hall and handed the baked goods to the potluck coordinator before walking to the sanctuary where he planned to wait for his parents near the door. Then he saw her.

Bailey walked in, causing his heart to pound so hard he was sure everyone around him could hear it. And then right behind her were his parents. Bailey glanced over her shoulder, said something, and his mother nodded. He gulped. It looked strangely like they'd already been talking.

When his dad spotted him, he tapped Bailey on the shoulder and pointed. She grinned at him, but he could see that she was nervous. Scott forced a smile through his confusion and walked toward the people he cared about most in the church.

"Bailey," he said softly before tentatively placing his arm around her. "Mom and Dad, it looks like you've already met the prettiest girl here."

His dad was the first to speak. "You were right, son. She is beautiful, but even better than that, she seems like a very sweet young woman."

Church that morning was surreal. Not only was he sitting next to the woman who kept his senses on high alert, both of his parents were on his other side for the first time since he was a little boy.

After the service ended, he asked his parents if they planned to stay. His dad shook his head. "No, we have some important business to attend to."

Scott suspected they were going to try to talk to Bailey's parents, but he wasn't sure if she knew that. So he didn't say anything about it.

"Have a great afternoon." He tugged at Bailey. "C'mon, let's get down to the fellowship hall. I'm starving." Once they were away from his parents, he pulled her close and whispered, "Are you okay?"

She nodded. "Did they tell you that I met your dad last night?"

"Where?"

She explained the open house she and Martina attended. "I recognized your mother pretty quickly. And I was surprised that your dad was as nice to me as he was."

"Something has changed."

They sat with Martina and several other people they knew from the Bible study that Bailey attended. After it was over, they did their part to help clean up.

"What now?" Scott asked. "Do you want to do something?"

"Sure. It's a nice day. Why don't we go for a long walk in the park or something?"

"Sounds perfect. We'll both go home and change, and I'll pick you up in about half an hour."

That afternoon was one of the best Scott could remember. Not only did he love being around Bailey, he felt free to express his feelings.

"Ya know, I can be pretty clueless about a lot of things," he said as they stood beneath a tree at the park. "But there's one thing I'm sure about." He wrapped his arms around her waist and clasped his hands behind her.

She leaned back and looked directly at him. "What's that?"

"I'm falling in love."

She sighed as he kissed her. Nothing could make this day any better.

*

Bailey walked around her house straightening up after she got in from her walk at the park with Scott. She couldn't remember ever having such a wonderful time on a date. Scott's profession of falling in love made her downright giddy. She didn't tell him she loved him back, but she planned to very soon. But first, she had to talk to her parents.

She dreaded placing the call since she had no idea what they'd say. But she finally picked up the phone, pulled up their number, and pressed CALL. Her dad answered.

"How's your day going?" she asked.

"Better than you can imagine."

"What happened?"

She could practically hear him smiling as he told her about the unexpected visit from Aaron and Ingrid Nixon. "It was pretty uncomfortable at first, but once your mother and Ingrid went off to chat in the kitchen, Aaron and I were able to get down to the nitty gritty."

"Nitty gritty of what?"

"Our old business deal that went south. And you could have knocked me over with a feather when he actually apologized." He chuckled. "I don't remember Aaron ever apologizing for anything—even when he knew he was wrong."

"I'm glad he did that. So are you back to being friends?"

"Let's just say we're working on it. I think that as long as we don't get into any business deals together, that's likely to happen."

"So how's Mom doing?"

"That's the best part about this whole thing. She and Ingrid made up for lost time, and they're planning to get together for lunch soon."

"I'm happy for y'all."

"And I'm happy for you too, sweetheart," he said softly. "Aaron said his son is completely head over heels for you."

"I like him a lot." She didn't want to admit the depth of her feelings until she was sure how her dad felt. "So what do you think?"

"If you like him … a lot … then I'm sure your mother and I will too."

As soon as Bailey got off the phone, she called Scott. "Did you know that our parents got together this afternoon?"

"Yes, I heard."

"Can you come over?"

"Now?" He didn't wait for an answer. "I'll be there in fifteen minutes."

As soon as he knocked, she flung open the door, threw her arms around his neck, and said, "I'm falling in love with you too."

He scooped her into his arms and kissed her. He pulled away for only a moment as they exchanged a look that said more than words ever could. And then she melted in his arms as he peppered her face with tiny kisses.

Epilogue

Six months later, Scott took a deep breath and walked into the Hug-a-Mug. After Bailey agreed to meet him there, he called everyone he knew—their families and friends—and filled them in on his plan.

Everyone was already sitting in the coffee shop, waiting. Bailey had the cutest confused expression on her face, but as soon as she saw him, she stood, walked over to him, and whispered, "What is going on?"

"You'll see. Do you want something to drink?"

"Your dad already bought everyone something—including you. I told him what you usually order."

"Okay then, let's get this show on the road."

"What are you talking about?" Bailey cocked her head to the side and stared at him.

"You are so cute, I should probably take a picture." He nudged her toward where she was sitting. "Go have a seat."

"Okay." She did as she was told.

With all eyes on him, Scott cleared his throat and held up his hands to get everyone's attention. "I love this woman with all my heart, which is why …" He knelt on the floor and opened the box that he'd been holding. "I'm asking her to be my wife." He looked her in the eyes. "Bailey, will you make me the happiest man in all of Summerville and marry me?"

Her eyes misted over as she nodded. He only took a brief moment to lift a victory fist. "She said yes!" And then he kissed her.

As everyone else surrounded them with their congratulations, both sets of parents stood off to the side and watched, looks of happiness on all of their faces. Scott couldn't remember ever being so happy and contented at the same time. He had no doubt that life would only get better from here.

The End

NEVER TOO LATE

A Runaway Bride Novella

By Debby Mayne

Forget Me Not Romances, a division of Winged Publications

Chapter 1

Stephanie Miller stood staring out the bridal room window in the Cornerstone Community Church of Summerville, South Carolina, the place where she'd started worshiping when some of her high school friends invited her for their youth group. She'd asked for a few minutes alone before it was time to walk down the aisle, so her bridesmaids had gone out into the lobby.

Her stomach hurt, her hands shook, and her mind reeled as she pondered what she was about to do. When Derrick had asked her to marry him on the way to go hang-gliding, she didn't waste a single second before saying, "Yes!" But shortly after she came back down to earth, doubts started creeping up.

When she mentioned her thoughts to Derrick, he just laughed it off and changed the subject. The one time she managed to get him to discuss it, he said it was normal to get cold feet—that after the wedding she'd be fine, and they'd be a power couple who got invited to all the best events.

The sound of a knock jolted her from her thoughts. The door opened a few inches, and Alyssa, her best friend from high school, gave her an empathetic smile. "Steph? May I come in?"

She sighed and nodded. "Yes, but just you."

Alyssa opened the door enough to get through it before closing it behind her. She stood there and held Stephanie's gaze for a few seconds. "You don't have to go through with this, you know. It's not to late to change your mind."

Stephanie swallowed hard and nodded as she fought back the tears that had threatened since she'd arrived at the church. "I know, but look at all of those people. They came just to watch Derrick and me get married. It wouldn't be right—"

"What's not right is going through with something you're not sure of." Alyssa took a step closer to Stephanie. "Why don't you let me see if the pastor can pause for a few minutes while you catch a breath and think about it some more? I'm sure the organist wouldn't mind playing an extra song or two."

Stephanie closed her eyes and shook her head. "I don't need a few minutes."

"So you're sure you want to go through with this?"

"No." Stephanie opened her eyes, lifted her gaze to Alyssa's, and sighed. "I'm sure I *don't* want to marry Derrick." She felt her chin quiver. "On the outside, he seems like the man of my dreams ... the man of any girl's dreams. But I've always known that something was missing, and now I'm here in church, I've finally figured out what that is. He keeps what little faith he has on the backburner." She cleared her throat. "And that's exactly what I've been doing for the past several years."

"Well then ..." Alyssa stepped even closer and lifted Stephanie's hand. "What do you want to do?"

The lump in Stephanie's throat grew bigger. "I need to let Derrick know that we can't do this."

"Do you want me to go get him?"

Stephanie shook her head again as she reached into her handbag and pulled out an envelope. "He won't listen." She handed the envelope to Alyssa. "So I wrote him a letter. I started to give it to him a couple of days ago, but I chickened out.

Alyssa glanced at it. "Are you breaking off your engagement with a letter?"

"Yes, I'm afraid so. He knows exactly what buttons to push to get me to do what he wants." Stephanie sighed. "I actually tried to end the engagement after I realized how out of control the wedding was becoming, but he said it was just my nerves and that it was normal, and ..." Her voice trailed off as the tears flowed freely. Now that they'd started, she couldn't stop crying.

"Okay, I'll take the letter to him." Alyssa started for the door but stopped and turned to face Stephanie. "I'll be right back. Get your stuff, and we'll leave before everyone else finds out. I don't think you're in good enough shape to deal with the onslaught of questions once word gets out." She stopped when she got to the door. "Don't take the time to change. We'll go to my place."

Stephanie quickly threw her belongings into a bag and waited by the side door. Alyssa joined her about a minute later.

"C'mon! Let's get out of here." Alyssa took the bag so Stephanie could lift her dress, and they ran to the car. She started her car, put it in gear, drove to the edge of the parking lot, and glanced in her rearview mirror. "Good thing I got a close parking spot. He's standing by the door."

Stephanie scooted lower in her seat as much as her wedding dress would allow. "I can't believe I'm actually doing this."

"I can't believe you let it get this far." Alyssa cast a quick glance in Stephanie's direction. "When you told me you were marrying him, and I asked you what you loved about him … well, I knew."

Stephanie gave her friend a curious look. "I only vaguely remember that, but I think I gave you a good answer."

Alyssa tilted her head back and laughed. "You said he was fun and that the two of you were never bored when you were together because you stayed so busy." She gave Stephanie a look of understanding. "That's not necessarily love."

"I'm not sure I know what love is." Stephanie paused. "Do you?"

"I don't know for sure what it is, but I do know that it's not just about having fun and staying busy and not being bored." Alyssa pulled into her apartment complex parking lot, found a spot by the entrance, and turned to Stephanie. "When was the last time you went to church … I mean before you started planning the wedding?"

Stephanie thought for a moment before groaning. "I went a couple of times, like when I was home for break. But you know how it is in college. There's so much going on—"

"I know. In fact, my first semester was such a whirlwind of activity that I think I only went once. Mom and Dad sat me down and had a long talk with me during semester break, and they said that if I wanted to continue getting their support, I needed to remember the important things they taught me."

"At least you have parents who attend church," Stephanie reminded her. "If it weren't for you, I never would have gone."

"It's obvious that's what's missing in your relationship with Derrick."

Stephanie let out a snort. "What relationship? I honestly think we were too busy to actually have a relationship."

"Yeah, I hear you." Alyssa pointed toward the apartment building. "Why don't we make a run for my place? Just be careful so you don't trip." She reached over the seat and lifted Stephanie's bag. "I'll carry this."

~

Brandon Walker stared straight ahead as the pastor explained that there wouldn't be a wedding. He hated to admit that he was relieved. He'd hung out with Stephanie ever since Alyssa brought her to church their freshman year of high school, and from what he could tell, she and this guy she'd met in college weren't a good match.

Yeah, he could be thinking that way because he'd had a monster-sized crush on her that developed over pizza night one summer and grew each time they were together. At first, he thought he stood a chance, but he never got the nerve to ask her out. He was shy back then, but he got over it during college. And now that he was the youth director at the church, he had to get up in front of people quite a bit.

"I'm sorry, folks," Pastor Keyes continued, pulling his attention back to the moment. "But since it's too late to cancel the reception, Mr. and Mrs. Miller said for everyone to go ahead and enjoy the party … without the bride and groom."

A low murmur filled the church as everyone wondered what had happened. The groom and his half of the wedding party had already taken their places at the front of the church, waiting for the bridesmaids and then the bride. Then the groom read a note that Alyssa brought up from the back of the church and left, so it was obvious that Stephanie had bolted.

The woman behind him mentioned how inconsiderate the bride was for letting it get this far, only to change her mind at the last minute. He knew Stephanie well enough to realize it was more than simply changing her mind. She was a tenderhearted person and kind to a fault—and not the least bit inconsiderate of anyone. Something terrible must have happened.

Brandon waited until everyone left the church before approaching Pastor Keyes. "Any idea what's going on?"

The pastor shook his head. "I didn't have the best feeling about this wedding, so I'm not completely surprised."

"Why did you agree to marry them?"

"I don't know." Pastor Keyes stared toward the back of the church for a few seconds before turning his attention back to Brandon. "Derrick handed me the letter she wrote to make sure he wasn't seeing something that wasn't there. She had the same feeling I had, so she changed her mind. Too bad she didn't come to this conclusion earlier."

"Any idea where she went?" Brandon asked.

"No, but I do know she's with Alyssa, so why don't you call and find out?"

"I'll do that." Brandon paused. "But I need to think about something first."

~

Alyssa's phone started ringing within minutes of when they got inside her apartment. The first call was from Pastor Keyes, so she answered. After she hung up, she turned to Stephanie. "He understands. Now we have to get through another hundred people."

"I really made a mess this time, didn't I?"

"Yes," Alyssa agreed. "You sure did. But it's easier to fix this mess than if you'd waited until after the wedding."

"I know, but what do I do now? Everyone probably hates me for doing that to Derrick."

"I don't hate you."

Stephanie snorted. "You're probably the only one."

"And Pastor Keyes said he understands."

"Okay, so that's two."

Alyssa's phone rang again. "I don't recognize the number." She clicked the ON button, said a few words, and clicked OFF. "If I don't know who's calling, I'm not answering. This is something you need to deal with after the shock wears off."

"I need to call my parents." She pulled her phone out of her bag and glanced at the list of missed calls. "I had it on silent. Looks like I missed a lot of calls."

Alyssa's phone rang. "Why don't you go in my bedroom and call your parents, and I'll take this call from Brandon."

"Tell him I'm sorry about what happened." She paused at the bedroom door, waiting for her friend to tell Brandon what she'd said.

Alyssa smiled as she answered her phone and gave him Stephanie's message. "He said you don't have to apologize to him. He doesn't want you marrying the wrong guy." Then she went back to her conversation with Brandon.

Stephanie had always liked Brandon, one of the sweetest boys she knew in high school. He'd always been one guy who seemed to understand her, even when she didn't understand herself. He was always the first person after Alyssa to be there when she needed someone to talk to. And she trusted him to a fault. There was actually a time when she thought there might be a spark, but since he never acted like anything but a friend, she pushed that to the back of her mind.

She put her bag down, got out of her wedding gown, slipped into the jeans she's worn to the church, and sat on the edge of the bed. Then she took a deep breath and called her mother's cell phone. Her dad answered.

"You have some explaining to do. What on earth were you thinking?"

"I couldn't—"

"You've already made a fool of yourself, but I'm sure everyone will understand if you let them know you were nervous and couldn't walk down the aisle in front of all those people."

"But I don't want to—"

"Guys like Derrick don't come along everyday, you know. He's the type of man your mother and I always hoped you'd marry."

"He's not—"

"Your mother and I have already spoken to him, and he agrees that you probably just have a case of cold feet. He said you've been a bundle of nerves for a while. Everyone will understand."

"No they won't." Before her father could interrupt again, she blurted. "I don't love Derrick. He's fun and nice and—"

"And well-to-do, which is important when you think about how difficult life is without the finer things in life. The love will come later. Sometimes it takes a while."

She let out a heavy sigh. "Dad, I can't marry Derrick. I never should have agreed to have a wedding in the first place."

"You are making the biggest mistake of your life, Stephanie. Your mother and I were looking forward to having Derrick as a son-in-law, and if you don't fix things now, you'll blow it."

"I'm sorry, Dad. I can't." She clicked the phone off and flopped back on the bed. She didn't expect her parents to understand, but she'd hoped they'd support her. She was obviously mistaken.

A knock came at the door. "Steph? Are you okay?"

"I don't know."

Alyssa opened the door. "Brandon is on his way here."

"Why?"

"He called his uncle and managed to get a cabin for you to stay in as long as you need to. We agreed that you needed a little time away from the craziness before you call everyone back."

Chapter 2

"Hi, Brandon." A wave of shyness washed over Stephanie. "I feel terrible."

"Not as terrible as you'll feel after some of those wedding guests talk to you." He gave her a warm smile. "Just kidding. They'll get over it, and if they're your real friends, they'll see that you did the right thing."

Alyssa gestured toward Stephanie's bag. "Is that all you have?"

Stephanie nodded. "Everything else is at my parents' house."

"Do you want to go get your things?"

"No. My parents are furious that I messed up their plans for me."

Alyssa glanced at Brandon before turning back to Stephanie. "I'm not going there either. You can borrow some of my clothes to get you through the next few days. I'll pick up some stuff on the way to the cabin."

Brandon gave Alyssa the address before gesturing toward the door. "I'll take you there now."

"What about my car?"

"We can get your car later. Right now, I agree that you're better off not having to face anyone." He offered a warm, sincere smile. "Unless you want to."

"No, you're right. I can't handle that right now."

"Then let's go."

Brandon played Christian music on the way to the cabin. She was thankful he wasn't a chatty person because her thoughts were swirling enough as it was.

When he pulled up to the cabin, she was pleasantly surprised. "It's really nice. I love the porch."

"Wait until you see inside. My uncle just had it remodeled."

The second they walked in, she felt as though she was in a dream. It wasn't elaborately decorated, but it was the coziest place she'd ever seen. The overstuffed sofa and chair looked inviting, and off to the side was a small round country table and chairs set. The kitchen had a delightful blend of conveniences and rustic décor.

"I might never want to leave," she said.

He nodded. "I know. My uncle plans to rent it out during the next tourist season. He said you can stay here as long as you need to."

"I'll never be able to thank him enough for this."

"He likes doing it."

Stephanie had met Brandon's uncle years ago when the church he pastored held a retirement party for him. She didn't know what else to say, but she didn't feel awkward with Brandon. A comfortable silence fell between them as they held gazes for a few seconds. Finally, Brandon backed toward the door.

"I need to go now. Alyssa said she'd be here soon with some food and other stuff you might need. Call me if you need me."

"Thanks, Brandon."

"Oh, do you mind if I stop by tomorrow night? I thought I would bring a pizza, and we could have a little Bible study."

Tears stung the back of her eyes as she nodded. "I would like that."

After Brandon left, she wandered around the rest of the cabin. It had two bedrooms—one of them with a queen-sized bed and the other with a pair of twin beds. The place was small but perfect for her to regroup. The wide hallway between the bedrooms was lined with bookcases filled with Bibles, Bible commentaries, classic fiction, mysteries, and Christian romance novels.

She noticed all the extra little touches as she walked around the entire cabin. All of the kitchen appliances were state-of-the-art, but the overall look was softened by the rustic cabinets and billowy curtains on the window over the sink. The bathroom was decorated in comforting shades of coral, peach, and green. Next to the claw-foot tub was a tile shower with a rain head.

Stephanie sighed. This was the perfect getaway spot that could help her heal from the stress she'd been feeling over the past several months.

She wandered back to the hallway with the bookshelves and selected a couple of books before settling on the sofa. Her eyelids grew heavy, so she allowed herself to close them.

The sound of a knock startled her awake. When she opened her eyes, it took a few seconds to remember where she was.

"Steph, it's me. Alyssa."

She got up and opened the door. "Sorry, I fell asleep."

"At least it didn't take long to get comfortable." Alyssa glanced around. "Wow! What a nice place. If I didn't think you needed some alone time, I'd talk you into letting me hang out here with you."

"If you want—"

Alyssa held up her hand. "Maybe after you have a little alone time. Can you help me with the stuff I brought?"

Stephanie laughed as she saw all the bags of things her friend had in her trunk. "I'm only one person, and I don't think I'll be here long."

"I just wanted to make sure you had everything you needed." Alyssa pointed to a tote. "I brought you some pajamas, but I had to guess your size."

"You are an amazing friend. I don't know what I'd do without you."

Alyssa grinned. "You've always been a good friend to me too. Remember when I got sick the day after my parents went on a ten-day cruise?"

Stephanie nodded. "You had to stay home because of school."

"And you brought me three meals a day, even after I started feeling better. I'll never forget that."

As they put everything away, they chattered about the beauty of the setting. Finally, when they were done, Alyssa planted her fists on her hips. "I'll need your car keys. Brandon said he'd go with me to get your car in a couple of days. We'd do it sooner, but we figured it would be better to let some of the steam evaporate before we confronted them. And it'll give you a chance to let them know what's going on."

"I'll call them in the morning."

"Good." Alyssa picked up her handbag and went to the door. "If you need anything else, give me a call, and I'll do whatever I can to help."

"Thanks."

"I've been praying for you ever since you got engaged." Alyssa tilted her head as she paused. "I'll call some of the people from our old prayer chain."

"I appreciate all the prayers I can get."

After Alyssa left, Stephanie went through the bag her friend had brought. Not only had she put a pair of cute pajamas with pictures of cats and dogs in there, she'd purchased underwear and a couple of T-shirts. She'd even added an extra pair of jeans.

Stephanie put everything away before sitting on the edge of the bed to think. Derrick would probably never forgive her, but she didn't want anything bad to happen to him. He truly was a sweet guy, but without the Lord in his life, he was lost … just like she'd been for the past several years.

Those thoughts reminded her that she hadn't said a heartfelt prayer in a very long time. She'd been *too busy*. Now that she was out here alone, with her family and many of her friends angry and hurt, she knew the Lord had found a way to make her be still and focus on what was really important.

She squeezed her eyes shut and lowered her head. As she prayed, she knew she was in good hands. God had never promised to make things easy, but He would always be there to lift her up when she fell.

~

Brandon had his car packed with a couple of games, a pizza, some ginger ale that he remembered being Stephanie's favorite soda, and a bouquet of flowers. His goal for the evening was to cheer her up and remind her that she had friends who cared about her, regardless of what she did.

And being honest with himself, he hoped she'd eventually see him in a different light. They'd been instant friends, but it didn't take long before he realized he wanted so much more.

He'd avoided asking her out for a romantic date because she was such a new Christian, and she needed to focus on her relationship with Christ first. They'd fallen into such a comfortable friendship that he hadn't taken the next step. And then college happened.

The drive out to the cabin was relaxing, until he made the final turn. His stomach lurched with anticipation, knowing that the woman who'd left a permanent imprint on his heart waited for him. He had to remind himself that they were still "just friends," but if the Lord saw fit and gave him the right signals, he'd let her know how he felt.

He couldn't help but grin when the door opened before he shut off his engine. It felt nice to see her standing on the porch, watching and waiting for him to arrive.

She walked down the steps and took the pizza from him. "I set the table, so all we have to do is dig in."

"Good. I'm starving." He reached over, picked up the ginger ale and flowers, and followed her into the cabin. "Let me go get the games. I'll be right back."

When he walked back inside, she'd already put slices of pizza on the plates and was now pouring the ginger ale. It all seemed so right and natural for them to be here together, but he had to remind himself that she was still injured.

"You are so sweet for doing this," she said.

"I'll say the blessing." He bowed his head and prayed aloud. When he opened his eyes, he saw that she was still praying, so he waited to pick up his fork. "So how do you like the place?"

"It's wonderful. I keep discovering new things about it. This morning I decided to have my coffee on the porch, and I had the pleasure of having some enjoyable company. Not only is there a bird feeder, there's a trough with nuts for squirrels attached to the rail."

"Uncle George loves wildlife, so I'm not surprised."

As they chatted, Brandon couldn't help but imagine this being his new normal. Stephanie's sweetness and gentle nature were still intact, in spite of what she'd just been through.

"Speaking of wildlife," she said with a half-smile that he could tell covered pain, "I bet there are some folks waiting for me to show up so they can take my head off."

"I'll protect you." Brandon chuckled. "But seriously, after a few days, things will calm down, and everyone will be back to their own personal daily drama."

"Good way to put it."

"It seems like so many people aren't satisfied unless there's excitement in their lives."

She nodded. "True but excitement is overrated."

"I agree." He helped himself to another slice of pizza. "So speaking of excitement, which game do you want to play after our Bible study? Scrabble or Monopoly?"

"What do you think?"

"Knowing you, Scrabble, so that's what we'll play."

He pulled out his cell phone and pulled up his Bible on the screen. As they discussed the verses he read, he was delighted to know she remembered what was truly important.

Finally, they closed in prayer. He opened his eyes to her teasing grin.

"Ready for a beating?" she asked.

*

Being with Brandon was so effortless it was almost like they shared the same heartbeat. He never insisted on getting his way. In fact, it seemed as though he wanted the same things she wanted.

"Who won last time we played?" she asked.

"You expect me to remember something that happened years ago?"

She nodded. "Yep."

"Okay, you're right. I do remember. You won. In fact, you beat the socks off me."

"And that's exactly what I plan to do tonight."

Brandon won, but being true to his nature, he didn't make a big deal over it. Stephanie hated comparing him to Derrick, but she couldn't help it. Derrick was never happy unless he won whatever he was doing, and then he enjoyed flaunting his victory and reminding her how *lucky* she was to be with him.

"I'll enjoy the win while I have it," Brandon said. "Because you'll probably beat me next time." He grinned. "We both know you have a better vocabulary."

"That's only because my degree is in English."

"Speaking of that, have you decided what to do, now that you've quit your job, and it looks like you'll be single for a while?"

"Actually, that has crossed my mind a time or two."

"Do you want to go back to teaching?"

She lifted her hands. "Maybe, but since the school year has already started, it's not exactly a good time to choose that path."

"You could substitute teach." He paused. "Or you could apply for the assistant youth director position at the church."

"I'm not exactly qualified."

"I disagree." He leaned forward on his elbows and looked her in the eyes. "You've worked with middle school kids, and you know the Bible as well as most adults."

"Don't forget it's been a while since I've gone to church on a regular basis."

"Well, there is that," he replied. "The position has been open for more than a month, so if you start attending after you return from the wilderness, that might not be an issue."

"Who would hire me?"

"Me."

Chapter 3

After Brandon left, Stephanie changed into her pajamas, picked up a book, and got comfortable on the sofa. She couldn't concentrate on the story because thoughts of Brandon's suggestion to apply for the assistant youth director job kept swimming in her head.

Now that she'd had time to think, she realized that a huge chunk of her life was missing. The church had provided the stability she'd never experienced growing up in a non-churched home. Mom and Dad were good people who claimed to believe in God, but they never embraced a deep relationship with Jesus. Most of their emphasis had been on the work they did for the community, and her father said that as long as he was good, he didn't have anything to worry about.

Until now, she never had an answer for him. But after feeling the emptiness of being away from the church, she knew she needed to share her faith with them. The only problem was that she'd been away from church for so long she feared a lack of credibility.

Her second night at the cabin was more restful than the first. She was over the initial shock of what she'd done.

She awoke the next morning with the realization that it was time to call her parents and at least try to talk to them, even though she suspected they still wouldn't understand. To her surprise, her mother answered with a light lilt to her voice.

"Hi, sweetie. I hope you're doing okay. I've been worried about you."

"You have?" Stephanie cleared her throat. She didn't expect that kind of reaction. "I mean, I wanted to make sure you and Dad weren't still angry with me."

"We were never really angry. Disappointed, yes, but after we had a chat with Derrick, we realized you just needed a little more time before you got married. Oh, and Derrick said it's probably better if the two of you went off on your own and had a destination wedding without so many distractions that can be quite overwhelming."

"Mom, I'm not going to marry Derrick."

"Oh, Stephanie, you're still on emotional overload. I get it. There were a lot of people in the church, and you've been so busy with the planning. Just give yourself a little more time, and I'm sure you'll realize how good of a husband Derrick will be."

"He'll be a great husband … just not for me."

Her mother sighed. "Whatever."

"I wanted to let you know that I gave my car key to Alyssa so she and Brandon can pick up my car."

"That's fine. Your car is in the driveway." Mom's tone had cooled a bit, but she still didn't sound angry.

"I love you, Mom. And tell Dad I love him too."

"I will."

Stephanie hung up and blew out a breath of frustration. It obviously still hadn't sunk in with her parents—or Derrick—that she had ended their relationship. Her mother was right about one thing. She'd been busy planning the wedding, and she was exhausted. But now that she looked back over the time since she started dating Derrick, she realized the exhaustion had set in long before the actually wedding plans began.

She decided it was time to immerse herself in God's word. Since it had been a while, she chose one of the Bible study books that appeared to deal with the basics. That was what she needed to clear her mind of all the worldly trappings she'd gotten caught up in since leaving for college. She graduated more than a year ago, and she had no excuses, so she was tempted to beat herself up over letting the most important thing go for so long.

As she read, everything came back to her. One thing she loved about the Bible was that, in spite of how crazy-busy people in the world around her got, God's word never changed.

Her rumbling stomach reminded her that it was time for lunch. She got up to make a sandwich when her cell phone rang. It was Alyssa.

"Brandon and I picked up your car, and we're on our way to bring it to you. I'm on my lunch break, so I can't stay long."

"I'll fix you a sandwich."

"Sounds good."

After Stephanie got off the phone, she prepared three sandwiches. It was nice to have company she could relax around and not have to worry about keeping them entertained.

She stopped and stared at the countertop as the realization came over her. Derrick's insatiable need for constant excitement went against her inner nature. She loved relaxing and having quiet evenings at home, while he always wanted to go out and be among people.

By the time her friends arrived, she had the food and drinks on the table. Alyssa's eyes widened as she walked in and saw the spread.

"Wow! You didn't waste any time, did you?" She sat down. "Come on, y'all. Let's eat so we can get back to work."

Brandon grinned at Stephanie. "You heard the boss. Have a seat, and I'll say the blessing."

As the three of them ate, Stephanie realized she hadn't felt this relaxed in years. Her friends liked her, regardless of her mood—even when she was quiet. Derrick, on the other hand, always did everything he could to pry a comment out of her. He was never mean, but he seemed to think everyone was like him.

Before she had a chance to lift a finger, Brandon started cleaning up. Alyssa hopped up and carried her plate to the sink. All of the dishes were washed and in the drying rack in less than five minutes.

Brandon dried his hands on the towel, turned, leaned against the counter, and looked directly at Stephanie. "What are you doing this afternoon?" he asked. "Got any plans?"

Stephanie shrugged. "I just got back to reading the Bible, so I thought I'd continue." She pointed to the book on the end table. "I started with a basic Bible study."

He glanced at Alyssa who nodded before turning back to Stephanie. "If you don't mind bringing me back to town this afternoon, I'd love to stick around for a little while. We can do a Bible study together and then maybe go for a walk. Uncle George told me about a couple of hiking trails that are pretty."

Stephanie grinned at him and nodded. "Yes, I'd like that."

"Then if y'all don't need me, I need to head back. The boss gave me an extra half hour for lunch, and I don't want to push it."

Once Brandon and Stephanie were alone, he gestured toward the sofa. "Let's talk about the important stuff."

She read the next scripture verse in the Bible study, and they discussed the commentary from the book. Then Brandon shared one of his personal experiences as it related to the verse.

Stephanie appreciated the depth of Brandon's knowledge of the

Bible, but even more, she loved the way he never made her feel stupid. In fact, he did the opposite.

"You've always been like a sponge with God's word," he said softly. "I'm glad you've come back to soak it up again."

Her emotions rendered her incapable of speaking. All she could do was smile and nod.

He smiled back, reached for her hands, and helped her to her feet. "I think it's time for us to go outdoors and enjoy some fresh air. It's a beautiful spring day."

They held hands as they walked along the trail, stopping every few minutes to observe fresh flowers and small wildlife. "This is so perfect for me right now," she said softly.

"You needed a chance to regroup, and what better way than to be still and allow God to lead you?"

"I know." She glanced down, letting her hair fall forward.

Next thing she knew, Brandon had repositioned himself in front of her, and he had his hand beneath her chin, gently lifting it so she'd face him. She wanted him to kiss her at that moment, but she knew it wouldn't be right—not so soon after she left Derrick at the altar.

Brandon gazed into her eyes for several seconds before dropping his hand. "You have quite a bit of healing to do. I hope you know that if you need anything, I'll be here for you. It's hard enough to deal with difficult situations, and I don't want you to have to do it alone."

"Thank you, Brandon."

"Why don't we head on back? One of the youth groups is meeting at the church for supper, and I still have to set up."

"Okay." They walked back to the cabin in a comfortable silence. The only thing that bothered Stephanie was the possibility of seeing someone she knew when she drove into town.

~

Brandon could tell that Stephanie was on edge as she drove toward town, so he decided to remain silent to give her some emotional space. He sank back in his seat and thought about how much fun he'd had that afternoon.

Stephanie's sweetness came natural to her. She never seemed forced or fake. That was why he'd almost kissed her when they stopped on the trail. It took every ounce of self-restraint to hold back.

He knew she needed more time to recover from what she'd been through. The other issue was that he wasn't totally positive she wouldn't go back to her fiancé, with all the pressure he heard she was getting. That would break his heart, but it would be worse if he allowed himself to get romantically involved with her.

Oh, who was he kidding? He was already in love with Stephanie. Had been for years. He'd managed to push her to the back of his mind after her engagement, but now it would be next to impossible.

One of the things he'd have to do, though, was refrain from giving her advice that would directly benefit him. Deep in his heart, he knew she was better off without Derrick, but he never wanted her to doubt his motives. If she chose not to go back to Derrick, it had to be all her and not based on something he said or did to persuade her.

She pulled up in front of the church and stopped. "Thank you so much for helping me with the car and spending the afternoon with me."

"My pleasure." He got out and leaned over. "I'll call you soon, if that's okay."

She nodded before pulling away from the curb. He watched as the woman he loved more than anyone else in the world disappeared around the corner.

When he turned around to go inside, he was faced by one of the women who worked in the church. She smiled and chuckled. "You look like a lovesick puppy."

Chapter 4

Stephanie couldn't get back to the cabin quickly enough. It had become a sanctuary in the short time she'd been there. It felt safe in its secluded coziness. Too bad she ever had to leave.

Once safely inside, she went through the refrigerator and pantry and decided to fix herself a nutritious meal. Alyssa had purchased some of her favorite foods, including salmon, rice, and the seasonings she liked.

She enjoyed the whole process of mixing and cooking. By the time she sat down, her appetite was at its peak.

She picked up her fork but remembered her blessing. Bowing her head, she gave thanks for all that the Lord had done for her. When she opened her eyes, the first thought that came to mind was how Brandon had been so kind and helpful, without asking for anything in return.

Every bite of her dinner was delicious. Instead of gulping it down as she had done with her meals over the past several years, she savored every single bite. The only thing that would have made it better would have been sharing it with Brandon.

It took her just a few minutes to clean the kitchen afterward. Once she had everything put away, she went back to her Bible study. Thoughts of Brandon kept popping into her head, but she forced herself not to think about him. Her emotions were too raw to get involved with another guy. Besides, she didn't want to run to him if there was even a chance it was a rebound. She finally got up and went to bed.

The next morning, she awoke to a light rain tapping on the roof. She kicked back the covers and stretched. The cabin had been a blessing, but she knew she couldn't stay there forever, so she got up and started thinking about what to do next as she got ready for the day.

One thing she knew was that she couldn't move back in with her parents. They'd already made it clear how they felt about her decision not to marry Derrick, and she didn't want to have to listen to their opinions everyday. However, she needed a job to be on her own.

Brandon had mentioned the assistant youth director position at the church, but she wasn't sure what that entailed or if it would pay enough for an apartment. She also wondered if it would work out, considering the fact that she'd be working directly with Brandon.

She picked up the Bible study guide and worked through several pages before she realized she'd done nearly a month's worth of reading in just a couple of days. She walked outside and took a deep breath, allowing the scent of rain and trees to fill her nostrils.

Brandon's image kept creeping back into her mind, so she finally decided she might as well call and talk to him about a number of things she'd been thinking about. He answered on the first ring.

"Hey, Steph. I'm with some kids now, but I'll be free later this evening. How about I bring some dinner, and we can chat then?"

"Okay." She hung up and decided to go back into town. Almost everyone she knew would be at work now, so she figured she could avoid anyone she didn't want to see.

As she drove past all the familiar places, she thought about how her life had changed so quickly in the course of a few days. A week ago, she was still in the throes of wedding planning, her mind racing, and her fears mounting. Now she felt as though she didn't have a care in the world, yet she had no idea what lay ahead.

It was weird to be in this position. After college, she taught for a year, but she and Derrick had decided that she should take some time to look for a house that they would raise their children in. He'd always said he wanted three children and a wife who stayed active on committees in the community because that would help his career and ability to provide for the family.

Stephanie never really thought about it all that much at the time, but as she looked back over her relationship with Derrick and how he told her how things would be without asking her opinion. She couldn't imagine Brandon being so demanding.

There she went again, thinking about Brandon. She admonished herself for getting carried away with her raw emotions. This was a time for healing, not bouncing off one guy and onto another.

She stopped at a bakery on the edge of town to pick up a few treats for after supper. She purchased a German chocolate cupcake for Brandon and a raspberry tart for herself. Then she went to the half-price rack and found an assortment of cookies for later.

~

All Brandon could think about throughout the afternoon was seeing Stephanie. One of the kids even noticed that his mind was elsewhere.

"You act like my brother did when he fell in love," Jeremiah teased after the other teenagers left. "Are you in love with someone?"

Brandon chuckled. "You're too smart for your own good."

"Then I'm right?" Jeremiah's grin widened.

"I'll tell you if and when you need to know, but in the meantime, let's get this place cleaned up so I can take you home."

Jeremiah laughed. "Girls sure do mess with guys' heads, don't they?"

"Yes, they do, and we love every minute of it."

"Not me. I don't want anyone trying to change me."

Brandon used this opportunity to dish some advice. "No one should ever try to change you, but if you love someone, you'll want to take her feelings into consideration."

"I don't know, man. Girls say and do strange things."

Now it was Brandon's turn to laugh. "You got that right."

As they straightened up the room, Brandon did his best to act as normal as possible, even though he couldn't erase Stephanie's image from his mind. Every now and then, he caught Jeremiah watching him and laughing.

They finally finished cleaning. After Brandon locked the church, he and Jeremiah went outside and started toward the parking lot. He held his breath in anticipation of more questions, but there weren't any—at least not until they got in the car and fastened their seatbelts.

Jeremiah turned to him before he turned the key in the ignition. "When are you going to bring her to church so we can meet her?"

Rather than continuing to deny his feelings, Brandon cast a look at Jeremiah. "I don't have to bring her. She already goes to church with us."

Jeremiah's eyebrows shot up. "She does? Who is she?"

Brandon let out a low chuckle and started the car. "That's for you to figure out, buddy. That's enough talk about my love life for now. It's your turn to tell me what's up with you." He put the car in gear and pulled out of the parking lot. "How did you do with your science project?"

Brandon managed to keep the subject off himself all the way to Jeremiah's house, where he lived with his single mother and younger sister. He pulled up to the curb. "See ya, buddy. Don't forget to practice for the church drama. We're counting on you."

Jeremiah got out and leaned over to face Brandon. "Don't let this girl get to you, Brandon. Remember what you told me when I thought I was in love with Tiffany. If it's meant to happen, it will." Then he straightened up, turned away, walked toward the house, and waved his hand over his shoulder as he ascended the porch steps.

Brandon had to stifle his laughter until he was sure Jeremiah couldn't see him. As he chuckled, he thought about how he'd prayed for the right woman to come into his life after he realized—or thought he realized—Stephanie was no longer available. He certainly hadn't expected what happened.

~

Stephanie couldn't get over the fact that she was so excited about seeing Brandon again. She was downright giddy.

After putting away her purchases, she went through the cabin and straightened up, even though not much was out of place. It was something to do to keep busy. Finally, she figured she might as well go out on the porch to enjoy some of the sweet, woodsy-smelling fresh air.

This was such a peaceful place—perfect for what she was going through. She sat down on one of the large rocking chairs and stared off into the distance as she thought about leaving the church like she had. It was out of character for her not to follow through with something she'd started, but ... well, a wedding was serious, and she knew it was all wrong.

The strangest thing, now that she had time to reflect, was that Derrick hadn't bothered calling her. She checked her phone to make sure, and his number wasn't on the call log. He'd gone to visit her parents, but she would have thought he'd at least try to talk to her.

It really bugged her to pieces that he told Mom and Dad that it would be better for her if they changed course and had a destination wedding. How could he say such a thing without consulting her?

She rocked a few more times as she pondered the situation. Now that she thought about it, she considered how he didn't consult her about much during their relationship. The only time he asked her anything was when he proposed ... and she suspected he wasn't listening when she said *yes*. He probably just assumed that would be her answer.

As she thought back on everything, she felt her anger level rising, until she remembered that she didn't have to worry about Derrick anymore. Sure, she'd eventually have to talk to him and give him his ring back, but she would never stay engaged to someone she knew wasn't a good fit for her.

What she needed was a man who listened, someone who cared

about her opinions, a guy who could be still and enjoy her company without constant excitement, and most of all, someone who loved the Lord. Someone like …

She glanced up as the sound of a car came toward the cabin. *Someone like Brandon.*

Her heart hammered at the realization that she felt the way she did for Brandon. Even after her initial crush, there had always been an attraction, but the timing had always been off for them to get together. Throughout high school, she had to keep her grades up because she needed a scholarship, so she didn't go out much, other than what she did with the church group.

Brandon got out of the car, opened the back door, and pulled out some bags and a bouquet of flowers. He handed the bouquet to her and lifted the bags.

"I hope you still like Thai food."

"I still *love* Thai food."

Derrick never once considered her feelings when they went out to dinner or ordered carryout. He liked steak, lobster, and pizza—so that was what they had. The one time she mentioned Thai food, he'd crinkled his nose and said it wasn't very good.

"I wasn't sure if you still had ginger ale, so I brought some more."

She laughed. "We can fill a pool with all the ginger ale I have in the cabin."

He made a face and laughed. "The kids from church would probably like that."

They went inside together. He opened the bags and pulled out the containers of a variety of dishes, while she got the plates, flatware, napkins, and glasses. Everything about setting the table together seemed right. They worked in harmony, without even a hint of awkwardness.

When they had everything out, they sat down. He reached across the table, so she took his hand for the blessing. Then he squeezed her hand and let go.

"This is delicious," she said between bites. "It's been a long time since I've had Panang curry."

He gave her a curious look. "Why?"

She shrugged. "Derrick never … well, he didn't care for anything he didn't grow up with."

Brandon pulled his lips between his teeth as he slowly shook his head. She could tell he had to bite back what he was thinking.

"But that's in the past. I don't want to wait so long to have it again." She lifted the lid on another of the dishes he'd brought. "What's this?"

"It's a green papaya salad." Brandon grinned and wiggled his eyebrows. "And very spicy."

"Yum!" She helped herself to the salad she'd never had before. Spicy food was another thing Derrick didn't care for, even though she loved it.

Brandon leaned back and smiled as he watched her. "I love to see you enjoying your food."

"You know exactly what I like."

His expression quickly changed. As her gaze met his, she sensed that he was holding something back.

"What's going on, Brandon?"

He shook his head before helping himself to some of the salad. "It's just nice to be here with you, having dinner, relaxing together."

"I know, right?" She stabbed another bite of food with her fork and shoved it into her mouth.

He clearly didn't want to tell her what had him so deep in thought, and she didn't want to pry it out of him. He'd tell her if and when he wanted to. In the meantime, she wanted to enjoy the evening.

After dinner, they started clearing the table when her phone rang. She glanced at it and saw Derrick's name. When she looked up at Brandon, she could tell he knew.

"Why don't I finish up here while you go in the bedroom and talk to him in private?" he offered.

She nodded. "I don't think I'll be long."

"Take your time. I'll be here as long as you need me."

As soon as she got to the bedroom, she answered the phone. Derrick cleared his throat before speaking.

"It's been several days, so I think you've had enough time to calm down. That was an awful lot to deal with."

"Yes," she agreed. "It was a lot."

"So are you ready to find a quieter place to get married?" The trepidation in his voice sounded strange. He'd always come across so sure of himself.

"No, Derrick. I can't."

"Would you rather have a wedding here, with just the family?"

"No, not that either." She swallowed hard. "I don't think … well, I know I don't want to … um … We're not right for—"

"We need to talk. What are you doing in an hour?"

He deserved more than a phone conversation, after getting left at the altar, but this obviously wasn't a good time for her. "I can't tonight."

"When?" His harsh tone stunned her.

"How about tomorrow?"

"Okay, tomorrow is fine. Do you want me to go to your parents' house?"

"No, why don't we meet somewhere?" She thought for a moment. "How about Chelsea's Diner?"

"Where is it?"

She gave him directions before hanging up. The joy she'd felt when Brandon first arrived had faded, but she knew it was temporary. Brandon had always brought out the best in her by allowing her to be herself—the opposite of what Derrick did.

She shoved the phone into her back pocket, took a deep breath, and slowly let it out before going back out to face Brandon. He smiled but didn't say anything at first.

"Derrick wants me to meet him tomorrow. We need to talk."

"Are you okay with that?" The concerned look on Brandon's face touched her.

She nodded. "After what I did to him, that's the least I can do. He deserves answers."

"Do you think you might—" He stopped himself.

She studied him for a few seconds. "What were you going to ask?"

Brandon shook his head. "It's really none of my business."

"If you were wondering if I might get back with Derrick, the answer is no. He's a nice guy, already successful in business, and a great catch for someone … but not me. I don't want the same things in life that he does."

"You don't have to explain anything to me, Stephanie."

"I know, and that's one of the reasons I like being around you."

He gave her a curious look. "What do you mean by that?"

She shrugged. "I never feel like I have to explain anything. You take me at face value, for who I am."

"Why would I do anything different?" He lifted his hands and let them flop back to his sides. "I like you just the way you are."

She looked into his eyes and saw the sincerity that made her want to reach out and pull him closer. But she didn't. Her breakup with Derrick was still too fresh. And she was going to see him tomorrow.

"I'm really tired," she said. "I think I'll do a little more reading and go to sleep early tonight."

He smiled at her. "Sounds good. If you need anything, just call. I'll be up a few more hours. I have some preparation to do before the next youth group get-together." He took a couple of steps toward the door before stopping. "Oh, by the way, have you thought about the assistant youth director position?"

"Can we talk about that some other time?" she asked.

"Yes, of course."

"Another thing we need to discuss is when I need to leave this cabin. I've probably already overstayed—"

"No, in fact, my uncle said you can stay here as long as you need to."

She smiled. "Please thank him for me."

"I already did."

After Brandon left, Stephanie closed the door and locked it before going to the sofa and picking up the Bible. She was thankful for Brandon's friendship and companionship, but she appreciated the fact that he understood her need to be alone at this time.

She'd barely gotten back into the next chapter when her phone rang again. She glanced at the screen and saw that it was Derrick.

Chapter 5

"I've thought about it, and I want to see you tonight," he said. "Where are you?"

She didn't want to tell him, but she didn't want to say that directly to him. "I'm really tired, Derrick."

"Look, Stephanie, I've always known that your energy wasn't what it should be. But after making me look foolish in front of so many people, I think you owe this to me."

She sighed at the clock and saw that it just a little past 8:00. "Okay, why don't we meet somewhere?"

"How about that place you told me about earlier? I went for a drive and found it."

"Okay, but it'll take me a half hour to get there."

"I'll be waiting for you."

Stephanie spent more time praying than she did freshening her makeup—something she'd failed to do the entire time she'd known Derrick. Things were different now. The only thing she had to worry about was dealing with his persuasive ways, and the only way to do that without buckling was to rely on the Lord to help her stand firm.

She drove straight to Chelsea's Diner, her hands gripping the steering wheel so tight her knuckles were white. When she pulled into the parking lot, she spotted Derrick's Lexus SUV by the door.

This was one of the most difficult moments of her life. After all, being a runaway bride wasn't anything she ever planned. She closed her eyes, prayed for guidance, and took another deep breath. Time to go in and face the man she'd left at the altar.

The second she walked in, she felt as though all the oxygen had been sucked from the room. Derrick sat at a booth in the corner, his gaze boring straight through her. She forced a smile and walked toward him, still praying for wisdom and strength.

"Hi, Derrick," she managed to say with a hint of a squeak in her voice.

His forehead crinkled. "You look different. What happened to you?"

"Different?" She sat down across from him. "How?"

He contorted his mouth and shook his head. "I don't know. Your makeup is different. You didn't do your hair the way I like it."

She slowly folded her hands on the table in front of her and held his gaze. "Derrick, I hate the lipstick you picked for me, and even worse …" She gave him an apologetic smile. "I hate the French twist even more."

"But it looks so good on you." He paused. "Very elegant, in fact. My mother and sister even like the way you look when you take the time to do your hair. This looks …" He waved his hands around his head. "You look somewhat disheveled."

"This is how I looked when we met."

"I know, but I saw the potential in you," he reminded her. "Your patrician nose, your high cheekbones, your well-sculpted eyebrows."

"The eyebrows came later, remember?" She cringed at the memory of how she felt when he told her she needed more polish. "You even booked my first appointment at the eyebrow bar."

He briefly smiled. "Yes, you did look a little shaggy when we met. But still, you're a beautiful woman who—"

"Who changed to what you wanted," she finished.

"I would think you would want to please your husband," he reminded her.

"That's why … I mean, that's one of the reasons you're not my husband." She glanced down before looking him in the eyes. "And you never will be." She took a breath and gave him a chance to process what she'd just said. "Look, Derrick, you're a sweet guy who will make someone very happy. But that's not me."

"I thought you were very happy." He looked hurt momentarily, but he quickly recovered. "I gave you everything you could possibly want."

She shook her head. "That's just it. I never wanted anything but acceptance for who I am. I'm not the girl you thought you knew."

He let out a snicker. "That's obvious."

"I'm really sorry I embarrassed you at the church a few days ago, but I didn't know any other way to stop the train."

"You could have told me before we got there."

"I tried." She cleared her throat. "Remember?"

"You didn't try hard enough."

She shook her head. "I'm so sorry, Derrick. I just felt so … I don't know … caged."

"Caged?" He closed his eyes and shook his head before glaring at her. "That's quite an accusation that I don't feel I deserve."

"I know," she said softly. "It's my fault for letting it get so out of hand."

"Fine, I'm not going to grovel. If you want a boring life with nothing but a bunch of church meetings and potluck dinners you can have it. But it's not enough for me." His expression became cold and guarded. "Do you have the ring?"

"Yes." She opened her handbag and pulled out the velvet bag she'd used to put the ring in. "Why don't you see if you can get your money back?"

"I doubt if I ever will," he said, "although I hope you realize this is not about the money."

The more they talked, she was surer than ever that she'd made the right decision. Why she'd ever let their relationship get as far as it had was beyond anything she could comprehend right now. Derrick was obviously not the right man for her, and she was not the type of woman he was looking for.

"So what do you plan to do now?" he asked.

"I don't know."

"Will you stay here in Summerville?"

She shrugged. "I might."

"This is a small town. There aren't many opportunities."

"Derrick, one thing I know for certain is that there are opportunities everywhere as long as my goal is to live for the Lord."

His forehead creased. "Are you seriously getting all religious now? I thought you'd outgrown that."

Anger flooded her body. "I've been a believer since high school, although the way I acted, no one would have known that when I was in college."

"You seemed happy." He forced a smile. "Unlike now."

"This is awkward." She fidgeted with her napkin as she gathered her thoughts. "I had a lapse, but now that I'm back, I see that I made a lot of mistakes."

"So you think I was a mistake?"

She shook her head. "No, you weren't a mistake at all. In fact, you helped me see what was really important in life. And now all I can do is pray that you see it too."

He stood, pulled out his wallet, extracted some money, and dropped it on the table. "You don't need to pray for me. I can take care of myself. I wanted to take care of you too, but you've clearly gone off the deep end."

She chose not to respond to his bitter comment. "I'm tired, Derrick. Since we've already said everything that we need to say—"

He stood and gestured toward the door. "I'll walk you to your car."

At least he was a gentleman. He placed his hand in the center of her back, guiding her toward the exit. Then, after they went out the parking lot, he held her car door, waited for her to fasten her seatbelt, and closed it.

~

Brandon had decided to pick up some muffins from Chelsea's Diner so he'd have something to bring to the church tomorrow. He sat off to the side to wait for the cashier to put them in a box when he spotted Stephanie walking out with Derrick.

His entire body suddenly felt numb. Derrick had his hand on Stephanie's back and was guiding her out the door, which could only mean one thing.

"Here you go, Brandon. A dozen assorted muffins."

"Thanks, Chelsea." He kept his head down as he handed her the money.

"What's wrong?" Chelsea walked around from behind the register. "You look like you just saw a ghost."

"I wish that was all I saw."

"Anything I can help you with?"

He shook his head. "No, this is something I have to work through on my own. Thanks for the muffins."

"I hope you enjoy them." She gave him an apologetic look. "And I hope things get better for you soon. I don't think I've ever seen you this down before."

"I'm sure everything will be just fine. See you on Sunday." Brandon lifted the box of muffins and headed out the door.

He felt like he was on top of the world when he first walked into Chelsea's Diner. All it had taken to knock him down was the single sighting of someone he'd allowed himself to care about. Why had she kept her date tonight a secret?

All the years he'd known Stephanie, she'd never been deceitful. He reflected on the last few minutes before he'd left the cabin. She said she was going to read for a little while and then turn in early.

He tossed the box of muffins onto the backseat of his car before getting in behind the steering wheel. *Lord, please help me do the right thing. If I can help Stephanie in any way, I will, but please don't make this more difficult by letting my personal feelings continue to grow.*

When he opened his eyes, he knew what he had to do. He'd continue talking to Stephanie, but he wouldn't initiate anything. If she wanted to see him—or discuss the job he'd told her about—it would have to be all up to her.

~

Stephanie awoke the next morning feeling as though she'd been in a wrestling match. She had a hard time going to sleep after her conversation with Derrick. Why hadn't she seen through him when she first started going out with him? It was so clear to her now, she couldn't believe she didn't notice before.

She reflected back on the early days of their time together. She'd gone to an intramural flag football game because Tabitha, the girl in the room across the hall from hers, liked a guy on one of the teams and didn't want to go alone.

When the game was over, her friend went to talk to the guy she liked. Next thing Stephanie knew, Derrick had approached and started chatting with her.

He told her he was on the team until he twisted his ankle, and although it had healed, the doctor advised him not to play again for a while. Then he asked her if she was seeing anyone. She said she wasn't, and before she left the field, she had a date planned for the next night.

On the way back to the dormitory, Tabitha filled her in on who Derrick was. "Do you realize he was voted most likely to succeed back in high school?"

"How do you know this?" Stephanie asked.

"One of the other guys on the team is from the same high school, and he told the rest of them." Tabitha shook her head. "Almost any girl would give her right arm for a date with Derrick, and look at you."

"At least I know he's not a serial killer."

Tabitha laughed. "I doubt he'd be playing flag football if he was a serial killer. No, I think you'll be just fine going out with him."

After the first date, Stephanie had an uneasy feeling about Derrick. All he could talk about was how he planned to be CEO of a large company someday. He told her he had a strategy planned out, and nothing would stop him.

Then he asked her out again. As tempting as it was to say she was busy, she figured she should probably give him another chance. After all, she wasn't seeing anyone else, so she didn't have anything to lose.

The second date was much better. He paid quite a bit of attention to her and spent less time talking about himself. He told her she was pretty and had an elegant profile that she could show off if she did her hair differently. He even gently brushed her hair away from her face and said her features were stunning. It actually felt good to hear such sweet compliments from a guy like Derrick. But looking back, she realized he was using psychology to change her into what he considered the perfect woman for a corporate executive.

As she drank her morning coffee, she thought more about her relationship with Derrick and pondered how it had happened. They were an item throughout the remainder of college. The one time they split up because she felt like she needed a little breathing room, every girl she knew told her she'd better hold onto Derrick because if she didn't, there would be someone else who'd snag him.

She should have said fine, but she didn't have the strength to do that. In fact, instead of growing more confident as she went through college, she felt less significant and figured her friends were right. So she went back to Derrick.

He did everything right before and during the engagement—at least from everyone else's perspective. He asked her father for her hand in marriage. Her parents were smitten and told her how proud they were that she had found such a wonderful man to marry.

Looking back, she realized she was never truly happy. She simply went through the motions, with her hair done the way Derrick liked it, dressing in clothes he thought were appropriate, and wearing the lipstick he gave her. Her opinions didn't seem to matter … and for a while, she was fine with that. At least she thought she was. Now, as she looked back, she realized that the entire time she was in college, she simply went through the motions of living what others saw as a charmed life. Derrick had kept her too busy to stop and think about what she wanted.

No wonder she'd had such crazy dreams last night. She stood and poured more coffee into her mug and then fixed herself a bowl of cereal. It was time to take action to do something she wanted to do rather than what someone else expected.

After she ate breakfast, showered, and dressed for the day, she called Brandon. His phone rang four times before he finally answered.

"Hey. What are you doing for lunch?" she asked.

"I brought a sandwich," he said in a monotone. "I'll probably stick around the church."

The lack of warmth in his voice caught her by surprise. "How about I pick something up and have lunch with you?"

"That's fine."

"Are you sure? You don't sound good. Are you not feeling well?"

"I feel fine."

"Well … did something happen?"

"No." He let out an audible sigh. "Nothing happened. I'm just swamped."

"Is that why you need an assistant?"

"Yes."

"Okay." She paused to reflect for a moment. "Tell you what. I'll grab some food and swing by the church. We can talk about the position over lunch."

"Okay."

"See you in a couple of hours."

After Stephanie hung up, she had a strange sensation in the pit of her stomach. If she didn't know better, she'd think Brandon was upset with her. But last time they saw each other was last night, and he left on a positive note.

She read another chapter from the second Bible study guide before Alyssa called. "Hey, girl. How's the hermit doing?"

"I haven't exactly been a hermit." Stephanie told her about Brandon's visits and her meeting with Derrick.

"Why did you do that?" Alyssa asked. "Isn't it dangerous to see him now? Aren't you worried you might cave to his demands?"

"Not really."

"Seems to me he's a control freak. I don't want you to get hurt."

"He might be bossy and full of himself, but he's actually a sweet guy deep down," Stephanie said. "He wouldn't hurt a fly."

"I'm not talking about physically dangerous. Weren't you concerned that he might try to talk you into doing something you don't want to do?"

"Not anymore. In fact, I told him exactly how I felt, including how I hated wearing my hair up, and the color of lipstick makes me feel like someone I'm not."

"Sounds intense," Alyssa said with a teasing tone. "Great reasons for leaving a guy at the altar. Lipstick can be pretty serious stuff." She let out a nervous giggle. "But you know what I mean. I agree that he's a sweet guy, but he's very persuasive."

"I know, which is why I have no doubt he'll be successful in business."

"Did you share the gospel?" Alyssa asked.

"I told him I'd pray for him, but he said he didn't need my prayers."

"He's going to wind up being a poor rich man if he continues to feel that way."

"I know, right?" Stephanie paused. "Hey, do you have any idea what might have happened to Brandon?"

"What do you mean?"

Stephanie explained his cool abruptness on the phone. "Last night, he was warm and fun, but today when we chatted, he sounded like he had better things to do than talk to me."

"I have no idea if anything's going on with him, but you've seen him more than I have lately. Did you ask him?"

"I did, and all he said was that he's swamped."

"Hmm. I wish I could tell you something."

"I'm sure it's nothing," Stephanie said. "I'm going to the church and having lunch with him, so I'll try to find out. I just thought you might have heard something."

"Actually, I've been so busy at work I haven't heard much of anything but my computer humming."

"Why don't we get together soon?" Stephanie thought for a moment. "Hey, I know. We can get a bunch of people to go skating, just like the old days."

"We were back in high school last time we did that," Alyssa reminded her. "We're getting old now. I'm afraid I might break a leg."

"Oh, yeah, twenty-four is so old."

Alyssa laughed. "You're right. Ask Brandon what he thinks. He might even want to include some of the high school kids."

"They'll make us feel even older."

"Or we can show them how to have a good time."

"True."

"I'll call you tonight," Alyssa said. "You can tell me what happens with Brandon."

After Stephanie hung up, she glanced at the time on her cell phone. She needed to get going.

She swung through the closest burger place and picked up some food before heading over to the church. Brandon was in the fellowship hall, sitting at a table, staring down at the rows of paper in front of him. She stood and watched for a few seconds, but when he didn't move, she cleared her throat.

He glanced up, and she smiled. And then he looked back down at the papers.

Her heart sank. He looked terrible. Whatever was bugging him must be serious.

Chapter 6

Brandon wasn't the least bit hungry, but he didn't need to let Stephanie know how she'd affected him. "My lunch is in the kitchen. Have a seat, and I'll be right back."

He left her sitting there, watching him with a confused expression. She clearly didn't know that he'd seen her last night.

When he returned with his food, she tilted her head and cleared her throat. "Brandon, I don't know what's bothering you, but I hope you feel comfortable enough with me to tell me about it. I'd like to help."

He pushed his food away and stared at it for a moment before looking directly at her. "Are you planning on going back with Derrick?"

"What?"

"You obviously still care about each other. Are you going to get back with him?"

She slowly shook her head. "No." With her forehead all scrunched up, she gave him a questioning look. "What on earth gave you the idea that I still care for him?"

He sighed. "I went to Chelsea's Diner last night."

Her eyes popped wide open. "Oh. Well …"

"You don't have to say anything." He did everything he could to keep her from seeing how distressed he was. "You don't owe me an explanation."

"No, I'm not getting back with Derrick. In fact, he called after you left last night and said he wanted to see me."

"Are you going to hop every time he tells you to?" The instant those words left Brandon's mouth, he wanted to kick himself. "I'm sorry. That was out of line."

She offered a sweet smile. "I understand."

Her phone rang. She glanced at it, and without taking the call, she put it on silent.

He wasn't sure what to say or do next, so he just sat there, staring at the table. This was the most awkward—and worst—conversation he could imagine.

"Since he insisted on seeing me, I figured it would be a good time to give him back his ring." She glanced down at her hand and then at him. "I let him know what I really thought."

"About …?"

"About him and me. About how I never liked the hairdo he wanted me to wear or the lipstick he bought for me."

Brandon felt a sense of relief, but he was still guarded as he smiled back at her. "How did he take that?"

She shrugged. "This is Derrick we're talking about. He always maintains his cool, no matter what."

"I suppose that's one of the things you liked about him."

"Actually, no." She reached for his hand on the table. "I like people to show how they really feel. Guarding every emotion and pretending that everything is fine when it's not …" She shrugged. "It just complicates things."

"So, would you say your relationship with Derrick is complicated now?"

She shook her head. "It's not complicated in the least. He knows exactly how I feel and that I will never marry him."

"Are you sure that's what you want?"

"Positive. Why?"

"Because—" He came to an abrupt stop, before admitting his feelings for her. This wasn't the time or place for that. "Why don't we discuss this some other time?"

"Okay." She started unwrapping her burger. "I'm starving."

He pulled his food closer. "Me too."

As they ate lunch, he told her about the position they were starting at the church. "It doesn't pay well, but the job satisfaction should more than make up for it."

"Do you think the pastor would want to hire me after what I did?"

Brandon swallowed the food in his mouth and laughed. "Are you kidding? I think that pretty much sealed the deal for you. He told me later that it took a lot of courage to back out like that."

"I'm not sure about courage."

"Stephanie, you are one of the most courageous women I know."

She put her burger on the table and studied his face. "Thank you, Brandon. I think I would like to be considered for the job."

"I'll let Pastor Keyes know."

"Oh, before I forget, Alyssa and I were talking about going skating with a bunch of old friends."

"Talk about courageous." Brandon laughed. "I've taken the kids skating, but I haven't actually done it in a while."

"I haven't either."

He shrugged. "I'll give it a try."

"Why don't you ask some of the high school kids if they want to join us?"

"Are you sure you want me to do that?"

"I think so. That would be like a job interview to see if they like me."

"Oh, trust me, they'll like you."

After they finished eating, she fished around in her purse to find her lipstick. He laughed at everything she pulled out and placed on the table.

"You're like Mary Poppins. Do you have a lamp in there?"

She chuckled. "Maybe."

"I've always been amazed by all the things women manage to cram into their purses."

Her smile warmed his heart, and everything in the room became much brighter. She stood and gathered her things. "I'd better let you get back to work. Let me know what the pastor says about the job."

"Let me know more about this skating get-together."

"See ya."

~

After Stephanie left the church, she thought about what Brandon had seen last night. She understood how it must have appeared.

What baffled her was why it bothered Brandon so much. Sure, she knew he cared about her wellbeing, but he seemed to have taken it personally.

She spent the afternoon on the porch, alternating between thinking about Brandon and reading. Having the use of this cabin had been such a huge blessing. It was close enough to town for convenience but far enough to escape the busyness that would muddy her mind. It gave her a chance to think about where she'd been and where she wanted to go. The job at the church sounded like the ideal position. Now all she'd have to figure out was how to make ends meet.

Alyssa called earlier than she expected. "Want to meet somewhere for dinner?"

"Sure. Where?"

Alyssa named a place that specialized Low Country cuisine. "My treat."

"You don't have to do that," Stephanie argued.

"I know, but I thought about having you to my place for dinner, but since I haven't cleaned in a while, I figured this would be better."

After they got off the phone, Stephanie went inside and freshened up. She was glad they were eating at a casual place so she could wear jeans.

"Hey!" Alyssa greeted her with a hug. "I figured you could use some comfort food, and they have the best shrimp and grits in town."

Stephanie patted her chest. "Be still, my heart."

After they placed their order, Alyssa leaned forward on her elbows. "I want to hear all about your conversation with Derrick … at least whatever you can tell me."

Stephanie told her as much as she could remember. "He seemed surprised that I had those feelings."

"Well, the stuff he picked out did look good on you, but you looked different—not like the Stephanie I always knew." Alyssa folded her arms. "Did he get mad and yell or anything?"

"No, Derrick would never do that. He's too composed." She paused. "But he did let his guard down a little, so I saw how he covered his surprise by being testy."

"I don't get it," Alyssa said. "He's a good looking guy who can probably have his pick of girls." She looked alarmed by what she'd said, and her face turned bright red. "Not that you aren't the best girl out there. It's just that … well …"

"I know what you're saying. He could have chosen someone who was more like what he wanted."

Alyssa nodded. "Yeah, that's what I'm saying. I wonder why he decided to make you over."

"I've wondered that for a long time. People kept telling me how lucky I was to have someone like Derrick. He was always so attentive—almost to the point of being smothering. Did I ever tell you that he always insisted on going shopping with me?"

"Why would he want to do that?"

"He liked picking out my clothes."

"That would drive me insane." Alyssa made a face. "I wonder what he's going to do now."

"Probably find someone who will be the perfect corporate wife. He has his whole life planned out, including the number of children he wants to have and the neighborhood he wants to raise them in."

"Wow. I wonder if he'll ever figure out what life is really all about."

"I certainly hope so. I always thought he'd make a good Christian. When he believes in something, there's no stopping him."

Alyssa chuckled. "I've always thought it was funny when people said someone else would make a good Christian."

"In his case, if he ever became a believer, he'd study the Bible and tell everyone he knew about Christ. He'd find out what Jesus called him to do, and that's exactly what he'd do. Derrick loves planning and setting goals."

"He just might do that one of these days."

"He'd have to stop and change direction. He always said he believed in God but didn't need the Bible. All of his plans have been carefully laid out based on what he thinks a corporate executive would do. The few times I mentioned my faith, he seemed like he was listening, but then he reminded me of all the *churchy* Christian hypocrites he knew." A lump formed in Stephanie's throat. "That might be one of the reasons I stuck with him. I thought that if I set a good example as a Christian, without being hypocritical, he'd want to follow. Now I realize that was wishful thinking."

"Maybe not. You might have planted a seed that will take root later." Alyssa glanced at the approaching server. "I'm starving."

As they ate, Stephanie talked about how she'd allowed her priorities to get messed up, and she pushed her beliefs to the back of her mind. "My faith was always there, even though I didn't put it first in my life. Now that I look back, I see how messed up things were."

"I'm glad you realized that."

Stephanie decided it was time to change the subject. "I mentioned the skating idea to Brandon. He said he hasn't worn a pair of skates in a long time."

Alyssa crinkled her nose. "I just hope we don't all wind up with broken bones."

After they finished eating, Alyssa asked Stephanie if she wanted to go to a movie. "Not tonight. I got up early this morning, and I'd like to get back and finish this chapter I'm reading."

"Good book, huh?"

Stephanie nodded. "Yeah, the best. It's the Bible."

Alyssa paid the check, and they walked out to the parking lot together. "Let's not wait too long for the skating party."

"So it's turning into a party?" Stephanie teased.

"You know me. I love parties."

"Why don't we plan it for this coming weekend?"

Alyssa nodded. "Perfect. I'll talk to some of our old friends and see if they can join us." She gave Stephanie another hug before they parted ways and went to their own cars.

All the way to the cabin, Stephanie couldn't help but smile. Things were definitely turning around for her. She'd gotten out of her engagement, she almost had a job, and she had a cozy place to stay for a while.

Keeping her eyes open, she thanked the Lord for His provisions. He had never let her down. Even when things didn't go her way, she knew it was all for a reason.

She slowed way down as she turned onto the road leading to the cabin. Once she rounded the last curve, she spotted Derrick's SUV. For a moment, she was tempted to turn around and run, but she couldn't do that.

Chapter 7

Stephanie parked her car, paused for a moment to gather her thoughts, and got out. Derrick remained standing on the porch, watching her as she slowly made her way toward the cabin.

"Quaint little place," he said softly, a hint of condescension in his voice.

"I like it."

"That's nice. Mind if I come in?"

"Um …"

"Look, Stephanie, I know I should have called first, but I was afraid you'd tell me not to come."

"How did you find out where I was?"

"Your parents told me."

"Oh." Stephanie glanced toward the front door. She was glad she'd left the front porch light on. It was bright enough to cover most of the yard and driveway. "I guess it's okay for a little while."

"I won't stay long. There's something I need to get off my chest."

She gestured toward the front door. "Then let's go on inside. I have plenty of ginger ale." She paused. "Did you know that I like ginger ale?"

He offered a closed-mouth smile and slowly shook his head. "Apparently there are a lot of things I don't know about you. I thought you liked tea."

"I do, but ginger ale is my favorite drink." She unlocked the door and led the way inside, turning on lights as she went. "My home for a while, until I figure out what I'm going to do."

Derrick looked around and then at her. "It's very … sweet."

She chuckled. "And it makes me happy. Ginger ale?"

"Sure."

She pointed toward the kitchen table. "Why don't we sit here?"

After she poured their drinks and brought them to the table, she sat down across from Derrick. It seemed weird, now that they were no longer a couple.

"So what did you want to talk about?"

He fidgeted with the edge of his napkin—something she'd never seen him do. Finally, he glanced up at her. "Stephanie, this is really difficult to say, but one of the reasons I liked you so much when we first met was because you were different. I never knew any girls like you before."

"What do you mean?"

He shrugged. "Everyone else seemed so impressed with the things I talked about and how successful I planned to be. You just took it in stride and acted like it didn't faze you."

"If you liked me so much, why did you want to change me?"

"I didn't realize I was doing that until you told me. I've always had order in my life—and I suppose some of that spilled over into our relationship. I'm really sorry."

She blinked and cleared her throat. "I appreciate your apology, but I still don't want to marry you."

"And I accept that. But I do have a favor I'd like to ask."

"What's that?"

"Can you tell me about your religion?"

"My religion?" she asked. "You mean my faith in God?"

He nodded. "See? I don't even know what to call it."

She didn't want to appear judgmental, so she tried to keep her expression neutral. "Jesus died for the sins of believers, and I just happen to be one of them."

"I don't understand all of that. I didn't grow up in a relig—I mean a home that got into all that kind of stuff. I mean, we went to church on Christmas Eve, and my dad gave them quite a bit of money, but in my family, success was more about making money, having a big house in the right neighborhood, and driving a car that showed you'd made it."

That was something Stephanie did understand since she'd lived in a similar type of home. "My parents were—and still are—like that too. They thought I'd lost my mind when I decided not to marry you."

"How did you find your faith?"

She studied his face and saw sincerity that she'd never seen in him before. "Jesus found me. When I was in high school, Alyssa was in several of my classes. She and I started talking between classes and lunch, and eventually we started hanging out after school. Then one Friday afternoon she asked me to spend Saturday night with her and go to church with her on Sunday."

"That sounds logical."

"I agree. The only problem was that I didn't know what to do. My parents rarely went to church—mostly on Christmas and Easter and weddings."

He nodded. "I have to admit that it had been a while since I'd been in a church, so going to visit your pastor for our counseling session and then the rehearsal and wedding … well, I was a bit uncomfortable."

"I couldn't tell."

A grin tweaked the corners of his lips. "I obviously hide my discomfort well."

"Is that the first time you were uncomfortable with me?"

He slowly shook his head. "No, there were many times, but I didn't want you to notice."

"But why? Isn't it important to be able to open up to the person you plan to marry?"

"I don't know."

"Derrick, what is the real reason you came here tonight?"

"I want to know more about God. After I left Chelsea's Diner, I thought about what I said." He glanced down at the table and then slowly lifted his gaze to hers. "All that talk about not needing your prayers was an act. Part of my image is to appear strong and sure of myself."

Stephanie's eyes widened. She couldn't believe Derrick was actually admitting this, and it happened so quickly. "So what do you want to know about God?"

"Is He really everywhere? Does he know what I'm doing, what I'm thinking, and what I'm feeling?"

"Yes, He knows everything."

"Then I'm doomed."

"No, you're not doomed. I'll be right back." She got up from the table and got the Bible study book she'd just finished reading. She placed it on the table in front of him. "This is a basic study about the nature of God and why He sent Jesus to save us from sin."

He pulled out his phone and started tapping on it before putting it back in his pocket. "Okay, I just ordered the electronic version."

"You didn't have to do that. You could have borrowed this one."

"I don't like borrowing things."

She remembered that about Derrick. "Start from the beginning, read the commentary, and answer the questions as you go. If you do that, you'll have a much better understanding of how a relationship with Jesus is the most important thing you can have."

"Why didn't you talk about this when we were together?"

"I tried a couple of times, but you didn't seem interested." She lowered her gaze. "And I have to admit that I got lazy about it when I went to college."

He gave her an apologetic look. "I'm sorry if I had anything to do with that."

That was a first. Stephanie couldn't remember a single time she'd heard Derrick apologize. She cleared her throat and did her best to disguise her surprise.

"No, don't be. I stopped going to church regularly before I met you, so it's not your fault."

She stood up to refresh her drink. He got up and followed her.

"Derrick—"

He held up both hands. "I'm not going to touch you. I just wanted to … well, I don't know."

"I understand." She glanced around, trying to figure out what to say or do next.

He shifted from one foot to the other, showing an uncharacteristic awkwardness as he pointed to the Bible study book. "Would you … um … can we start working on this now?"

She took a deep breath and slowly let it out before shaking her head. "I'm sorry, Derrick, but not tonight. I'm exhausted."

"Okay, that's fine. But I do have one question before I leave."

"What's that?"

He reached for her hand—the one that once sported an engagement ring but was now glaringly bare. "Is there any chance for us in the future? I mean, do you think you'll ever want to get back together?"

"I—"

He held up a hand. "I have to admit, I was shocked that you ran away from the wedding … at least at first."

"But you were sweet about it," she said. "I appreciate how you didn't trash me. You very well could have justified showing your anger."

"That wouldn't have done any good." He offered a hint of a smile. "Besides, that would have been bad for my image."

"Your image is difficult to live up to."

He lifted an eyebrow and made a face. "Tell me about it. Try being me for a week, and you'll see how hard it is."

"Then why do you continue to worry about it?"

He shrugged. "I don't know. I suppose I'm concerned that it's the only way people will like or respect me."

"Anyone who truly matters will respect you for who you really are." She patted her chest. "You've heard the saying that it's what's inside that matters."

"Yes, and it's a cliché that I'm not sure everyone subscribes to."

"You can't make everyone happy, Derrick."

He leaned over and took her hand in his again, kissed the back of it, and continued to hold it. "That's why I still have hope for us, Stephanie. You're good for me."

~

Brandon couldn't believe Stephanie had left her wallet at the church. As much as he wanted to consider it an inconvenience to drive all the way out to the cabin to return it, he welcomed another opportunity to see Stephanie today. He'd tried to call, but she didn't answer. She must have left her phone on silent.

As soon as he pulled onto the road that led to the cabin, he spotted the Lexus SUV parked in front. His heart hammered at the thought of something happening to Stephanie—that maybe that ex of hers had come out here to hurt her—and a sense of urgency washed over him.

He threw his car into park, turned off the ignition, got out, and ran up the walkway. As soon as he got to the porch, he glanced through the open window.

Chapter 8

Stephanie was there with her ex, all right. But she didn't appear to be struggling in the least. Derrick was holding her hand as they gazed into each other's eyes.

Brandon felt as though all the blood had been drained from his body, as he remained frozen to one place on the porch. It wasn't until they let go of each other's hands before he could move.

He jumped off the porch and pretended he'd just arrived when the front door opened. Stephanie's eyes widened when she saw him.

"Hey, Brandon. I didn't hear your car."

He held up her wallet. "You left this at the church."

Derrick glanced back and forth between Stephanie and Brandon before settling his gaze on Stephanie. "Where have I seen this guy? Who is he?"

Stephanie appeared nervous as she gestured toward Brandon. "Derrick, I'd like for you to meet Brandon. We've been friends since I first started high school."

"An old high school buddy, huh?" Derrick grinned as he approached Brandon. "It's nice to meet you, Brennan."

Brandon's first thought was that the mistake was intentional. He cleared his throat before correcting Derrick.

"Oh, sorry. It's just that I haven't heard about you before."

Brandon glanced at Stephanie. "I tried to call you, but when you didn't answer, I figured you'd forgotten to take your phone off silent."

"Thank you so much for bringing it all the way out here," she said.

"Derrick was just leaving, weren't you?"

Derrick nodded and smiled. "Unless you'd like for me to stick around and chat with your friend. I think it's a good idea to get to know the people who helped make you who you are today."

Brandon narrowed his eyes as he tried to figure out what was going on. Stephanie obviously wasn't over her relationship with Derrick, as she'd led him to believe. He thought back to their conversation and distinctly remembered her saying she would never marry this guy. Either she couldn't make up her mind, or she couldn't be trusted. Whatever the case, he didn't want to get involved where he would only complicate matters more than they already were.

Stephanie broke the silence. "I'm exhausted, so I think I'll take a pass on that." Then she turned to Brandon. "Please let Pastor Keyes know that I'd like to meet with him soon."

"That Pastor Keyes is quite a guy, isn't he?" Derrick said. "In fact, while I'm in town, I might even call him to take him up on that golf match he mentioned."

"He just said—" Stephanie began.

Derrick lifted his hand in a half-wave. "C'mon, buddy. Let's get going so our girl can rest. She's been through a lot over the past week."

Brandon cringed at Derrick's casual use of the word *buddy*. He doubted they'd ever be buddies, but he thought about what Christ would want him to do. "You're right. I need to get on home anyway." He forced a smile in Stephanie's direction. "I'll talk to the pastor and let him know. He'll probably call you to set up an appointment."

After Stephanie closed the door, Derrick tried to strike up a conversation. "So you've been friends with our girl for a long time, huh?"

Brandon nodded. "Yeah, we've been friends for a while."

Derrick chuckled. "Looks like you're feeling more than friendship. Can't say I blame you, though. She's quite a girl."

"Yes, she certainly is." Without another word, Brandon got in his car, started it, and drove away. He couldn't continue this conversation that made his blood boil.

All he could think about as he drove home was how Stephanie could have lied to him. As he thought back to their conversation, he tried to remember whether or not she'd given him any reason to think he had a chance with her. Nothing came to mind, but then it was still too soon after her split with Derrick to expect anything. One thing was obvious, though. She wasn't telling him everything.

The more he thought about it, the more he realized that hoping for something more than friendship with her wasn't realistic. That was all they'd ever been, and it appeared that was all it ever would be. And if she got back with Derrick, they might not even be friends. It wasn't likely he'd ever be buddies with Derrick, regardless of what the guy called him.

~

Stephanie wasn't sure what Brandon saw, but it appeared he might be jumping to conclusions. Sure, Derrick still acted possessive toward her, and some of his comments emphasized that, but she didn't want Brandon to think she had any plans to reunite with the man who clearly wasn't right for her.

Although it was late, she decided to take a chance and call Alyssa who answered on the second ring. "No, I wasn't asleep. What's up?"

Stephanie told Alyssa what had happened. "I'm happy that Derrick has decided to read the Bible, but I'm afraid Brandon might have gotten the wrong idea."

"First of all, I want to make sure I'm clear on something, "Alyssa said. "If Derrick becomes a believer, and he takes his faith seriously, do you think you might change your mind about marrying him?"

"No. After everything that's been going on, I can't see that ever happening. Besides, the chemistry simply isn't there for me."

"Okay, so I have another question, but it's probably too soon to ask you."

"You can ask me anything, Alyssa. You know me better than anyone else."

"Do you have feelings for Brandon?"

"Feelings?" Stephanie swallowed hard as she tried to push the thoughts she'd been having about Brandon to the back of her mind. "I've been friends with him for a long time—practically as long as I've known you."

"Yes, I know, but that still doesn't answer my question."

Stephanie sighed. Alyssa was right—it was too early. But she couldn't hide something so obvious to her best friend. "Yes, I do have feelings for Brandon. In fact, I've had a crush on him since high school."

"I remember that, but you seemed to have gotten over him while you were in college."

"That might be why I went on such a dating frenzy," Stephanie admitted.

"And why you pushed away from your faith."

"Probably."

"What do you want to do now?"

"I don't know. But I do know that Derrick and I are over."

"And you're worried that Brandon will think you're getting back with him, right?" Before Stephanie had a chance to answer, Alyssa continued. "Are you getting signals from Brandon that he might have the same feelings for you?"

"That's another thing I don't know. My emotions have been weird lately, so I'm all mixed up right now."

"Okay, I get the picture … and I have some advice if you want me to give it to you."

"Yes, please."

"You need to do nothing."

"Nothing?" Stephanie repeated.

"Yes, nothing … at least for now. Time and separation are the only things that will prove to Brandon that you're over Derrick. After Derrick gets the message that it's over between the two of you, I assume he'll eventually go away. When that happens, let your relationship with Brandon grow naturally."

"What if Brandon finds someone else before that happens?"

"We'll deal with that if and when it happens. But for now, I don't think you're ready to be in a relationship with anyone."

"You're right."

They chatted for a few more minutes. After Stephanie got off the phone, she knelt beside the bed and prayed.

Lord, I'm so mixed up right now. But I do know that marrying Derrick would have been the biggest mistake I could have made, so thank you for saving me from that. Please guide me to do what's right by both men.

After she opened her eyes, she got ready for bed. She got her Bible and read it until her eyelids grew heavy.

The next morning, she awoke to the sound of her phone ringing. It was Pastor Keyes.

A glance at the clock on the nightstand let her know she'd slept later than usual. It was 8:15.

"I have to do some hospital visitations this afternoon," Pastor Keyes said, "but if you're in the area sometime this morning, I'd love to chat with you about the position."

She sat up and rubbed her eyes. "I can be there in an hour."

"Perfect." Pastor Keyes paused. "Stephanie, I'm relieved that you didn't go through with something you weren't sure about."

"Thanks, Pastor. I just wish I'd acted sooner. What I did hurt some people, including my parents."

"They'll come around. The slight pain they're feeling now is nothing compared to what it would be if you came to the same conclusion later."

"Thank you so much for understanding. I'll see you in an hour."

As soon as she got off the phone, she jumped out of bed, started the coffee, and hopped into the shower. It took her another half hour to get ready and drink her coffee before heading out the door. Her stomach rumbled, but she didn't have time to eat.

Pastor Keyes and Brandon were in the church's front office waiting for her when she arrived. "Would you like a bagel?" the pastor asked.

She nodded. "Sounds good."

"I'll get it for you," Brandon said. "Do you still like a light smear of cream cheese?"

"Yes, please."

After Brandon left, the pastor gestured toward his office in the back. "Let's go ahead and get started. Brandon has already filled me in on what he needs from an assistant."

He explained the duties of the assistant youth director. "Unfortunately, we can't afford to offer much this year, but when the finance committee does next year's budget, we might be able to pay more."

Brandon arrived with bagels and coffee. Stephanie couldn't help but notice that he seemed uncomfortable. She'd have to talk to him later but not in front of the pastor.

"Now that you know about the job, is it something you'd consider?" Pastor Keyes asked.

She nodded. "I would. In fact, I would like to accept if there's an offer."

"There is an offer," the pastor said. "I've already gotten permission from the church council, so now all I need to know is whether or not you can start in two weeks."

"In two weeks?" she asked.

Pastor Keyes glanced at Brandon before looking at her. "Is that too soon?"

"Two weeks from now is fine."

"Good. Now I'll leave the two of you to discuss the job while I gather everything for my visitations." He stood up. "Welcome to the church staff, Stephanie. I hope you experience the blessings the rest of us have."

"I'm sure I will."

After he left, she turned to Brandon who seemed rather intent on studying his shoes. He finally lifted his head and met her gaze.

"Congratulations," he said. His expression was difficult to read.

"What hours do you want me to work?"

"When we have something going on. Most of the time, things start in the afternoon, so you'll have your mornings free … at least until summer."

She nodded. I guess I should let you get back to work now. See you on Sunday."

The next two weeks seemed to drag. Derrick called a couple of times, but he didn't press. However, he still sounded like he thought this was a minor blip on the relationship. Finally, she asked him to stop calling.

"I will for a while, but Stephanie, you know I can't wait forever for you to make a decision."

"I already made a decision, Derrick. I'm not marrying you."

After she hung up, she prayed that Derrick would get the message that she had no intention of marrying him. She suspected that his pride was what kept him calling. He'd gone back to Charlotte, but that was close enough that she feared he might pop over to Summerville at the least expected time. She hated being caught off-guard.

On the day before she was supposed to start her job, she drove to the church. Brandon was in his office looking through some papers.

"I don't want to bother you. I just wanted to know what time you need me to come in tomorrow."

"Can you be here after lunch? I have a program for the middle and high school kids, so I can use your help setting up." His tone was light, but it seemed forced, and he appeared to be avoiding eye contact with her.

She nodded. "Yes, of course I can be here."

"All right. I thought it would be best to slowly get you involved with the kids. A lot of them have trust issues with new people."

"Okay." She understood that a lot of the kids in the youth program had difficult home lives. It might have helped if they'd gotten together for a skating party like she'd hoped.

He inhaled as he stood and then slowly let out his breath. "That's about it."

"Don't you want me to do anything else?"

"Not really. After the program tomorrow, I'll send you home with a roster of all the kids we work with and what programs they like."

His demeanor toward her had changed so much she wasn't sure how to react. So she simply nodded, said, "Thank you," and left.

All the way home, she wondered what she could do to at least get him back to his jovial mood. This was totally unlike she'd ever seen him act before, and it threw her off.

She called Alyssa before starting her car. "I start my new job at the church tomorrow."

"Wonderful! Now you'll be able to see Brandon more often, and that'll probably take care of the whole problem."

"Or make it worse," Stephanie replied.

"Since when did you become a pessimist? You've always been so positive about everything."

"Sorry. It's just that my whole world has been turned upside-down lately."

"I know," Alyssa said. "But don't forget that you had a hand in making that happen."

"True."

"Now go on home and try to get some rest. Call me after work tomorrow and tell me all about your new job."

Stephanie hung up and headed toward the cabin. She spotted Derrick's SUV as soon as she made the turn. She was tempted to turn around, but that wouldn't be the right thing to do.

He stood up from the rocking chair on the porch and walked toward her car. "I've been waiting for a while, Stephanie. Where've you been?"

"It doesn't matter," she said.

He hung his head. "Okay, I suppose that makes sense, considering the fact that we haven't officially gotten back together yet."

"Nor will we ever."

"C'mon, Stephanie. You know you and I are good together."

"We're not good together, Derrick. I don't know what it'll take to get it through your head. I think you're a great guy and all, but we have different goals in life."

"Would it help if I told you that I finished the entire Bible study book? I can even recite some of the verses."

"No, Derrick. Please don't do this."

"Why did you bother telling me to do this Bible study if you had no intention of getting back with me?"

"Because that's what I'm called to do. The Lord wants believers to share His message with others."

He rolled his eyes and backed away. "If I'd known this, I wouldn't have bothered with you in the first place. I'm outta here."

Stephanie blinked as he strode toward his SUV, got in, and peeled out. A part of her felt terrible, but another part was relieved. She was pretty sure he wouldn't bother again.

~

Brandon had finally gotten all his calls made and was now able to go home. He was thankful he didn't have any programs tonight, after dealing with the emotional roller coaster he'd been on with Stephanie and then seeing her today. He'd spotted her at church and spoken with her in passing, but otherwise, he'd avoided too much contact, hoping that time would help him deal with his feelings.

He'd barely pulled the church door closed when he heard the sound of a car coming to a stop and Derrick's voice behind him. He turned around to face the man who'd won the girl. The driver's side window was open, so Brandon got a good look at the smirk on Derrick's face.

"She's all yours, man."

Brandon squinted. "What are you talking about, Derrick?"

"I thought that if I gave in and played Bible study with her for a little while, she'd eventually come to her senses. But no, she's convinced that God has a different plan for her." Derrick shook his head and pounded his palm on the steering wheel. "She and I made a great team. If she weren't so brainwashed on this Christianity stuff, she'd make a great corporate wife."

"I still don't understand what you're saying."

"I did everything short of beg her to come back to me, and she's still not budging." He let out a snort.

"Did she tell you that?"

Derrick nodded. "Afraid so. After my last conversation with her, I wouldn't take her back, even if she begged. It's time to cut bait and find a real woman who knows how to be a good wife." He put his car into gear, waved, and added, "Good luck with her. Like I said, she's all yours." And then he sped away, leaving Brandon standing there trying to figure out what had just happened.

Chapter 9

He stared off toward the road before he finally got in his car and headed home. Regardless of all the angles he contemplated, the only thing that made sense was the basic fact that Stephanie and Derrick weren't an item anymore. Beyond that, nothing was clear. Whether she blew him off or he was turned off by her faith, the very thought of what Derrick had said made him smile.

One thing he'd learned from his past was that he needed to act quickly, or he might miss out on the opportunity to have a chance with Stephanie. However, he didn't want to move too fast—not after what she'd been through over the past few weeks.

Brandon didn't have much experience in the romance department, so he decided to talk to someone who knew about such things. He called Pastor Keyes.

The older gentleman laughed. "I already knew. In fact, I've known for years that there was a strong chemistry between the two of you, and it started long before y'all ever went your separate ways to college."

"Why didn't you say something?" Brandon asked.

"It wasn't my place to bring it up. The Lord has His own way and timing that I didn't want to interfere with. So how can I help you?"

Brandon explained what had just happened and how he felt about not missing the opportunity. "I don't want to take a chance on someone else coming into the picture, but I don't want to rush her right after she broke her engagement."

"I understand." The pastor paused. "There are two things to consider. First of all, it's not like the two of you just met. Tell her that you would like to date her when she's ready. She's smart. She'll let you know when that is. And secondly, the fact that you both are attracted to each other gives you an edge over anyone else."

"Okay, I'll tell her that I want to hang out with her."

"No, I don't think you heard me correctly. Tell her you want to *date* her. There's a big difference between hanging out and dating. In fact, you've already been *hanging out* with her quite a bit."

"True … at least until a couple of weeks ago." Brandon sighed. "It'll seem strange since she and I have been friends for so long."

"Do you still think you can work with her?"

"Oh yes. In fact, I can't think of anyone more suited to the job than Stephanie, and we've always worked well together on committees. I hope you don't have a problem with that."

"I don't. Some of the best youth group leaders are young husband-and-wife teams. They give the kids a healthy relationship to look up to."

"Wait a minute. We're not husband and wife."

"Not yet." Pastor Keyes chuckled. "But if you make your move at the right time, I can see it happening in the not-so-distant future."

Brandon could too, but he wasn't about to come out and say it … at least not until he talked to Stephanie. "I'll start with the dating thing first."

"Good idea. One thing I want you to remember, Brandon, is that you need to put your heart on the line if you want to win hers."

"Okay." As Brandon hung up, he pondered what the pastor had said. The main reason he never acted on his feelings for Stephanie years ago was because of his fear of having his heart broken. It was time to take the biggest risk of his life.

~

Stephanie awoke the next morning with mixed emotions—excited about starting her new job but nervous about the way Brandon acted toward her yesterday. But she knew she shouldn't worry too much. People had moods, and maybe that was all it was. A mood.

She showered and dressed for the day. Since the church was casual and this was a youth event, which was even more casual, she wore jeans, a fitted T-shirt, and a lightweight khaki jacket. Derrick definitely wouldn't approve. She'd barely finished putting on her makeup when she heard someone knocking at the door.

On the way to the door, she held her breath, hoping it wasn't Derrick. To her surprise when she opened it, Brandon stood on the other side, smiling.

"Mind if I come in?" he asked.

"Um ... sure." She took a step back and let him in. "It's early. Is everything okay?"

He nodded. "Everything is perfect. I have the church set up for the youth program, so all we have to do is show up."

"I thought you wanted me to help with that this afternoon after lunch." Now worry filled her as she thought that perhaps he didn't need an assistant, after all.

"I did, but there's something more important that came up." He looked her over and widened his smile. "You look nice."

"Thank you." Brandon was definitely acting different, and she had no idea why. "I hope I'm dressed okay for the youth group."

"You're perfect ... I mean you're dressed just fine."

Finally, she couldn't stand it anymore. She had to find out what was going on. "So why are you here?"

"Can we go for a walk? Like on that nature trail behind the cabin?"

"Sounds good. Let me grab my key and phone, and we can go."

It took her all of a minute to get what she needed. As they headed for the trail, he took her hand and laced his fingers with hers. This wasn't the first time he'd held her hand, but it felt different—almost possessive. And she liked it.

As they walked, he pointed out some trees that were native to South Carolina. She laughed. "If I didn't know better, I'd think you were a country boy."

"Who says I'm not?" he said.

"Well, I just happen to know where you grew up."

"Yeah, you're right. But I used to hang out with my uncle during the summer when he wasn't so busy with regular church duties. He taught me how to fish and hunt." Brandon gestured around. "And he taught me how to identify a lot of trees and plants."

"I'm impressed." She squeezed his hand.

He stopped and turned her toward him. "Are you really?"

"Am I really what?"

"Impressed." He paused. "You just said you were impressed."

The tenderness in his expression caught her off-guard. She nodded. "Yes, I really am, and not just about your knowledge of foliage."

She had the urge to kiss him, but she was worried that he'd reject her. So she looked away instead.

Brandon didn't make any moves, so she turned back around to see his expression. He smiled at her. "I like you, Stephanie."

"I like you too, Brandon."

"I mean, I really like you, as in ..." He glanced down at his feet and then back up at her, a goofy look taking over his face. "I'd like to … well, if it's not too soon after …" He stopped and coughed. "This is hard for me."

"You'd like to what, Brandon?"

He closed his eyes, and his lips moved, as though he might be mouthing a silent prayer. When he opened his eyes, he looked directly at her. "There's no other way to do this but tell you I like you a lot more than just as friends, and I'd like to date you when you're ready."

"You do?" Her heart hammered. "You would?"

He nodded. "Yes, but I understand if you're not ready."

She lifted her fingers to his lips to quiet him. "I'd like to date you too, Brandon. In fact, I wanted this a long time ago, but I didn't think you were that interested in me."

"Funny you say that. I thought the same thing back in high school."

"Well, now that we've decided to date, is there any way I can get a kiss?" She smiled up at him.

He paused only for a moment before pulling her into his arms and dropping a brief, tender kiss on her lips. "That'll have to do for now. It's time for us to head to the church and get ready for the youth group."

Epilogue

One year later, Stephanie stood at the window in the bridal room at the back of the church, looking outside at the parking lot. There weren't as many cars this time, but that didn't matter. All she cared about was the fact that she was with the man she truly loved—the one who allowed her to be herself and accepted her the way she was.

"It's never too late, is it?"

Stephanie spun around at the sound of Alyssa's voice. Both of them had tears in their eyes, so they laughed. "No, and I can't believe this is actually happening. Thank you so much for stopping me from making the biggest mistake of my life last year."

"Somehow, I knew we'd be here again." Alyssa took a step back and looked Stephanie up and down. "Even this dress fits better. You look amazing," she added. "And very happy."

"You know I am."

"Why don't I go take a peek at the altar and let you have a few minutes alone?"

Stephanie nodded. "Okay, that sounds good. Just don't stay gone long, okay? I don't want to be late for Brandon."

"I agree. Both of you have waited long enough for this."

After Alyssa left her alone, Stephanie lowered her head and said a prayer of thanksgiving for Brandon's love, her parents' willingness to eventually listen, and her friends who stuck with her through the most difficult of times. By the time Alyssa returned, the music had started.

"Looks like the show is about to start," Alyssa said. "Are you ready?"

"Oh yeah."

The sound of the music caused Stephanie's heart rate to increase, only this time it was due to pure joy that swelled inside her. Her father came to the door to get her.

"Love you, sweetie. I think you found the right man this time." He bent over and kissed her cheek before straightening and offering his arm. "Let's go."

As they walked up the aisle toward the man she loved, she had no doubt she was doing the right thing. Brandon beamed with the same joy she felt.

Throughout the ceremony, she had to force herself to focus on the pastor's words. All she wanted to do was grab Brandon and plaster a huge kiss on his lips. But she managed to get through the vows without making a fool of herself. When Pastor Keyes said, "You may kiss the bride," she thought she'd explode with happiness.

Brandon chuckled and whispered, "I've been waiting a long time for this. Are you ready to go live our lives together, Mrs. Walker?"

She nodded and then kissed him again. Pastor Keyes cleared his throat and pointed toward the back of the church. "They're waiting for y'all to go."

"We'd better do that now." Brandon squeezed her hand.

"Then come on. Let's get the party started."

I hope you enjoyed *Never Too Late*. Please don't forget to leave a review. Below you'll find more of my books and novellas that I wrote to entertain and inspire.

Thank you!
Debby Mayne

Unraveled Hearts

Debby Mayne

Threads of Faith
Forget Me Not Romances

Forget Me Not Romances, a division of Winged Publications

Chapter 1

"Put some lipstick on, Ruby Lynn." Ruby braced herself for what she knew would come next. "And for heaven's sake, suck in that stomach. You don't want—"

"Mama, please. I need to finish this email."

As soon as Ruby was sure Mama wouldn't interrupt her again, she read her acceptance, took a deep breath, placed her finger on the SEND button, and pressed. Okay, now she was committed to attending Plantersville High School's ten-year reunion for her class.

"Are you done?" Mama's voice grated on her last nerve.

"Yes, I'm finished."

"Then come on to supper. I don't want Nate to think you don't want to see him."

"I told you …" Ruby let her voice trail off since there wasn't any way around Mama's matchmaking attempts—especially when it came to Nate Harwell who just happened to be the son of Mama's best friend from college.

"Just hurry up, okay?" Mama narrowed her eyes. "It's not polite, you sittin' in your daddy's study while we have company."

"Give me a couple more minutes. I have to look at one more thing."

Mama shook her head in her typical disapproving fashion. "Okay, but you'd better hurry."

After the invitation arrived in the mail yesterday, her first thought was to avoid it at all costs, simply because she didn't want to see Antonio Fontana in such an up-close and personal way. It was bad enough to occasionally spot him around town when she ate in his restaurant, but at least she could do an about-face or pretend not to see him.

When Mama called and invited her to come over for supper, she had no idea Nate would be there. But she should have guessed since the last time she and Mama had talked, it was all about her biological clock and how she wasn't getting any younger.

She fished around in her handbag, found her brightest red lipstick, and carefully applied it to her lips. Then she tousled her hair, hung her head upside down, and pulled the whole mess of it up into an elastic band she kept on her wrist for times like this. She knew Mama hated the messy bun look, but that didn't matter anymore. Ruby could wear her hair any way she pleased, now that she was out on her own, supporting herself, and not accepting a dime of the money Mama and Daddy kept trying to throw at her. The only handouts she ever took were the occasional meals they guilted her into coming over for.

The blended aroma of pot roast and something chocolaty filled her nostrils as she rounded the corner of the oversized house Mama and Daddy insisted on maintaining—even though they didn't have a single young'un still living at home. Ruby's brother Trey left for college and never came back to Plantersville. He took a job with one of the Wall Street firms, one of the few things outside of South Carolina Daddy would have accepted. Last Ruby had heard, Trey was on his way up the corporate ladder and dating his boss's daughter.

She stopped short of the arched doorway to the dining room and took another breath. If she didn't stop this deep breathing soon, she'd hyperventilate.

"I think I hear her coming." Mama's sweeter-than-honey voice irritated Ruby every bit as much as her matchmaking.

Ruby squared her shoulders, lifted her head, and sucked in her gut, just as Mama had taught her. She even managed a half smile to greet Nate.

"Hey, Ruby." He stood up and gestured toward the chair beside him. "You're lookin' mighty good."

"Thanks, Nate."

"Your mama tells me you're going to the reunion. I thought you said you wouldn't go anywhere near it. You said—"

She dropped her smile. "I changed my mind."

Mama cleared her throat. "I have a great idea. Why don't y'all go together? I'm sure everyone will be happy to see that you're still …" She glanced back and forth between Ruby and Nate. "They'll like to see the two of you together, since you were inseparable when you were in school."

Nate grinned at Ruby, but she detected a hint of discomfort in his eyes. Was it possible that he didn't want to go with her any more than she wanted to go with him?

"I'm not sure Ruby wants—" Nate began before Mama cut him off.

"Of course Ruby wants to go to the reunion with you." Mama lifted her iced tea glass and held it in front of her face, with her eyes peeking from above it. She tilted her head ever so slightly, letting Ruby know she meant business. "Don't you, Ruby?"

"I guess."

"Then it's settled." Mama took a sip of tea and set her glass on the table in a triumphant gesture. "Y'all can make arrangements for when you pick her up later. But now I want y'all to enjoy your supper. I'm sure Ruby has some interesting stories to tell about the children in her class." Mama sighed. "I imagine they're just the sweetest little things."

If only Mama knew the half of it. Ruby now taught fifth grade, and she learned as much from them as they did her. She taught what was in the books, and they shared what they'd learned from the reality shows their parents let them watch … or worse, the things their moms, dads, and significant others let them see first hand. When she was their age, she had no idea people did some of the stuff they talked about.

Nate gave her a knowing look. "You have older kids, right?"

She nodded, paused, and then shrugged. "Well, older for elementary school."

"From what I've seen, kids become quite worldly at an early age these days … not at all like us when we were little."

"Some of the kids in my class are as tall as me."

Ruby kept the conversation on her class as long as Mama would allow, but she knew that wouldn't be long. The discussion quickly turned back to things Mama deemed more important … like the Junior League.

"I still don't see why you don't want to join the Junior League, Ruby. They do a lot of wonderful things for the community, and I know you love helping people." She put on her biggest smile, showing all her very expensive, sparkling white teeth. "Otherwise, why would you resort to the low pay of teaching at a public school?"

Ruby tensed. Her parents had always said it wasn't polite to discuss money with anyone outside the family, so she was caught off guard. "I'm doing just fine, Mama."

"I don't see how, since you won't accept a dime from your daddy and me." Mama turned her attention to Nate, clearly trying to get him to team up with her. "Can you imagine trying to live off what they pay schoolteachers?"

Nate opened his mouth, but as soon as he locked gazes with Ruby, he slowly shook his head. "I'm staying out of this one, Mrs. Wilson."

Mama chuckled. "Probably a good idea. I don't need to start a quarrel between the two of you."

Throughout all of this discussion, Ruby noticed that Daddy hadn't uttered a single solitary word. He just sat there nibbling on pot roast and potatoes, letting the conversation swirl around him. It was high time to get him involved.

"So what do you think about the Carolina Panthers, Daddy? Will they ever manage to win the Super Bowl?"

Before he had a chance to respond, Mama piped up. "How on earth would your daddy know something like that, Ruby? What kind of question is that?"

Daddy cleared his throat. "It's actually a very good question, Janet." He looked back at Ruby. "If they keep doing what they're doing and not let small backslides psyche them out, I believe they'll eventually come away with a Super Bowl win." He looked at Nate. "What do you think?"

"Oh, I agree."

From that moment on, the conversation had completely shifted away from Ruby—exactly what she'd intended. She also noticed that Mama had glazed over with all that football talk. It took every ounce of self-restraint to keep from laughing.

~

The next evening, Antonio took another glance at the invitation before opening his laptop to respond. He wanted to go, mainly to see Ruby Wilson … and he wasn't even sure she'd be there.

Oh well. He'd take a chance and go. The only problem he could imagine was if Marla Sumrall showed up and decided to make another attempt to win him over. He liked Marla, and he certainly appreciated all the things she made for him, including all of the sweaters she'd knitted over the years. But the chemistry wasn't there for him. She worked in a hair salon next to her mother, but she still seemed to have the high school mindset he'd tried hard to shed, now that he was a successful businessman.

After high school, he managed to get through college on a needs based scholarship—making him the first person in his family to get a post-secondary education. Pop had told him he didn't need college to follow his footsteps in the restaurant business, but he wanted to do it anyway, if nothing else but to prove he could do it.

Now he was glad he'd done that because when Pop's boss lost his business to bankruptcy, he had the knowledge from his business management degree to pick up the restaurant for practically nothing and turn the business around. The Italian Eatery was now one of the most popular Italian restaurants in the Low Country. And he'd managed to open two more restaurants—one in Charleston and the other in Myrtle Beach. His hope was to eventually expand to other southern states, but for the time being, he was happy with what he'd done.

When he'd first purchased the restaurant in Plantersville, Marla came by at least once a week, bringing gifts she'd made. Pop started warning him as soon as he spotted her car pulling into the parking lot. So he'd made a quick dash out the back door so no one would have to lie about his not being there. Eventually, he stopped doing that, and he finally agreed to join her for dinner.

That was all she needed to be encouraged. It seemed as though every single week, she showed up with something new she'd baked, sewed, or knitted. He finally had to have a heart-to-heart with her, letting her know that although he appreciated everything, it had to end. She stopped coming around, and the only time he saw her after that was during one of the festivals on Main Street—usually from a distance.

And now he'd have to face her again if she decided to show up at the reunion. There was no reason to believe she wouldn't be there since she was so involved with everything at the school.

"Hey, Antonio." Pop slid into the chair across the table from him. "What's got you so worked up?" He pointed to the computer. "I read about people bullying folks on social media." He lifted an eyebrow. "Is that happening to you?"

Antonio smiled at his dad. "No, it's nothing like that. I was just thinking about the ten-year reunion."

"It's been ten years already? Seems like it was only yesterday your mom and I sat in the auditorium watching you walk up there in your cap and gown." He grinned and puffed out his chest. "We were so proud of our boy."

"Yeah, that was a proud day." He pressed the SEND button and shut the computer. "So did you finish that catering order for the Whitehall wedding?"

Pop brushed his hands together. "All done. That was an easy one. All they wanted was lasagna and salad."

"And bread and cannoli."

"Goes without saying." Pop chuckled. "I could've done all that with my eyes closed."

"I think it's going to be a slow night, so if you have someplace else you'd rather be—"

"Tuesday is always a slow night, but I like being here with you. Your mother said she might stop by for a bite to eat after she gets everything put away." His smile widened. "You know how your mother is after she goes shopping. She can't stand to leave everything in the bags. She has to pull everything out and admire it."

"I'm just glad she's able to shop."

Pop's smile faded. "That's only because you pay me so well."

"You earn every penny."

"I'd like to do more if you'd let me."

The door to the restaurant opened, and when he glanced up and saw that it was Ruby, he had to do a double take. This was only the second time he'd seen her here. She looked around the restaurant until she met his gaze. Then it took every ounce of strength to maintain his composure.

"You look like you just saw a ghost, son." Pop glanced over his shoulder. "Well, I'll be."

Chapter 2

It took every ounce of courage Ruby had to stop off at the Italian Eatery. She'd been there before with her parents, but it wasn't because she was brave. Mama was always craving their famous meatballs, and once she got a craving, there was no stopping her.

Her eyes had barely adjusted to the dim lighting when her gaze locked with Antonio's. Then everything else around them blurred and faded away. The sound of her own heartbeat echoed in her head as she tried to pull her eyes away, but she couldn't. The warmth of his smile drew her in … and this wasn't the first time.

Before she had a chance to turn and run, he got up and headed straight toward her, still smiling, still looking directly at her. The older man who'd been sitting across from him watched with narrowed eyes and a hint of a smile playing on his lips.

"Ruby, come on over and have a seat." Antonio glanced behind her. "Are you alone?"

She opened her mouth, but nothing came out, so she nodded. Now that she was here, she wasn't sure what to do.

"I hope you're hungry. Our special today is veal Parmesan … plus we have some fresh tiramisu."

Under any other circumstances, that would have sounded good, but Ruby doubted she'd be able to eat much. "I … um … I think I'll just have a salad."

"Perfect. I'll let the chef know to fix you our house antipasto salad. House dressing?"

She nodded. "Yes, please."

He stopped at a table and pulled out a chair. Once she was seated, he nodded toward her. "Be right back."

As Ruby sat and waited for Antonio to return, she wondered what she'd been thinking, coming in here alone. She hadn't planned to stop, but after passing the restaurant and wondering about Antonio and whether or not he'd be there at this time, she figured it would be interesting to find out. Ever since she clicked on the acceptance to go to the reunion, she couldn't get him out of her mind. So she did a U-turn and drove straight to the parking lot. She figured he'd either not be there or would be too busy to talk. The surprise was on her, though, when she walked in and saw that it wasn't very busy. She knew this was odd because most of the time, according to her parents, the place was packed, and there was at least a half hour wait if they didn't make reservations.

She looked around the room and noticed several small touches that added to the intimate ambience. The ornate sconces on the wall flickered with light against the rich wood-grain paneling. The exposed stained beams on the ceiling provided an extra layer of texture and detail. Antonio had once told her he'd be somebody important someday. To her, he already was, but now as she continued to let her gaze wander around the dining room, she realized he wanted something to show off. And now he had what he was looking for.

~

"I haven't seen you like this in a while, son." Pop came up from behind, talking the minute he was within hearing range. "Isn't that Ruby, the girl you introduced your mom and me to when you were still in school?"

Antonio nodded and allowed himself to smile. "The one and only."

"If I recall correctly, you were always sweet on her."

"I never told you that."

"You didn't have to. You said it with your eyes and the way your voice softened when you said her name." Pop stepped up beside him. "So what's she doing here?"

"Same thing everyone else is doing here. She came to have dinner."

"Then why are you so nervous?"

Antonio started to argue, but there was no point. Pop could see right through him. "It's special for her to be here."

"For her, it is." Pop placed a hand on his shoulder and smiled. "Why don't you sit down and have dinner with her?"

"I don't know …" Antonio glanced down. "She might not want me to."

"You can ask."

Antonio nodded. He knew better than to let on that he was worried about rejection. Pop had always said it's better to get rejected than to never try.

"Go on out there and ask her, son. Tell her you haven't eaten yet, and you'd love the honor of having dinner with her."

"That sounds kind of stuffy."

Pop leaned back and shook his head. "Girls like that kind of thing. It's sort of their image of what a dashing prince would say."

Now Antonio couldn't help but laugh. "Dashing prince, huh? What if she thinks I'm more of a toad?"

"You? Toad?" Pop snorted. "No way. If there ever was a dashing prince, that would be you." He lowered his voice. "Your mother and I always thought you were the closest thing to an Italian prince we'd ever see in this town."

"You could be biased."

"Of course I'm biased." Pop gestured toward the dining room. "Go on out there and ask if you can join her. I'll bring your order when it's ready."

Antonio hesitated and then nodded. Pop was right. If he didn't at least ask her a question, how would he ever know what she thought?

He turned and started toward the dining room, but when he got to the door, he noticed that she wasn't there. So he turned back around and walked over to Pop.

"She's gone."

"She's what?" Pop scrunched his face. "Why would she place an order and leave? That wouldn't be right."

"Go see for yourself."

"Okay, I think I will." With that, Pop went straight out to the dining room.

Antonio stood there with his arms crossed, waiting for him to return. But he didn't. So Antonio went and peeked around the corner and spotted her sitting there laughing at Pop who sat across the table from her. That was strange. But what would be even stranger was what Pop might be telling her.

Time to run interference. He didn't waste another second before going out to the dining room to save Ruby from whatever Pop was saying.

Both of them glanced up as he arrived at the table. Pop stood and gestured toward the chair. "Sit down, son. I'll bring your food when it's ready." He started to walk away.

"How do you know what I want?" Antonio said loud enough for Pop to hear.

"I don't think you much care right now. I'll bring you whatever the chef has ready."

Once Pop disappeared back into the kitchen, Antonio gave Ruby an apologetic smile. "Sorry about him. He's rather old school sometimes."

He chuckled. "And I'm not talking old-school American. When he does stuff like this, he tells me that's the way they did things back home. Who knows if he's telling the truth?"

She laughed as she lifted her water glass. "I think he's charming. He told me all about how you bought this place when it was on the brink of closing, and now it's making a killing."

"Pop told you that? He was only out here for a few minutes."

"That's not all he said."

A sense of dread washed over Antonio. "What else did he tell you?"

"He said you were going to the reunion."

That wasn't so bad. "I am. How about you?"

She licked her lips as she slowly nodded. "Yes, I plan to be there."

"Would you like to go with me?" He wanted to kick himself for speaking before thinking it through. "I mean, do you … um, do you have a date?"

~

Ruby wished she'd done a better job of stopping Mama when she arranged for her and Nate to go to the reunion together. From the moment she first laid eyes on Antonio, she'd wanted to get his attention. He might have asked her to go with him to the reunion because she was there, and it was convenient, but she would have loved to say yes. And she couldn't. She felt like she was in high school all over again, and her old insecurities bubbled over.

"I do …" She looked him in the eyes and instantly lowered her gaze. "I have a date. Sorry."

"Oh, that's okay. I'm sure we'll both have fun anyway."

She wanted to ask about Marla. Last Ruby had heard, Antonio was still seeing her and wearing sweaters she'd knit for him. In fact, her best friend since preschool, Charlene, had said she heard through the grapevine that Marla was hoping for a ring soon.

"I thought you were seeing Marla." The instant those words left Ruby's mouth, she felt like kicking herself.

"I was … I mean … yeah, I guess I am … sort of."

Ruby forced a smile. "I always admired her for her domestic talents. I never knew anyone who could knit like she did."

He nodded. "I still have most of the sweaters she made me."

"That's nice." She racked her brain, trying to think of something to say, but Antonio's father saved the moment as he came toward them carrying a tray filled with a variety of dishes.

"That is way too much food," Antonio argued.

Mr. Fontana grinned at Ruby. "He's always had a hearty appetite."

"Not that much of one."

"Then eat what you want, share some with this lovely lady, and leave the rest." Mr. Fontana began unloading the tray, placing everything on the table. "Enjoy. If you want anything else, son, you know where the kitchen is." And then he left.

Ruby leaned back, stared at the multitude of dishes on the table, and laughed. "I'm sure I'll find my salad somewhere around here."

"Yeah, I'm sure it's there somewhere." Antonio lifted a plate from the edge of the table, and after rearranging a few things, placed it in front of her. "Here ya go. And please help yourself to anything else that looks good. There's no way I'll ever be able to eat the rest of it." He shook his head. "I have no idea what Pop was thinking."

Ruby laughed again. "He wants to make sure we don't go hungry."

"I've never gone hungry." At first he laughed, but then he paused, and his tone grew more serious. "Even when I was growing up, Mom made sure we had good food. I knew we were struggling back then, but she somehow managed to put delicious meals on the table."

Ruby pondered that for a moment. She didn't remember there ever being a time when her family struggled, but Mama had never been the best cook. When she was younger, they hired kitchen help, but as she got older, the only domestic help they had was a once-a-week cleaning lady. And since Mama still didn't have many dishes in her culinary repertoire, they had a lot of salads, sandwiches, and canned soup. And they ate out quite a bit.

It wasn't until Ruby graduated from college and moved into her own apartment that she learned how to cook. It was rough going at first, but she learned from her mistakes and figured out how to make some decent meals.

She felt his gaze on her, so she glanced up. "This salad is good."

"Is that what you were thinking about?" He tilted his head and gave her a doubtful look.

"Um …" She couldn't lie. "Not really."

"Were you wondering how a poor guy from the wrong side of the tracks could wind up owning a small chain of restaurants?"

Her face flamed. "No. I wasn't thinking that at all."

Chapter 3

The instant those words left Antonio's mouth, he wanted to kick himself in the backside. He heard the bitterness in his own statement, so there was no doubt she did too.

"I'm so sorry. What was I thinking?" He paused and cleared his throat. "More important, what are you thinking?"

Her expression instantly appeared glazed. "It really doesn't matter, does it?"

"I think it does."

"No. You have some preconceived idea of what I'm thinking or who I am. It doesn't seem like you're the least bit interested in what or who I really am."

He hated the fact that he'd blurted his thoughts, but they were true. He didn't harbor any delusions that anyone who knew him before he left for college would think he deserved all he had. "No, I suppose it doesn't matter."

He'd lost his appetite, and now he wanted to run to the kitchen … to go cower somewhere and never show his face around her, ever again. But he couldn't do that … at least not in Plantersville.

Ruby had taken all of two bites of her salad, but she didn't bother pretending to be hungry anymore. She'd put down her fork and stared at the table.

"I'm sorry." There was nothing else he could say.

She blinked a couple of times before raising her gaze to his. "I'm going to the reunion with Nate, and I'm sure we'll have a wonderful time."

He managed a smile even though he'd prayed she was over that guy she used to date. "I didn't realize the two of you were still …" He swallowed hard. "I didn't know you were still an item."

"We're not." She lifted her napkin from her lap, blotted her lips, and placed it on the table beside her plate. "We're just going to the reunion together because our mothers thought that would be a good idea."

Of course they did. Antonio had heard that Mrs. Wilson and Mrs. Harwell had been sorority sisters in college, and that bond trumped everything. He thought about his own mom and wondered if Mrs. Wilson would ever bother getting to know her, even though she'd never stepped foot on a college campus before she visited Antonio when he moved into the dorm.

"I suppose it's time for me to leave now." Ruby placed her napkin beside her plate, stood, and put some money on the table. "Please let the chef know that I enjoyed the salad." And then she left before he could say another word or give her back her money.

~

Ruby couldn't get out of there fast enough. She willed herself not to run or cry, until she got to her car where she let the tears fall. This hadn't gone anything like she'd hoped.

But what did she expect? Antonio had always had a chip on his shoulder about status or class. Why did she bother thinking there could ever be anything different between them?

She didn't have to think too long to remember the moments when his shield had come down. Like when she was locked out of the school and needed to get something out of her locker. He'd been waiting outside for a ride from one of his friends when he glanced over and saw her pulling on the door. To this day, she had no idea how he did it, but within minutes, he was inside the school and holding the door open for her.

The look they exchanged would forever be etched on her heart. She even thought he looked like he wanted to kiss her. But he didn't. She thanked him and went home, wishing she'd been more creative and found a way to talk to him. That night she lay awake in bed thinking about how Antonio had saved her. He'd been her hero that day.

There were other times when he'd made her heart skip a few beats. Like when she wasn't paying attention and almost missed a step in the steep stairwell leading to the second floor. He'd reached out and effortlessly caught her, keeping her from tumbling down. When she looked up into his eyes, the smoldering gaze took her breath away. Or another time when she'd almost passed out on the football practice field while rehearsing for graduation. He miraculously appeared with a cup of water.

~

"What did you say to make her leave so abruptly?" Pop asked.

Antonio shrugged as he tried to pretend it was no big deal. "Nothing. She just decided she was finished, and it was time to leave."

"Don't lie to me, son." Pop tilted his head forward and glared at him from beneath his bushy salt-and-pepper eyebrows. "That would be rude, and she doesn't strike me as someone who would act so impulsively. Did you say something to upset her?"

"I … well …" Antonio rubbed the back of his neck as he pondered how much to tell Pop. He knew better than to lie, but he didn't want to tell everything, or he knew his parents would be furious. "Maybe I did say something."

"Okay, I'm waiting."

"You're gonna be mad." Antonio cast a wary glance at his father. "I didn't mean it in a disrespectful way, and it's no reflection on you."

Pop snorted. "That tells me what you said was disrespectful, and somehow it has something to do with me." He planted his fists on his hips and widened his stance. "Just tell me what you said."

Antonio sucked in a deep breath and relayed the conversation—at least as much as he could—to his father. As he spoke, Pop's face remained expressionless. Finally, he shook his head and took a step back. "I didn't mean it as bad as it sounded. It's just that Ruby will never understand what it's like to be us."

"That was very bad, Antonio."

"It's not that I don't appreciate all you did for us—"

"I'm not talking about bad for me. It reflects on you more than anyone else. Yes, I did work hard … still do. And there is absolutely no shame in what we did or what we had. Your mother and I both did everything in our power to make sure you had a nice home. The problem I see is that you didn't appreciate it."

"Oh, but I did."

"Doesn't sound like it to me. You need to apologize."

"I'm really sorry, Pop."

"Not to me, Antonio. Apologize to Ruby. I believe she sees what's real, and I have a feeling she understands more than you realize. You're the one with the head in the cloud."

"But she's always had everything handed to her."

"And how would you know that? Did she tell you she gets everything she wants?"

"No." Antonio pondered Pop's question. "Have you seen where she lives?"

"Do you mean where her parents live?"

"Yes, sir."

"I shouldn't have to do this, but I'm going to answer your question.

I haven't seen where her parents live, but that has nothing to do with who she is in here." Pop made a fist and tapped his chest. "I'm sure her parents provided well for her, just as your mother and I did for you. Maybe they live in a bigger house in a fancy neighborhood, but they didn't have anything we didn't have … that is, anything of importance."

Antonio looked down at the floor. He knew his father's words were sincere and from the heart, but he still didn't understand what it was like to be the poor kid wanting approval from his classmates.

"You had all the love you needed, more than enough food to keep you healthy, and now you have a good education."

Antonio slowly nodded as he finally met Pop's gaze again. "And a great business that is growing."

"Don't forget about your wonderful pop who works hard for you."

"I'll never forget about you, Pop." Antonio opened his arms, and his father came toward him, pulling him to his chest. "I really am sorry for acting so …" He grimaced as he looked at his father.

"Like such a brat?" Pop chuckled. "I forgive you, but that doesn't let you off the hook with Ruby. She's the one you owe an apology to."

"But—"

Pop held up a hand to stop him. "No excuses. You need to apologize to this girl and invite her back as your guest."

"You're right. I'll do that sometime this week."

"Now that that's settled, are you going to bring a date to the reunion?"

"I don't know." Antonio was tempted to skip the reunion so he wouldn't have to face Ruby any more than he needed to. But he knew Pop would argue that he shouldn't let what happened change his plans. "Maybe I'll see if Marla wants to go."

Pop frowned. "You know how your mother and I feel about Marla. She's a sweet girl … sometimes, even though she's also rather … um … immature and aggressive. But you also know how we feel about you stringing her along. If you can't see yourself in a more … um … permanent relationship with her, it's time to let her go find someone who appreciates what she has to offer."

"I know. It's just that—"

"It's just that she's always there for you." Pop shook his head. "Don't take advantage of that girl's affection."

"You're right."

"I know I am." Pop glanced at his watch. "It's almost quitting time for me, and I promised your mother I'd bring her some rigatoni."

"Then you'd better do it. I don't want to make Mom mad too. It's bad enough that I angered you."

"Oh, I'm not mad. Just disappointed." Pop gave him a quick wink. "But you'll do the right thing and come out of this situation just fine."

After Pop left him standing there, Antonio wished he could be as sure of himself as Pop was. Apologizing to Ruby wouldn't be an easy task—especially since he'd hidden behind prideful arrogance since the first time they'd interacted.

He remembered the time he'd forgotten the sandwich Mom had packed, so he went without lunch. Ruby saw him sitting with his friends, all of them with food, while he sat and watched. She walked to his table, leaned over, and whispered that she could lend him the money for lunch. He'd leaned back and laughed at her, saying he didn't need her charity and that he was fasting for an Italian holiday. Of course, that holiday didn't exist, but he figured she wouldn't know that.

Another time he remembered was when she stood outside in the freezing rain, shivering and waiting for her ride. He'd taken off his jacket, walked up to her, and draped it over her shoulders. That was when he noticed how ratty it looked next to her pristine outfit, so he grabbed it back and took off. He cringed as he remembered the look on her face before he turned away from her. At first, he tried to rationalize that it was a mocking expression, but now he was pretty sure it was one of confusion.

The rest of the evening was pretty slow, which was typical for a Tuesday night. That was fine, though, because the rest of the week they were booked with reservations, and it was nice to have some down time.

He got up early the next morning, poured himself a cup of coffee, and sat down at his computer. The first thing he did was offer to bring something from the restaurant to the reunion to help defray some of the costs. Then he composed an email to Ruby to ask if he could call her later. After he wrote it, he sat and stared at his computer screen for several minutes before he finally hit SEND. Then he jotted a quick note to Marla, asking her if he could talk to her soon about something important that was long overdue. After he sent that, he got up, popped some bread in the toaster, and scrambled a couple of eggs. At least his day had gotten off to a productive start.

Chapter 4

Ruby's students were taking a test, so she used this opportunity to read her email. When she saw Antonio's name, she paused before clicking on it.

After she read his message, she was torn about what to do. She'd already decided she never wanted to see him again—at least not up close and personal. There was no avoiding him with both of them living in the same small town or going to the same reunion. But an occasional wave from across a parking lot or even at the reunion was quite different from agreeing to *see* him again.

She'd have to think about this before replying. A shadow from the classroom door caught her attention. It was Deanna Spears, who taught in the class next to hers. Ruby got up and walked over to the door.

"Just wanted to check and see if you're interested in hanging out after school."

"Sure, sounds good. What are you thinking about doing?"

Deanna lifted a shoulder and let it drop. "I don't know. Maybe stop off at the craft store and then find a place where we can sit down and have dinner in peace."

"I've never been much of a crafty person, but I can tag along with you."

"To be honest, I'm not much into crafts either, but my sister is coming to town in a couple of weeks, so I figured I'd get her kids some crafts to do while they're here."

"Sounds good." Ruby glanced over her shoulder to check on her class and then turned back around. "See you later."

The rest of the afternoon went by without incident, so after she finished posting information to the kids' files, she grabbed her handbag and went to Deanna's classroom. "Ready?" Deanna said.

Ruby nodded. "Why don't I follow you to your place, and you can leave your car there."

Fifteen minutes later, they were both in Ruby's car, on their way to the craft store. Deanna pulled a slip of paper out of her handbag. "I have crayons, sketch paper, and beading supplies. Any other ideas for a couple of girls—one eight and one six?"

"I have no idea. Why don't we just walk around and see what they have?"

"That's what I was thinking."

As soon as they walked into the massive store, they took a quick glance around and then looked at each other with wide eyes. "This place is monstrous," Deanna said. "I don't even know where to begin."

"How about over there?" Ruby pointed toward the left, where there appeared to be rows and rows of beads.

They walked up and down each aisle, pulling strings and bags of beads off the shelf and dropping them into the cart. When they got to the end of it, Deanna pointed toward a woman sitting at a table in front of the yarn section. "Looks like she's doing a knitting demonstration."

An image of one of the sweaters Marla knitted for Antonio popped into Ruby's mind. "Let's go see how she does it."

"Sure, why not?"

They walked up to the table where only a couple other women were watching the woman demonstrate how to cast the yarn onto the hook. Ruby leaned toward Deanna and whispered, "That doesn't look too hard."

"I don't think it is. Both of my sisters started knitting when they first got married, so it can't be too difficult."

As she watched the demonstration go from putting yarn on the hook to knitting several rows of a basic stitch, she decided that was something she wanted to try. "I think I'll pick up a few things of yarn and some knitting needles while we're here."

Deanna made a face and laughed. "You're kidding, right? I totally can't see you sitting still long enough to knit."

"I can do it." The other women had backed away from the demonstrator's table, so Ruby approached the lady. "What all do I need to get started?"

"C'mon, dear, let me show you." The woman stood up and walked over toward the section with the knitting needles. "Why don't you start with this small multi-pack? It's an economical set that provides three different sizes of needles."

"Okay." Ruby took one of the packs. "Now I need to get some

yarn." She glanced around and got a little dizzy from the vast assortment of choices.

"What do you plan to knit?"

Ruby shrugged. "I have no idea. I just want to start with something super easy."

"Then how about a scarf? There's nothing complicated about that."

"Okay."

"You'll want to get something soft." The woman led her around the corner. "Any idea what color you'd like to work with?"

"Blue?" Ruby remembered seeing Antonio wearing a lot of blue.

The woman waved her hand toward the blue yarns. "Take your pick."

Ruby looked around before pulling out a sky-blue yarn. "This one looks good."

"Why don't you get two skeins so you can make a hat to go with it?"

"Skeins?"

The woman smiled as she nodded. "Yes, that's what we call the bundle of yarn."

"Okay." Ruby looked at one of the knitted hats on display and then turned back to the woman. "I'm not sure I can make a hat."

"It's not that hard. I can send you home with some basic instructions, and if you have any questions, you can call or stop by, and I can help you work through whatever you need."

Deanna nudged her. "Or you can watch a YouTube video."

Ruby nodded. "True." She paused for a moment, glancing at the yarn and trying to imagine it turning into a scarf and hat. Antonio's image popped into her head again, and that was when she decided she'd give it a try.

"I can't wait to see what you wind up with."

"If the scarf and hat turn out, who knows? Maybe I'll try a sweater next." Ruby smiled. "Wouldn't that be something?"

Deanna chuckled. "That'll be something, all right. I'm just not sure what."

"Can you imagine a closet full of sweaters I knitted myself?"

"You want the truth?" Deanna waited a couple of seconds. "Not really."

"You might be surprised. If I get good enough, I might even knit for friends." Ruby had never done anything like this before, but everything else she tried, she had at least some degree of success. She didn't see why it would be any different with knitting. "Besides, how hard can it be? Millions of people knit."

"True." Deanna offered a comforting smile that Ruby had always appreciated. "And if you like it, maybe you can show me how."

"Why don't you try it with me?"

Deanna shook her head. "I have enough going on in my life right now. I don't need to add something else."

After they had everything they needed and paid for it, they sat in the car to decide where to go for dinner. "It's not like we have a lot of choices in Plantersville … or we could drive to Charleston."

"I'm not in the mood to drive far."

Deanna tapped her chin, and then her eyes lit up. "How about the Italian Eatery? They have the best veal."

Ruby opened her mouth to say she'd rather go somewhere else, but she quickly closed it because she didn't feel like explaining her feelings to Deanna. She glanced out the window to gather her thoughts.

"What's the matter? I know you like Italian food. Are you not in the mood for it?"

"No, that's fine. We can go there."

"Okay, if you're sure you're okay with it …" Deanna continued looking at her with an expression of concern.

"Oh, I'm totally fine with it. They do have good veal, but I think I'll probably go for the lasagna." Ruby knew that putting more emphasis on the food would get Deanna's mind off her reaction.

"Yeah, that sounds good too."

Ruby drove slowly to the restaurant, hoping Deanna wouldn't notice. And as Deanna chattered about what went on in her class that day, Ruby let her mind wander to Antonio. She had mixed feelings about seeing him and prayed he wouldn't be there. As upset as she was last time, she wished more time had passed. But she knew there would still be an attraction that she couldn't deny or let go of that fast.

"I cannot wait to chow down." Deanna led the way to the front door. "Did I ever tell you that this is my favorite restaurant? I've heard that the owner took this place from failing to success in a matter of months."

Ruby didn't say anything since she knew quite a bit about the success story. She'd never doubted that Antonio would be successful someday, and she often wondered if he realized that.

A man Ruby had never seen before greeted them at the door, led them to a table, and handed them each a menu. He told them about the specials before going to get their water.

"Even the people who work here are top-notch." Deanna leaned toward her. "Have you ever seen the owner? He's totally the whole package—good looking, charming, and obviously rich." She giggled. "Oh, did I mention how good looking he is?"

Ruby managed a half smile and nodded. "Yes, I believe you did."

"Anyway, I heard he was dating someone from high school, and they're practically engaged. Too bad, or I'd find a way to get his attention." Deanna's eyes widened as she glanced at something behind Ruby. "Oh man, I can't believe this. He's coming this way."

"Who?" Ruby glanced over her shoulder in time to see Antonio walking toward them. She wanted to crawl under the table, but that would be too obvious. Instead, she took a deep breath, blew it out, and took a sip of water.

"Well, hello there, Ruby. I'm a little surprised to see you here, but I'm glad you came. I want to apologize for what I said the other day."

Ruby felt Deanna's gaze boring through her as Antonio stood there, waiting. "That's okay. Don't worry about it."

"No, I want to make it up to you. Whatever you and your friend order is on the house."

"You don't have to—" Ruby began.

"I know I don't have to, but I want to. It's the least I can do." Antonio turned toward Deanna and extended his hand. "I'm Antonio Fontana."

"Um …" Deanna's bottom lip twitched, letting Ruby know how flustered she was. "My name's Deanna Spears, and I teach school with Ruby."

His smile widened, making the corners of his eyes crinkle. "If my teachers looked half as good as the two of you, I'm sure I would have done much better in class."

"Thank you." Even though the lighting was dim in the restaurant, Ruby knew Deanna's face must be tomato red.

"If you ladies know what you want, I can take your order now."

After he took their orders and left, Deanna leaned toward Ruby and glared at her. "Why didn't you tell me you knew him? Now you have to tell me all about this Antonio guy. How did you meet him, and is it true about him and his girlfriend?"

Ruby took a deep breath before talking so she could have time to think about each word. What she didn't want to do was overreact, but that was hard, considering how she'd felt about Antonio for so long.

"Well?" Deanna leaned closer. "Do tell."

"I've known Antonio since high school. As for his girlfriend, he's been dating the same girl since then, but I don't know anything about an engagement."

"Maybe there's hope for me …" Deanna narrowed her eyes and scrunched her forehead. "Uh oh. Don't tell me there's something going on between you and him."

"Okay, I won't because there isn't."

"Whew. The look on your face had me worried."

Ruby managed a smile as she changed the subject. "I'm excited about starting my knitting project. I just hope I can remember how to put the yarn on the needle."

"Like I said, you can watch a YouTube video." Deanna glanced behind Ruby and smiled as she lowered her voice. "Here comes Mr. Gorgeous."

Antonio placed a couple of salads on the table and gestured toward one of the empty chairs. "Mind if I join you ladies for a few minutes?"

Ruby's heart sank. She worried that she wouldn't be able to hide her feelings if he hung around too long.

"Be our guest." Deanna pointed to the chair next to her. "We were just talking about Ruby's knitting project."

A look of surprise came over him. "I didn't know you were a knitter."

Ruby swallowed hard. "I'm not yet."

"But she will be," Deanna said. "We watched some lady do a demonstration, and she decided she wanted to give it a try." She smiled at Ruby before turning back to Antonio. "She said after she practices on a scarf and hat, she wants to make a sweater."

Ruby wanted to crawl under the table. "I'm not sure—"

Antonio's face lit up. "A sweater, huh?"

"That's only if I don't mess up with the scarf and hat." Ruby's voice cracked.

Deanna laughed. "You have to admit, it's pretty ambitious for someone who's never picked up a knitting needle before today."

"Maybe not." Antonio held her gaze. "Ruby has been good at everything she's ever tried, and I'm sure this will be no exception."

Deanna tilted her head. "Would you wear the first sweater Ruby knits?"

Antonio slowly nodded. "Yes, I absolutely would."

Chapter 5

Antonio saw the look on Ruby's face and wished he could talk to her alone. He didn't want to say or do anything that might embarrass her in front of her friend.

Deanna's face lit up with amusement. "Wonderful! We'll have to have a fashion show. Ruby, you can wear the scarf, I get the hat, and Antonio can wear the sweater."

Antonio leaned back and folded his arms, meeting Deanna's expression with one of his own. "And where will this fashion show be held?"

"Why not right here?" She placed her forearms on the table and leaned toward him. "We can launch Ruby's knit collection right here in the restaurant."

Was she flirting with him? That was the last thing he needed at the moment, so he turned his attention to Ruby.

"What are you thinking?" He paused. "Are you up for a fashion show?"

Her lips momentarily tightened into a straight line as she looked down and then back up to meet his gaze. "This sounds a bit silly to me."

He held her gaze for several seconds, until he feared she might bolt. "We're just having a little fun, but I want you to know that I'll wear anything you make for me."

Her lips parted, but she quickly closed them. He glanced at her friend. Deanna didn't say a word. Instead, she remained quiet as she looked back and forth between Ruby and him. He could tell she knew something was happening, but he doubted she had any idea what it was.

He pushed his chair back and stood. "If you ladies will excuse me, I'll go check on your order."

~

Deanna didn't waste a second after Antonio got up. "Why didn't you tell me you had a history with this guy?"

"Because I don't."

"Ruby, honey, I'd have to be blind to miss the fact that this guy is crazy about you, and you have something going on that I can't figure out yet … but I suspect there are some deep feelings in there somewhere."

"I don't know about that."

"You might be fighting it, but it's obviously there. When did it start? Back in high school?"

"He dated Marla Sumrall when we were in high school, and I … well, I went to prom with Nate."

Deanna tilted her head back and laughed. "Seriously? You don't have to date someone to harbor feelings for him." She shook her head. "And to think I was going on and on about how handsome I thought he was and that I—" She covered her lips with her fingertips. "You know I'd never try to come between you and whatever you have going on with him."

"I don't have anything going on with him." Ruby now regretted not driving to Charleston for dinner. "If you like him, go for it."

"No way. I'm taking a step back, and you …" She tilted her head as she started to grin. "You're going to come back here and have a talk with this guy. Y'all have some unfinished business that needs to be resolved."

"Not really." Ruby forced herself to look Deanna in the eyes, but the scrutiny proved to be too much, so she looked down at the napkin she'd been nervously rubbing.

"Really. And you can't convince me otherwise." Deanna leaned closer. "Here he comes with the food."

~

After Ruby and her friend left, Antonio leaned against the counter by the beverage station and pondered what had just happened. First, he wondered why they chose to have dinner at his restaurant. Second, he tried to imagine Ruby Wilson with a pair of knitting needles in her hand and a ball of yarn by her side. That brought a quick smile to his face because it didn't fit his image of her. And third, he wondered what Ruby's friend thought about him.

"Did they leave yet?"

Antonio turned around at the sound of Pop's voice. "Yes, they left."

"I hope you appreciate that I didn't embarrass you."

"You embarrass me?" Antonio shook his head. "You've never embarrassed me."

"Never? Not even when I picked you up from school in that old beat-up car I used to drive?"

"Not even then." Antonio loved his parents, even though he knew they didn't fit in with many of his classmates' families. "In fact, I'm proud of you and Mom."

"What's there to be proud of?" Pop looked uncomfortable as he always did when someone paid him a compliment. "I was nothing but a working stiff all my life."

"That's why I'm so proud of you. In spite of the fact that nothing came easy for you and Mom, you held your head up and did what you had to do to put food on the table. And Mom …" Antonio grinned. "She's the first girl I ever loved."

"Well, we're both mighty proud of you, son. We always knew you'd amount to something, but even in our wildest dreams, we never imagined this." He gestured around the room. "When I first came to work here when you were a little boy, it bugged me that it was so worn down. But I kept my head down and did my job. There's no telling where I'd be if you hadn't come along and saved the place."

"You would have found a job … maybe even a better one."

"There's no job better than one where I get to work with family. Even your Mom likes coming here to help out when you let her."

"I'll let her come whenever she wants. But I also know she likes having a little time to herself."

Pop gave a clipped nod. "She always has been a homebody and doing things around the house."

"Speaking of doing things around the house, you'll never guess what Ruby's about to start doing."

"Then you'd better tell me."

"She's taking up knitting."

"Knitting?" Pop made a face. "What on earth for?"

Antonio shrugged. "She and her friend went to the craft store before they came here, and some lady was doing a knitting demonstration."

"Do you think you … or Marla might have anything to do with it?"

"Why would Marla or I have something to do with it?"

"I don't know. Maybe she thinks that's the way to your heart, since you dated a girl who was constantly showering you with things she knitted."

That was something Antonio hadn't considered. Even if that wasn't the case, it made him smile. "Interesting thought, but I doubt it."

"I'm serious, son. I've been around that girl enough to know she has way more pride than is good for her. I don't think she realizes that's what she's doing."

"Ruby is a smart woman," Antonio countered.

"Oh, I never said she wasn't smart. What I'm saying is she doesn't know her heart." Pop paused and narrowed his eyes. "Sound familiar?"

"So you're saying I don't know my own heart?"

Pop laughed as he nodded. "Yep, you nailed it. That's exactly what I'm saying."

Antonio rubbed the back of his neck. "I don't know about any of this. It's so confusing."

"Welcome to the world of romance. Anyone who's been in love knows it's more complicated than rocket science or brain surgery."

"Who said I was in love?"

Pop's lips tilted into a smirk. "Who says you're not?"

~

The next morning, Ruby arrived at the school an hour early to prepare for the next series of lessons. She hadn't been there more than five minutes when Deanna showed up at her classroom door.

"Got a minute?" Deanna asked.

Ruby smiled. "That's about all I have. What's up?"

"I just wanted to say that I learned more about you last night than the past five years we've been teaching together."

"Oh?"

Deanna walked closer. "I never realized until we were having dinner that you never talk about your past, other than stuff related to your family."

Ruby shrugged. "That's because there's not much to say."

"Oh, but I think there is … a lot more."

Before Ruby could say another word, Deanna backed toward the door. She paused momentarily, waved, and disappeared around the corner.

It took a while to wrap her mind back around her lessons, but she managed to get through the afternoon without too much trouble. But when she spotted Deanna in the parking lot at the end of the day, she was torn between avoiding her friend and confronting the situation head-on. Her choice was made when Deanna ran toward her.

"I want you to know that I'm not going to bug you about your love life, but if you ever want to talk, I'm all ears."

Ruby was surprised. Deanna was always the friend who wanted information, and until now, she never let up until she got it.

"Thanks."

Deanna tilted her head and grinned. "So do you feel like talking now?"

Laughter escaped Ruby's throat. Deanna had a kind heart, and it sounded like she was seriously trying to be a good friend, but she couldn't help herself. She was just being Deanna. "There's really nothing to talk about."

"C'mon, Ruby, you know you can trust me. Maybe if you get your feelings off your chest, you'll feel better."

"Who said I don't feel great?"

Deanna rolled her eyes. "Okay, what I should have said is *I'll* feel better." She tilted her head and gave a puppy dog look. "Please?"

"Okay, we can talk. Why don't you follow me to my place?"

"Are you sure you don't mind?"

Ruby knew better than to tell her what she was really thinking. "I'll see you in a few minutes."

As soon as they walked into Ruby's apartment a few minutes later, Deanna spotted Ruby's knitting project on the end table. "Wow! You didn't waste any time, did you?" She picked it up and inspected it.

"Be careful. It's easy to lose the stitches."

"This is amazing. How did you remember how to do this? We just watched that lady for a few minutes."

Ruby pointed to her laptop beside the yarn. "YouTube, remember?"

"Oh yeah. Is this the scarf?"

"Either that or a very long hat." Ruby took it from Deanna and set it back on the table. "It took me forever to get that much done, and I don't want it to unravel."

"You'll probably have it finished in a few days. Don't forget to bring it to school and let me see it before you give it to Antonio."

Ruby let out a groan. "Who said I was giving it to Antonio?"

"Well …" Deanna shrugged. "I assumed … but I guess I shouldn't be doing that, should I?"

"No, you absolutely shouldn't." Ruby gestured for Deanna to follow her to the kitchen. "C'mon, I'll fix you some tea."

As they sat at the small table sipping their tea, Ruby's thoughts kept drifting back to Antonio and how Deanna had let it slip that she was taking up knitting. Deanna did most of the talking, and then she stopped, stared at Ruby for a few seconds, and then started laughing.

"What?"

Deanna shook her head. "You haven't been listening to a word I said, have you?"

"Sorry."

"I understand. If I had a lifetime crush on someone who clearly felt the same way, I'd be off on Cloud Nine too."

"Lifetime crush?" Ruby made a face and shook her head. "I don't think so."

Deanna pushed away from the table, stood, and carried her cup to the sink. "Okay, so you're still in denial. I totally get it."

"I'm not—" Ruby stopped herself since she realized there was no point in arguing about something that didn't matter anyway. "He's still seeing Marla, so it's a moot point."

Deanna leaned against the kitchen counter, folded her arms, and grinned at Ruby. "Maybe he's just seeing this Marla you keep talking about because he doesn't think he can have you."

"You've been reading too many romance novels. That kind of stuff doesn't happen in real life."

"I beg to differ, but I can tell you're not ready to deal with your feelings about Antonio."

Ruby sighed. There was no point in going on and on about how she didn't have a crush on Antonio. In fact, she suspected the more she denied it the less believable she seemed to Deanna. Even if she did daydream about him, she needed to keep it to herself. Her feelings were nothing but that—feelings. Acting on them would serve no purpose but to frustrate her and embarrass anyone else around her.

"I reckon it's time for me to leave. I just wanted to give you a chance to unload, but that was a bust." Deanna gave her a big smile. "That's fine. When you're ready, I'll be here for you."

"Thanks." Ruby walked her friend to the door, where they said their goodbyes. Once Deanna was inside her car, Ruby closed the door and leaned against it.

Now that she was alone, she was free to let her thoughts wander. And now that she could ponder her feelings for Antonio, she knew that not a day had gone by that she didn't think about him.

Chapter 6

Antonio stood in the restaurant kitchen, trying his best to psyche himself into being ready to face Marla who'd just entered the dining area. He'd avoided her ever since the reunion invitations went out, but he knew he couldn't continue doing that, which was why he'd asked to talk to her. And now he regretted it.

"You'd better go out there and tell that sweet young lady you don't want to go with her." Pop placed his hand on his shoulder and gave him a gentle shove toward the door, until Antonio resisted.

"Easier said than done."

"I know, but you can't keep stringing her along."

"Shouldn't she know by now that I'm not interested?"

"You'd think, but sometimes infatuation can be blinding." Pop smiled. "Just tell her. It's like ripping off a bandage. It hurts like the dickens at first, but once you toss it in the trash can, you know you did the right thing."

"Toss it in the trash can?" Antonio cringed. "I don't want her to think—"

"You know I didn't mean it that way. All I'm saying is that the sooner you tell her the better it will be. Just think. If you'd done it last year or the year before, she would have had time to move on."

"But I didn't."

"Remember, son, that another year will go by, regardless of what you do. If you tell her, this time next year you and Marla will be able to look back and laugh about it …" Pop paused and rubbed his chin. "Well, maybe not laugh about it, but you would have done the right thing so both of you can move on."

"Okay, I'll tell her."

"Why don't you take the table over in the corner, and I'll make sure no one is seated at any of the nearby tables."

"Thanks, Pop." Antonio sucked in a deep breath, rotated his shoulders a few times, and headed out toward Marla who was being seated.

Her face lit up when she saw him. "I was so happy you wanted to see me." She gave him a shy grin. "I brought you something."

A feeling of dread washed over him. She was clearly not going to make this easy for him.

She reached into a bag and pulled out a gray sweater. "I had a hard time finding this yarn, and it wasn't the easiest to work with." She held it up for him to look at. "I have to admit it took forever to knit, and if I didn't have the experience, I never would have been able to finish it."

He glanced at it but didn't take it, even when she held it out toward him. "Marla, I really appreciate all the work you put into it." He swallowed hard. "I really do. But—"

Her eyebrows shot up. "You don't like the color? I knew I should have shown it to you before I started knitting." She waved her hands around, showing off her fresh manicure with the incredibly long fingernails, making him wonder how on earth she managed to be such a prolific knitter. "Oh, never mind. I'll just make you another one. What color do you want?"

"No, it's not that. The color is perfect."

"Then what's the problem?" Her forehead scrunched up. "You don't like the design?"

"The design is good too."

She dropped the sweater into her lap. "But I don't understand. What is it you don't like about it?"

"I like the sweater just fine." He closed his eyes and took another breath. When he opened his eyes, he saw her looking at him from narrowed eyes. "It's just that I don't think …" He cleared his throat. "I like you just fine and all, but I don't see us as …" He glanced away before turning back to her. "I don't think of us as anything more than friends."

Her expression became extremely pinched as she tightened her jaw. The silence nearly drove him batty.

Finally, she managed a smile. "That's all we ever were, isn't it?" Her lips quivered, and she coughed. "I mean, you're a nice guy and everything, and I like knitting, so I thought it would be fun to make stuff for you." She reached down and gripped the sweater. "And I thought you liked what I made."

"Oh, I absolutely do."

"Do you want it or not?" Her voice quivered, showing emotion she was clearly trying to hide.

Antonio didn't know how to answer, and he felt awful. The sweater wasn't something he would have chosen if he'd gone out looking for something, but she had put quite a bit of time into it.

She widened her eyes and bobbed her head. "Well?"

"It's a very nice sweater."

"But?"

Now he felt as though he had no choice but to accept the gift … the very extravagant gift. "I would love to have it."

She dropped the sweater back into the bag, and using her feet, she moved it toward him. "Then take it."

"So what would you like to have for dinner? It's on the house."

She stood so quickly she bumped the table and caused her water glass to tip over and splash all down the front of his trousers. "Oops. Sorry." She shrugged. "I'm not really hungry. You said you wanted to see me. I was busy, but I figured it wouldn't hurt to stop off and bring you the sweater."

He lifted a hand to summon one of the bussers. "Are you sure?"

"Positive. In fact …" She made a big issue of looking at her watch. "I have to be somewhere in just a few minutes. If you don't mind, I'll just leave now."

Before he had a chance to say a word, she darted toward the door and left. Pop showed up a few seconds later.

"What was that all about?" He looked at the mess the busser was sopping up with some big towels. "Don't tell me she threw her water at you."

"No, it was an accident." It would almost have been better if she'd thrown it at him. "I feel horrible."

"So she didn't take your news very well."

"No," Antonio said. "She took it just fine … maybe even too fine. She said all we ever were was friends, nothing else."

Pop chuckled. "Did she put it like that?"

"Not exactly, but close enough."

"Well, it's done. You might think she took it well and that this …" Pop gestured around at the mess. "That this was an accident. But trust me, it wasn't. She had to do something to let out her frustration and maybe even her embarrassment." He looked down at the bag. "What's that?"

"A sweater she knitted."

"Oh wow. I'm surprised she didn't take it with her."

Antonio shrugged. He didn't know what to say now, and the guilt over what he'd done was so intense he couldn't quite think straight.

"You doing okay?"

Antonio shrugged. "Not really."

"Then go on home. I can close up for you tonight. There's really nothing you can do here that I can't take care of for you."

Normally, that would be out of the question, but Antonio wanted to be alone with his thoughts. "Thanks, Pop."

~

Ruby had mixed feelings about going to the reunion now. She was excited about seeing everyone—especially those who'd moved away and were returning just for the event. But it sure would be awkward to see Antonio and Marla.

Friday during lunch, Deanna offered to let her borrow something to wear to the big dinner on the last night. "I have all these cute cocktail dresses that I've only worn once and will probably never wear again."

"I don't know," Ruby told her. "I hate borrowing clothes. What if I spill something on it?"

Deanna shrugged it off. "You can have it cleaned. Most of what I have was from the clearance rack, so I'm not too worried about it."

One of the other teachers gave her an incredulous look. "She's offering you the free use of a dress. It's not like you're making a killing as a teacher."

Another teacher nodded. "Yeah, you need to jump on that offer."

Deanna smiled at the other teachers and turned back to Ruby. "See? They agree with me."

"Well, maybe …"

"Tell you what. Why don't you come over tonight and see if there's anything you like? If you don't like what I have, it won't hurt my feelings. In fact, I'll even go shopping with you to help you find something. How about it? Will you at least take a look at my stuff?"

"Are you sure?"

"Positive. I think it'll be fun to have you try stuff on. We can order a pizza and make a night of it."

Ruby finally nodded. "All right, sounds good."

"So the pizza sold you, huh?" Deanna teased. "I figured that might do the trick."

After school, Ruby went home and changed into some comfortable clothes before heading over to Deanna's place. As soon as she walked inside, she was accosted by the vision of at least a dozen dresses draped over the sofa and chairs.

"I pulled out what I thought you might like," Deanna explained. "There's more if you don't like these."

Ruby glanced around at the colorful offerings. "There's not a single black dress in the bunch."

"Don't tell me you want to wear black to your high school reunion."

"What's wrong with black? It's classic."

Deanna rolled her eyes. "That's what everyone else will be wearing because they couldn't manage to stay on their diets and lose the weight."

"I'm not exactly skinny."

"No, but that doesn't really matter, does it? You look fabulous just as you are, and you don't need to be hiding behind a black dress."

"But—"

Deanna picked up a bright red dress with an off-shoulder neckline. "I think this will look amazing on you."

"You're kidding, right? I'll stick out if I wear that."

"I know, right?" Deanna held the dress up to Ruby. "And that's the whole point. Plus it goes with your name." She put it down and moved on to a turquoise dress. "This one will look good with your coloring."

"Okay, I'll try both of those on."

"Try them all on. And if you want, you can take a couple of them." She gave a sly grin. "I just happen to know there's more than one event, so you'll need a couple of outfits."

Ruby picked up the red dress first. "I'll start with this one."

"Take the other one, and I'll start looking for some accessories."

"I can't—"

"Yes, you can, and you will." Deanna grinned as she shoved the turquoise dressed toward her.

As Ruby went into the second bedroom to try on the dresses, she thought about how she had never been comfortable borrowing clothes from anyone—including people like Deanna who had more than she'd ever be able to wear more than once in a lifetime.

She slipped out of her work clothes and into the red silk dress. Even before she turned around and looked in the full-length mirror, she knew it was a perfect fit.

"Do you have it on yet?" Deanna hollered. "Don't take it off before I have a chance to see it."

Ruby swallowed hard as she gazed at herself in the mirror. This dress was unlike anything she'd ever worn, but she liked it. "Okay, you can come in now."

Deanna opened the door, and as she gave Ruby a once-over, her chin dropped. "That dress looks like it was made for you. You have to wear it to the big event." She walked around Ruby and laughed. "It never looked that good on me."

"I'm sure it did."

"No, red isn't my color, but it sure is yours. Now take it off and try the other dress. You'll need something for the night before."

"We're having a bonfire the night before."

"Oh, then you won't want to wear a dress."

"I have some new jeans."

Deanna nodded and lifted her eyebrows. "And I have the perfect top for you." She disappeared and came back holding an off-shoulder tunic in swirling shades of red, turquoise, black, and white.

"I don't know about that. It might be a bit too …"

"Colorful?" Deanna asked.

"Yeah, I'll stand out like a—"

"Like the beautiful woman you are. Stop trying to melt into the background."

"But—" Ruby stopped herself. She'd grown up buying clothes from all the ultra conservative stores Mama shopped at. Not only did she rarely wear prints, she couldn't remember ever having a top that bared the shoulders.

"I'll leave you alone to put it on. Don't forget to let me see it."

After Deanna left the room, Ruby stood and stared at the top. Finally, she figured she might as well get it over with. Surely Deanna would see that it wasn't her style. She took it off the hanger and pulled it over her head.

Instead of looking in the mirror, she flung open the door so Deanna could have a good laugh. But that wasn't what she saw. Instead, Deanna's eyes widened so big it looked like they might pop right out of her head. "Girl, if you wear that, you'll slay the entire male population of your graduating class."

Chapter 7

Antonio couldn't believe how quickly time flew. He'd thrown himself even more deeply into his work, which was the only way he could keep his mind off of Ruby.

Every now and then, he thought he saw her out of the corner of his eye. But when he looked directly at whoever it was, he was disappointed.

A couple of days before the reunion started, Marla made an appearance. She walked into the restaurant, said something to the maître d', and glanced over at him. Once they made eye contact, he knew he couldn't avoid her, so he decided to confront the situation and see what she wanted.

"Hey, Antonio, I wanted to stop by and apologize. I know I'll be seeing you in a few days, and …" She grimaced and then offered a hint of a smile. "I didn't want it to get awkward."

Relief flooded his body. "Apology accepted."

"Well?" She folded her arms. "Don't you have anything to say?"

Now he was confused. "Like what?"

"I just happen to know you don't have a date, and I don't either …" She held out her hands and smiled even bigger as she bobbed her head. "There's no point in both of us going alone."

The relief turned into a sour feeling in the pit of his stomach. He had no desire to be Marla's date, and she'd put him in a terrible position. He had to say something.

"Um … I'm sorry, Marla, but I do have a date."

A frown quickly took over her expression. "Wait a minute. I spoke to the reunion chairman, and he said you were going alone."

"I haven't had a chance to talk to him yet."

"You were supposed to have done that weeks ago so they could make sure to have enough food and tables. I don't know if—"

"It doesn't matter because I'm taking Ruby." The instant he said that, he wanted to kick himself in the backside. But now that it had come out, he decided to stay with it. "She already accepted the invitation."

"Oh." She closed her mouth and tightened her lips in a disapproving manner. "In that case, I guess ... maybe I'll just ..." She scrunched her face so tight he thought she might implode. "I ... I ..." She glanced over her shoulder at the door. "I have to go now." Before he could say another word, she turned and ran out the door.

"What did you go and do this time, son?" Pop approached from behind, chuckling softly.

"Boy, I sure did get myself in a mess this time."

"Why don't you tell me about it, and I'll see what I can do to help you get out of it."

As Antonio explained to Pop what he'd done, he got absolutely no sympathy. Instead, his father laughed. "Sounds like you're going to have to convince Ruby to be your date." He held out his hands. "Either that or apologize to Marla and take her up on her offer."

Antonio hung his head. "I don't want to take Marla, but I don't know how to convince Ruby she should go with me since she already committed to Nate."

"I'm sure you'll think of something." Pop gestured around the restaurant. "If you can turn this place from a run-down hole of a restaurant to one of the most popular eating establishments in Plantersville, and then add two more that are equally successful, surely you can sweet-talk Ruby into giving you a chance."

Antonio sighed. "I'll try."

"It doesn't sound to me like she and Nate are all that into each other, so it shouldn't be too difficult."

~

Ruby didn't mind knitting, but it was slower than she'd thought. It took her hours and hours, and she still wasn't finished with the scarf. She'd brought it to school to work on it during lunch.

"It's looking pretty good," Deanna said. "Looks like you're about three-fourths done."

"You think that'll be long enough?"

Deanna studied it for a few minutes and then nodded. "Yeah, I think another foot and a half should do it. Are you planning to wear it?"

"I don't know."

"Or do you plan to give it to a special person?" Deanna gave her a teasing grin. "I know the perfect guy who will love it. Rumor has it he enjoys homemade gifts."

"He said he would, but he's used to well made things like sweaters, not some amateurish attempt at a simple scarf."

"Well, I just happen to think he'd rather have your so-called attempt at a beautiful blue ..." She reached out and stroked it. "A beautiful blue and oh-so-soft scarf than a sweater knitted by someone who has been chasing him since high school."

"I ... no, I don't think so."

"Okay, whatever. So are you excited about the barbecue?"

Ruby was glad Deanna finally got off the topic of her attempt at knitting. "I am. I haven't seen a lot of the people in ten years, so I'm eager to catch up on what everyone's doing."

"You'll have a blast." A dreamy look came over Deanna's face. "I had my tenth two years ago, and I loved every single minute of it. What was funny was the guys I thought were so cool didn't seem so great, but the biggest geeks of all were super successful and happy."

"I've heard that happens."

"Yeah, reputations are hard to change in high school, but once people grow up and figure out what they want to do with their lives, you can see who really has it together."

Ruby slowly nodded as she thought about Antonio and how his image had changed, even in her mind. She'd been intrigued by him when she was a teenager, but now she admired him and respected what he'd done with his life. And she loved how he treated his parents.

As her lunch break came to a close, Ruby picked up her knitting and left the teacher's lunchroom to go to her classroom. The kids hadn't gotten back yet, so she had time to put everything away.

Her phone rang as she headed out to the parking lot after school. It was Charlene. "I'm so sorry I've been out of pocket for a while. How's everything going?"

Ruby hesitated momentarily, but then she told her best childhood friend everything—from the knitting project to the outfits she'd borrowed from Deanna. "I'm doing several things way out of my comfort zone."

"It's about time. I wish I didn't have so much going on in my life right now so we could get together soon, but I'll catch up with you at the reunion."

"Sounds good."

After Ruby hung up, she thought about how she and Charlene used to share their deepest secrets with each other. The only person she'd ever told about her crush on Antonio was Charlene, who'd encouraged her to act on her feelings, saying she'd never get what she wanted if she didn't go for it.

~

A couple of hours later, Antonio stood at the door of her apartment, trying to remember what he needed to say. Pop had coached him, but none of it seemed appropriate.

Finally, he just lifted his hand and knocked. The door opened thirty seconds later, and Ruby looked like she might fall over backward.

"What are you doing … I mean, why didn't you call and tell me you were coming?"

He opened his mouth but closed it and chuckled. "I was going to say I was just in the neighborhood and thought I'd stop by to say hi, but that wouldn't be the truth."

She smiled. "So you drove all the way over here just to see me?"

He nodded. "Guilty as charged."

She remained standing there staring at him for a few very uncomfortable seconds before opening the door all the way. "Come on in. I wasn't expecting company, so the place is a mess."

He looked around and saw that nothing was out of place, except for a ball of yarn and what looked like a long rectangle draped over the sofa arm. "What's that?"

"My knitting project."

"It looks … nice."

She giggled. "You don't have to say that. I obviously have no idea what I'm doing yet, but I actually do enjoy knitting. It gives me something to do with my hands."

"What is it going to be when you're finished?"

"A scarf."

"Oh, I should have figured that out. You mentioned that was what you were going to make. Whoever you're making it for is very fortunate." He held her gaze, hoping she'd tell him who the scarf was for. But she didn't, so he decided to be assertive and ask. "Who are you knitting it for?"

She grimaced and shook her head. "I can't imagine anyone wanting to wear it, so actually, no one."

"I'd wear it."

Her eyebrows shot up. "You would?"

"Absolutely." He picked up the end of it, stroked it a couple of times, and then put it back down on the arm of the sofa. "It's a great color that will go with a lot of my fall clothes, and it's soft, so I'm sure it'll be comfortable."

"So …" She narrowed her eyes as she glanced at the scarf and then back at him. "If I gave it to you, you'd actually wear it?"

"That's what I just said."

"Okay, when I'm done it'll be yours."

That made him about as happy as anything else had. So he decided to go after what he came for. "Now I have a special favor to ask."

"Other than begging for a poorly made scarf?"

"It's not poorly made. And yes, something besides begging for the scarf."

"Okay, what's the favor?"

"Will you to go the reunion with me?"

"I told you I was going with Nate."

Chapter 8

"Good for you!" Deanna looked like she was about to burst with excitement as soon as Ruby told her the next day at lunch. Then a look of concern crossed her face. "But what about Nate?"

"I called and asked if he minded not going with me. He was relieved because there was someone else he wanted to ask."

Deanna's grin returned. "I have a feeling some wonderful things are about to happen between you and Antonio."

"Don't get too worked up. We're just going to the reunion together. Nothing else."

"It's a start."

Ruby shook her head. "He just doesn't want to go alone."

"You really think that?"

"Absolutely. Why wouldn't I?"

"Because it's not true?" Deanna bobbed her head. "You've always been so smart when helping other people. I can't believe how dense you're being with your own love life."

If anyone else had said that, Ruby would have been offended, but she knew Deanna had her best interest at heart. "Love life? Honestly, Deanna, you can think that all day long, but it doesn't make it so."

"We'll see about that, won't we? In the meantime, you'd better get going on that scarf if you want to give it to him before the reunion."

"I finished it last night, and now I'm starting on the sweater."

Deanna narrowed her eyes and gave her a curious look. "What happened to the hat?"

Ruby shrugged. "I went to the craft store and picked up some really pretty dark gray yarn last night, and one of the other customers told me about a tutorial online that taught her how to knit."

"Oh, okay." Deanna tightened her lips.

"So you don't think I can do it?"

"I didn't say that."

Ruby laughed. "But you were thinking it. I'll have you know that I started on it last night, and it's coming along rather nicely."

"Have you done a sleeve yet?"

"No."

"Then you won't have the sweater done by the reunion."

"Of course not." Ruby paused and did some mental calculation. "At the rate I'm going, it'll take me a couple of months."

"At least you don't have unreal expectations."

Ruby tilted her head toward her friend. "That's right. I don't." She hoped Deanna got the message.

After school let out that afternoon, Ruby went straight home and tried on her outfits again for the reunion. She couldn't believe how different she looked. Mama had always told her that she needed to maintain understated elegance, but when she saw herself in the mirror wearing these bold, bright colors, her heart hammered with excitement. She looked like the fun person she always wanted to be—not some drab homebody who didn't know how to have a good time.

The next couple of days went by without incident, which disappointed Ruby. She'd started getting used to excitement of the unknown—from Antonio asking her to go to the reunion with him to seeing herself in these cute outfits.

~

On the night of the first reunion event, Antonio stopped by the restaurant to see Pop and make sure everything was running smoothly. He walked in and took a long look around. He let out a sigh of relief when he saw that there was nothing out of the ordinary.

"Can't stay away, can you, son?" Pop came up from the side. He leaned back and took a long look at Antonio. "You sure do clean up well. She'll be impressed."

Antonio felt like a teenager getting ready for prom as his father gave his approval. He laughed to cover his nervousness. "It's just a casual outfit for the bonfire, Pop. Nothing special."

"Then let me take the price tag off the back of those pants. We don't want her to think you went out and bought something special, just for her."

"Oops. I'm glad you noticed."

Pop stepped behind the host stand and came toward him with a pair of scissors. After he snipped the tag, he took a look at it and raised his eyebrows. "Whoa, son. I don't think I've ever paid this much for a complete outfit, let alone a pair of trousers."

"They had a sale." Antonio grinned at Pop. "I didn't pay full price."

"Good thing. I don't want you thinking expensive clothes is the way to a decent woman's heart."

Antonio thought about Ruby and how she'd dated that guy Nate who always wore the latest and obviously most expensive styles from an exclusive men's store in Charleston. And in case people didn't know it, Nate told his classmates. Antonio had never been able to afford even one item in that store, so he never bothered to walk inside. The times he'd gone to Downtown Charleston, he'd mostly window-shopped.

"You look real nice, Antonio. I hope you have a wonderful time."

"I'm sure I will." He pulled his cell phone out of his back pocket. "I'll have this with me, so if you need something you can call or text."

Pop laughed, shook his head, and led Antonio to the door. "Stop worrying about us. We'll do just fine. Anyone who can't get away for a couple of nights hasn't hired the right people, and that's not the case with you."

"I know." Antonio smiled. "I have you, and you're the best."

"So go on and have fun." Pop gave him one last push out the door and then closed it.

He stood at the edge of the parking lot and stared at his car. Having a date with Ruby Wilson was something he'd been dreaming of since the first time he saw her their freshman year of high school. He never thought it would happen, and now he worried he'd mess things up.

All the way to her place, he gave himself a mental lecture. *Don't say anything to embarrass her. Don't try to be someone you're not. Don't let on how desperately you want to be with her.*

Then it dawned on him. All he was thinking were negative thoughts. *Don't this* and *don't that.* He cringed. It was time to force out those *don'ts* and come up with some *dos*.

So he took another deep breath and tried to think about positive things. He knew he was more successful than anyone thought he'd be. And to put it in his mother's words, he cleaned up well.

As he got closer to Ruby's place, his pulse quickened. He kept taking deep breaths and thinking about what to say and how to act.

When he pulled into the parking lot of Ruby's apartment complex, he took one more deep breath as he got out of the car. This was what he'd been waiting for nearly half his life, and he didn't want to blow it.

He'd barely knocked when the door opened. The instant he saw her, his mouth went dry. She'd always been beautiful, but wow! He'd never seen such a stunning creature in his entire life.

~

Ruby had to blink to believe the guy of her dreams stood at her door, waiting for her to let him in so they could get started on their date. Well, maybe it wasn't a date, but they were going somewhere together, and she could dream, couldn't she?

"You look …" He paused and gave her a once-over. "Amazing." He tipped his head forward. "Mind if I come in, or are you ready to go now?"

"Oh." She stepped back. "Come on in. Would you like something to drink before we leave?"

"Sure. What do you have?"

"Iced tea, water, and …" She made a face. "That's pretty much all I have, unless you'd like a glass of almond milk."

"Water is just fine."

She wasn't sure what he was thinking, but she figured he must think she was pretty lame for not having more to offer. "Have a seat, and I'll bring it out."

It took her almost a minute to pour both of them a glass of water. When she got back to the living room, she saw him inspecting her knitting projects.

He glanced up and smiled. "The scarf turned out great." He pointed to the gray yarn with the knitting needles stuck in it. "Is that the sweater?"

"It will be."

"Nice color." He lifted the scarf again. "But I really like this."

"You do?"

He nodded. "There's something special about the first time you finish a new skill. I'll never forget the first spaghetti I made from scratch."

"Was it delicious?"

He shook his head and laughed. "Not really, but it was special because it was the first time I made it. Does that make sense?"

"Yeah, I think so."

"Do you plan to wear this?" He rubbed his hand over the scarf.

"I doubt it."

He gently placed it around his neck and looped it in the front. "Do you mind if I wear it?"

"Are you serious?"

"Absolutely. It's very soft, and since you made it …" He rubbed it against his face. "It's pretty special."

"If you want to wear it, go right ahead. I was thinking of it as a practice item." She put his water glass on the table next to him. "Here's your water."

They both took a couple of sips of their water before he stood. "A practice item, huh? Well, I think it's perfect for those cool nights … like maybe at a high school reunion barbecue. It starts out nice but gets cooler as the night wears on, and you find yourself wishing you had a nice, soft scarf to keep your neck warm."

"Are you sure you want to wear it tonight?"

"Yes, it would be my honor." His eyes crinkled as he smiled at her.

Her heart thudded. "Okay."

"Why don't we head on over to the barbecue? Some of the people said they were getting there early, so I know we won't be the first ones there."

She nodded. She knew Nate wouldn't be there yet because he enjoyed making an entrance—especially now that he had the Alfa Romeo. Showing off was one of the things he did best.

As Antonio held the door of his late-model Buick, she thought about how much work Antonio had to do to get to the point of affording this car. Nate had a trust fund, so he'd never know what it was like to scrimp and save to get what he wanted.

"You can adjust the heat according to how warm you want it." Antonio proudly pointed to the temperature control on her side.

"This is a nice car, Antonio."

"I really like it. Pop was worried I might have over-extended, but I think he's proud of what I've managed to do. This is my second car, but you wouldn't want to see what I used to drive." He shuddered. "It was a heap."

"But it got you where you needed to go, right?"

"Yes, you're right."

"Then it was a nice car."

He reached for her hand and squeezed it as he smiled. "And you're a really nice woman."

"Thank you." She appreciated his compliment, but it would have made her happier if he'd told her she made his heart go crazy … like he did hers.

"I think folks will be shocked to see us together."

She scrunched her forehead as she looked at his profile. "Why?"

"I don't know. It's just that …" His chest rose and fell as he sighed. "You come from a different background, and people will probably wonder why you'd want to go on a date with me."

So it *was* a date. Deanna had been right. In spite of the things he was saying, she couldn't help but smile.

"Why are you grinning?"

"I was thinking the same thing, only in reverse. You could have your pick of people to take to the reunion, so why would you want me to go with you?"

"Want to know the truth?"

She swallowed hard. She wasn't sure if she really wanted to know, but she nodded. "Of course."

"Going out with you has been a dream of mine since the first time I saw you." He pulled up to a stop sign and gave her a look letting her know that he meant every word he said.

Chapter 9

He wasn't sure if he should have told her how he felt so early in the evening, but now that it was out, there was no taking it back. The look on her face didn't give him any indication of how she felt, so he hoped that was a good sign. At least she didn't look repulsed.

When they arrived at the big open field where the bonfire was already underway, she sat and stared at the crowd. He reached over and squeezed her hand again. "You okay?"

She nodded. "I'm fine."

He had a momentary thought that maybe she was embarrassed to be seen with him, but before he let it get hold of his nerves, he opened the door. "Let's get this show on the road."

As they walked toward the crowd, he pondered whether or not to take her hand. He'd decided against it, but right before they reached the edge of the group, she grabbed his arm.

He turned and looked at her, and for the first time since he'd known her, she looked scared. "You're not okay, are you?"

"I don't know what's coming over me." Her voice was low, and he could barely hear her. "I've never been shy before, but that's how I'm feeling right now."

"You'll be fine." He put his arm around her and guided her to the beverage table. "Maybe a soda will make you feel better."

"Soda?" The voice behind them caught his attention, so he turned around to see Douglas, one of the guys who had always fancied himself a ladies' man. "Give her something good … not some lame can of soda. We have plenty of beer and wine."

"A soda is fine," she said.

"Thanks, Doug," Antonio said as he picked up a soda and handed it to Ruby before getting one for himself.

The guy glared at him. “That’s *Douglas* to you.”

“Sorry, Douglas.” Antonio could tell Douglas had been hitting the beverage table a little too hard, so he steered Ruby over to another area, where the people appeared more sober. He leaned over and whispered, “Looks like some people haven’t changed since high school.”

“I know.” Her smile warmed him from the inside out, which reminded him of something he’d put in his pocket.

“Look what I have.” He pulled out the scarf she’d knitted and showed it to her.

Her eyebrows shot up. “You brought that?”

He nodded. “Ya never know when you’ll need it this time of year.”

“I know, but …” Her expression became unreadable. “I didn’t expect you to actually wear it tonight. I don’t want you to be embarrassed by something so …”

“Oh, trust me, this will not embarrass me. If anything, I’ll wear it with pride.” He paused and gave her the biggest grin he could manage. “In fact, I think I’ll put it on now, and if anyone asks me, I’ll tell them the prettiest girl who ever graduated from Plantersville High School made it.”

She pulled her lips between her teeth, so now he had no idea what she was thinking. But that was okay. He figured she’d come right out and tell him if she didn’t want him to wear it.

As they made their way through the crowd, Antonio noticed the double takes from people as they realized who he was with. He was proud to be with her, but he wasn’t so sure about how she felt. He pulled her off to the side to talk to her about it.

“Are you okay being here with me?” he asked.

She gave him a confused look. “Why wouldn’t I be?”

He shrugged. “I don’t know. Maybe because I don’t exactly match up to you socially.”

“Would you please stop it?” Her forehead was scrunched up as she pursed her lips.

“You were … well, you fit in.” He paused and shrugged. “And I didn’t.”

“That’s a silly thing to worry about. First of all, you fit in as much as the rest of us did, and secondly, that was a long time ago.”

“True.”

“I was worried you might be embarrassed to be seen with me.”

Now he was stunned. “That makes absolutely no sense. How can you think such a thing?”

“Because I was a silly, shallow girl who had no idea what was going on in the world?"

It took every ounce of self-restraint for him not to laugh. He'd never seen Ruby Wilson as silly or shallow. All he'd seen was a girl who was always pulled together and acted like she knew where she was going.

"You, on the other hand, didn't care about some of the unimportant stuff. I always thought you had your act together."

This time he didn't hold back his laughter. "That's about as far from reality as it could possibly be. I totally didn't have my act together."

Charlene approached, grinning back and forth between them. "Looks like destiny has finally found you."

Antonio gave Ruby a curious look, and she laughed. "I'll tell you later."

"Stan's talking to someone he hasn't seen in a while, so I told him I'd get us some drinks. See y'all later." She waved as she walked toward the beverage area.

After she walked away, Antonio looked down at Ruby. "She and Stan seem like a match made in heaven. I'm glad he finally came to his senses and proposed. Any idea when they're getting married?"

She shook her head. "I don't think they're in any hurry, but I don't think it'll be too much longer, now that they're both settled in their jobs and can afford a house. They both want kids."

"It doesn't seem all that long ago that we were all kids."

Now she smiled, and relief washed over him. At least she didn't seem mad. "I know, right? Isn't it amazing how we've grown so much since high school?"

Before he had a chance to respond, he heard Marla's voice from behind. "What on earth are you wearing around your neck, Antonio? It looks like something you got out of the bargain bin at the discount store."

Anger flooded his veins, so he didn't dare turn around to face the woman who clearly had no manners. Instead, he tugged on Ruby's hand and tried to pull her away. But she resisted.

He glanced down at her and saw the frustration on her face. "I told you I didn't think you should wear it. I don't want you to be embar—"

"I am not embarrassed," he said in as stern of a tone as he could manage. "In fact, I'm proud to wear something you worked so hard on."

"But Marla said—"

"I can't believe you're talking about me like I'm not here." The sound of Marla's voice rang in his ears. "I don't get it at all. The two of you …" He spun around in time to see her pointing back and forth between him and Ruby. "You're out of your league, Antonio."

"You don't know what you're talking about," Ruby said. "I'm the one—"

She was interrupted by Marla's laughter. "Actually, I do get it. She's decided to go slumming."

Before he had a chance to say a word, Ruby spoke up again. "Marla, you are about the rudest person I have ever known. I didn't want to say anything because I know you and Antonio used to date. But now I don't even care. Go ahead and insult me and the scarf I made, but you have no right to say that about—"

Antonio pulled her back and whispered, "That's okay, Ruby. You don't have to do this."

"No, I know I don't, but we can't let her get away with being so mean."

Marla tilted her head back and cackled. "Antonio, you're clearly clueless, but you'll learn." She turned to Ruby and gave a fake smile. "I know plenty of people like you. Once you get whatever it is you want from him, you'll leave him in the dust." Now she looked at Antonio. "And I'll be waiting for you when you're ready to crawl back to me."

Antonio felt Ruby stiffen, but at least she didn't try to make a comeback. He suspected she was too shocked to say anything.

He narrowed his eyes and glared back at the woman who had refused to leave him alone since high school. "That's enough, Marla."

"Oh, I'm sure it is." She reached out and grabbed for the scarf, but he was faster and managed to keep her from taking it, but not until a couple of rows unraveled.

Ruby's eyes widened as her mouth opened. "No …" She flinched and closed her eyes.

Marla laughed. "Looks like whoever made this rag didn't know how to finish it off. Imagine that. One little bitty touch, and it came unraveled … just like you will when she's done with you."

"Stop being childish, Marla."

She lifted an eyebrow. "Childish?" She nodded toward the scarf. "If you want to know childish, take a look at your sorry excuse for a scarf."

He glanced down and focused on the loose thread that Marla had pulled. Anger welled in his chest, but he knew better than to let it show. He leaned over and whispered to Ruby. "Do you want to leave now?"

She hesitated for several seconds before shaking her head. "No, I don't think so. But I do want to get away from her."

"C'mon." He took her by the hand and led her over to another area, where several people whose names he couldn't remember congregated. "I am so sorry about this." He lifted the scarf. "If I'd known—"

She placed a couple of fingers over his lips. "No, don't worry about it. I did a lousy job, and she's right. I didn't finish it off correctly, or that never would have happened." She cleared her throat. "I have no idea why

I ever thought I could do something like that. It's obvious that I'm in over my head with knitting if I can't even make a simple scarf. I'm better off sticking to stuff I'm familiar with."

His heart felt as though someone had ripped it from his chest. He hated the fact that Marla had insulted Ruby's efforts. "Don't be like that. This is the first thing you've ever made."

"I know, and I think it's best if it's my last."

"No, I can't accept that."

"What?"

"I think you heard me. Don't give up so easily. If I'd done that, I'd be sweeping floors in some office building now."

"But I'm not you," she reminded him. "When things get rough for me, I have no idea what to do."

"You just keep plowing ahead and doing whatever it takes to make things work out." Nothing had been easy for him, so that was all he ever knew how to do—get knocked down and then get back up. He'd had to do that so many times he wouldn't have known what to do if everything had worked out the first time he tried.

"Yeah, I'm glad that works for you."

He still wasn't sure what was going on in her head, but he heard defeat in her voice. The rest of the evening, he did what he could to get her to smile, and when she did, it didn't last long.

~

Neither of them could eat much, so they left the event early. Antonio walked her to her door, and they stood there not looking directly at each other. Finally, he tipped her chin up to face him. "See you tomorrow night."

She shook her head. "I hate to break our date, but I think it's better if I don't go."

"Please?" He felt as though all his blood had been drained. "Can we at least talk about it?"

Her heart hammered. "Not now."

"I'll call you tomorrow."

She nodded. "That's fine."

After Ruby closed her apartment door, she leaned against it and closed her eyes. She'd never been so torn in her life. On the one hand, she loved being with Antonio, but on the other hand, she'd never been so happy to have the evening end. The very sight of Marla as she made her rounds at the reunion made Ruby's stomach hurt.

She changed into some pajamas, got a drink of water, and walked over to her knitting project. She stared down at it and wondered what on earth she'd been thinking when she decided to take up knitting. She had no idea how difficult it would be, but like she told Antonio, she should have stuck to what she knew rather than try something so foreign to her.

Antonio had tried to reassure her, but the more he spoke the more she realized she was out of her league. He had something she'd never had—and that was the ability to get past her inadequacies. She obviously had plenty of them.

One thing she couldn't figure out was why Antonio had gone to the trouble of being with her. Marla might have been mean, but she was gorgeous, smart, and incredibly talented at things Ruby couldn't imagine ever being able to do. The girl had won awards for her cooking and crafting, and she clearly knew how to knit. She was one of the most sought after hairdressers in Plantersville. Back in high school, Marla was runner up for "Most Likely Girl to Succeed," but she'd lost it to a cheerleader who just happened to have a lot of friends who campaigned for her.

Ruby, on the other hand, had been in the top five finalists in the Miss Plantersville beauty pageant. Her talent of doing a dramatic reading wasn't strong enough to come in first or second. Those positions went to girls who could sing and dance.

She'd also been accepted into several different colleges—one with a full academic scholarship. But since she didn't want to go far from home, she chose to go to the community college for the first two years.

Antonio was more of a risk taker. She knew he'd applied at dozens of universities and in spite of the rejections, he still persisted and managed to get offered a couple of needs-based scholarships. He left the area for the time it took to get his business degree, and when he came back, he risked everything and purchased a failing restaurant. While she admired his skills and confidence, she knew she never would have been able to do that. She would have been too defeated. She clearly didn't have what it took to deal with half of what he did. He was a fighter, just like Marla was.

Yeah, she needed to stick to what she was capable of doing and forget about trying something new that she didn't stand a chance of succeeding at. She picked up the start of the sweater she'd been working on, looked it over for a few seconds, and then walked into the kitchen and dropped it in the garbage can.

Chapter 10

Antonio felt terrible about everything that happened when they got to the barbecue. He thought he'd made things clear to Marla, but the message had obviously not sunk in with her. Another thing that was painful was how he'd let things get so out of hand with her, even though he knew a long time ago nothing would come of their relationship.

Pop was right. He should have ended it sooner. Now that he looked back over the years he'd kept quiet about his feelings, he realized her immaturity wasn't nearly as bad as his inability to confront the inevitable. He was responsible for what had happened, and he fully intended to make things right.

He went to bed that night, wishing he could have a do-over with both Marla and Ruby. But he obviously couldn't, so he had to make things right from where he was now. His desire was to ignore Marla, but his instincts told him he needed to address the problem there first and make everything extremely clear to her. Otherwise, there wouldn't be any way he could start fresh with Ruby.

The next morning he called Marla, hoping she hadn't left for work yet. She answered on the second ring. "I knew you'd call. Have you come to your senses yet?"

"Yes, I absolutely have." He cleared his throat. "Do you have a few minutes to talk?"

"On the phone?"

"No, in person."

"I have to work a couple of hours this afternoon, and I don't want to miss the last night of the reunion. If you want to talk, it'll have to be this morning. Why don't you come on over to my place?" The sound of joy in her voice grated his last nerve.

"I think it's better if we meet somewhere … someplace like IHOP. Can you be ready in a half hour?"

"Give me an hour, and I'll be there."

After he hung up, he called Ruby. It was Saturday, so he knew she wasn't at school. As the phone rang, he held his breath, praying she wouldn't ignore his call. He let his breath out in a whoosh when she finally answered.

"Can I see you sometime today?" he asked.

"I don't know. I already told you I'm not going back to the reunion."

"That's fine, but I still need to talk to you. I had some things I wanted to tell you last night, but after what happened, I thought it would be better to wait until today."

There was a long several seconds of silence before she finally spoke. "Okay. What time?"

"Can I take you to lunch?"

"Sure."

~

As soon as Ruby hung up, she called Charlene and told her what happened last night. "I feel so stupid."

"Why on earth would you feel stupid? Marla is the one who should be ashamed of herself. Don't let that girl get to you."

"It's just that—"

Charlene interrupted her. "It's just that you have always had a certain image of how things are supposed to be, but let me tell you something, girlie …" She laughed. "I just became my mother. Sorry about that. But I've always been frustrated by how little you think of yourself. You're one of the sweetest, prettiest, most unassuming people I know. There is no doubt in my mind that Antonio likes you every bit as much as you like him … maybe even more. But you don't seem to get that."

"He's a self-made man. I'm just—"

"You're just a wonderful woman who follows her heart and spends all your time with children, teaching them and making them love you to pieces. You have never realized how gorgeous you are, so that makes you even prettier. And you're smart as a whip, except when it comes to your own love life."

"Okay, okay, I don't need a lecture now."

Charlene laughed. "Oh, but I think you do. You finally have the opportunity to have something … I mean someone you've always wanted, and I want to make sure you don't blow it."

"It'll never work between Antonio and me."

"It won't if you don't give it a chance. Look, Ruby, he's going to all kinds of trouble to see you. Can't you see it?" Before Ruby had a chance to reply, Charlene continued. "No man is going to try so hard to make things right if he's not crazy about you. Trust me on this."

"Well …" Ruby's mind had been wrapped around the negatives, and she hadn't given much thought to the trouble Antonio had gone to.

"If he wasn't crazy about you, he wouldn't have worn the scarf to the reunion where he'd see everyone he knew in high school, and he definitely wouldn't have called and begged to see you today."

Now that Ruby thought about it, she considered that there might be some truth to what Charlene was saying. But she still didn't want to assume anything, or she could wind up making a fool of herself like she did when she let him out of her apartment with the scarf.

"I reckon I'd better go," Charlene said. "I'll see you tonight."

"I'm afraid I won't be there."

"You'd better be, or I'll have to resort to some drastic measures."

"What?" Ruby thought for a moment. "What are you talking about?"

"Trust me, if you're not there, I'll show those pictures we took after graduation."

"Not the pudding pictures."

"Yep, the pudding pictures."

Ruby groaned. Neither she nor Charlene had dates after graduation, so they decided to have a movie marathon. They started out eating popcorn and then moved on to pudding. They started getting silly, so when Charlene challenged her to a pudding competition with no spoons allowed, they got ridiculously silly and took it outside for a food fight. Charlene's brother caught them and snapped some pictures of them with pudding all over themselves.

"I'll have them in my purse, so you'd better be there."

Then something dawned on Ruby. "You're in the pictures too. Aren't you embarrassed?"

"Not in the least. Stan has already seen them, so I have nothing to lose."

"But I trusted you."

"I know." Charlene laughed. "And I love making people laugh. No one will believe that the sweet, reserved Ruby Wilson they all know would resort to being involved in something as rowdy as a pudding fight."

After Ruby got off the phone, she pondered the worst thing that could happen if everyone saw the photos, and she laughed. It was so silly and out of character for her, but it was also ten years ago. No one would think anything about that now.

She took her time getting ready to go to lunch with Antonio. In spite of the fact that she didn't think anything would ever come of her feelings for him, she spent a little extra time making sure her makeup was just so and picking the perfect necklace for the V-neck top she'd decided to wear. Then she added a stack of bracelets. In the past, she wore button-up collars, but Charlene had convinced her that V-necks were more flattering on most people.

After she finished getting ready, she stood in front of her full-length mirror and realized she looked like she was trying too hard. So she took off her bracelets and looked again. Yeah, this was a much more natural look for her.

She expected to have to wait, since she was ready early, but he got there fifteen minutes before he was due. He looked her up and down and grinned. "You look amazing … but then you always do."

"Thank you." He looked really good too, as he always did, but it didn't feel right to tell him—at least not now.

He drove straight to Sweetgrass Diner, a place that was known for their shrimp and grits entrée. It also happened to be Ruby's favorite restaurant.

"I remember you telling me you like this place."

Her lips twitched into a smile. "Thank you."

After they were seated and their order placed, he planted his forearms on the table and leaned forward to look her in the eyes. "Okay, so since I begged you to come out with me, I need to tell you why." He pulled his lips between his teeth, closed his eyes, and appeared to take a deep breath. "This is extremely hard for me to say, since I don't know how you're going to take it, but I know I don't have much time, and I have to make it count." He paused. "I've been absolutely crazy about you ever since high school." He paused. "I mean head over heels. And now I think I could easily fall in love with you."

She blinked as she heard words she never expected. In spite of the fact that she was pretty sure she was in love with him, she wasn't ready to come right out and say it.

The server brought their food. Once she was gone, he bowed his head to say a silent blessing, so she did the same. When they looked back up at each other, her heart felt as though it just might melt.

He picked up his fork and stabbed a shrimp, but before he put it in his mouth, he paused and gazed at her. "Is there any way I can convince you to go to the event tonight? I'll do everything in my power to keep Marla away from you."

"You don't have to do that. I'll go."

He tilted his head and gave her a look of concern. "But you were so upset last night … and this morning when I called, you reminded me that you didn't want to go to the event tonight."

"That's because I was caught off guard last night." What she didn't say was that his admission to being crazy about her made everything Marla had said and done insignificant.

"So you do want to go?"

She nodded. "Yes, I do."

"With me?"

She smiled. "With you."

~

Later that afternoon, Antonio rushed to get ready for the final night of the reunion. Pop had practically kicked him out of the restaurant, reminding him what time it was.

"If you want to impress the girl, you have to take a shower and put on some nice clothes."

"Okay, okay. I'm outta here."

"Just remember, son, focus on the prize and keep your eyes open for whatever opportunity presents itself."

"Opportunity?"

Pop smiled. "Yep. You'll know what I'm talking about when it happens. Now go have yourself some fun."

After a quick shower and shave, Antonio pulled on one of the sweaters he'd purchased, not one Marla had made. He'd already gathered all of those up and put them in a bag to return to her. When he told her that he didn't want to be with her, even if Ruby wasn't in the picture, she'd taken it hard and sobbed. But she finally nodded her acceptance through the tears.

He brushed his teeth and combed his hair. Then he looked in the full-length mirror to make sure he got all the price tags off his clothes before leaving to pick up Ruby.

As soon as she opened her apartment door, his mouth went completely dry. Even before tonight, he thought she was the prettiest girl in Plantersville. But now, here she was wearing a cherry-red dress with bare shoulders and shiny pearls around her neck, showing off her stunning face and hair that flowed in waves. He was so mesmerized he couldn't speak.

She smiled at him. "Ready?"

He nodded. "Am I ever."

All the way to the event hall, they chatted about very lightweight things, until they pulled into the parking lot. He remembered Pop's comment about keeping his eyes open for opportunity and decided to create that moment.

As soon as he stopped the car, he reached for her hand. "Can we talk for a minute before we go inside?"

Her eyes widened as she nodded. "Sure."

"I've already told you that I'm crazy about you and that I think I can fall in love with you." He paused to make sure she was able to process that. "Well, that has changed."

She lowered her gaze, almost as though she was disappointed. This gave him the strength to continue.

"It's changed because I know for sure that I'm already in love with you."

Her head popped up, and she looked him in the eyes. "You are?"

"Yes. Very much so."

Her lips widened into a smile. "Want to know a secret?"

"Of course."

"I feel the same way about you."

"So you're saying you … you love me?"

She nodded. "Yes."

A couple of people walked past his car. "I think we should probably go on inside, but can we continue this conversation later?"

"I would like that very much."

The night felt like he was living a dream. They sat across from Charlene and her fiancé during dinner, telling stories about their teenage years. Afterward, they danced to some music that had been popular when they were in high school.

And then Marla approached. "Mind if I chat with your girlfriend?"

"Not at all." He smiled at Ruby. "I'll be waiting for you right here."

~

Ruby was surprised when Antonio encouraged her to talk to Marla. If he hadn't been there, she would have turned and run as fast as her legs would carry her.

Marla led her to a quiet hallway and stopped. As she turned around, Ruby felt her heart pounding in her throat from apprehension.

"I had breakfast with Antonio today," Marla said. "He told me that he was madly in love with you and that whatever I thought we had was based on my imagination and not reality."

"He told you that?"

"Yep, and that's not all. He said he wanted me to take back everything I ever gave him because he didn't want anything to come between you and him."

Ruby was speechless. She opened her mouth, but nothing would come out.

"To be honest, I sort of knew, even back when we were teenagers. He used to watch you, and when I asked him what he was thinking, he always said how nice you were and how different you were from some of the other kids in your group."

"My group?"

Marla nodded. "Yeah, the group we used to call the over-privileged kids. Even I noticed that you didn't seem spoiled. Remember when we had that art project together?"

How could Ruby forget? She nodded.

"You were so nice to me, and that really bugged me because it would have been so much easier to hate you if you were mean and snobby." Marla looked around and then placed her hand on Ruby's arm. "I can see why Antonio is so smitten with you. Please treat him well. He deserves a nice woman."

All kinds of thoughts flittered through Ruby's head as emotions overwhelmed her. She still couldn't talk.

"Go on out there and have fun. It's time for me to move on and find someone who loves me the way he loves you."

After Marla left her in the hallway, Ruby remained standing there staring at the wall. A shadow appeared, so she glanced up and spotted Antonio standing there. As their gazes met, he slowly walked toward her. Once he was close enough, he pulled her into his arms. "I'm warning you. I feel a kiss coming on."

"Me too." She tilted her face up to his for the best kiss she'd ever had.

Epilogue

"Whatcha doing?" Antonio looked over Ruby's shoulder as she maneuvered the yarn to the other side of her growing belly to make it easier to work with.

"Trying to figure out this new pattern."

"Haven't you made enough blankets? The baby is going to burn up with all the things you've crocheted for her."

"Just one more." She smiled up at her husband of a year and a half.

"Okay. Just don't tire yourself out." He leaned over and kissed her on the nose. "I'll bring supper home from the restaurant so you don't have to cook. How does lasagna sound?"

"Perfect."

After he left, she walked over to the window and watched his car until he turned the corner. Then she picked up her yarn and crochet hook and went back to her current project. She'd discovered that she enjoyed crocheting much more than knitting, so she bought every single color of yarn she liked and started making blankets … so many that Antonio, Deanna, and Charlene all teased her about being the crochet queen of Plantersville.

Mama and Daddy did kick up a fuss when she first announced she was in love with Antonio and wanted to marry him. But after they met him and got to know him on a more personal level, they loved him almost as much as she did.

She had just started a new row when her phone rang. It was Antonio.

"We're about to get slammed, but I wanted to remind you that I love you. Our baby is going to be the best swaddled child in all of South Carolina."

Ruby laughed. “I love you too. Now get back to work, and I’ll see you when you get home.”

After she hung up, she sighed with contentment. Life couldn’t be any better than this.

Dear Reader,

I hope you enjoyed *Unraveled Hearts* as much as I loved writing it. Please take a couple of minutes to leave an honest review on Amazon or Goodreads.

Thanks!
Debby Mayne

More books by Debby Mayne:

Trouble in Paradise (contemporary romance – first book in the Belles in the City series)
Julia's Arranged Marriage (historical romance – first book in the Hollister Sisters Mail Order Brides series)
Murder Under the Mistletoe (mystery – first book in the Summer Walsh series)

Romance

Hollister Sisters Mail Order Brides series:
Julia's Arranged Marriage
Lenora's Inconvenient Marriage
Mary's Improbable Marriage
Sarah's Suitable Marriage
John's Christmas Bride

Belles in the City series:
Trouble in Paradise
One Foot Out the Door
Can't Fool Me Twice

The Bouchers of Biloxi series:
Kathryn's Pride

Christmas and Holiday Romance:
Mistletoe and Holly
Silver Bells
Kissing Carly
Christmas in Winter Creek

More Romance:
Love Finds You on Christmas Morning
Love Finds You in Treasure Island, Florida
Lured by Love
Waiting for a View
For the Love of Pete
Sarasota Dreams
Shades of the Past
Trusting Her Heart
Unlikely Match
Noah's Ark
Love's Image
Double Blessing
If the Dress Fits
Lessons in Love
A New Beginning
A New Attitude
A New Understanding
A New Image
Sweet Baklava
Dixie Belle
Aloha Reunion
Forever Aloha
Magnolia Lane

Women's Fiction:
Pretty Is as Pretty Does
Bless Her Heart
Tickled Pink

Mysteries:
Murder Under the Mistletoe
Gun in the Garden
Offed at the Office
Summer Walsh Mystery Collection
Corpse on the Court

Printed in Great Britain
by Amazon

57940857R00161